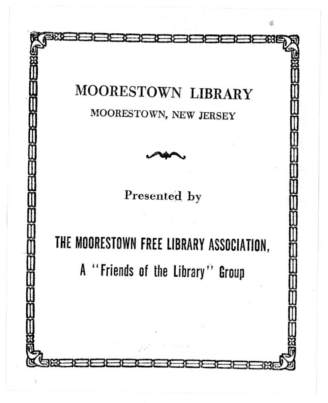

The Captive

Also by Victoria Holt
in Thorndike Large Print

Secret for a Nightingale

The Captive

VICTORIA HOLT

Thorndike Press • Thorndike, Maine

LP
Fiction
Hol

Library of Congress Cataloging in Publication Data:

Holt, Victoria, 1906-
    The captive / Victoria Holt.
        p. cm.
    ISBN 1-56054-022-2 (alk. paper : lg. print)
    ISBN 0-89621-997-6 (alk. paper : lg. print : pbk.)
    1. Large type books. I. Title.
[PR6015.I3C35   1990]   90-34617
                                        CIP

Thorndike Press Large Print edition published in 1990 by arrangement with Doubleday, a division of Bantam Doubleday Dell Publishing Group, Inc.

Cover illustration by Linda Fennimore.
Cover typography by David Gatti.

The tree indicium is a trademark of Thorndike Press.

This book is printed on acid-free, high opacity paper.

Contents

The House
in Bloomsbury

I was seventeen when I experienced one of the most extraordinary adventures which could ever have befallen a young woman, and which gave me a glimpse into a world which was alien to all that I had been brought up to expect; and from then on the whole course of my life was changed.

I always had the impression that I must have been conceived in a moment of absent-mindedness on the part of my parents. I could picture their amazement, consternation, and acute dismay when signs of my impending arrival must have become apparent. I remember when I was very young, having temporarily escaped from the supervision of my nurse, encountering my father on the stairs. We met so rarely that on this occasion we regarded each other as strangers. His spectacles were pushed up onto his forehead and he pulled them down to look more closely at this strange creature who had strayed into his world, as though trying to remember what it was. Then my mother appeared; she apparently recognised me immediately for she said, "Oh, it's the child. Where is the nurse?"

I was quickly snatched up into a pair of familiar arms and hustled away, and when we were out of earshot I heard mutterings. "Unnatural lot. Never mind. You've got your dear old Nanny who loves you."

Indeed I had and I was content, for besides my dear old Nanny I had Mr. Dolland the butler, Mrs. Harlow the cook, the parlourmaid Dot and the housemaid Meg, and Emily the tweeny. And later Miss Felicity Wills.

There were two distinct zones in our house, and I knew to which one I belonged.

It was a tall house in a London square in a district known as Bloomsbury. The reason it had been chosen as our residence was because of its proximity to the British Museum, which was always referred to belowstairs with such reverence that when I was first considered old enough to enter its sacred portals I expected to hear a voice from Heaven commanding me to take the shoes from off my feet, for the place whereon I was standing was holy ground.

My father was Professor Cranleigh, and he was attached to the Egyptian section of the

Museum. He was an authority on Ancient Egypt and in particular Hieroglyphics. Nor did my mother live in his shadow. She shared in his work, accompanied him on his frequent lecture tours, and was the author of a sizable tome entitled *The Significance of the Rosetta Stone*, which stood in a prominent place of honour, side by side with the half dozen works by my father in the room next to his study, which was called the library.

They had named me Rosetta, which was a great honour. It linked me with their work, which made me feel that at one time they must have had some regard for me. The first thing I wanted to see when Miss Felicity Wills took me to the Museum was this ancient stone. I gazed at it in wonder and listened enraptured while she told me that the strange characters supplied the key to deciphering the writings of ancient Egypt. I could not take my eyes from that basalt tablet which had been so important to my parents, but what gave it real significance in my eyes was that it bore the same name as myself.

When I was about five years old my parents became concerned about me. I must be educated and there was some trepidation in our zone at the prospect of a governess.

"Governesses," pronounced Mrs. Harlow, when we were all seated at the kitchen table, "is funny things. Neither fish nor fowl."

"No," I put in. "They are ladies."

"That's as may be," went on Mrs. Harlow. "Too grand for us, not good enough for them." She pointed to the ceiling, indicating the upper regions of the house. "They throw their weight about something shocking . . . and upstairs, well, they're as mild as milk. Yes, funny things, governesses."

"I've heard," said Mr. Dolland, "that it's to be the niece of some professor or other."

Mr. Dolland picked up all the news. He was "sharp as a wagonload of monkeys," according to Mrs. Harlow.

Dot had her own sources, gathered when waiting at table. "It's this Professor Wills," she said. "They was together at the university, only he went on to something else — science or something. Well, he's got this niece and they want a place for her. It looks certain we're going to have this Professor Wills's niece in our house."

"Will she be clever?" I asked in trepidation.

"Too clever by half, if you ask me," said Mrs. Harlow.

"I'm not having her interfering in the nursery," announced Nanny Pollock.

"She'll be too grand for that. It'll be meals on trays. Up them stairs for you, Dot . . . or you, Meg. I can tell you we're going to

10

get a real madam."

"I don't want her here," I announced. "I can learn from you."

That made them laugh.

"Say what you will, lovey," said Mrs. Harlow. "We're not what you'd call eddicated . . . except perhaps Mr. Dolland."

We all gazed fondly at Mr. Dolland. Not only did he uphold the dignity of our region but he kept us amused, and at times he could be persuaded to do one of his little "turns." He was a man of many parts, which was not surprising because at one time he had been an actor. I had seen him preparing to go upstairs, formally dressed, the dignified butler, and at other times with his green baize apron round his rather ample waist, cleaning the silver and breaking into song. I would sit there listening and the others would creep up to share in the pleasure and enjoy this one of Mr. Dolland's many talents.

"Mind you," he told us modestly, "singing's not my line. I was never one for the halls. It was always the straight theatre for me. In the blood . . . from the moment I was born."

Some of my happiest memories of those days are of sitting at that big kitchen table. I remember evenings — it must have been winter because it was dark, and Mrs. Harlow

11

would light the paraffin-filled lamp and set it in the centre of the table. The kitchen fire would be roaring away and, with my parents absent on some lecture tour, a wonderful sense of peace and security would settle upon us.

Mr. Dolland would talk of the days of his youth when he was on the way to becoming a great actor. It hadn't worked out as he had planned, otherwise we should not have had him with us, for which we must be grateful although it was a pity for Mr. Dolland. He had had several walk-on parts and had once played the ghost in *Hamlet;* he had actually worked in the same company as Henry Irving. He followed the progress of the great actor, and some years earlier he had seen his hero's much acclaimed Mathias in *The Bells.*

Sometimes he would beguile us with scenes from the play. A hushed silence would prevail. Seated beside Nanny Pollock, I would grip her hand to assure myself that she was close. It was most effective when the wind howled and we could hear the rain beating against the windows.

"It was such a night as this that the Polish Jew was murdered," Mr. Dolland would proclaim in hollow tones, and we would sit there shivering; and I used to lie in bed afterwards, gazing fearfully at the shadows in the room and wondering whether they were going to form themselves into the murderer.

Mr. Dolland was greatly respected throughout the household, which he would have been in any case, but his talent to amuse had made us love him, and if the theatrical world had failed to appreciate him that was not the case in the house in Bloomsbury.

Happy memories they were. These were my family and I felt safe and happy with them.

In those days the only times I ventured into the dining room were under the sheltering wing of Dot when she laid the table. I used to hold the cutlery for her while she placed it round the table. I would watch with admiration while she dexterously flicked the table napkins into fancy shapes and set them out.

"Don't it look lovely?" she would say, surveying her handiwork. "Not that they'll notice. It's just talk, talk, talk with them, and you don't have a blooming notion of what they're talking about. Get quite aerated, some of them do. You'd think they was all going up in smoke . . . all about things that happened long ago, places and people you've never heard of. They get so wild about them, too."

Then I would go round with Meg. When she stripped the beds I would take off my shoes and jump on the feather mattresses because I loved the way my feet sank into them.

We would make the beds together.

"First the heel and then the head, that's the way to make a bed," we would sing.

"Here," said Meg. "Tuck in a bit more. Don't want their feet falling out, do you? They'd be as cold as that there stone what you was named after."

Yes, it was a good life and I felt in no sense deprived by a lack of parental interest. I was only grateful to my namesake and all those Egyptian kings and queens who took up so much of their attention that they had none to spare for me. Happy days spent making beds, laying tables, watching Mrs. Harlow chop meat and stir puddings, getting the occasional titbit thrust into my mouth, listening to dramatic scenes from Mr. Dolland's frustrated past; and always there were the loving arms of Nanny Pollock, for those moments when comfort was needed.

It was a happy childhood in which I could safely dispense with the attention of my parents.

Then came the day when Miss Felicity Wills, niece of Professor Wills, was to come to the household to be governess to me and concern herself with the rudiments of my education until further plans were made for my future.

I heard the cab draw up at the door. We were at the nursery window: myself, Nanny Pollock, Mrs. Harlow, Dot, Meg, and Emily.

I saw her alight and the cabby brought her bags to the door. She looked young and help-less and certainly not in the least terrifying.

"Just a slip of a thing," commented Nanny.

"You wait," said Mrs. Harlow, determined to be pessimistic. "As I've told you often, looks ain't everything to go by."

The summons to the drawing room which we were expecting came at length. Nanny had put me into a clean dress and combed my hair.

"Remember to answer up sharp," she told me. "And don't be afraid of them. You're all right, you are, and Nanny loves you."

I kissed her fervently and went to the draw-ing room, where my parents were waiting for me with Miss Felicity Wills.

"Ah, Rosetta," said my mother, recognis-ing me, I supposed, because she was expect-ing me. "This is your governess, Miss Felicity Wills. Our daughter, Rosetta, Miss Wills."

She came towards me and I think I loved her from that moment. She was so dainty and pretty, like a picture I had seen somewhere. She took both my hands and smiled at me. I returned the smile.

"I am afraid you will have to begin on virgin soil, Miss Wills," said my mother. "Rosetta has had no tuition as yet."

"I am sure she has already learned quite a good deal," said Miss Wills.

My mother lifted her shoulders.

"Rosetta could show you the schoolroom," said my father.

"That would be an excellent idea," said Miss Wills. She turned to me, still smiling.

The worst was over. We left the drawing room together.

"It's right at the top of the house," I said.

"Yes. Schoolrooms often are. To leave us undisturbed, I suppose. I hope we shall get along together. So I am your first governess."

I nodded.

"I'll tell you something," she went on. "You're my first pupil. So we are beginners . . . both of us."

It made an immediate bond between us. I felt a great deal happier than I had when I had awakened that morning and the first thing I had thought of was her arrival. I had imagined a fierce old woman and here was a pretty young girl. She could not have been more than seventeen; and she had already confessed that she had never taught before.

It was a lovely surprise. I knew I was going to be all right.

Life had taken on a new dimension. It was a great joy to me to discover that I was not as ignorant as I had feared.

Somehow I had taught myself to read with the help of Mr. Dolland. I had studied the pictures in the Bible and had loved the stories told by him with dramatic emphasis. They had fascinated me, those pictures: Rachel at the well; Adam and Eve being turned out of the Garden of Eden, looking back over their shoulders at the angels with flaming swords; John the Baptist standing in the water and preaching. Then of course I had listened to Mr. Dolland's rendering of the speech before Harfleur and I could recite it, as well as some of "To be or not to be." Mr. Dolland had greatly fancied himself as Hamlet.

Miss Wills was delighted with me, and we were friends from the start.

It was true there was a certain amount of hostility to be overcome with my friends in the kitchen. But Felicity — I was soon calling her Felicity when we were alone — was so gracious, and by no means as arrogant as Mrs. Harlow had feared, that she soon broke through the barrier between the kitchen and those who, Mrs. Harlow said, thought themselves to be "a cut above." Soon the meals on trays were no more and Felicity joined us at the kitchen table.

Of course it was a state of affairs which would never have been accepted in a well-ordered household, but one of the advantages of having parents who lived in a remote atmosphere of scholarship, apart from the mundane ménage of a household, was that it gave us freedom. And how we revelled in it! When I look back on what many would call my neglected childhood, I can only rejoice in it, because it was one of the most wonderful and loving any child could have. But, of course, when one is living it, one does not realise how good it is. It is only when it is over that that becomes clear.

Learning was fun with Felicity. We did our lessons every morning. She made it all so interesting. In fact, she gave the impression that we were finding out things together. She never pretended to know. If I asked a question she would say frankly, "I'll have to look that up." She told me about herself. Her father had died some years ago and they were very poor. She had two sisters, of whom she was the eldest. She was fortunate to have her uncle, Professor Wills, her father's brother, who had helped the family and found this post for her.

She admitted that she had been terrified, expecting a very clever child who would know more than she did.

18

We laughed about that. "Well," she said, "the daughter of Professor Cranleigh. He's a great authority, you know, and very highly respected in the academic world."

I wasn't sure what the academic world was but I felt a glow of pride. After all, he was my father, and it was pleasant to know that he was highly thought of.

"He and your mother have many demands made on them," she explained. That was further good news. It would keep them out of our way.

"I thought there would be a great deal of supervision and guidance and that sort of thing. So it has all turned out much better than I expected."

"I thought you'd be terrible . . . neither fish nor fowl."

That seemed very funny and we laughed. We were always laughing. So I was learning fast. History was about people, some very odd, not just names and a string of dates. Geography was like an exciting tour round the world. We had a big globe which we turned round and round; we picked out places and imagined we were there.

I was sure that my parents would not have approved of this method of teaching, but it worked well. They would never have engaged anyone who looked like Felicity, and who admitted that she had no qualifications and had never taught before, if she had not been the niece of Professor Wills.

So we had a great deal to be thankful for and we knew it.

Then there were our walks. We learned what an interesting place Bloomsbury was. It became a game to us to find out how it had become as it was. It was exciting to discover that a century before it had been an isolated village called Lomesbury and between St. Pancras Church and the British Museum were fields and open country. We found the house where Sir Godfrey Kneller had lived; then there were the rookeries, that area into which we could not venture — a maze of streets in which the very poor lived side by side with the criminal classes, where the latter could rest in safety because no one would dare enter the place.

Mr. Dolland, who had been born and bred in Bloomsbury, loved to talk about the old days and, as was to be expected, he knew a good deal about it. There were many interesting conversations on the subject during meals.

We would sit there on winter evenings, the lamp shedding its light on the remains of Mrs. Harlow's pies or puddings and empty vegetable dishes, while Mr. Dolland talked of his early life in Bloomsbury.

He had been born in Gray's Inn Road and in his boyhood he had explored his surroundings and had many stories to tell of it.

I remember details from those days so well. He really had dramatic powers and, as do most actors, liked to enthral an audience. He certainly could not have had a more appreciative one — even though it was smaller than he might have wished.

"Shut your eyes," he would say, "and think of it. Buildings make a difference. Think of this place . . . when it were all country. I was never one for the country myself."

"You're like me, Mr. Dolland," said Mrs. Harlow. "You like a bit of life."

"Don't we all?" asked Dot.

"I don't know," put in Nanny Pollock. "There's some as swears by the country."

"I was born and bred in the country," piped up the tweeny.

"I like it here," I said, "with all of us."

Nanny nodded her approval of that sentiment.

I could see Mr. Dolland was in the mood to entertain us, and I was wondering whether to ask for "Once more unto the breach" or *The Bells*.

"Ah," he said, "there's been a lot going on round here. If you could only see back to years ago."

"It's a pity we have to rely on hearsay," said Felicity. "I think it's fascinating to hear people talk of the past."

"Mind you," said Mr. Dolland, "I can't go back all that way, but I've had stories from my granny. She was here before they put up all these buildings. She used to talk about a farm that used to be just about where the top of Russell Street is now. She remembered the Miss Cappers who lived there."

I settled happily in my chair, hoping for a story about the Miss Cappers. Mr. Dolland saw this. He smiled at me and said, "You want to hear what she told me about them, don't you, Miss Rosetta?"

I nodded and he began.

"They were two old maids, the Misses Capper. One was crossed in love and the other never had a chance to be. It made them sort of bitter against all men. Well-to-do they were. They had the farm left to them by their father. Ran it themselves, they did. Wouldn't have a man about the place. They managed with a dairy maid or two. It was this dislike of the opposite sex."

"Because one was crossed in love," said Emily.

"And the other never had a chance to be," I added.

"Sh," admonished Nanny. "Let Mr. Dolland go on."

"A queer pair they were. Used to ride out on old grey mares. They didn't like the sex but they dressed just as though they belonged to it . . . in top hats and riding habits. They looked like a couple of old witches. They were known all round as the Mad Cappers."

I thought that was a good joke and laughed heartily, only to receive another reproving shake of the head from Nanny. I should have known better. One should never interrupt Mr. Dolland when he was in full flow.

"It was not that they did anything that was really wicked. It was just that they liked to do a bit of harm here and there. It was a place where boys used to like to fly their kites, it being all open to the sky. One of the Miss Cappers used to ride round with a pair of shears. She'd gallop after the ones with the kites and cut the strings so that the little boys were standing there . . . the string in their hands, watching their kites flying off to Kingdom Come."

"Oh, poor little boys. What a shame," said Felicity.

"That was the Miss Cappers for you. There was a little stream nearby where the boys used to bathe. There was nothing they liked more on a hot summer's day than a dip in the water.

They'd leave their clothes behind a bush while they went in. This other Miss Capper used to watch them. Then she'd swoop down and steal their clothes."

"What a nasty old woman," said Dot.

"She said the boys were trespassing on her land and trespassers should be punished."

"Surely a little warning would have done?" said Felicity.

"That wasn't the Miss Cappers' way. They caused a bit of gossip, those two. I wish I'd been around when they were alive. I'd like to have seen them."

"You would never have let them cut *your* kite and send it to Kingdom Come, Mr. Dolland," I said.

"They were pretty sharp, those two. Then, of course, there were the forty steps."

We all settled back in our seats to hear the story of the forty steps.

"Is it a ghost story?" I asked eagerly.

"Well, sort of."

"Perhaps we'd better have it in the morning," said Nanny, her eyes on me. "Miss gets a bit excited about ghost stories at the end of the day. I don't want her awake half the night fancying she hears things."

"Oh, Mr. Dolland," I begged. "Please tell us now. I can't wait. I want to hear about the forty steps."

Felicity was smiling at me. "She'll be all right," she said, wanting to hear as much as I did, and, having whetted our appetites, Mr. Dolland saw that he must go on.

Nanny looked a little displeased. She was not as fond of Felicity as the rest of us were. I believed it was because she knew of my affection for her and was afraid it detracted from what I had for her. She need have had no qualms. I was able to love them both.

Mr. Dolland cleared his throat and put on the expression he must have worn when he was waiting in the wings to go on the stage and do his part.

He began dramatically. "There were two brothers. This was a long time ago when King Charles was on the throne. Well, the King died and his son, the Duke of Monmouth, thought he himself would make a better king than Charles's brother James, and there was a battle between them. One of the brothers was for Monmouth and the other for James, so they were enemies fighting on different sides. But what was more important to them was their admiration for a certain young lady. Yes, the two brothers loved the same woman and it got to such a state that they made up their minds to fight it out between them, for this young lady was the Beauty of Bloomsbury and she thought quite a lot of herself, as such young ladies do. She was proud because they were going to fight over her. They were to fight with swords, which was how they did it in those days. It was what they called a duel. There was a patch of ground close to Cappers' farm. It was wasteland and it always had had a bad reputation. It was the haunt of the highwaymen, and no one with any sense walked there after dark. It seemed a good place for a duel."

Mr. Dolland picked up the large carving knife from the table and brandished it deftly, stepping back and forth as he battled with an invisible opponent. Gracefully he held the knife but with such realism that I could almost see the two men fighting together.

He paused for a moment and, pointing to the kitchen stove, said, "There on a bank, enjoying every minute, seeing each brother prepared to kill the other for her sake, sat the cause of the trouble."

The kitchen stove became a bank. I could see the girl, looking a little like Felicity, only Felicity was too good and kind to want anyone to die for her. It was all so vivid; and that was how it always was with Mr. Dolland's turns.

He made a dramatic thrust and went on in hollow tones. "Just as one brother caught the other in the neck, severing a vein, the other struck his brother through the heart. So . . .

26

both brothers died on Long Fields, as it was called then, though afterwards the name was changed to Southampton Fields."

"Well, I never!" said Mrs. Harlow. "The things people do for love."

"Which one haunted her?" I asked.

"You and your ghosts," said Nanny disapprovingly. "There always has to be a ghost for this one."

"Listen to this," said Mr. Dolland. "While they were going back and forth" — he did a little more swordplay to illustrate his meaning — "they made forty steps on that blood-stained patch, and where those brothers had trod nothing would ever grow again. People used to go out and look at them. According to my granny they could see the footsteps clearly and the earth was red as though stained with blood. Nobody ever went there after dark."

"They didn't before," I reminded him.

"But the highwaymen didn't go there either . . . and still nobody went."

"Did they *see* anything?" asked Dot.

"No. There was just this brooding feeling of something not quite natural. They said that when it rained and the ground was soggy you could still see the footsteps and they were tinged with red. Things were planted but nothing would grow. The footsteps remained."

"What happened to the girl for whom they

fought?" asked Felicity.

"She fades out of the story."

"I hope they haunted her," I said.

"They shouldn't have been such fools," said Nanny. "I've no patience with fools. Never have had, never will have."

"It's rather sad, I think, that they both died," I commented. "It would have been better if one of them had remained to suffer remorse . . . and the girl wasn't worth all that trouble anyway."

"You have to accept what is," Felicity told me. "You can't change life to make a neat ending."

Mr. Dolland went on. "There was a play written about it. It was called *The Field of the Forty Steps.*"

"Were you in it, Mr. Dolland?" asked Dot.

"No. A bit before my day. I heard of it, though, and it made me interested in the story of the brothers. Somebody called Mayhew wrote it with *his* brother, which was a nice touch — brothers writing about brothers, so to speak. They played it at the theatre in Tottenham Street. It ran for quite a while."

"Fancy all that happening round here," said Emily.

"Well, we never know what's going to happen to any of us at any time," commented Felicity seriously.

★

So the time passed, weeks merging into months and months into years: happy, unruffled days with little to disturb our serenity. I was approaching my twelfth birthday. I suppose Felicity would have been about twenty-four then. Mr. Dolland was greying at the temples, which we declared made him look very distinguished and that added a certain grandeur to his turns. Nanny complained more of her rheumatics and Dot left to get married. We missed her but Meg took her place and Emily took Meg's, and it was thought unnecessary to engage a new tweeny. In time Dot produced a beautiful fat baby whom she proudly brought round for us all to see.

There were many happy memories in those days; but I should have realised that they could not go on forever. I was growing out of childhood and Felicity had become a beautiful young woman.

Change comes about in the most insidious way.

There had been the odd occasion since Felicity had come to us when she had been invited to join one of the dinner parties given by my parents. Of course, Felicity explained to me, it was because they needed another female to balance the sexes, and as she was the niece of Professor Wills she was a suitable guest, although only the governess. She did not look forward to these occasions. I remember the one dinner dress she had. It was made of black lace and she looked very pretty in it, but it hung in her wardrobe, a depressing reminder of the dinner parties which were the only occasions when she wore it. She was always thankful when my parents went away, for the reason that then there could be no invitations to dinner parties. She was never sure when they would be forced on her, for to invite her was generally a last-minute decision. She was, as she said, a most reluctant makeshift.

As I grew older I saw a little more of my parents. I would take tea with them at certain times. I believe they felt even more embarrassed in my presence than I did in theirs. They were never unkind. They asked a great many questions about what I was learning and, as I had an aptitude for gathering facts and a fondness for literature, I was able to give a fair account of myself. So although they were not particularly elated by my progress, they were not as displeased as they might have been.

Then the first signs of the change began, although I did not recognise them as such at the time.

There was to be a dinner party and Felicity was summoned to attend.

"My dress is getting that tired and dusty look which black gets," she told me.

"You look very nice in it, Felicity," I assured her.

"I feel so . . . apart, the outsider. Everyone knows I'm the governess called in to make up the numbers."

"Well, you look nicer than any of them and you're more interesting, too."

That made her laugh. "All those deedy old professors think I'm a frivolous empty-headed idiot."

"*They* are the empty-headed idiots," I said.

I was with her when she dressed. Her lovely hair was piled high on her head, and her nervousness had put a becoming touch of pink into her cheeks.

"You look lovely," I told her. "They'll all be envious."

That made her laugh again and I was pleased to have lightened her mood a little.

The awesome thought struck me: Soon I shall have to go to those boring dinner parties.

She came to my room at eleven that night. I had never seen her look so beautiful. I sat up in bed. She was laughing. "Oh, Rosetta, I had to tell you."

"Sh," I said. "Nanny Pollock will hear.

31

She'll say you ought not to disturb my slumbers."

We giggled and she sat on the edge of my bed.

"It was such . . . fun."

"What?" I cried. "Dinner with the old professors, fun?"

"They weren't all old. There was one . . . "

"Yes?"

"He was quite interesting. After dinner — "

"I know," I broke in. "The ladies leave the gentlemen to sit over the port to discuss matters which are too weighty or too indelicate for female ears."

We were laughing again.

"Tell me more about this not-so-old professor," I said. "I didn't know there were such things. I thought they were all born old."

"Learning can sit lightly on some."

There was a radiance about her, I noticed then.

"I never thought to see you enjoy a dinner party," I said. "You give me hope. It has occurred to me that one day I shall be expected to attend them."

"It depends on who is there," she said, smiling to herself.

"You haven't told me about the young man."

"Well, he was about thirty, I should say."

"Oh, not so young."

"Young for a professor."

"What's his subject?"

"Egypt."

"That seems a popular one."

"Your parents tend to move in that particular circle."

"Did you tell him I was named after the Rosetta Stone?"

"As a matter of fact I did."

"I hope he was suitably impressed."

And so we went on with our frivolous conversation, but just because Felicity had enjoyed one of the dinner parties it did not occur to me that this might be the beginning of change.

The very next day I made the acquaintance of James Grafton. We had taken our morning walk, Felicity and I, and since we had heard the story of the forty steps and located them, we often went that way. There was indeed a patch of ground where the grass grew sparsely and it really did look desolate enough to confirm one's belief in the story.

There was a seat close by. I liked to sit on it, and so vivid had been Mr. Dolland's reconstruction of the affair that I could imagine the brothers in their fatal battle.

Almost by force of habit we made our way to the seat and sat down. We had not been there very long when a man approached. He took off his hat and bowed. He stood smiling at us while Felicity blushed becomingly.

"Why," he said, "it really is Miss Wills."

She laughed. "Oh, good morning, Mr. Grafton. This is Miss Rosetta Cranleigh."

He bowed in my direction.

"How do you do?" he said. "May I sit for a moment?"

"Please do," said Felicity.

Instinctively I knew he was the young man whom she had met at the dinner party on the previous night and that this meeting had been arranged.

There was a little conversation about the weather.

"This is a favourite spot of yours," he said, and I had a feeling he was telling himself that he must include me in the conversation.

"We come here often," I told him.

"The story of the forty steps intrigued us," said Felicity.

"Do you know it?" I asked.

He did not, so I told him.

"When I sit here I can imagine it all," I said.

"Rosetta's a romantic," Felicity told him.

"Most of us are at heart," he said, smiling at me warmly.

He told us that he was on his way to the

Museum. Some papyri had come to light and Professor Cranleigh was going to allow him to have a look at them.

"It is very exciting when something turns up which might increase our knowledge," he added. "Professor Cranleigh was telling us last night about some of the wonderful discoveries which have been made recently."

He went on talking about them and Felicity listened enraptured.

I was suddenly aware that something momentous was happening. She was slipping away from me. It seemed ridiculous to think such a thing. She was as sweet and caring as ever, but she did seem a little absent-minded, as though when she was talking to me she was thinking of something else.

But it did not immediately strike me on that first encounter with the attractive Professor Grafton that Felicity was in love.

We met him several times after that, and I knew that none of these meetings was by chance. He dined at the house once or twice, and on each occasion Felicity joined the party. It occurred to me that my parents were in the secret.

Felicity bought a new dinner dress. We went together to the shop. It was not really what she would have liked but it was the best she could afford, and since she had met James

Grafton she had become even prettier and she looked lovely in it. It was blue, the colour of her eyes, and she was radiant.

Mr. Dolland and Mrs. Harlow soon became aware of what was going on.

"A good thing for her," said Mrs. Harlow. "Governesses have a poor time of it. They get attached, like, and when they're no longer wanted it's off to the next one until they get too old . . . and then what's to become of them? She's a pretty young thing and it's time she had a man to look after her."

I had to admit I was dismayed. If Felicity married Mr. Grafton she would not be with me. I tried to imagine life without her.

She was taking a great interest in ancient Egypt, and we paid many visits to the British Museum. I no longer felt the awe of my childhood and was quite fascinated, and, spurred on by Felicity, I was almost as enthralled by the Egyptian Room as she was.

The mummies in particular attracted me . . . in a rather morbid way. I felt that if I were alone in that room with them they would come to life.

James Grafton used to meet us there sometimes. I would wander off and leave him to whisper with Felicity while I studied the faces of Osiris and Isis just as those who thought they were divine must have seen them all those years ago.

One day my father came into the room and saw us there. There was a moment of puzzlement until it dawned on him that here in this holy of holies was his own daughter.

I was standing by the mummy-shaped coffin of King Menkaure — one of the oldest in the collection — when he came upon me. His eyes lit up with sudden pleasure.

"Well, Rosetta, I am pleased to find you here."

"I have come with Miss Wills," I said.

He turned slowly to where Felicity and James were standing.

"I see." There was a look on his face which in others might have seemed quite puckish but with him it was just rather indulgently knowledgeable.

"You are attracted by the mummies, I see."

"Yes," I replied. "It's incredible . . . the remains of these people being here after all those years."

"I am delighted to see your interest. Come with me."

I followed him to where Felicity and James were standing.

"I am taking Rosetta to my room," he said. "Perhaps you would join us in, say, an hour?"

"Oh, thank you, sir," said James.

I knew what my father was doing. He was

giving them a little time alone. It was amusing to think of my father playing Cupid.

I was taken to his room, which I had never seen before. It was lined with books from floor to high ceiling, and there were several glass-doored cabinets which contained all sorts of objects, such as stones covered in hieroglyphics and carved images.

"This is the first time you have seen where I work," he said.

"Yes, Father."

"I am pleased that you are displaying some interest. We do wonderful work here. If you had been a boy I should have wanted you to follow me."

I felt I ought to apologise for and defend my sex. "My mother — " I began.

"She is an exceptional woman."

Yes, of course. I could hardly aspire to that. Exceptional I was not. I had spent my happy childhood with people belowstairs who had entertained me, loved me, and made me contented with my lot.

As the embarrassment which our encounters never failed to engender seemed to be building up, he plunged into a description of embalming processes to which I listened entranced, all the time marvelling that I was in the British Museum talking to my father.

Felicity and James Grafton eventually

joined us. It was an unusual morning, but by this time I had realised that change was on the way.

Very soon after that, Felicity became engaged to James Grafton. I was both excited and apprehensive. It was good to see Felicity so happy and to know something which had never occurred to me until Mrs. Harlow pointed it out: that she was secure.

But there was, of course, the question of what would become of me.

My parents were taking more interest in me, which was in itself disconcerting. I had been discovered by my father showing interest in the exhibits in the Egyptian Room of the British Museum. We had had a little talk in his room there. I was not exactly the ignoramus they had previously thought me. I had a brain which had lain dormant for all these years, but I might possibly grow up to be one of them.

Felicity was to be married in March of the following year. I had passed my thirteenth birthday. Felicity was to stay with us until a week before the marriage; then she would go to the house of Professor Wills, who had been responsible for her admission into our household, and from there be married; and in due course she and James would set up house in

Oxford, to whose university he was attached. The big question was, What course should my education now take?

Having received a gift of money from her uncle, Felicity was now able to indulge in replenishing her scanty wardrobe, a task in which I joined with great enthusiasm, though never able to escape from the big question of my future and the prospect of facing the emptiness which her departure must inevitably mean.

I tried to imagine what it would be like without her. She had become part of my life, and closer even than the others. Would there be a new governess of the more traditional sort — at cross-purposes with Mrs. Harlow and the rest? There was only one Felicity in the world and I had been lucky to have her with me all those years. But there is little comfort in recalling past luck which is about to be snatched away so that the future looks uncertain.

About three weeks before the date fixed for the wedding, my parents sent for me.

Since my meeting with my father in the British Museum there had been a subtle change in our relationship. They had certainly become more interested in me and, in spite of the fact that I had always told myself I was happy to be without their attention, I was now faintly pleased to have it.

"Rosetta," said my mother. "Your father and I have decided that it is time you went away to school."

This was not unexpected, of course. Felicity had talked to me about it.

"It's a distinct possibility," she had said, "and really it's the best thing. Governesses are all very well but you'll meet people of your own age, and you will enjoy that."

I could not believe I would enjoy anything as much as being with her and I told her so.

She hugged me tightly. "There'll be holidays and you can come and stay with us."

I remembered that now, so I was prepared.

"Gresham's is a very good school," said my father. "It has been highly recommended. I think it will be most suitable."

"You will be going there in September," went on my mother. "It's the start of the term. There will be certain preparations. Then there is Nanny Pollock, of course."

Nanny Pollock! So I was to lose her too. I felt a great sadness. I remembered those loving arms, those whispered endearments, the comfort I had received.

"We shall give her a good reference," said my mother.

"She has been excellent," added my father.

The only one who was moving to a happier

state was Felicity. There was always some good in everything, Mr. Dolland had said.

But how I hated change.

The weeks passed too quickly. Every morning I awoke with an uneasy feeling in the pit of my stomach. The future loomed before me, unfamiliar and therefore alarming. I had lived too long in unruffled serenity.

Nanny Pollock was very sad.

"It always comes," she said. "Little chicks don't stay that way forever. You've cared for them like they was your own . . . and then comes the day. They've grown up. They're not your babies any more."

"Oh, Nanny, Nanny. I'll never forget you."

"Nor I you, lovey. I've had my pets, but them upstairs being as they are, made you more my little baby . . . if you know what I mean."

"I do, Nanny."

"It's not that they was cruel, or hard-hearted . . . no, none of that. They was just absent-minded, like, so deep in all that unnatural writing and what it means and all them kings and queens kept in their coffins all them years. It was unhealthy as well as unnatural and I never did think much of it. Little babies is more important than a lot of dead kings and queens and all the signs they made because they didn't know how to write properly."

I laughed and she was glad to see me smile.

She cheered up a little. "I'm all right," she said. "I've got a cousin in Somerset. Keeps her own chickens. I always like a real fresh egg for breakfast, laid that morning. I might go to her. I don't feel like taking on another . . . but I might. Anyway, there's no worry on that score. Your mother says not to hurry. I can stay here if I want till I find something I like."

At length Felicity was married from the house of Professor Wills in Oxford. I went down with my parents for the wedding. We drank the health of the newly married pair and I saw Felicity in her strawberry-coloured going-away costume which I had seen before and in fact helped her to choose. She looked radiant and I told myself I must be glad for her while feeling sorry for myself.

When I returned to London they wanted to know all about the wedding.

"She must have made a lovely bride," said Mrs. Harlow. "I hope she's happy. God bless her. She deserves to be. You never know with them professors. They're funny things."

"Like governesses, you used to say," I reminded her.

"Well, I reckon she wasn't a real governess.

43

She was one on her own."

Mr. Dolland said we should all drink to the health and happiness of the happy pair. So we did.

The conversation was doleful. Nanny Pollock had almost decided to go to her cousin in Somerset for a spell. She had drunk a little too much wine and had become maudlin.

"Governesses . . . nannies . . . it's their fate. They should know better. They shouldn't get attached to other people's children."

"But we're not going to lose each other, Nanny," I reminded her.

"No. You'll come and see me, won't you?"

"Of course."

"But it won't be the same. You'll be a grown-up young lady. Them schools . . . they do something to you."

"They're supposed to educate you."

"It won't be the same," insisted Nanny Pollock, shaking her head dolefully.

"I know how Nanny is feeling," said Mr. Dolland. "Felicity has gone. That was the start. And that's how it always is with change. A little bit here, a little bit there, and you realise everything is becoming different."

"And before you can say Jack Robinson," added Mrs. Harlow, "it's another kettle of fish."

"Well, you can't stand still in life," said

Mr. Dolland philosophically.

"I don't want change!" I cried out. "I want us all to go on as we always did. I didn't want Felicity to get married. I wanted it to stay like it always has been."

Mr. Dolland cleared his throat and solemnly quoted:

> The Moving Finger writes; and, having
> writ,
> Moves on: nor all thy Piety nor Wit
> Shall lure it back to cancel half a Line,
> Nor all thy Tears wash out a Word of it.

Mr. Dolland sat back and folded his arms and there was silence. He had pointed out with his usual dramatic emphasis that this was life and we must all accept what we could not alter.

Storm at Sea

In due course I went away to school. I was wretched for a time but I soon settled in. I found community life to my liking. I had always been interested in other people and I was soon making friends and joining in school activities.

Felicity had done quite well with my education, and I was neither outstandingly brilliant nor dull. I was like so many others, which is perhaps the best thing to be for it makes life easier. No one envied me my scholarship and no one despised me for my lack of it. I soon mingled with the rest and became a very average schoolgirl.

The days passed quickly. School joys, dramas, and triumphs became part of my life although I often thought nostalgically of the kitchen at mealtimes and particularly of Mr. Dolland's turns. We had drama classes, and plays were put on in the gymnasium for the entertainment of the school. I was Bassanio in *The Merchant of Venice,* and scored a modest success, which I was sure was due to what I had learned from Mr. Dolland's technique.

Then there were the holidays. Nanny Pollock had decided to go to Somerset after all and I spent a week with her and her cousin; she had become reconciled to life in the country and, a year or so after she left Bloomsbury, the death of a distant relative brought complete contentment back to her life.

The deceased was a young woman who had left a two-year-old child, and there was consternation in the family as to who would take care of the orphan. It was a heaven-sent opportunity for Nanny Pollock: a child to care for, one whom she could make her own and who would not be snatched from her as those of other people were.

When I went home I was expected now to dine with my parents, and although my relationship with them had changed considerably I longed for the old kitchen meals. However, when they went away from London researching or lecturing, I was able to revert to the old customs.

We missed Felicity and Nanny Pollock, of course, but Mr. Dolland was in as sparkling a form as ever and Mrs. Harlow's comments retained the flavour of the old days.

Then of course there was Felicity. She was always delighted to see me.

She was very happy and had a baby named James and had thrown herself wholeheartedly into the task of being a good wife and mother. She was a good hostess, too. It was necessary, she told me, for a man in James's position to entertain now and then, so that was something she had had to learn. Growing up as I was, I could attend her dinner parties and I found that I enjoyed them.

It was at one of them that I made the acquaintance of Lucas Lorimer. Felicity told me something of him before I met him.

"By the way," she said. "Lucas Lorimer is coming tonight. You'll like him. Most people do. He is charming, good-looking . . . well, good-looking enough . . . and he has the trick of making everyone feel they're enormously interesting. You know what I mean. Don't be deceived. He's like that with everyone. He's rather a restless sort of person, I imagine. He was in the Army for a spell. But he retired from that. He's the younger son. His elder brother, Carleton, has just inherited the estate in Cornwall, which is quite considerable, I think. The father died only a few months ago, and Lucas is rather at a loose end. There is plenty to do on the estate but I imagine he's the sort who would want to be in command. He's a little unsure of what he wants to do at the moment. A few years ago he found a charm, a relic of some sort, in the gardens of Trecorn Manor — that's the name of the place in Cornwall. There was a certain excitement about this find. It was Egyptian, and there was some speculation as to how it came to be there. Your father is connected with it."

"I expect it was covered in hieroglyphics."

"At the time, Lucas wrote a book about it. He did some research and found out that it was a medal awarded for some special military service. That led him on to the ancient customs of Egypt and he came upon some which had not been heard of till he made his discovery. This interested people like your father. Anyway, you'll meet him and judge for yourself."

I did meet him that night.

He was tall, slim, and lithe; one was immediately aware of his vitality.

"This is Rosetta Cranleigh," said Felicity.

"How delightful to meet you," he said, taking both my hands and gazing at me.

She was right. He did make one feel important and as though his words were not merely a formality. I felt myself believing him in spite of Felicity's warning.

Felicity went on. "Professor Cranleigh's daughter and my one-time pupil. In fact, the only one I ever had."

"This is so exciting," he said. "I have met

your father — a brilliant man."

Felicity left us to talk together. He did most of the talking. He told me how helpful my father had been and how grateful he was to have had so much of the important gentleman's time.

Then he wanted to know about me. I confessed that I was still at school: that this was my holiday and I had another two or three terms to come.

"And then what shall you do?"

I lifted my shoulders.

"You'll be married before long, I daresay," he said, implying that my charms were such that prospective husbands would be vying with each other to win me.

"One never knows what will happen to us."

"How very true," he remarked as though my trite remark made a sage of me.

Felicity was right. He set out to please. It was rather transparent when one had been warned, but pleasant, I had to admit.

I found myself seated beside him at dinner. He was very easy to talk to. He told me about the find in the garden and how to a certain extent it had changed his life.

"The family have always been connected with the Army and I have broken the tradition. My uncle was a colonel of the regiment, hardly ever in England, always doing his duty at some outpost of Empire. I discovered it wasn't the life for me so I got out."

"It must have been very exciting, finding this relic."

"It was. When I was in the Army I spent some time in Egypt. That made it rather specially interesting. I just saw it lying there. The soil was damp and one of the gardeners was doing some planting. It was covered in hieroglyphics."

"You needed the Rosetta Stone."

He laughed. "Oh, not quite so obscure as that. Your father translated it."

"I'm glad of that. I was named after the stone, you know."

"Yes, I did know. Felicity told me. How proud you must be."

"I used to be. When I first went to the Museum I gazed at it in wonder."

He laughed. "Names are important. You would never guess what my first name is."

"Tell me."

"Hadrian. Just imagine being burdened with such a name. People would constantly be asking how you were getting on with the wall. Hadrian Edward Lucas Lorimer. Hadrian was out, for the reasons I've mentioned. Edward — well, there are a great number of Edwards in the world. Lucas is less used . . . so I became Lucas. But you realise what my initials spell? It's rather extraordinary: H E L L."

"I am sure it is most inappropriate," I said with a laugh.

"Ah, but you do not know me. Have you another name?"

"No, just Rosetta Cranleigh."

"R.C."

"Not nearly so amusing as yours."

"Yours suggests someone very devout, whereas I could be an imp of Satan. It's significant, don't you think: the suggestion of people in opposite spheres? I am sure it means something concerning our friendship to come. You are going to turn me from my evil ways and be a good influence on my life. I'd like to think it meant that."

I laughed and we were silent for a while; then he said, "You are interested in the mysteries of Egypt, I daresay. As your parents' daughter you must be."

"Well, in a mild way. At school one doesn't have much time to be interested in what isn't going on there."

"I'd like to know what the words on my stone really meant."

"I thought you said they had been translated."

"Yes . . . in a way. All these things are so cryptic. The meaning is couched in words which are not quite clear."

"Why do people have to be so obscure?"

"To bring in an element of mystery, don't you think? It adds to the interest. It's the same with people. When you discover subtleties in their characters you become more interested."

He smiled at me, his eyes saying something which I did not understand.

"You will eventually discover that I am right," he said.

"You mean when I'm older?"

"I believe you resent people referring to your youth."

"Well, I suppose it implies that one is not yet capable of understanding much."

"You should revel in your youth. The poets have said it passes too quickly. 'Gather ye rosebuds while ye may.'" He smiled at me with a benignity which was almost tender.

I was a little thoughtful after that and I guessed that he was aware of it.

After dinner I went out with the ladies and when the men joined us I did not talk to him again.

Later Felicity asked me how I had liked him. "I saw you were getting on very well with him," she said.

"I think he is the sort who would get on well with anyone . . . superficially."

She hesitated for a second; then she said,

"Yes. You are right."

It seemed significant afterwards that what I remembered most clearly about that visit was my meeting with Hadrian Edward Lucas Lorimer.

When I came home for the Christmas holiday my parents seemed more animated than usual, even excited. The only thing I imagined which could make them feel so would be some new knowledge they had acquired. A breakthrough in their understanding of their work? A new stone to replace the Rosetta?

It was nothing of the sort.

As soon as I arrived they wanted to talk to me.

"Something rather interesting has occurred," said my mother.

My father smiled at me, rather indulgently, I thought. "And," he added, "it concerns you."

I was startled.

"Let us explain," said my mother. "We have been invited to do a most interesting lecture tour. This takes us to Cape Town and, on the way back, to Philadelphia and New York."

"Oh? You will be away for a long time."

"Your mother thinks it would be interesting to combine a holiday with work," said my father.

"He has been working far too hard recently. Of course we will not leave it altogether. He can be working on his new book. . . . "

"Of course," I murmured.

"We plan to go by ship to Cape Town, a long sea voyage. We shall stay a few days there while your father does one of his lectures. Meanwhile, the ship goes on to Durban and we shall pick it up again when it returns to Cape Town. It is calling at Philadelphia, where we shall leave it again — another lecture — then we shall travel up to New York by land, where your father will give the last of his lectures, and then we shall take another ship for home."

"It sounds very interesting."

There was a slight pause.

My father looked at my mother and said, "We have decided that you shall accompany us."

I was too astonished to speak. Then I stammered, "You . . . you really mean that?"

"It will be good for you to see a little of the world," said my father benignly.

"When . . . when?" I asked.

"We are setting forth at the end of April. There will be a great many preparations to make."

"I shall be at school."

"You would be leaving at the end of the

summer term in any case. We thought that little could be lost by cutting it short. After all, you will be nearly eighteen years of age. That is quite mature."

"I hope you are pleased," said my father.

"I am just . . . so surprised."

They smiled at me.

"You will need to make your own preparations. You could consult Felicity Wills . . . or, rather, Grafton. She has become quite worldly since her marriage. She would know what you needed. Perhaps two or three evening dresses for functions, and some . . . er . . . suitable garments."

"Oh, yes . . . yes," I said.

After brooding on the matter I was not sure whether I was pleased or not. The idea of travelling and seeing new places enthralled me. On the other hand I would be in the company of my parents and, I presumed, people so weighed down by their own scholarship that they would naturally reduce me to the status of an ignorant girl.

The prospect of new clothes was pleasant. I could not wait to consult Felicity.

I wrote to her and told her of the project.

She replied at once. *How thrilling! James has to go up North for a few days in March. I have a wonderful nanny who adores Jamie and he her. So I could come to London for a few days and we'll have an orgy of shopping.*

As the weeks passed the prospect of travelling abroad so enchanted me that I forgot the disadvantages that would go with it.

In due course Felicity came to London and, as I had expected, she threw herself wholeheartedly into the business of finding the right clothes. I was aware that she regarded me in a different light now that I was no longer a schoolgirl.

"Your hair is most striking," she said. "Your greatest asset. We'll have to plan with that in mind."

"My hair?" I had not thought about it before, except that it was unusually fair. It was long, straight, and thick.

"It's the colour of corn," said Felicity. "It's what they call golden. It really is very attractive. You'll be able to do all sorts of things with it. You can wear it piled high on your head when you want to be dignified, or tied back with a ribbon, or even plaited when you want to look demure. You can have a lot of fun with it. And we'll concentrate on blue to bring out the colour of your eyes."

My parents had gone to Oxford so we reverted to old customs and had our meals in the kitchen. It was just like old times and we prevailed on Mr. Dolland to do his Hamlet or Henry V and the eerie excerpts from *The Bells* for the sake of the old days.

We missed Nanny Pollock, but I wrote and told her what was happening; she was now very happy, completely absorbed by little Evelyn, who was a "pickle" and reminded her of what I had been at her age.

I paraded round the kitchen in my new garments, which resulted in oohs and ahs from Meg and Emily and a few caustic comments from Mrs. Harlow, who muttered something about fashions nowadays.

It was a very happy time, and it did occur to me now and then that the preliminaries of travel might be more pleasant than the actuality.

It was with regret that I said goodbye to Felicity and she returned to Oxford. The day was fast approaching when we would set out for Tilbury to board the *Atlantic Star*.

There was constant talk of the coming trip in the kitchen. None of them had been abroad, not even Mr. Dolland, although he had almost gone to Ireland once; but that, as Mrs. Harlow pointed out, was another kettle of fish. I was going to see real foreign parts, and that could be hazardous.

You never knew where you were with foreigners, commented Mrs. Harlow, and I'd be seeing a lot of them. She wouldn't have wanted to go, not even if she was offered a hundred pounds to do so.

Meg said, "Well, nobody's going to offer you a hundred pounds to go abroad, Mrs. H. So you're safe."

Mrs. Harlow looked sourly at Meg, who, according to her, was now getting above herself.

However, the constant talk of abroad — its attractions and its drawbacks — was suddenly overshadowed by the murder.

We first heard of it from the newsboys shouting in the streets. " 'Orrible murder! Man found shot through the head in empty farmhouse!"

Emily was sent out to buy a paper and Mr. Dolland sat at the table, wearing his spectacles and reading to the assembled company.

The murder was the main news at this time, there being nothing else of importance going on. It was called the Bindon Boys Murder, and the press dealt with it in lurid fashion so that people everywhere were reading of the case and wondering what was going to happen next.

Mr. Dolland had his own theory, and Mrs. Harlow reckoned that Mr. Dolland had as good a notion of such things as any of the police. It was because of the plays he knew so much about; many of them were concerned with murder.

"They ought to call him in, I reckon," she pronounced. "He'd soon put them to rights."

Meanwhile, basking in the glory of such admiration, Mr. Dolland would sit at the table and expound his views.

"It must be this young man," he said. "It all points to him, living with the family and not being one of them. That can be tricky, that can."

"One wonders why he was brought in," I said.

"Adopted son, it seems. I reckon he was jealous of this young man. Jealousy can drive people to great lengths."

"I could never abide empty houses," said Mrs. Harlow. "They give me the creeps."

"Of course, the story is that he went into this empty farmhouse, Bindon Boys as they call it, and shot him there," went on Mr. Dolland. "You see, this Cosmo was the eldest son and that alone would have made the young man a bit jealous, he being the outsider as it were. Then there was this widow: Mirabel, they call her. He wanted her for himself and Cosmo takes her. Well, there's your motive. He lures Cosmo to this empty farmhouse and shoots him."

"He might have got away with it," I said, "if the younger brother, Tristan — wasn't that his name? — if he hadn't come in and

60

caught him red-handed."

I pieced the story together. There were two sons of Sir Edward Perrivale — Cosmo and Tristan — and also in the household was the adopted son, Simon, who had been brought there when he was five years old. Simon had been educated as a member of the family but, according to the evidence, he had always been aware that he was not quite one of them.

Sir Edward was a sick man and in fact had died at the time of the murder so he would probably have been quite unaware of it. Bindon Boys — originally Bindon Bois, the press told us, because of a copse nearby — was a farmhouse on the Perrivale estate. It was in need of renovation and all three young men were concerned in the management of the estate, which was a large one on the coast of Cornwall. The implication was that Simon had lured Cosmo to the derelict farmhouse and calmly shot him. He probably had plans for disposing of the body but Tristan had come in and caught him with the gun in his hand. There seemed to be ample motive. The adopted son must have been jealous of the other two, and it seemed he was in love with the widow to whom Cosmo was engaged to be married.

It was a source of great satisfaction to the servants, and I must admit that I too began to be caught up in it.

Perhaps I was getting a little apprehensive about the coming trip with my parents and seized on something to take my thoughts away from it. I would become as animated as any of them when we sat round the kitchen table listening to Mr. Dolland pitting his wits against Scotland Yard.

"It's what they call an open-and-shut case," he pronounced.

"It would make a good play," said Mrs. Harlow.

"Well, I am not sure of that," replied Mr. Dolland. "You know from the start who the murderer is. In a play there has to be a good deal of questioning and clues and things and then you come up with the surprise ending."

"Perhaps it is not as simple as it appears," I suggested. "It might *seem* as if this Simon did it . . . but he says he didn't."

"Well, he would, wouldn't he?" put in Mrs. Harlow. "They all say that to save themselves and put the blame on someone else."

Mr. Dolland pressed the palms of his hands together and looked up at the ceiling. "Take the facts," he said. "A man brings a stranger into the house and treats him as his son. The others don't want him . . . and the boy resents not being treated like one of the family. It builds up over the years. There'd be hatred in that house. Then there's this widow. Cosmo's going to marry her. There's always been this feeling between them . . . so he kills Cosmo, and Tristan comes in and finds him."

"What fancy names," said Meg with a little giggle. "I've always been partial to fancy names."

Everyone ignored the interruption and waited for Mr. Dolland to go on. "Then there's the widow woman. That would be the last straw. Cosmo gets everything. And what's Simon? Just a bit better than a servant. Resentment flares up. There you have the planned murder. Ah . . . but before he could dispose of the body Tristan comes in and foils his plan. Murders always go wrong in plays. They always have to or there wouldn't have been a play . . . and plays are based on real life."

We all hung on his words.

Emily said, "I can't help feeling sorry for that Simon."

"Sorry for a murderer!" cried Mrs. Harlow. "You're out of your mind, girl. How would you like him to come along and put a bullet through your head?"

"He wouldn't, would he? I'm not Cosmo."

"You thank your lucky stars you're not," said Mrs. Harlow. "And don't interrupt Mr. Dolland."

"All we can do," went on the sage, "is wait and see."

We did not have to wait long. The newsboys were shouting in the streets. "Dramatic turn in Bindon Boys case! Read all about it!"

We did, avidly. It seemed that the police had been on the point of arresting Simon Perrivale — why they had delayed was a mystery to Mr. Dolland — and now Simon had disappeared.

WHERE IS SIMON PERRIVALE? demanded the headlines. HAVE YOU SEEN THIS MAN? Then, *Police on trail. Arrest expected hourly.*

"So," pronounced Mr. Dolland. "He has run away. He could not have said more clearly, I'm guilty. They'll find him, never fear."

"It's to be hoped so," added Mrs. Harlow. "A body don't feel safe in bed of nights with murderers running around."

"He wouldn't have reason to murder you, Mrs. Harlow," said Meg.

"I wouldn't trust him," retorted Mrs. Harlow.

"They'll soon find him," said Mr. Dolland reassuringly. "They'll have their men searching everywhere."

But the days passed and there was no news of a capture.

Then the case ceased to be headline news.

The Queen's Golden Jubilee was taking up the space, and there was no room for a sordid murder with the chief suspect having left the scene. No doubt when he was captured there would be a fresh surge of interest, but in the meantime the news of Bindon Boys was banished to the back pages.

Three days before we were due to depart, we had a caller.

I was in my room when my parents sent for me. I was to go to the drawing room immediately. A surprise awaited me there. As I entered, Lucas Lorimer came forward to greet me.

"Mr. Lorimer tells me that you met at Mr. and Mrs. Graftons' house," said my mother.

"Why, yes," I said, naïvely betraying my pleasure.

He took my hand, smiling into my eyes.

"It was such a pleasure to meet Professor Cranleigh's daughter," he said, complimenting both my father and me at the same time.

My parents were smiling on me indulgently.

"We have some good news," said my father.

The three of them were watching me as though they were about to inform a child of a treat in store.

"Mr. Lorimer is sailing on the *Atlantic*

Star," said my mother.

"Really!" I cried in amazement.

Lucas Lorimer nodded. "A great surprise for me and a great honour. I have been asked to give a talk on my discovery at the same time as Professor Cranleigh gives his lecture."

I felt laughter bubbling up within me. I was amused by the fine distinction implied between a talk and a lecture. I could not really believe he was as modest as he sounded. The look in his eyes did not somehow fit his words.

"So," went on my father, "Mr. Lorimer will be travelling with us."

"That," I replied with truth, "will be very pleasant."

"I can't tell you how delighted I am to be going," he said. "I have often thought what a lucky day it was for me when I made that find in the garden."

My father smiled and remarked that the message on the stone was a little difficult to decipher — not the hieroglyphics, of course, but the meaning . . . the accurate meaning. It was typical, he went on to say, of the Arabic mind. Always fraught with obscurity.

"But that is what makes it all so interesting," put in Lucas Lorimer.

"It was good of you to come and tell us of your invitation," my father went on, "and your decision to accept."

"My dear Professor, how could I refuse the honour of sharing a platform with you . . . well, not exactly sharing, but being allowed to follow in your footsteps, shall I say?"

My parents were clearly delighted, which showed they could emerge from the rarefied atmosphere in which they usually lived to bask in a little flattery.

He was asked to luncheon, when we discussed the journey and my father, encouraged by my mother, went on to talk of the subject of the lectures he would be giving in South Africa and North America.

I could only think, He will be on the ship with us. He will be in foreign places with us. A considerable excitement had been injected into the prospect.

In a way it took the edge off my apprehension.

Lucas Lorimer's presence would certainly add a spice to the adventure.

Boarding a ship for the first time was an exhilarating experience. I had driven to Tilbury with my parents and had sat demurely listening to their conversation on the way down, which was mainly about the lectures my father would give. I was rather pleased about this because it relieved me of the strain of talking. He did refer to Lucas Lorimer and wondered how his talk would be received.

"He has only a superficial knowledge of the subject, of course, but I have heard he has a lighthearted way of representing it. Not the right approach, but a little lightness seems to be acceptable now and then."

"He will be talking to people of knowledge, I hope," said my mother.

"Oh, yes." My father turned to smile at me. "If there are any questions you wish to ask, you must not hesitate to do so, Rosetta."

"Yes," added my mother. "If you know a little it will enhance your enjoyment of the lectures."

I thanked them and fancied they were not entirely dissatisfied with me.

I had a cabin next to my parents which I was to share with a girl who was going to South Africa to join her parents, who were farming there. She had just left school, and we were of an age. Her name was Mary Kelpin and she was pleasant enough. She had travelled this way several times and was more knowledgeable than I.

She chose the lower of the two bunks, which I did not mind in the least. I imagined I should have felt a little stifled sleeping below. She meticulously divided the wardrobe we had to share, and I thought that, for the time we were at sea, we should get on well.

It was early evening when we set sail, and almost immediately Lucas Lorimer discovered us. I heard his voice in my parents' cabin. I did not join them but decided to explore the ship. I went up the companionway to the public rooms and then out to the deck to take a last glimpse of the dock before we sailed. I was leaning on the rail studying the activity below when he came upon me.

"I guessed you'd be here," he said. "You'd want to see the ship sail."

"Yes, I do," I replied.

"Isn't it amusing that we are taking the trip together?"

"Amusing?"

"I am sure it will be. A delightful coincidence."

"It has all come about very naturally. Can you call that a coincidence?"

"I can see you are a stickler for the niceties of the English language. You must help me compile my speech."

"Haven't you done it yet? My father has been working on his for ages."

"He's a professional. Mine will be very different. I shall go on about the mysticism of the East. A sort of *Arabian Nights* flavour."

"Don't forget you will be talking to experts."

"Oh, I hope to appeal to a wider audience, the imaginative romantic sort."

"I am sure you will."

"I'm so glad we're sailing together," he said. "And now you are no longer a schoolgirl. That is exciting in itself, is it not?"

"Yes, I suppose so."

"On the threshold of life . . . and adventure."

The sound of a hooter rent the air.

"I think that means we are about to sail. Yes, it does. Adieu, England. Welcome new lands . . . new sights . . . new adventures."

He was laughing. I felt exhilarated and glad because he was with us.

I continued to be so. My parents were made much of by the Captain and certain other travellers. The information that they were going to lecture in Cape Town and North America quickly spread, and they were regarded with some awe. Lucas was very popular and in great demand. I knew why. He was one of those people who are without inhibitions; when he arrived at a gathering there was immediate laughter and general animation. He had the ability of making everything seem amusing.

He was charming to me, but then he was to

everybody. He went through life smoothly and easily and, I imagine, getting his own way because of this rare gift of his.

My cabin mate was greatly impressed.

"What a charming man!" she said. "And you knew him before you came on board. Lucky you!"

"Well, I met him briefly at a dinner party, and then he called to tell us he would be on board."

"It's because of your father, I suppose."

"What do you mean?"

"That he is so friendly."

"He's friendly with everyone."

"He's very attractive . . . too attractive," she added ominously, and watched me speculatively. She was inclined to regard me as a simpleton because I had foolishly told her that I had cut school short to come on this trip. She had left the previous year and must have been a year or so older than I.

I had an idea she was warning me against Lucas. There was no need, I wanted to tell her fiercely, and then I feared I might be too fierce. She was right in one thing; I was ignorant of the ways of the world.

But the time I spent with Lucas was certainly enjoyable.

During the first days we found a sheltered spot on the deck, for at that time the sea was a little rough and the wind strong. My parents spent a good deal of time in their cabin and I was left free to explore.

This I did with great interest and soon learned my way about the ship. I found the small cabin restricting, especially as it had to be shared with the rather loquacious and faintly patronising Mary. I was glad to get out of it as much as possible. I found my top bunk a little stifling. I would wake early and lie there waiting for it to be time to get up.

Then I discovered that I could descend the ladder without waking Mary, slip on a few things, and go out on deck. The early morning was exhilarating. I would sit in our sheltered spot and look out over the sea, watching the sun rise. I loved to see the morning sky, sometimes delicately pearl, at other times blood red. I would picture figures in the formation of the clouds as they drifted across the sky and listen to the waves swishing against the sides of the ship. It was never quite the same at any other time of the day.

There was a man in blue overalls who used to swab that part of the deck where I sat each morning. I had struck up an acquaintance with him . . . if it could be called that. He would come along with his mop and pail, tip out the water, and swab away.

At such an hour the deck was almost deserted.

As he approached I said, "Good morning. I came out for a breath of fresh air. It was stifling in the cabin."

"Oh, yes," he said, and went on swabbing.

"Am I in your way? I'd better move."

"Oh, no. It's all right. I'll go round and do that bit later."

It was a cultured voice devoid of accent. I studied him: fairly tall, light brown hair, and rather sad eyes.

"You don't get many people sitting out at this hour," I said.

"No."

"I expect you think I'm crazy."

"No . . . no. I understand you want to get the air. And this is the best time of the day."

"Oh, I do agree."

I insisted on getting up, and he moved my chair and went on swabbing.

That was the first morning I saw him, and on the next one I met him again. By the third morning I imagined he looked for me. It was not exactly an assignation, but it seemed to have become part of the day's ritual. We exchanged a few words — "Good morning . . . it's a nice day" — and so on. He always kept his head down when he was swabbing, as though completely absorbed by what he was doing.

"You like the sea, don't you?" he said on

the fourth morning.

I said I believed I did. I was not sure yet as it was the first time I'd been on it.

"It takes a grip on you. It's fascinating. It can change so quickly."

"Like life," I said, thinking of the changes in mine.

He did not answer and I went on. "I suppose you've had great experience of the sea?"

He shook his head and moved away.

Mealtimes on board were interesting. Lucas Lorimer, as a friend, sat at our table and Captain Graysom had made a pleasant custom of taking his seat at each table in turn during the voyage so that he could get to know most of his passengers. He had many stories to tell of his adventures at sea, and that happy custom made it possible for all to hear of them.

"It is easy for him," said Lucas. "He has his repertoire, and all he has to do is give a repeat performance at each table. You notice he knows just where to pause for the laugh and get the best dramatic effects."

"You are a little like that," I told him. "Oh, I wasn't suggesting repetition, but you know where the pauses should come too."

"I see that you know me too well for my comfort."

"Well, then, let me comfort you. I think one of the greatest gifts one can have is the ability to make people laugh."

He took my hand and kissed it.

My parents, who were at the table when this dialogue took place, were a little startled. I think it must have brought home to them that I was growing up.

Lucas and I were taking a walk round the deck when we encountered Captain Graysom. He used to walk round the ship every day to assure himself, I supposed, that everything was in order.

"All well?" he asked as he approached.

"Very well indeed," answered Lucas.

"Getting your sea legs now? They don't always come at once. But we've been moderately lucky in the weather . . . so far."

"Isn't it going to continue?" I asked.

"You need a wiser man than I am to tell you that, Miss Cranleigh. We can only forecast, and never with absolute certainty. The weather is unpredictable. All the signs look good and then something quite unforeseen appears on the horizon and our forecasts go awry."

"Predictability can be a little dull," said Lucas. "There is always a certain attraction in the unexpected."

"I'm not sure that applies to the weather," said the Captain. "We'll shortly be putting into Madeira. You'll go ashore?"

"Oh, yes," I cried. "I'm looking forward to that."

"It's a pity we only have one day there," said Lucas.

"Just long enough to pick up stores. You'll like the island. You must sample the wine. It's good."

Then he left us.

"What plans have you for Madeira?" asked Lucas.

"My parents haven't said anything yet."

"I should like to escort you round the place."

"Oh, thank you. Have you been there before?"

"Yes," he replied. "So you will be safe with me."

It was exhilarating to wake up in the morning and see land. I was on deck early to watch our approach. I could see the lush green island rising out of a pellucid aquamarine-coloured sea. The sun was warm and there was no wind to disturb the water.

My father had a slight cold and was staying on board; he had plenty to occupy him, and my mother would be with him. They thought it would be an excellent idea if I went ashore with Mr. Lorimer, who had kindly offered to take me.

I was content, feeling, somewhat guiltily, how much more enjoyable it would be without them. Lucas did not say so, but I felt sure he shared my view.

"Having been here before, I shall know something about it," he said. "And if there is anything of which I am ignorant . . ."

"Which is most unlikely."

" . . . we shall discover it together," he finished.

And on that note we set out.

I drew deep breaths of air which seemed scented with flowers. Indeed, there were flowers everywhere. Stalls were overflowing with brilliantly coloured blossoms, as well as baskets, embroidered bags, shawls and tablecloths and mats.

The sunshine, the chatter of people in a foreign language — Portuguese, I presumed — as they proffered their goods, the excitement of being in a foreign land, and the company of Lucas Lorimer: all these things made me realise that I was enjoying myself as I had not done for a long time.

It was indeed a day to remember. Lucas was the perfect companion. His smiles charmed people wherever we went, and I thought he was one of the nicest people I had ever met.

It was true that he did know a good deal about the place.

"It's quite small," he said. "I was here for a week, and in that time I was able to go almost everywhere."

He engaged one of the bullock-drawn carts and we drove through the town: past the cathedral, where we called a halt that we might explore, past the market with more flowers, baskets, and wickerwork tables and chairs.

From the town we caught glimpses of the *Atlantic Star* lying a little way out to sea and the launches which were ferrying the passengers between the shore and the ship.

Lucas said we must try the wine, and we went into one of the wine cellars and there sat at one of the little tublike tables while glasses were brought to us containing a sample of Madeira wine in the hope I supposed that we should be so delighted that we would buy some.

It was dark in the cellar — a contrast to the bright light outside. We sat on stools and surveyed each other. Lucas lifted his glass.

"To you . . . to us . . . and many more days like this."

"The next stop is Cape Town, I believe."

"Well, you and I may have a chance to repeat this pleasure while we are there."

"You will be busy with your lecture."

"Please don't call it a lecture. That's for

sterner stuff. It makes it sound so severe. There are connotations in that word. It can mean a severe talking to, a reprimand. When they asked me to come, it was as a light contrast to the Professor. I was honoured — and look, it has led to this. So . . . call it a talk. That's much more cosy. As a matter of fact, I have a feeling it will shock your parents. It's about gruesome things like curses and tomb robbers."

"People might enjoy hearing about that sort of thing rather than — "

"I'm not letting it bother me. If they don't like it, that will be that. So . . . I refuse to allow preparations to overshadow my pleasure. It's the greatest good luck that we are travelling together."

"It's certainly pleasant for me."

"We're getting maudlin. It's the wine perhaps. It's good, isn't it? We must buy a bottle to show our appreciation of the free sample."

"I hope all the free samples make it worthwhile."

"Must do, or they wouldn't continue with the old custom, would they? In the meantime it is very pleasant sitting here in this darkish room, on these uncomfortable stools, sipping their excellent Madeira wine."

Several of our fellow passengers came into the cellar. We called greetings to each other.

They all looked as though they were enjoying the day.

Then a young man walked past our table.

"Hello," said Lucas.

The young man paused.

"Oh," said Lucas. "I thought I knew you."

The young man stared at Lucas stonily, and then I recognised him, which I had not done previously because he was not on this occasion wearing the overalls in which I had always seen him before. He was the young man who swabbed the decks in the morning.

"No," he said. "I don't think . . . "

"Sorry. I just thought for the moment I'd met you somewhere."

I smiled and said, "You must have seen each other on board."

The deckhand had drawn himself up rather tensely and was studying Lucas, I thought, with a hint of uneasiness.

"That must be it," said Lucas.

The young man passed on and sat at a table in a dark corner of the cellar.

I whispered to Lucas, "He is one of the deckhands."

"You seem to be acquainted with him."

"I have met him on several mornings. I go up there to watch the sunrise and he comes round at that time swabbing the decks."

"He doesn't look like a deck swabber."

"That's because he's not in overalls."

"Well, thanks for enlightening me. The poor chap seemed a bit embarrassed. I hope he enjoys the wine as much as we have done. Come on. Let's buy a bottle to take back to the ship. Perhaps we'd better get two. We'll drink it at dinner tonight."

We bought the wine and came out into the sunshine.

Slowly we made our way back to the launch which would take us to the ship. On the quay we stopped at a stall and Lucas bought one of the bags for me. It was heavily embroidered with scarlet and blue flowers.

"A memento of a happy day," he said. "To say thank you for letting me share it with you."

I thought how gracious and charming he was; he had certainly given *me* a happy day.

"I shall always remember it when I see this bag," I told him. "The flowers . . . the bullock carts . . . the wine. . . ."

"And even the swabber of decks."

"I shall remember every minute of it," I assured him.

Friendships grow quickly at sea.

After Madeira we were in balmy weather with smooth seas. Lucas and I seemed to have become even firmer friends since our day ashore. Without making arrangements we met regularly on deck. He would seat himself beside me and we would talk desultorily as we watched the calm sea glide past.

He told me a great deal about himself, how he had broken the tradition in his family that one of the sons should have a career in the Army. But it was not for him. He was not really sure what was for him. He was restless and travelled a good deal, usually in the company of Dick Duvane, his ex-batman and friend. Dick had left the Army when he had and they had been together ever since. Dick was in Cornwall now, making himself useful on the estate, which Lucas supposed was something he would have to come to eventually.

"Just at the moment I'm uncertain," he said. "There is enough to do on the estate to keep both my brother and me occupied. I suppose it would have been different if I had inherited. My brother, Carleton, is in charge and he's the perfect squire ... such as I should never be. He's the best fellow in the world, but I don't like playing second fiddle. It's against my arrogant nature. So, since leaving the Army, I've drifted a bit. . . . I've travelled a great deal. Egypt has always fascinated me, and when I found the stone in the garden it seemed like fate. And so it was, because here am I at the moment, travelling with the

élite such as your parents — and of course
their charming daughter. And all because I
found a stone in the garden. But I am talking
all this time about myself. What of you? What
are your plans?"

"I haven't made any. I've cut school, you
know, to come here. Who knows what the
future holds?"

"No one can be sure, of course, but sometimes one has the opportunity to mould it."

"Have you moulded yours?"

"I am in the process of doing so."

"And your brother's estate is in Cornwall."

"Yes. As a matter of fact, it's not far from
that place which has been in the papers recently."

"Oh? What's that?"

"Did you read about the young man who
was on the point of being arrested and disappeared?"

"Oh, yes. I remember. Wasn't it Simon
somebody? Perrivale, was it?"

"That's it. He took his name from the man
who adopted him, Sir Edward Perrivale.
Their place is some six or eight miles from
ours: Perrivale Court. It's a wonderful old
mansion. I went there once, long ago. It was
about something to do with the neighbourhood which my father was involved in, and
Sir Edward was interested. I rode over with

my father. When I read about the case in the papers it all came back. There were two brothers and the adopted one. We were all shocked when we read about it. One doesn't expect that sort of thing to happen to people one knows, however slightly."

"How very interesting. There was a lot of talk about it in our house — among the servants, not my parents."

While we were talking, the deck swabber came by, trundling a trolley on which were bottles of beer.

"Good morning," I called.

He nodded his head in acknowledgement and went on wheeling.

"A friend of yours?" said Lucas.

"He's the one who swabs the deck. Remember? He was in the wine cellar."

"Oh, yes ... I remember. Seems a bit surly, doesn't he?"

"He's a little reserved perhaps. It may be that they are not supposed to talk to passengers."

"He seems different from the others."

"Yes, I thought so. He never says much more than good morning and perhaps a comment on the weather."

We dismissed the man from our minds and talked of other things. He told me about the estate in Cornwall and some of the eccentric people who lived there. I told him about my home life and Mr. Dolland's turns, and I had him laughing at my descriptions of kitchen life.

"You seem to have enjoyed it very much."

"Oh, I was fortunate."

"Do your parents know?"

"They are not really interested in anything that happened after the birth of Christ."

And so we talked.

The next morning when I took my seat on deck in the early morning, I saw the deck swabber, but he did not come near me.

We were heading for Cape Town and the wind had been rising all day. I had seen little of my parents. They spent a lot of time in their cabin. My father was perfecting his lecture and working on his book and my mother was helping him. I saw them at meals, when they regarded me with that benign absent-mindedness to which I had become accustomed. My father asked if I had plenty to do; if not, I might come to his cabin where he would give me something to read. I assured him I was enjoying shipboard life: I already had something to read and Mr. Lorimer and I had become good friends. This seemed to bring some relief and they went back to their work.

The Captain, who dined with us occasionally, told us that some of the worst storms he had encountered had been round the Cape. It was known to ancient mariners as the Cape of Storms. In any case we could not expect the calm weather we had enjoyed so far to be always with us. We must take the rough with the smooth. We were certainly about to take the rough.

My parents stayed in their cabin but I felt the need for fresh air and went out onto the open deck.

I was unprepared for the fury which met me. The ship was being roughly buffeted and felt as though she were made of cork. She pitched and tossed to such an extent that I thought she was about to turn over. The tall waves rose like menacing mountains as they fell and drenched the deck. The wind tore at my hair and clothes. I felt as though the angry sea were attempting to lift me up and take me overboard.

It was alarming and yet at the same time exhilarating.

I was wet through with seawater and found it almost impossible to stand up. Breathlessly I clung to the rail.

As I stood there debating whether it was wise to cross the slippery deck and at least get away from the direct fury of the gale, I saw the deckhand. He swayed towards me, his clothes damp. The spray had darkened his hair so that it looked like a black cap and seawater glistened on his face.

"Are you all right?" he shouted at me.

"Yes!" I shouted back.

"Shouldn't be up here. Ought to get down!"

"Yes!" I cried.

"Come on. I'll help you."

He staggered over and fell against me.

"Is it often as rough as this?" I panted.

"Haven't seen it. My first voyage."

He had taken my arm and we rolled drunkenly across the deck. He opened a door and pushed me inside.

"There," he said. "Don't venture out in a sea like this again."

Before I could thank him, he was gone.

Staggering, I made my way to my cabin. Mary Kelpin was lying on the lower bunk. She was feeling decidedly unwell.

I said I would look in on my parents. They were both prostrate. I came back to my cabin, took a book, climbed to the top bunk, and tried to read. It was not very easy.

All through the afternoon we waited for the storm to abate. The ship went on her rocky way, creaking and groaning as though in agony.

By evening the wind had dropped a little. I

managed to get down to the dining room. The fiddles were up on the tables to keep the crockery from sliding off and there were very few people there. I soon saw Lucas.

"Ah," he said. "Not many of us brave enough to face the dining room."

"Have you ever seen such a storm?"

"Yes, once when I was coming home from Egypt. We passed Gibraltar and were coming up to the Bay. I thought my last hour had come."

"That is what I thought this afternoon."

"She'll weather the storm. Tomorrow the sea may be as calm as a lake, and we shall wonder what all the fuss was about. Where are your parents?"

"In their cabin. They did not feel like coming down."

"In common with many others obviously."

I told him I had been on deck and had been rather severely reprimanded by the deckhand.

"He was quite right," said Lucas. "It must have been highly dangerous. You could easily have been washed overboard. I reckon we were on the edge of a hurricane."

"It makes you realise how hazardous the sea can be."

"Indeed it does. One should never take the elements lightly. The sea — like fire — is a good friend but a bad enemy."

"I wonder what it is like to be ship-wrecked."

"Horrendous."

"Adrift in an open boat," I murmured.

"Much more disagreeable than it sounds."

"Yes, I imagine so. But it seems the storm is dying down now."

"I'd never trust it. We have to be prepared for all weathers. This has been a salutary lesson to us, perhaps."

"People don't always learn their lessons."

"I don't know why when they have a good example of how treacherous the sea can be. Smiling one moment, angry . . . venomous . . . the next."

"I hope we shall encounter no more hurricanes."

It was past ten o'clock when I reached my cabin. Mary Kelpin was in her bed. I went to the next cabin to say good night to my parents. My father was lying down and my mother was reading some papers.

I told them I had dined with Lucas Lorimer and was now going to bed.

"Let's hope the ship is a little steadier by morning," said my mother. "This perpetual motion disturbs your father's train of thought, and there is still some work to do on the lecture."

I slept fitfully and woke in the early hours

of the morning. The wind was rising and the ship was moving even more erratically than it had during the day. I was in danger of being thrown out of my bunk and sleep was impossible. I lay still, listening to the wailing and shrieking of the gale and the sound of the heavy waves as they lashed the sides of the ship.

And then . . . suddenly I heard a violent clanging of bells. I knew at once what this meant, for on our first day at sea we had taken part in a drill which would make us prepared, in some small way, for an emergency. We were told then that we were to put on warm clothing together with our life jackets, which were kept in the cupboard in our cabins, and make for the assembly point which had been chosen for us.

I leaped down from my bunk. Mary Kelpin was already dressing.

"This is it," she said. "That ghastly wind, and now . . . this."

Her teeth were chattering and space was limited. It was not easy for us both to dress at the same time.

She was ready before I was, and when I had fumbled with buttons and donned my life jacket I hurried from the cabin to that of my parents.

The bells continued to sound their alarming note. My parents were looking bewildered, my father agitatedly gathering papers together.

"There is no time for that now," I said. "Come along. Get these warm things on. And where are your life jackets?"

I then had the unique experience of realising that a little quiet common sense has its advantages over erudition. They were pathetically meek and put themselves in my hands, and at last we were ready to leave the cabin.

The alleyway was deserted. My father stopped short and some papers he was carrying fell from his hands. I hurriedly picked them up.

"Oh!" he said in horror. "I've left behind the notes I made yesterday."

"Never mind. Our lives are more important than your notes," I said.

He stood still. "I can't . . . I couldn't . . . I must go and get them."

My mother said, "Your father must have his notes, Rosetta."

I saw the stubborn look in their faces and I said hurriedly, "I'll go and get them. You go up to the lounge where we are supposed to assemble. I'll get the notes. Where are they?"

"In the top drawer," said my mother.

I gave them a little push towards the companionway which led to the lounge and turned back. The notes were not in the top drawer. I searched and found them in a lower one. My life jacket rendered movement rather difficult. I grabbed the notes and hurried out.

The bells had stopped ringing. It was difficult to stand upright. The ship lurched and I almost fell as I mounted the companionway. There was no sign of my parents. I guessed they must have joined others at the assembly point and been hustled on deck to where the lifeboats would be waiting for them.

The violence of the storm had increased. I stumbled and slid until I came to rest at the bulkhead. Picking myself up, feeling dazed, I looked about for my parents. I wondered where they could have gone in the short time I had taken to retrieve the notes. I was clutching them in my hands now as I managed to make my way to the deck. There was pandemonium. People were surging towards the rail. In vain I looked among them for my parents. I suddenly felt terrifyingly alone among that pushing screaming crowd.

It was horrific. The wind seemed to take a malicious delight in tormenting us. My hair was loose and flying wildly about my head, being tossed over my eyes so that I could not see. The notes were pulled from my hands. For a few seconds I watched them doing a frivolous dance above my head before they were snatched up by the violent wind, fluttered, and fell into that seething mass of water.

We should have stayed together, I thought. And then: Why? We have never been together. But this was different. This was danger. It was Death staring us in the face. Surely a few notes were not worth parting at such a time.

Some people were getting into boats. I realised that my turn would not come for a long time, and when I saw the frail boats descending into that malignant sea, I was not sure that I wanted to trust myself to one of them.

The ship gave a sudden shivering groan as though it could endure no more. We seemed to keel over and I was standing in water. Then I saw one of the boats turn over as it was lowered. I heard the shrieks of its occupants as the sea caught them hungrily and drew them down.

I felt dazed and somewhat aloof from the scene. Death seemed almost certain. I was going to lose my life almost before it had begun. I started thinking of the past, which people say you do when you are drowning. But I was not drowning . . . yet. Here I was on this leaky frail vessel, facing the unprecedented fury of the elements, and I knew that at any moment I could be flung from the comparative safety of the deck into that grey sea in which no one could have a hope of survival. The noise was deafening — the shrieks and prayers of people calling to God to save them from the fury of the sea . . . the sound of the raging tempest . . . the violent howling of the wind and the mountainous seas — it was like something out of Dante's *Inferno*.

There was nothing to be done. I suppose the first thought of people faced with death is to save themselves. Perhaps when one is young death seems so remote that one cannot take it seriously. It is something which happens to other people, old people at that; one cannot imagine a world without oneself; one feels oneself to be immortal. I knew that many this night would lie in a watery grave, but I could not really believe that I should be one of them.

I stood there — dazed, waiting — striving to catch a glimpse of my parents. I thought of Lucas Lorimer. Where was he? I wished I could see him. I thought fleetingly that he would probably still be calm and a little cynical. Would he talk of death as nonchalantly as he did of life?

Then I saw the overturned boat. It was being tossed about in the water. It came close to the spot where I was standing. Then it righted itself and was bobbing about below me.

Someone had roughly caught my arm.

"You'll be washed overboard in a minute

if you stay here."

I turned. It was the deckhand.

"She's finished. She'll turn over . . . it's certain."

I turned. His face was wet with spray. He was staring at the boat which the violent wind had brought close to the ship's side. A giant wave brought it almost level with us.

"It's a chance," he shouted. "Come on. Jump!"

I was surprised to find that I obeyed. He had my arm still in a grip. It seemed unreal. I was sailing through the air and then plunging right down into that seething sea.

We were beside the boat.

"Grip!" he shouted above the tumult.

Instinctively I obeyed. He was very close to me. It seemed minutes but it could only have been seconds before he was in the boat. I was still clinging to the side. Then his hands were on me and he was hauling me in beside him.

It was just in time. The boat was lifted up on the crest of an enormous wave. His arms were about me and he was holding me tightly.

"Hang on . . . hang on . . . for your life," he cried.

It was a miracle. We were still in the boat.

We were breathless.

"Hang on. Hang on!" he kept shouting.

I am not sure what happened in the minutes

that followed. I just knew that I was roughly buffeted and that the velocity of the wind took my breath away. I was aware of a violent crash as the *Atlantic Star* seemed to rise in the air and then keel over. I was blinded by the sea; my mouth was full of it. We were on the crest of the waves one moment, down in the depths of the ocean the next.

I had escaped from the sinking ship to a small boat which, it seemed certain, could not survive in such a sea.

This must be the end.

Time had ceased to register. I had no idea how long I clung to the sides of the boat, while only one thing seemed important: to hang on.

I was aware of the man close to me.

He shouted against the wind. "We're still afloat! How long — "

His voice was lost in the turmoil.

I could just make out the *Atlantic Star*. She was still in the water but at an unusual angle. Her prow seemed to have disappeared. I knew that there could be little chance of anyone's surviving on her.

We continued to rock uncertainly, waiting for each new wave which might end our lives. All about us the sea roared and raged . . . such a flimsy craft to defy that monster sea. I found myself wondering what would have happened to me if this man had not come along when he did and made me jump with him. What a miracle! I could scarcely believe it had happened. I thought of my parents. Where were they? Could they have escaped?

Then it seemed as though the storm was a little less fierce. Was it my fancy? Perhaps it was a temporary lull. But it was a small respite. One of the lifeboats was coming close to us. I scanned it anxiously in the hope that my parents might be in it. I saw the strained white faces . . . unrecognisable . . . unfamiliar. Then suddenly a wave caught the boat. For a second or so it hung suspended in the air and then it was completely enveloped by another giant wave. I heard the screams. The boat was still there. It was lifted high again. It seemed to stand perpendicular. I saw bodies tipped into the sea. Then the boat fell back and overturned. It was upside down in the water before it rose again as the sea tossed it aside as a child might have done when a toy it had been playing with suddenly bored it.

I saw heads bobbing in the water for what seemed interminable minutes and then disappear.

I heard my rescuer shouting, "Look. Someone's drifting towards us."

It was a man. His head suddenly appeared close to us.

"Let's get him on board, quick, or he'll go

under and take us with him."

I stretched out my arms and was immediately overcome by the emotions which assailed me, for the man we were attempting to haul into the boat was Lucas Lorimer.

It was a long time before we succeeded. Then he collapsed and lay face downward in the boat. He was very still.

I wanted to shout at him, You're safe Lucas. Oh, thank God.

Recognising him, my companion caught his breath. Then he shouted to me, "He's in a bad way."

"What can we do?"

"He's half drowned."

He bent over Lucas and started to pump the water out of his lungs. He was trying to save Lucas's life and I wondered then how long he would be able to keep it.

It was helpful to have something to do. He was succeeding. Lucas looked a little more alive.

I noticed there was something odd about his left leg. Every now and then one of his hands would move to it and touch it. He was only half conscious, but he was aware that something there was wrong.

"Can't do any more," murmured my rescuer.

"Will he be all right?"

He lifted his shoulders.

It must have been two hours or so before the wind started to subside. The gusts were less frequent.

Lucas had not opened his eyes; he lay at the bottom of the boat, inert. My other companion was tinkering with the boat. I did not know what he was doing but it seemed important, and the fact that we had kept afloat told me that he must have some knowledge of how the thing worked.

He looked up and caught me watching him. "Get some sleep. You're exhausted," he said.

"You too. . . ."

"Oh, there's enough to keep me awake."

"It's better now, isn't it? Have we a chance?"

"Of being picked up? Perhaps. We're in luck. There's a can of water and a tin of biscuits here, shut away under the seat. Put there as emergency rations. That will help us to keep going for a bit. Water's most important. We can survive on that. . . for a while."

"And him?" I pointed to Lucas.

"In a bad way. He's breathing, though. He was half drowned . . . and it looks as though his leg's broken."

"Can we do anything?"

He shook his head. "Nothing. No supplies.

He'll have to wait. We've got to look for a sail. Nothing you can do, so try to sleep. You'll feel better."

"What about you?"

"Later perhaps. Nothing more we can do for him. Have to go the way the wind takes us. Can't steer. If we're lucky we'll hit the trade routes. If not . . . " He shrugged his shoulders. Then he said almost gently, "Best thing for you is to get some sleep. That will work wonders."

I closed my eyes and, to my later amazement, I obeyed.

When I awoke the sun had risen. So a new day had broken. I looked about me. The sky was stained red, which threw a pink reflection over the sea. There was still a strong breeze, which set white crests on the waves. It meant that we were moving along at a fair pace. Where to, was anyone's guess. We were at the mercy of the wind.

Lucas lay still at the bottom of the boat. The other man was watching me intently.

"You sleep?" he asked.

"Yes, for a long time, it seems."

"You needed it. Feel better?"

I nodded. "What's happened?"

"You can see we are in calmer waters."

"The storm has gone."

"Keep your fingers crossed. It's abated for the time being. Of course, it can spring up in a matter of minutes . . . but at the same time we've got a second chance."

"Do you think there is a hope of our being picked up?"

"Fifty-fifty chance."

"And if not?"

"The water won't last long."

"You said something about biscuits."

"Mm. But water is most important. We'll have to ration it."

"What about him?" I asked, indicating Lucas.

"You know him." It was a statement, not a question.

"Yes. We were friends on board."

"I've seen you talking to him."

"Is he badly hurt?"

"I don't know. We can't do anything about it."

"What of his leg?"

"Needs setting, I expect. We've nothing here."

"I wish — "

"Don't wish for too much. Fate might think you were greedy. We've just had what must be one of the most miraculous escapes possible."

"I know. Thanks to you."

He smiled at me rather shyly. "We've still got to go on hoping for miracles," he said.

"I wish we could do something for him."

He shook his head. "We have to be careful. We could overturn in half a second. He's got to take a chance just as we have."

I nodded.

"My parents . . . " I began.

"It could be that they got into one of the boats."

"I saw one of the boats go off . . . and go under."

"Not much hope for any of them."

"I'm amazed that this little craft survived. If we get out of this it will be entirely due to you."

We fell into silence, and after a while he took out the water can. We each took a mouthful.

He screwed it up carefully. "We'll have to eke it out," he said. "It's life blood to us, remember."

I nodded.

The hours slipped by. Lucas opened his eyes and they alighted on me. "Rosetta?" he murmured.

"Yes, Lucas?"

"Where . . . " His lips formed the word but hardly any sound came.

"We're in a lifeboat. The ship has sunk, I think. You're all right. You're with me and — "

It was absurd not to know his name. He might have once been a deckhand but now he was our saviour, the man in charge of our brilliant rescue.

Lucas could not hear properly in any case. He showed no surprise but shut his eyes. He said something. I had to lean over him to catch it. "My leg . . . "

We ought to do something about it. But what? We had no medical supplies, and we had to be careful how we moved about in the boat. Even on this mild sea it bobbed about in an alarming fashion, and I knew it would be easy for one of us to be thrown overboard.

The sun came up and the heat was intense. Fortunately the breeze — now a light one — persisted. It was blowing us gently along but neither of us had any notion in what direction.

"It will be easier when the stars come out," he said.

I had learned his name which was John Player. I fancied he admitted to it with a certain reluctance. "Do you mind if I call you John?" I had asked, and he had replied, "Then I shall call you Rosetta. We are on equal terms now . . . no longer passenger and deckhand. The fear of death is a good leveller." I had replied, "I do not need such fear

103

to call you by your Christian name. It would be absurd to shout, 'Mr. Player, I am drowning. Please rescue me.' " "Quite absurd," he had agreed. "But I hope you will never have to do that."

I asked him now, "Shall you be able to steer by the stars, John?" He shrugged his shoulders. "I am no trained navigator, but one picks up a bit at sea. At least if we get a clear night we might have some idea of where we are headed. It was too cloudy last night to see anything."

"The direction could change. After all, you said it depended on the wind."

"Yes, we have to go where we are taken. That gives one a great sense of helplessness."

"Like depending on others for the essential things in life. Do you think Mr. Lorimer is going to die?"

"He looks strong enough. I think the main trouble is his leg. He must have got a battering when the lifeboat overturned."

"I wish we could do something."

"The best thing is to keep our eyes open. If we see the smallest sign on the horizon we must do something to attract attention. Put up a flag."

"Where could we find a flag?"

"One of your petticoats on a stick . . . something like that."

"I think you are very resourceful."

"Maybe, but what I am looking for now is another piece of luck."

"It may be that we had our share when we got away from the wreck."

"Well, we need a little bit more. In the meantime, let's do our best to find it. Keep your eyes open. The least speck on the horizon, and we'll send up a signal of some sort."

The morning passed slowly. It was afternoon. We drifted slowly along. Lucas opened his eyes now and then and spoke, although it was clear that he was not fully aware of the situation.

The sun was fortunately obscured by a few clouds, which made it more bearable. I did not know what would be worse, rain, which might mean another storm, or this burning heat. John Player had suddenly dropped into a sleep of exhaustion. He looked very young thus. I wondered about him. It took my mind off the present desperate situation. Why had he come to be a deckhand? I was sure there was some hidden past. There was an air of mystery about him. He was secretive . . . almost furtively watchful. At least during the last hours I had not noticed these qualities because he was intent on one thing, saving our lives. That had brought about a certain relationship between us. I suppose it was natural that it should.

I could not keep my mind from my parents. I tried to imagine their coming out onto the deck in that childlike, bewildered way in which they faced life which did not centre round the British Museum. They were quite unaware of the practicalities of life. They had never had to bother about them. Others had done that, leaving them free to pursue their studies.

Where were they now? I thought of them with a kind of tender exasperation.

I imagined their being hustled into a lifeboat, my father still mourning the loss of his notes rather than his daughter.

Perhaps I was wrong. Perhaps they had cared for me more than I realised. Hadn't they called me Rosetta, after the precious stone?

I scanned the horizon. I must not forget that I was on watch. I must be ready if a ship came into sight. I had removed my petticoat and it was attached to a piece of wood. If I saw anything like another craft, I would wake John and lose no time in waving my improvised flag madly.

The day wore on and there was nothing — only that wide expanse of water all around us . . . everywhere . . . to the horizon. Wherever I looked there was emptiness.

Darkness had fallen. John Player awakened. He was ashamed to have slept so long.

"You needed it," I told him. "You were absolutely worn out."

"And you kept watch?"

"I swear to you there has been no sign of a ship anywhere."

"There must be sometime."

We had more water and a biscuit.

"What of Mr. Lorimer?" I asked.

"If he wakes up we'll give him something."

"Should he be unconscious so long?"

"He shouldn't be, but it seems he is. Perhaps it's as well. That leg must be rather painful."

"I wish we could do something about it."

He shook his head. "We can't do anything. We hauled him aboard. That was all we could do."

"And you gave him artificial respiration."

"As best I could. I think it worked, though. Well, that was all we could do."

"How I wish a ship would come."

"I am heartily in agreement with you."

The night descended on us . . . our second night. I dozed a little and dreamed I was in the kitchen of the house in Bloomsbury. "It was such a night as this that the Polish Jew was murdered. . . ."

Such a night as this! And then I was awake.

The boat was scarcely moving. I could just make out John Player staring ahead.

I closed my eyes. I wanted to get back into the past.

We were into our second day. The sea was calm and I was struck afresh by the loneliness of that expanse of water. Only us and our boat in the whole world, it seemed.

Lucas became conscious during the morning. He said, "What's the matter with my leg?"

"I think the bone may be broken," I told him. "We can't do anything about it. We'll be picked up by a ship soon, John thinks."

"John?" he asked.

"John Player. He's been wonderful. He saved our lives."

Lucas nodded. "Who else is there?"

"Only the three of us. We're in the lifeboat. We've had amazing luck."

"I can't help being glad you're here, Rosetta."

I smiled at him.

We gave him some water.

"That was good," he said. "I feel so helpless."

"We all are," I replied. "So much depends on that ship."

During the afternoon John sighted what he

thought was land. He called to me excitedly and pointed to the horizon. I could just make out a dark hump. I stared at it. Was it a mirage? Did we long so much for it that our tortured imaginations had conjured it up? We had been adrift for only two days and nights but it seemed like an eternity. I kept my eyes fixed on the horizon.

The boat seemed not to be moving. There we were on a tranquil sea and if there really was land close by we might not be able to reach it.

The afternoon wore on. The land had disappeared and our spirits sank.

"Our only hope is a ship," said John. "Goodness knows if that is possible. How far we are from the trade routes, I do not know."

A slight breeze arose. It carried us along for a while. I was on the lookout and I saw land again. It was close now.

I called to John.

"It looks like an island," he said. "If only the wind is in the right direction . . . "

Several hours passed. The land came nearer and then receded. The wind rose and there were dark clouds on the horizon. I could see that John was anxious.

Quite suddenly he gave a shout of joy. "We're getting nearer. Oh, God . . . please help. The wind . . . the blessed wind . . . it's going to take us there."

A tense excitement gripped me. Lucas opened his eyes and said, "What is it?"

"I think we're near land," I told him. "If only . . ."

John was right beside me. "It's an island," he said. "Look, we're going in!"

"Oh, John," I murmured, "can it be that our prayers are answered?"

He turned to me suddenly and kissed my cheek. I smiled and he gripped my hand hard. We were too full of emotion in that moment for more words.

We were in shallow water and the boat scraped land. John leaped out and I joined him. I felt an immense triumph, standing there with the water washing above my ankles.

It took a long time for us to drag the boat onto dry land.

The island on which we had landed was small, little more than rocks jutting out of the sea. We saw a few stunted palm trees and sparse foliage. The land rose steeply from the beach, which I supposed was the reason why it was not completely submerged. To John's delight in another compartment under the seat he found more biscuits and another can of water, a first-aid box containing bandages, and some rope which enabled us to tether the boat to a tree, and this gave us a wonderful sense of security.

Finding the water particularly delighted John. "It will keep us alive for another few days."

My first thought was for Lucas's leg. I remembered that Dot had once broken an arm and Mr. Dolland had set it before the doctor had arrived and commended him for his prompt action. It had been related to me in some detail and I now tried to recall what Mr. Dolland had done.

With John's help I did what I could. We discovered the broken bone and tried to piece it together. We found a piece of wood which served as a splint, and the bandages were useful. Lucas said it felt more comfortable as a result, but I feared our efforts were not very successful and they had in any case come far too late.

It was strange to see this hitherto self-sufficient man of the world so helpless and dependent upon us.

John had taken charge. He was a natural leader. He told us that he had attended drills on board the *Atlantic Star*, which every crewman was expected to do, and he had learned something about how to act in an emergency. That stood him in good stead now. He wished he had paid more attention but at least he remembered something of what he had been taught.

We were impatient to explore the island. We found a few coconuts. He shook them and heard the rattle of milk.

He turned his eyes to the sky. "Someone up there is looking after us," he said.

Those days I spent on the island stand out in my memory, never to be forgotten. John turned out to be quite ingenious; he was practical and resourceful and was constantly trying to find ways to help us survive.

We must keep an account of the time, he said. He was going to make notches in a stick for this purpose. He knew we had been at sea three nights and so we had a start. Lucas was now fully aware of what was happening. It was maddening for him to be unable to move but I think his main concern was that he might be a hindrance.

We tried to assure him that this was not so and we needed someone to be on watch all the time. He could stay in the boat and keep a lookout while John and I were exploring the island, searching for food, or doing any jobs that needed to be done. We had been provided with whistles with our life jackets, and if he spotted a sail or anything unusual happened he could summon us immediately.

It is amazing how very close one can become to another human being in such circumstances. Thus it was with John and me. Lucas had been my companion before this shipwreck. John had been almost a stranger. Now we seemed like close friends.

He would talk to me more frankly when we were alone than he did when Lucas was present. There was something very kind about him. He understood Lucas's feelings, realising how he would feel in his position, and he never mentioned before him his fears about the water supply running out. He did to me, though. He had installed a system of rationing. We took water at sunrise, midday, and sunset.

"Water is the most precious thing we have," he said. "Without it we're finished. We could very shortly become dehydrated. A healthy young person can do without food for perhaps a month, but that person must have water. It is only a little we're getting. Drink it slowly. Hold it in your mouth, roll it round to get the utmost from it. As long as we have water we can survive. We'll preserve some if it rains. We'll manage."

I felt comforted to be with him. I had an immense confidence in him. He knew it and I believe my faith in him gave him courage and the power to do what might have seemed impossible.

He and I explored the island, looking for likely food, while Lucas kept watch. Sometimes we walked in silence, sometimes we talked.

We had gone a mile or so from the shore and climbed to the top of a slope. From there we could see the island clearly and gaze right out to the horizon.

A feeling of utter aloneness swept over me. I think he felt it too.

"Sit down awhile, Rosetta," he said. "I think I work you too hard."

I laughed. "You, John, are the one who works hard. We should never have survived if it had not been for you."

"Sometimes I think we shall never get off this island."

"Of course we shall. We have been here only a few days. Of course we'll get off. Look how we found land. Who would have believed that? A ship will come by . . . you'll see."

"And if it does — " he stopped, frowning into the distance.

I waited for him to go on.

Instead he said, "I think this can't be the route that ships take."

"Why shouldn't it be? You wait and see — "

"Let's face it. We're going to run out of water."

"It'll rain. We'll collect it."

"We've got to find food. The biscuits are running out."

"Why do you talk like this? It is not like you."

"How do you know? You don't know me very well, do you?"

"I know you as well as you know me. At times like this people get to know each other quickly. There is not all the fuss of conventions and great gaps in acquaintanceship which you get at home. We are together all the time . . . night and day. We've shared incredible dangers together. You get to know people quickly when it is like that."

"Tell me about yourself," he said.

"Well, what do you want to know? You saw my parents on board, perhaps. I keep wondering what has happened to them. Could they have got into one of the boats? They are so vague. I don't think they realised what was happening. Their minds were in the past. They often seemed to forget about me, except when they saw me. They would have been more interested in me if I had been a tablet covered in hieroglyphics. At least they named me after the Rosetta Stone."

He was smiling and I told him of my happy childhood, mostly spent belowstairs, of the maids who were my companions, of kitchen meals, Mrs. Harlow, Nanny Pollock, and Mr. Dolland's turns.

"I can see I do not have to feel sorry for you."

"By no means. I often wonder what Mr. Dolland and the rest are doing now. They will have heard of the shipwreck. Oh, dear . . . they'll be dreadfully upset. And what will happen to the house? And to them? I do hope my parents were saved. If not, I don't know what will happen to them all."

"Perhaps you will never know."

"There you go again. It's your turn. What about you?"

He was silent for a while. Then he said, "Rosetta, I'm sorry."

"It's all right if you don't want to tell me."

"I do. I feel a compulsion to tell you. I think you ought to know. Rosetta . . . my name is not John Player."

"No? I thought it might not be."

"It's Simon Perrivale."

I was silent. Memories came rushing back: sitting at the kitchen table . . . Mr. Dolland putting on his glasses and reading from the newspaper.

"Not the . . . " I stammered.

He nodded.

"Oh — " I began.

He interrupted. "You're startled. Of course you are. I'm sorry. Perhaps I shouldn't have told you. I am innocent. I wanted you to know. You may not believe — "

"I do believe you," I said sincerely.

116

"Thank you, Rosetta. You know now I am, as they say, 'on the run.' "

"So you worked on the ship as — "

"Deckhand," he said. "I was lucky. I knew that my arrest was imminent. I was sure they would find me guilty. I wouldn't have a chance. There was so much against me. But I *am* innocent, Rosetta. I swear it. I had to get right away, and perhaps later on — if it were possible — find some way of proving my innocence."

"Perhaps it would have been better to have remained and faced it."

"Perhaps. Perhaps not. He was already dead when I got there. The gun was beside him. I picked it up . . . it looked as though I were guilty."

"You might have proved your innocence."

"Not then. Everything was against me. The press had made up its mind that I was a murderer . . . so had everyone else. I felt then that I didn't stand a chance against them all. I wanted to get out of the country in some way so I made my way to Tilbury. I had what I thought was an amazing stroke of luck there. I talked to a sailor in a tavern. He was drinking heavily because he didn't want to go back to sea. His wife was going to have a baby and he couldn't bear to leave her. He was heartbroken. I took advantage of the fact that he

117

was drunk. I shouldn't have done so but I was desperate. I felt I had to get out of the country, give myself a chance. It occurred to me that I might take his place . . . and this is what I did. He was a deckhand on the *Atlantic Star*, John Player. The ship was sailing that day . . . it was going to South Africa. I thought if I could get there, I could start a new life and perhaps some day the truth would come out and I could go home. I was desperate, Rosetta. It was a crazy plan but it worked. I was constantly in fear that someone might find out . . . but no one did. And then this happened."

"I guessed at once that there was something different about you. You didn't fit somehow."

"On our morning meetings, of course."

"Yes."

"Was it so obvious?"

"A little."

"I was afraid of Lorimer."

"Oh, I understand. He did say something about his home being not far from the Perrivale house."

"Yes. He actually came there once. I was about seventeen, I imagine. I was in the stables when he rode in. It was a very brief meeting and one changes a lot in the years. He couldn't have recognised me, but I was afraid."

"And now?" I said. "What now?"

"It looks as though this could be the end of the story."

"What happened on that day? Can you bear to talk of it?"

"I think I could tell you. One wants to talk to someone and you and I . . . well, we've become friends, real friends. We trust each other, and even if I felt you might betray me, you couldn't do much harm here, could you? To whom could you betray me here?"

"I would not dream of betraying you anywhere! You've told me you were innocent."

"I never felt that I belonged at Perrivale. That's rather sad for a child, you know. I have vague memories of what I used to think of as Before. Life was comfortable and easy then. I was five years old before it changed into what I called Now. There was someone I called Angel. She was plump, cosy, and smelt of lavender; she was always there to comfort me. There was another one too. She was Aunt Ada. She did not live in the cottage with us but she came there often. On the days when she came I used to hide under a table which was covered with a red cloth, velvety and smooth. I can feel that cloth now and the faint odour of moth balls, and I can hear the strident voice saying, 'Why don't you, Alice?' in tones of reproach. Alice was the cosy lavender-smelling Angel.

"I remember once going in a train with Angel. We were going to Aunt Ada, to Witch's Home. I believed then that Aunt Ada was a witch. She must be if she lived in Witch's Home. I clung to Angel's hand as we entered. It was a little house with leaded windows which made it dark but everything in it shone brightly. All the time Aunt Ada was telling Angel what she ought to do. I was sent out to the garden. There was water at the bottom of it. I was afraid because I was separated from Angel and I thought Aunt Ada might tell her that she ought to leave me there. I can remember now my great joy when I was in the train once more with Angel beside me. I said, 'Angel, don't let's go to the Witch's Home any more.'

"We did not go again but Aunt Ada came to us. I would hear her saying, 'You should do this, you should not do that,' and Angel would say, 'Well, you see, Ada, it's like this. . . . ' And they would talk about the Boy, which I knew referred to me. Aunt Ada was sure I would grow into a criminal if a little more discipline was not shown. Some would say she was right. But it wasn't so, Rosetta. I am innocent."

"I do believe you," I told him.

He was silent for a while and his eyes looked

dreamily back into the past.

He went on. "There was a man who used to come and visit us. I found out in due course that he was Sir Edward Perrivale. He brought presents for Angel and for me. She always looked pleased when he came so I was, too. I used to be put on his knee, and he would look at me and every now and then give a little chuckle. Then he would say, 'Good boy. Fine boy.' And that was all. But I thought it was rather nice and a change from Aunt Ada.

"One day I had been playing in the garden and came into the cottage to find Angel seated in a chair by the table. She had her hand to her breast; she looked pale and was gasping. I cried, 'Angel, Angel, *I'm* here.' I was frightened and bewildered because she didn't look at me. And then suddenly she shut her eyes and she wasn't like Angel at all. I was frightened and went on calling her name, but she fell forward with her head down. I started to scream. People came in. They took me away then and I knew something dreadful had happened. Aunt Ada came and it was no use hiding under the tablecloth. She soon found me and told me I was a wicked boy. I didn't care what she called me, I just wanted Angel to be there.

"She was dead. It was a strange, bewildering time. I can't remember much of it, except that there was a constant stream of people coming to the cottage and it wasn't the same place any more. She lay in a coffin in the parlour with the blinds drawn down. Aunt Ada took me to have 'a last look at her.' She made me kiss her cold face. I screamed and tried to run away. It wasn't the Angel I had known lying there, indifferent to me and my need of her. . . . Why am I telling you all this, and telling it as a child? Why don't I just say she died, and that's that?"

"You are telling it as it should be told," I said. "You make me see it as it was . . . as you lived it . . . and that is how I want to see it."

He went on. "I can hear the tolling of the funeral bell. I can see these black-clad figures and Aunt Ada like some grisly prophet of disaster . . . watching me all the time, menacing me.

"Sir Edward came down for the funeral. There was a great deal of talk and it concerned 'the Boy.' I knew my future was in the balance and I was very frightened.

"I asked Mrs. Stubbs, who used to come to the cottage to scrub the floors, where Angel was and she said, 'Don't you worry your little head about her. She's safe enough. She's in Heaven with the angels.' Then I heard someone say, 'Of course he'll go to Ada.'

"I could not imagine a worse fate. I had half

suspected it. Ada was Angel's sister, and since Angel was in Heaven, someone had to look after the Boy. I knew there was one thing I had to do. I had to find Angel, so I set out to go to Heaven, where I should see her and tell her that she must come back or I would stay with her there.

"I did not get very far before I met one of the farmworkers driving a cartload of hay. He stopped and called down to me, 'Where are you off to, young fellow me lad?' And I replied, 'I'm going to Heaven.' 'That's a long way,' he said. 'You going on your own?' 'Yes,' I told him. 'Angel is there. I'm going to her.' He said, 'You're little Simon, ain't you? I've heard about you. Here. Hop in and I'll give you a lift.' 'Are you going to Heaven then?' I said. 'Not yet, I hope,' he said. 'But I know the way you ought to go.' He lifted me up beside him. And what he did was take me back to the cottage. Sir Edward was the first to see me. Touching his forehead, the man who had betrayed me said, 'Begging your pardon, sir, but the little lad belongs here. I picked him up on the road. On his way to Heaven, he tells me. Thought I'd best bring him back, sir.'

"Sir Edward had a strange look on his face. He gave the man money and thanked him and then he said to me, 'We'll have a talk, shall we?' He took me into the cottage and we went into the parlour which still smelt of lilies, but the coffin wasn't there and I knew with a terrible sense of loneliness that she would not be there any more.

"Sir Edward put me on his knee. I thought he was going to say 'Fine boy,' but he didn't. What he said was, 'So you were trying to find your way to Heaven, were you, boy?' I nodded. 'It's a place you can't reach.' I watched his mouth moving as he spoke. He had a line of hair above the top lip and a pointed beard — a Vandyke actually. 'Why did you go?' he asked. I was not able to express myself with lucidity. I said, 'Aunt Ada.' He seemed to understand. 'You don't want to go with her. She *is* your aunt.' I shook my head. 'No, no, no,' I said. 'You don't like her?' I shook my head again. 'Well, well,' he said. 'Let's see what we can do.' He was very thoughtful. I think he must have made up his mind then, for a day or so later I heard that I was going away to a big house. Sir Edward was going to take me into his family."

He smiled at me.

"You have drawn your own conclusions. I am sure they are correct. I was his son, his illegitimate son — though it was hard to believe that, he being the man I came to know later. I was sure he loved my mother, Angel.

124

Anybody must. I had sensed it when they were together, but of course he couldn't marry her. She was not the right sort for him. He must have fallen in love with her and set her up in the cottage, and he came to visit her from time to time. I was never told this by Sir Edward or anyone. It was an assumption, but so plausible that it was accepted by all. Why else should he have taken me into his household and educated me with his sons?"

"So," I said. "That is how you came to Perrivale Court."

"Yes. I was two years older than Cosmo and three older than Tristan. That was fortunate for me, otherwise I should have had a bad time, I think. Those two years gave me an advantage. I needed it, for, having installed me in his nursery, Sir Edward seemed to lose interest in me, though sometimes I saw him watching me furtively. The servants resented me. If it hadn't been for the nanny I should probably have been as badly off as with Aunt Ada. But the nanny took pity on me. She loved me and protected me. I will always remember how much I owe to that good woman.

"Then we had a tutor when I was about seven years old, a Mr. Welling, I remember, and I got on well with him. He must have heard the gossip but it did not affect him. I was more serious than Cosmo and Tristan and I had those two years as an advantage.

"There was, of course, Lady Perrivale. She was a terrifying person and I was glad she seemed quite unaware of my existence. She very rarely spoke to me and I had the impression that she did not see me. She was a large woman and everyone — apart from Sir Edward — was afraid of her. It was well known in the house that her money had saved Perrivale Court and that she was the daughter of a millionaire coal owner or ironmaster; there seemed to be a divergence of opinion as to which. She had been an only daughter and he had wanted a title for her. He was ready to pay a price for it and much of the money made from iron or coal had gone into bolstering up the roof and walls of Perrivale Court. It must have seemed a good arrangement to Sir Edward for, as well as keeping the roof over his head, she provided him with two sons as well. I had one desire — to keep out of her way. So now you have a picture of the sort of household I was in."

"Yes. And then you went away to school?"

"Which was decidedly better for me. There I was equal with the others. I was good at lessons, fair at sports, and I did well. I lost a little of that aggressiveness which I had built up in the early years. I was ready to defend myself before there was any need to do so. I looked for slights and insults where there were none. School was good for me.

"Too soon it was over. We had ceased to be boys. There was enough work on the estate to keep us all busy, and we worked comparatively well together. We were reasonable adults now . . . all of us.

"I was about twenty-four when Major Durrell came to the neighbourhood. His daughter came with him. She was a widow with a small child, a girl. The widow was startlingly beautiful — red-haired and green-eyed. Very unusual. We were all fascinated by her, Cosmo and Tristan in particular, but she chose Cosmo and their engagement was announced."

I looked at him steadily. Had he cared for the widow, as had been suggested? Did the prospect of her marriage to someone else arouse his anger, despair, jealousy? Had he planned to have the widow for himself? No. I did believe him. He had spoken with such sincerity. He had made me see the nursery presided over by the kindly nanny and the arrival in their midst of the fascinating widow — Mirabel was what the papers had called her.

"Yes," he went on, "she chose Cosmo. Lady Perrivale was very pleased. She was very eager for her sons to marry and give her grandchildren and she was delighted that

Cosmo's bride was to be Mirabel. Mirabel's mother, it seemed, had been an old school friend of hers — her best friend, we heard. She had married Major Durrell and, although she was now dead, Lady Perrivale gave a warm welcome to the widower and his daughter. She had known the major when her friend had married him, and he had written telling her that he had retired from the Army and was thinking of settling somewhere. What about Cornwall? Lady Perrivale was delighted and found Seashell Cottage for them. That was how they came to be there. And then, of course, there was the engagement to Cosmo which followed very soon. You see how the stage was set."

"I am beginning to see it very clearly," I said.

"We were all working on the estate and there was this farmhouse, Bindon Boys. The farmer who had lived there and worked the farm had died some three years before and the land had been let out to a farmer on a temporary basis but no one had taken on the house. It was in a bad state and needed a bit of restoration as well as decorating."

"There was a good deal in the papers about Bindon Boys."

"Yes . . . it was originally Bindon Bois, after the copse nearby. It was called Bindon

Boys by the natives and that had become its official name. We had all inspected the house and were deciding what should be done."

I nodded. I visualised the heavy black headlines: BINDON BOYS CASE. *Police expect an arrest shortly.* I was seeing it all so differently now from when Mr. Dolland had sat at the kitchen table and we had tried to piece the story together.

"We had been over there several times. There was a great deal of work to be done. I remember the day clearly. I was meeting Cosmo at the farmhouse so that we could discuss some plan on the spot. I went to the house and found him there . . . dead . . . the gun by his side. I could not believe it. I knelt beside him. There was blood on my coat, his blood. I picked up the gun — and it was then that Tristan came in and found me. I remember his words. 'Good God, Simon! You've killed him!' I told him I had just come in, that I had found him like this. He stared at the gun in my hand . . . and I could see what he was thinking."

He stopped short and closed his eyes as though he were trying to shut out the memory. I laid my hand on his shoulder.

I said, "You know you're innocent, Simon. You'll prove it one day."

"If we never get away from this island, no

one will ever know the truth."

"We're going to get away," I said. "I feel it."

"It's just hope."

"Hope is a good thing."

"It's heartbreaking when it is proved unfounded."

"But it isn't in this case. A ship *will* come. I know it. And then . . . "

"Yes, what then? I must hide myself away. I must never go back. I dare not. If I did they would capture me, and they would say I had proved my guilt by having run away."

"What really happened? Have you any idea?"

"I think there is a possibility that it might have been old Harry Tench. He hated Cosmo. He had rented one of the farms some years before. He drank too much and the place went to ruin. Cosmo turned him out and put in another man. Tench went away but he came back. He was tramping the road. He'd become a sort of tinker. People said he had sworn vengeance on the Perrivales and Cosmo in particular. He hadn't been seen in the neighbourhood for some weeks, but of course, if he'd planned to kill Cosmo, he would naturally be careful about being seen nearby. His name was mentioned during the investigation, but he was dismissed and no longer a suspect. I was a more likely one. They made a great play about the enmity between Cosmo and me. People all around seemed to remember signs of it which I was unaware of. They made much of Mirabel and Cosmo's engagement to her."

"I know. The *crime passionnel*. Were you . . . in love with her?"

"Oh, no. We were all a little dazzled by her . . . but no."

"And when her engagement to Cosmo was announced, did you show that you were disappointed?"

"Tristan and I probably said how lucky Cosmo was and that we envied him or something like that. I don't think we meant it very seriously."

There was silence between us.

Then he said, "Now you know. I'm glad. It is like a weight being lifted from my shoulders. Tell me . . . are you shocked to find you have a suspected murderer with you?"

"I can only think that he saved my life . . . Lucas's too."

"Along with my own, of course."

"Well, if you hadn't saved your own, none of us would be here. I am glad you told me. I wish something could be done . . . to make things right . . . so you could go back. Perhaps one day you will."

"You are an optimist. You think we are going to get off this godforsaken island. You believe in miracles."

"I think I have seen a few in the last days."

Again he took my hand and pressed it.

"You are right and I am ungrateful. We shall be picked up in time . . . and someday, perhaps, I shall go back to Perrivale Court and they will know the truth."

"I am sure of it," I said. I stood up. "We have talked for a long time. Lucas will be wondering where we are."

Two more days passed. The water stock was very low and we were running out of coconuts. Simon had found a stout stick which Lucas used as a crutch. His leg was slightly less painful, he said, but I had little confidence in our attempts to set it. Still, he could hobble a few steps and that cheered him considerably.

When we were alone, Simon told me further incidents from his life and I began to get a clearer picture of what it had been like. I was fascinated by it all. I longed to be of help in uncovering the truth and establishing his innocence. I wanted to hear more of Harry Tench. I had decided that he was the murderer. Simon said Cosmo should not have been so hard on the man. True, Harry Tench was a poor farmer and if the estate was to prosper it must be maintained in a proper manner, but he could have kept Harry Tench on in some other capacity. Cosmo had insisted that he was useless as a worker; moreover, he had been insolent, which was something Cosmo would not accept.

We used to discuss how it would have been possible for Harry Tench to have killed Cosmo. He had no fixed home; he often slept in barns; he had admitted sleeping in Bindon Boys. Perhaps he had been there when Cosmo arrived at the house a short time before Simon came in. Perhaps he had seized his opportunity. But there was the gun. That needed a little explanation. It had been discovered that it came from the gunroom at Perrivale Court. How could Harry Tench have got his hands on it?

And so on . . . but I am sure it was a great relief to Simon to be able to talk.

It was our fifth day on the island and late in the afternoon. Simon and I had been wandering round all the morning. We had found some berries which we thought might be edible and were considering the risk of trying them when we heard a shout, followed by a whistle.

It was Lucas. We hurried back to him. He was pointing excitedly to the horizon. It was just a speck. Were we imagining this or were we conjuring up in our minds something we so desperately wanted to see?

In breathless silence we watched. It had begun to take shape.

"It is. It *is!*" cried Simon.

In the Seraglio

Having been close to death for so long, I had thought that anything would have been preferable, but the fears of the next weeks were beyond anything I could ever have imagined.

How often did I tell myself that it would have been better to go down with the ship or that our little boat had been destroyed in a hurricane?

I recall now our joy when we first saw that ship on the horizon and then, so soon after we had been rescued, I became sure that it would have been better if we had remained on the island, still vainly looking for help. Who knows, we might have found some means of surviving; at least we were together, enjoying a certain peace and security.

From the moment those dark, swarthy men waded ashore, red caps on their heads, cutlasses at their sides, our euphoria at being rescued was replaced by a fearful apprehension. It was immediately clear that we could not understand their language. I guessed they must be of Arabic origin. Their ship was no *Atlantic Star*. It looked like an ancient galley. It had not occurred to me that there could still be pirates on the high seas, but I remembered the captain of the *Atlantic Star* one night at dinner had told us that there were ships which still roamed about in certain waters, following some nefarious trade or other. And it instantly occurred to me that we had fallen into the hands of such men.

I did not like the ship, I did not like these men, and it was clear to me that my suspicions were shared by both Simon and Lucas.

We stood close as though to shield each other. There were about ten of them. They gabbled together and stared searchingly at us. One of them approached and took a lock of my hair in his hands. They were crowding round and chattering excitedly. My hair was fairer now that it was bleached by the sun, and I could only believe that they were astonished by my colouring, which was so different from theirs.

I sensed the uneasiness of Simon and Lucas. They had edged closer to me. I knew they would both fight to the death for me, which brought a modicum of comfort.

Their attention turned to Lucas, who was standing there, leaning on the stick we had found for him. He looked pale and ill.

The men were chattering and shaking their heads. They gazed at me and then at Simon. They laughed and nodded to each other. I had a terrible fear that they were going to take us and leave Lucas.

I said, "We'll all stand together."

"Yes," muttered Simon. "I don't like the look of them."

"Bad luck they found us," murmured Lucas. "Better . . ."

"What do you think they are?"

Simon shook his head, and I felt numb with fear. I was afraid of these men, their chattering voices, their sly sidelong glances, their implication as to what they would do with us.

Suddenly they made a decision. One, whom I took to be the leader, signed to them and four of them went to our boat, examined it, and turned to nod at the others. They were taking our boat out to the galley.

Simon took a step forward but he was barred by a man with a cutlass.

"Let them take it," I hissed.

It was our turn. The leader nodded and two men, their cutlasses drawn, came and stood behind us. They gave us all a little push and we saw what was indicated. We were to go out to the galley. Lucas hobbled between us . . . but the three of us were at least together.

Simon murmured, "We wouldn't have lasted long on that island anyway."

It was difficult getting Lucas on board. None of them helped us. We had to mount a rope ladder, which was almost an impossibility for Lucas. I think Simon half carried him up.

Then we were all three standing on the deck surrounded by curious men. They all seemed to be staring at me. Several of them touched my hair. They laughed together, twisting it round their fingers and pulling it.

There was a sudden silence. A man had appeared. I guessed he was the captain of the vessel. He was taller than the others and his dark lively eyes held a hint of humour. Moreover, there was a certain refinement in his well-defined features which gave me a brief glow of hope.

He shouted something and the men fell back.

He looked at the three of us and bowed his head in a form of greeting. "English?" he said.

"Yes . . . yes!" we cried.

He nodded. That seemed to be the extent of his knowledge of our language, but his courtesy was comforting. He turned to the men and talked in a way which seemed threatening. They were clearly subdued.

He turned to us and said, "Come."

We followed him and were put into a small cabin. There was a bunk there and we sat down thankfully.

The captain lifted his hand. "Eat," he said.

He went out and locked the door behind him.

"What does it mean?" I asked.

Lucas thought that the object would be to hold us for ransom. "It's a thriving business," he said. "I feel sure that is what they have in mind."

"Do you mean to say they roam the seas looking for shipwrecked mariners?"

"Oh, no. They'll have another trade. Smuggling, perhaps . . . or even seizing ships where possible . . . like the pirates of old. They'd turn their hands to anything if there's a profit in it. They would assume we must have a home somewhere and we're English. They are inclined to regard all English abroad as millionaires."

"How glad I am we remained together."

"Yes," said Lucas. "I think they were wondering whether I should be worth the effort."

"What are we going to do?" asked Simon. He looked at me steadily. "We must do everything in our power to stay together."

"I pray that we do."

Food was brought to us. It was hot and

spicy. In the ordinary way I should have declined it, but we were near starvation and any food seemed palatable. Lucas advised us to eat sparingly.

I felt a little better afterwards. I wondered how they would send home for ransoms. To whom would they send? My father had a sister whom we had scarcely seen for the last ten years or so. Would she be ready to pay a ransom for her niece? Perhaps my parents had reached home, but they had never been rich.

And Simon? The last thing he would want was for his identity to be known. As for Lucas ... regarding a ransom, he was probably in the best position of all of us, for he came from a wealthy family.

"I wish I knew where we were," said Simon. "That would be a help."

I wondered if he had plans for escaping. He had shown himself to be very resourceful by escaping from England. If he had done that, it was possible that he might be able to escape again.

So we brooded and all three of us, I am sure, were wishing we were back on the island. Food might have been scarce, hopes of survival slim, but at least we had been free.

I had an unpleasant experience on the first night. It was dark and we were trying to sleep when I heard stealthy footsteps outside the door and then the sound of a key being turned in the lock.

I started up as the door opened quietly.

Two men came in. I believed they were two of those who had come ashore to take us in but I could not be certain at this stage as one looked very like another to me.

They had come to take me. They seized me. I screamed. Lucas and Simon were immediately awake.

The two men were trying to drag me out of the cabin, and I could guess by their grunts and expressions what their intentions were.

"Let me go!" I cried.

Simon struck one of the men. He was knocked across the cabin by the other. Lucas brandished his stick and hit out at them.

There was a great deal of shouting and others appeared at the door. They were all laughing and chattering. Simon got up; he came to me, seized me, and thrust me behind him. I saw that his hand was bleeding.

A terrible fear swept over me. I knew I was in great danger.

I dare not imagine what would have happened to me if the captain had not appeared. He shouted an order. The men looked sheepish. He saw me cowering behind Simon and Lucas beside me.

Simon seemed somehow to indicate that if any one of them attempted to harm me that he would have to face him, and he was formidable. Lucas was equally protective, but of course he was crippled.

The captain had clearly summed up the whole situation. He knew what the motive of these men had been. I was different; I had long yellow hair such as they had not seen before; moreover, I was a woman, and that was enough for them.

The captain bowed to me and his gesture suggested an apology for the crude behaviour of his men.

He indicated that I must follow him.

Simon stepped forward.

The captain shook his head. "I see . . . safe," he said. "I . . . only I . . . captain."

Oddly enough, I trusted him. I knew he was the captain of a ship engaged in some nefarious trade, but for some reason I believed he would help me. In any case he was the captain. If we had attempted to disobey him, we should not have done so for long. We were at his mercy. For all their gestures, neither Simon nor Lucas could help me. I had to trust the captain.

I walked behind him through those men. Some of them put out their hands to touch my hair but none of them did. I could see that they were greatly in awe of the captain, and his orders obviously were that none was to touch me.

I was taken to a small cabin which I think adjoined his. He stood aside for me to enter. It was more comfortable than the one I had left. There were covers and cushions on a bunk which was like a divan. I could rest more comfortably here. Behind a curtain was a basin and ewer. I could wash!

The captain spread his hands, indicating the cabin. He said, "Safe here . . . I see safe."

"Thank you," I said.

I don't know whether he understood but my tone must have expressed my gratitude.

He bowed, went out, and locked the door behind him.

I sank onto the bed. I started to tremble violently as I contemplated the ordeal from which the captain had saved me.

It was a long time before I could regain my composure.

I wondered what *his* intentions were. Perhaps Lucas was right. I felt sure he must be. It was a ransom they were thinking of; and if this were the case, they would want to return us unharmed.

I pulled aside the curtain and indulged in the luxury of washing myself.

I returned to the divan. I lay down. I was

exhausted, physically, mentally, and emotionally, and for a brief spell forgot the hazards about me.

I slept.

I think perhaps I tried to forget those days when I lived in a state of perpetual terror. Every time I heard a footstep, every time my door opened, I would be seized by an overwhelming apprehension. One's imagination in such situations can be one's greatest enemy.

Food was brought to me regularly, and because of this I felt a respite from being constantly on the alert for danger; yet I knew it was all around me. I was not sure what their purpose was, but it was obvious that they were planning something for me. The captain certainly stood between me and a certain fate, and at least I had to be thankful for that. I trusted the man, not because I believed in his chivalry but his attitude meant that I must be treated with a certain respect because of what he had in mind for me.

I found I could eat a little. My creature comforts were attended to. It was a great blessing to be able to wash frequently. I wished I knew where the ship was going and what fate was planned for me. I wished I knew where Simon and Lucas were.

The captain came to my cabin once. I had

washed my hair and it was just drying when the knock came. He kept staring at my hair, but he was very polite. I knew that he wanted to talk to me but his knowledge of English was exasperatingly limited.

"You . . . come . . . ship . . . England?"

"Yes," I said. "But we were wrecked."

"From England . . . alone? No?" He shook his head.

"With my parents . . . my father and mother."

It was hopeless. I imagined he was trying to find out what kind of family I came from. Was there money? How much would it be worth to have me back?

He gave it up as hopeless, but I knew by the way in which he kept looking at my hair and smiling to himself that he was pleased with what he saw.

Then one morning when I awoke the ship was no longer moving. The sun had risen and when I looked out through the small porthole I caught a glimpse of white buildings.

I became aware of noise and bustle. People were shouting to each other in excited voices. One thing was certain. We had reached our destination and I must soon learn my fate.

During that morning it gradually dawned on me what it was to be, and I was filled with the utmost horror. I began to ask myself if it

145

would not have been better if I had never experienced my miraculous escape from the sea.

The captain came to my cabin. He brought with him a black cloak, a yasmak, and a snood. He made it clear that these were for me to wear. My hair had to be piled into the snood and when I was fully clad I looked like any Arab woman who might be met within the souks of an eastern town.

I was taken ashore and to my great delight I caught a glimpse of Simon. But I was immediately anxious because there was no sign of Lucas.

Simon recognised me in spite of my covering and I was aware of his fear as he did so. We tried to reach each other but we were roughly held back.

The sun was dazzling and I was very hot in my robes. A man walked on either side of Simon, and with the captain beside me we waded ashore.

I shall never forget that walk. We were in what I took to be the Kasbah. The streets were narrow, cobbled and winding, and crowded with men in robes and women dressed as I was now. Goats ran among us; there were a few hungry-looking dogs who sniffed at us hopefully. I caught a glimpse of a rat feeding in the refuge on the cobbles. There were small shops — little more than caves —

open to the streets, with stalls on which lay trinkets, brass ornaments, small leather goods, and food — exotic, spicy, and unappetising in my eyes. The smell was sickening.

Some of the traders called a greeting to the captain and his men. I was becoming more and more apprehensive about my eventual fate for they seemed to know the purpose of his visit and I wondered how many other young women had walked along these streets with him. If only I could get to Simon. And what had they done with Lucas?

At length we moved into a wider street. Some trees grew here — dusty palms, mostly. The houses were bigger; we turned in at a gate and were in a courtyard where a fountain played. Around this squatted several men — servants, I presumed, for they jumped up as we entered and started to talk excitedly.

One of them came up and bowed very low to the captain, who nodded an acknowledgement and waved his hand. We were led through a door into a large hall. The windows were heavily draped and set in alcoves designed I was sure to let in the minimum of heat.

A man in splendid robes bowed to the captain and seemed eager to show him the utmost respect. He was obviously telling him to follow, for he led us through another door and there, seated on a dais on an ornate chair, was a little old man.

He was flamboyantly dressed, but so small and wizened that his clothes only seemed to accentuate his age. He was very ancient except for his eyes, which were dark and lively; they reminded me of a monkey's.

The captain went to the chair and bowed and the old man waved in greeting. Then the captain obviously told his men to leave him with Simon and me.

The captain pushed me forward. He let the cloak fall to the ground and pulled off my yasmak and snood so that my hair fell about my shoulders. The lively dark eyes opened wide. He muttered something which seemed to please the captain. The old man's eyes were fixed on my hair, and he and the captain began to talk excitedly. How I wished I knew what they were saying.

Then Simon was brought forward. The old man's shrewd eyes ranged over him, weighing him up and down. He looked very tall and strong, and it seemed that his physical strength made as good an impression as my hair.

The old man nodded and I guessed that was a sign of approval.

The captain moved closer to the old man and they were in deep conversation. That

gave Simon and me a chance to get close together.

"Where is Lucas?" I whispered.

"I don't know. I was taken away and
brought here. He wasn't with me."

"I do hope he's all right. Where are we?"

"Somewhere along the north coast of
Africa, I imagine."

"What are they going to do with us? What
are they talking about?"

"Probably bargaining."

"Bargaining?"

"It looks as if we are being sold."

"Like slaves?"

"It would seem so."

"What shall we *do?*"

"I don't know. Wait for our opportunity.
We are helpless just now. We'll have to wait
for the right moment and then get away . . . if
we can."

"Shall we be together?"

"I don't know."

"Oh, Simon, I do hope we don't lose each
other."

"Let's pray for it."

"I'm frightened, Simon."

"I feel very much the same myself."

"This old man . . . what is he?"

"A trader, I imagine."

"A trader . . . in people?"

"That amongst other things. Anything that comes to hand, I imagine, if it's worthwhile. And that would include people."

"We must get away somehow."

"How?"

"Run . . . anywhere."

"How far do you think we'd get? No, wait. If we can keep together, we will. Who knows, the opportunity may come. We'll manage it."

"Oh, Simon, I believe we shall."

I remember now the look which passed between us. I treasured it to remember in my darkest and most frightened moments. I was to think of it often during the weeks to come.

There are some things one does not wish to remember. One wants to shut them out and make believe they did not happen. Sometimes the mind helps so that they become a blurred memory. And that is what seemed to have happened to me.

I remember being in the trader's house. It must have been for just one night. I recall my terrible apprehension, the pictures supplied by a cruel imagination which continually taunted me as to what my fate would be. The old man seemed like a horrible ogre. There was only one comfort to me. Simon was in the house. The transaction with the captain concerned us both.

Later on the day of our arrival the captain left the house and I never saw him again.

The next day I was enveloped in the robes in which I had arrived and my hair was completely hidden as before. Then Simon and I were taken through the streets of the Kasbah to the harbour, where a ship was waiting. The old man was clearly in charge of us but he took no notice of us and I had the impression that he was only there to protect his property, which we now were.

We could not imagine where he was taking us.

Simon and I found one or two opportunities on board to talk to each other. Our main topic was Lucas.

Simon told me that there had been one or two meetings with the captain. They had not been ill-treated. He said the captain had been very interested in Lucas. Simon thought he had been taken away somewhere. They had been separated and not able to talk, but he fancied Lucas was hopeful — at least not unduly alarmed.

"I think he thought at one time that they might throw him overboard because he would be no use for work. I imagine that is what they want of me."

I was silent, dreading to think what my fate might be.

Simon thought the place we had left was very probably Algeria.

"It used to be a refuge for pirates in the old days. They had the protection of the Turkish government. Perhaps it still remains a haven for them. The Kasbah must be an ideal spot for underhand business of any sort. I imagine few would want to venture there at certain times."

He was probably right.

We pursued our journey along the Syrian coast to the Dardanelles and then to our destination, which we learned in due course was Constantinople.

As we were approaching the Bosphorus, a woman came to my cabin. She had a girl with her, and the girl was carrying what looked like an armful of diaphanous material. It turned out to be garments and these were laid out on the bunk. Then they turned their attention to me. I had seen these women about the ship and had wondered what their duties were. I soon realised they had come to the cabin to help me dress in these splendid garments.

There were long trousers made of flimsy silky material, baggy and caught in at the ankles. Over them went a gown of beautiful transparent material. It was sparkling with sequins which looked like stars. They un-

152

pinned my hair and spread it round my shoulders. They combed it and looked at one another, nudging and giggling.

When I was dressed they stood back and clapped their hands.

I said, "I want my other clothes."

They could not understand me. They just went on giggling and nudging each other. They stroked my hair and smiled at me.

The old man came into the cabin. He looked at me and rubbed his hands together.

My fear was greater than ever. I knew that Simon's surmise was correct. We were going to be sold into slavery — he as a strong man to work as directed while I was destined for a more sinister purpose.

I sensed that Simon was more worried about my fate than his own.

The cloak, yasmak, and snood were brought in and my splendour was hidden from view. With Simon beside me, I was taken off the ship where a carriage was waiting for us and, with the old man and a younger one who, I imagined, was some sort of clerk or assistant, we were driven through the streets of Constantinople.

I was too concerned with my impending fate to take much note of my surroundings, but I learned later that there are two distinct parts of the city, the Christian and the Turkish, and these are connected by two bridges, rather clumsily constructed but adequate and very necessary. I was vaguely aware of mosques and minarets, and I felt, with great desolation, that we were very far from home.

It was to the Turkish section that we were taken.

I felt lost and very frightened. I kept looking at Simon to reassure myself that he was still there.

It seemed that we drove for a long time. It was like another world — narrow streets, incredibly dirty; fine buildings, their dazzlingly white spires reaching to the bluest of skies; mosques, bazaars; wooden houses little more than hovels; noise; people everywhere. They scattered before the oncoming carriage and again and again I thought we should run someone down, but they always managed to escape from under the horses' feet.

At length we turned into a quiet avenue. The trees and bushes were bright with colourful flowers. We slowed down before a tall white building which stood back from the road.

When we alighted from the carriage a man in white robes came out to greet us. The old man bowed to him rather obsequiously and the greeting was returned in a somewhat condescending manner. We were taken inside, into a room which seemed dark after the brilliance of the sun. The windows were similar to those which I had seen before, recessed and heavily draped.

A tall man came forward. He wore a turban with a jewel in it and long white robes. He sat down in a chair like a throne, and I noticed that the old man became more deferential than ever.

I thought in trepidation, Is this to be my new owner?

My cloak was removed and my hair displayed. The man in the chair was clearly impressed by it. I had never felt so humiliated in my life. He looked at Simon and nodded.

There had been two men standing at the door — guards, I supposed. One of them clapped his hands and a woman came in. She was plump, middle-aged, and elaborately dressed in the same style as I was.

She came to me, studied me, took a strand of my hair in her hands, and smiled faintly. Then she rolled up the sleeves of my gown and prodded me. She frowned and, shaking her head, made little sounds which I was sure indicated disapproval.

The old man started to talk very quickly; the other was reasoning. The woman said a word or two and nodded judiciously. It was maddening not to know what they were saying. All I could gather was that it was something about me and they were not as pleased with me as the old man had hoped they would be.

However, they appeared to come to some agreement. The old man was clasping his hands and the other was nodding. The woman nodded too. She was explaining something to them. The man was listening intently to her and she seemed to be reassuring him.

She signed to me to follow her.

Simon was left behind. I gave him an agonised look and he started after me. One of the guards stepped forward and barred his way, his hand on the hilt of his sword.

I saw the helplessness in Simon's face; then my arm was firmly taken by the plump woman and I was led away.

I was to learn that I was destined for the seraglio — the harem — of one of the most important pashas in Constantinople. All the men I had seen so far were merely his minions.

The harem is a community of women into which no man is allowed to appear except eunuchs, such as this important gentleman I had seen bargaining with the old man. He, I discovered, was the Chief Eunuch, and I was to see him frequently.

It took me some time to realise that I had reason to be thankful for the hardship I had suffered, because my physical state was the reason why, during the next weeks, I was left unmolested. My yellow hair had made me outstanding. I was a prize object because I was so different from the women around me. They were all dark-haired and dark-eyed. My eyes were a definite blue and they and my yellow hair set me apart.

It seemed to those whose duty it was to relieve the Pasha's jaded senses that my very difference might make me especially acceptable. There was something else which I discovered later they had noticed about me. These women were subservient by nature; they had been brought up in the certain knowledge that they were the inferior sex and their mission on earth was to pander to men's desires. But there was a spirit of independence about me. I came of a different culture, and it set me apart almost as much as did my blue eyes and yellow hair.

However, when I was stripped and subjected to one of the scented baths which had been prepared for me, it was seen by the watchful lady who was in charge of us all that my skin, where it had not been exposed to the sun, was very white and soft. Before I was offered up to the Pasha the whiteness of my skin must be restored to every part of my body. Moreover I had become very ill-nourished, and the Pasha did not like women to be too thin. The potential was there but it had to be recovered, and this process would take a little time.

How grateful I was! I had time to adjust myself, to learn the ways of the harem, and perhaps to find out what had happened to Simon. Who knew? I had been remarkably fortunate as yet. What if there might still be hope of escape before I had reached that state which would render me worthy of submission to the man who had bought me?

As soon as I learned that I was safe — if only for a short time — my spirits revived. Hope came flooding back. I wanted to learn all I could about my surroundings, and naturally I wondered a great deal about my companions.

The most important person in the harem was Rani, the middle-aged woman who had inspected me and decided that as yet I was unworthy to be submitted to the Pasha. If only we had had a common language I could have learned a great deal from her. The other women were very much in awe of her. They all flattered her and were most obsequious to her, for she was the one who selected those who were to be presented to the Pasha. When the order came she would give great thought to the matter, and during that time it was amusing to see how they all tried to call attention to themselves. I was amazed to realise that that which I so much dreaded was greatly sought after by the rest.

There were some young girls in the harem who could not have been more than ten years old and women who must have been close on thirty. It was a strange life these girls lived, and I discovered later that some of them had been there since childhood . . . trained to give pleasure to some rich man.

There was little for them to do all day. I had to have my daily baths and to be massaged with ointments. It was a world remote from reality. The air was heavy with the scent of musk, sandalwood, patchouli, and attar of roses. The girls would sit by the fountains, talking idly; sometimes I would hear the tinkle of a musical instrument. They picked flowers and entwined them in their hair; they studied their faces in little hand mirrors or gazed at their reflections in the pools; sometimes they played games; they would chatter together, giggle, tell fortunes.

They slept in a large and airy room on divans; there were beautiful clothes for them to wear. It was an extraordinary life to while away the days, thinking of nothing but how to beautify themselves, how to idle through the day hoping that that evening they might be selected to share the Pasha's bed.

There was a great deal of rivalry for this honour. I soon sensed that. I attracted a great deal of attention. I was so different from them it was almost a certainty that, when I was considered worthy, I should be chosen for my very strangeness, if for nothing else.

Meanwhile the attempts to wipe out the results of the hardships I had suffered went on. I felt like a goose being fattened up for Christmas. I found it difficult to eat the highly spiced food. It was a little game, trying to dispose of it without Rani's knowing what I was doing.

It was an exciting day when I found out that one of the more mature women — and I think one of the most beautiful — was French. Her name was Nicole and I noticed from the first that she was different from the others. She also seemed to be the most important — after Rani, of course.

One day I was sitting by the fountain when she came up and sat beside me.

She asked me in French if I spoke the language.

Communication at last! It was wonderful. My French was not very adequate but at least it existed and we were able to talk.

"You are English?" she asked.

I told her I was.

"And how did you come here?"

In halting French I told her of the ship-wreck and how we had been picked up.

She replied that she had been in the harem for nine years. She was Creole and had come from Martinique to go to school in France. On the way she too had been shipwrecked and taken by corsairs, brought here, and sold, just as I had been.

"You have been here all those years?" I said. "How have you endured it?"

She shrugged her shoulders. "At first," she said, "there is great fear. I was only sixteen years old. I had hated the convent. It was easy here. I liked the clothes . . . the idle life, I suppose. And I was different . . . as you are. The Pasha liked me."

"You were the favourite of the harem, I believe," I said.

She nodded. "Because," she said, "I have Samir."

I had seen Samir, a beautiful child of about four years old. He was made much of by the women. He was the eldest of the harem chil-dren. There was one other, Feisal, who was only a year younger and also a very attractive boy. I had seen him with a woman, a few years younger, I imagined, than Nicole. Her name was Fatima.

Fatima was a voluptuous beauty with masses of black hair and languid dark eyes. She was self-indulgent in the extreme, indolent, and vain. She would sit by the pool for hours, eating sweetmeats and feeding them to one of the two King Charles spaniels who were her constant companions. Fatima cared passionately for four beings — herself, Feisal, and her two little dogs.

Both the boys were taken away at times and there was a great deal of preparation then. They went to see the Pasha. There were two other little boys in the harem but they were as yet only babies. There were no girls. At first I wondered why it was that all the Pasha's children were boys.

Nicole was very informative. She told me that if a woman gave birth to a girl child she went away, to her family perhaps. The Pasha was not interested in daughters, only sons; and if a woman gave birth to a son who was beautiful and intelligent such as Samir she was in high favour.

Samir, being the eldest, would be the Pasha's heir. That was why the other women were jealous of Nicole. She had first been set above them by the Pasha's preference, but that could be fleeting, whereas Samir was always there, a reminder to the Pasha that he

162

could beget fine boys — and he favoured the women who helped him prove this.

She told me that she had secretly taught Samir French, and when the Pasha had discovered this she had been terrified of what he would do. But she had heard through the Chief Eunuch that he was pleased for the boy to learn as much as he could and she might continue teaching him.

It surprised me that a woman of the Western world could so adjust herself to this way of life and that she could be proud of her position and intensely hate anyone who tried to snatch it from her.

But how pleased I was to be able to talk to her and discover something of those around me!

I learned of the tremendous rivalry between her and Fatima, who had great ambitions for her son, Feisal.

"You see," said Nicole, "but for Samir, Feisal would be the Pasha's heir and she would be First Lady. She wants very much to take my place."

"She will never do that. You are more beautiful and much cleverer. Moreover, Samir is a wonderful boy."

"Feisal is not bad," she admitted. "And if I were to die . . ."

"Why should you die?"

She shrugged her shoulders. "Fatima is a very jealous woman. Once, long ago, one of the women poisoned another. It would not be difficult."

"She would not dare."

"One woman dared."

"But she was discovered."

"It was long ago, before the Pasha's day, but they still talk about it. They took her out. They buried her up to her neck in the grounds out there. They left her in the sun . . . to die. It was her punishment."

I shivered.

"I would wish the same for Fatima if she harmed my son."

"You must make sure that she does not."

"It is what I intend to do."

Life was easier now that I had made contact with Nicole. There were our beautiful clothes, our scents, our unguents, our sweetmeats, our lazy days; we were like birds of paradise in cages. After the hardships I had suffered this was a strange life to come to.

I wondered how long it would go on.

The Pasha was away — news which delighted me.

A lethargy fell upon the harem. The women lay about, dreamily admiring themselves in hand mirrors which they carried in the pockets of their capacious trousers, nibbling their sweetmeats, singing or playing their little musical instruments, quarrelling together.

Two of them quarrelled very fiercely, rolling on the mosaic floor, tugging at each other's hair and kicking wildly until Rani came and beat them both, sent them off in disgrace, and said they would not have a chance with the Pasha for three months. That soon sobered them.

Then he returned and there was great excitement. They all became docile and eager to please, displaying their charms, although there were only their companions and the occasional eunuch to see them.

Rani made her selections. I saw her eyes rest on me, and horror was replaced by relief when I realised that she considered me still not ripe for the great honour.

Six girls were selected — two who had been before and found special favour and four novices.

We all watched them being prepared. They were bathed first, their skins anointed, and scent rubbed into their hair. Henna was applied to the soles of their feet and the palms of their hands. Their lips were reddened with beeswax and their eyes made large with kohl. Flowers were set in their hair, bracelets on their wrists and ankles, and they were dressed in sequined garments.

We all waited to see who would be sent back.

It was one of the youngest who was chosen on that occasion.

"She will give herself airs when she returns," Nicole said to me. "They always do . . . particularly the young ones. I thought it might be your turn."

I must have betrayed my revulsion, for she said, "You do not want?"

"I wish with all my heart that I could get away."

"If he saw you . . . you would be the one."

"I . . . no . . . no!"

"It will come. Perhaps soon."

"I would do anything to escape."

She was thoughtful.

Nicole told me that if one was to receive those little privileges which were such an important part of harem life, one must be on good terms with two people. One was Rani, of course; the other was the Chief Eunuch.

"He is the important one. He is pasha of the harem. I have made him a very good friend of mine."

"I can see you are very wise."

"So long I have been here. It is the only home I know."

"And you are reconciled to all this . . . to being one of many?"

"It is the way of life here," she replied. "Samir is my son. He will be Pasha one day. I shall be the Pasha's mother, and that is a very honourable state, I can tell you."

"Would you not like a normal marriage, a husband and children, not all the time wondering if someone will replace you?"

"I have always known this." She waved her arms, indicating the harem. "It is so with all of them here. They know nothing else. They want to be the Pasha's favourite. They want to have a son who surpasses all others . . . and makes for his mother the grand position from which none can shake her."

"Can that be?"

"It can be."

"And that is your ambition?"

"My ambition is in Samir. Tell me of your ambition."

"To get away from here. To get back to my home, to my own people. To find those who were with me when I was shipwrecked."

"It is almost certain that you will be the chosen of the Pasha. When Rani thinks you are ready, she will send you to him. He will like you because you are different. He must be tired of these dark-skinned beauties. You are something quite new. If you have a son, your future is made."

"I would do anything to escape it. Nicole, I am frightened. I do not want this. It is not what I have been brought up to understand. I feel unclean . . . cheapened . . . a slave . . . a woman without a personality . . . with no life of her own."

"You talk strangely and yet I understand. I did not begin as one of them either."

"But you have accepted this way of life."

"I was too young for anything else, and now there is Samir. I want this . . . for him. He will be Pasha one day. That is what I want more than anything."

"You will get your wish. He is the eldest."

"Sometimes I am afraid of Fatima. When she goes to the Pasha she takes with her a powerful draught. I know she brews it. There is a way of rousing a man's desire. I have heard it talked of. It is made of crushed rubies, peacock's bones, and the testicles of a ram. They are mixed and slipped into the wine. I think when she goes to the Pasha she tries this."

"Where . . . where would she find these things?"

"Rani has a secret cupboard in which are many strange things. Herbs . . . potions . . . all sorts of mixtures. Rani knows much of these things. She may have this draught among her scents and unguents."

"But you say it is a secret cupboard."

"She keeps it locked, but there may be a means of finding the key. Fatima would be wise in this matter. I know her. She would do anything . . . just anything. That is why I am afraid."

"But when does she see the Pasha?"

"We are the mothers of his favourite sons, she and I. He sends for us now and then . . . a sort of courtesy visit . . . to talk of our sons and to spend the night. Oh, I fear that woman! She is determined. She would do anything . . . anything. Her hopes are in Feisal. The Pasha is fond of him. Chief Eunuch tells me this. Chief Eunuch does not like Fatima. That is not good for her. She is very foolish sometimes . . . and foolish women do rash things. When she was favoured she gave herself such airs. She thought she was First Lady already. She was disrespectful to Chief Eunuch, so they are now enemies. Silly Fatima. If she could she would harm Samir and me in some way."

"But Samir is the eldest, and so bright and clever."

"That I know, but it is in the hands of the Pasha. Now he likes Samir. He is proud of Samir. He is the eldest and the favourite. While he is so, all is well. But it is the Pasha who decides, and he will have many sons. If Fatima could do me or Samir some harm, it would be done."

"I cannot believe she would attempt it."

"It happened once . . . in the harem."

"But it will not again. Everyone knows what happened last time. That would be enough to deter them."

"I do not know. Fatima is a determined woman. She would risk much for Feisal and her own advantage. I must be watchful."

"I will be watchful too."

"And now there will be you. You will have a son. That son would be different. He would be like you. In Samir and Feisal — well, there is a likeness. But your son would be quite different."

I was filled with horror at the thought of it and recoiled from her.

"It's true," she said. "And do you really mean that you would not want this?"

"I could almost wish I had not been saved from the ship. I wish we had stayed on the island. If only I could get away. Oh, Nicole, if only that were possible! I would do anything . . . anything!"

She was staring ahead of her, deep in thought.

A few days later I was sitting by the fountain when she approached and sat down beside me.

"I have something for you," she said.

"For me?" I asked in surprise.

"I think you will be pleased. Chief Eunuch gave it to me for you. It is from the man who came with you."

"Do you mean . . . Nicole, where is it?"

"Be careful. We may be watched. Fatima watches everything. Rest your hand on the seat. In a moment I will slip a paper into it."

"No one is looking."

"How can you be sure? There are watchful eyes everywhere. These women seem idle. They *are* idle . . . but because they have nothing to do, they invent intrigue, even when it is not there. They are bored, looking for excitement, and when it does not come they try to make it. They have nothing to do but watch and gossip. Do as I say if you want this note."

"Oh, I do. I do."

"You must be careful then. Chief Eunuch says it is very important. He could lose his life for doing this. He does it for me . . . because I ask."

My hand was lying on the seat. She laid hers beside it, and after a few moments a crumpled paper was slipped under mine.

"Do not look at it now. Hide it."

I slipped it into my trouser pocket. I could

scarcely sit still. But she said it would be unwise of me to get up and hurry away. Someone might suspect something and that could mean dire consequences for us all.

I knew that for a man to communicate with the women of the harem could result in a cruel and lingering death, not only for the man but for the woman concerned. This had been the rule for centuries and I could believe that it still prevailed in this place, which seemed to have slipped back into — or never emerged from — another era.

I had to suppress my impatience until at length I felt I could wander off without arousing any undue curiosity. They were used to my being alone when I was not with Nicole, for she was the only one to whom I could talk. I went into the room where we slept. It was deserted, so I sat on my divan, brought out the piece of paper, and read it.

Rosetta,
I am nearby. I was brought here with you, and I am working in the gardens just outside the harem. We are close. I am thinking hard. I will do something. Never fear. Don't give up hope.

S.

I felt limp with relief. I screwed up the

paper. I wanted to keep it, to hide it away under my clothes, to feel it against my skin, to remind me that he had written it and that he was nearby and thinking of me.

But I must destroy it. If it were discovered, it could destroy us. It was dangerous. I tore it into as many pieces as I could. I would scatter them . . . a few pieces at a time so that they would never be discovered.

Later I talked to Nicole.

"You are happier," she said. "What I brought pleased you."

"Oh, yes, but it is difficult to see how there can be change. Does anyone ever escape from here?"

"Husbands are sometimes found if the Pasha is no longer interested and knows he never will be again. A few have been returned to their families."

"But does anyone ever run away?"

She shook her head. "I do not think that would be possible."

"Nicole," I said, "I must. I must."

"Yes," she said slowly, "you must. If you do not, soon you will be sent to the Pasha. Your skin is becoming very white. You have put on flesh and no longer look like a skeleton. You are different from when you came. Rani is pleased with you. It will be soon . . . perhaps next time he sends."

"He is away now."

"Yes, but he will come back. When he comes back he always sends.... Rani will think, Yes, the fair one, she is ready now. How pleased he will be with me for giving him such a prize ... something he has not had before.

"He will like you, I daresay. He may keep you with him. You will surely have a child. The Pasha will like you very much because you are different. He may like your child more than Feisal, more than Samir. Chief Eunuch says that Pasha is very interested in the West ... in England, particularly. He wants to know more of it. He wants to hear about the great Queen."

"No, no," I cried. "I hate it! I won't stay here. I'll get away somehow. I don't care what they do to me, but I won't stay for that. I'll do anything ... anything. Nicole, can you help me?"

She looked steadily at me and a smile played about her lips.

She said slowly, "Chief Eunuch is a friend of mine. He would not want me to be replaced as Chief Lady. He wants me to stay the mother of the next Pasha. Then we work together. We are friends, you see. I learn from him of outside and he learns from me of here ... inside. I know what goes on here. I can tell him. He pays me back with information from outside. Perhaps . . . "

"Perhaps?"

"Well, just perhaps . . . I might discover something."

I took her arm and shook her. "If you can help me, Nicole, if you know something — "

"I will help," she said. "No one must replace Samir. Besides, we are good friends."

Hope. It was the last thing left to me, and I was learning that it can mean everything to those in desperate straits.

The note and what I had heard from Nicole gave me that much-needed hope now.

I thought of all the dangers through which I had passed since that night when disaster had overtaken the *Atlantic Star*. I had had amazing good luck. Could it continue? Nicole would help if she could, I knew. Not only were we friends, she thought I might be a threat to her position. And the Chief Eunuch favoured her. No doubt he had his reasons. But did it matter what they were, as long as they served to help me?

I was desperate. I needed all the help I could get.

I had reason to hope. Two of the most important people in the seraglio were on my side. And Simon was not far off.

Indeed there was hope. For the first time

since I had entered this place, escape did not seem a complete impossibility.

Rani was indicating pleasure in my appearance. She grunted with satisfaction when she massaged my person.

My heart sank. In the cold light of reason, escape seemed remote. I had allowed myself to be carried away on a wave of euphoria. How could I escape?

That afternoon, I went into the dormitory and lay on my divan. The blinds were drawn and the heavy drapes made the room cool and dark. Someone crept into the room. Through half-closed eyes I saw Nicole.

"You are sick?" she whispered.

"Sick with fear," I replied.

She sat down on the divan.

"I am afraid that nothing is going to save me," I went on.

She said, "Rani plans . . . next time . . . she will send you."

"I . . . I won't go."

She shrugged her shoulders, a habitual gesture with her.

"Chief Eunuch says the Pasha will be away for a week. When he comes back he will send."

"A week. Oh, Nicole, what can I do?"

"We have a week," she said.

"What can we do?"

She regarded me steadily. "Chief Eunuch likes your man. He wants to help him. They have talked. Rani wants very much to show you to the Pasha. She wants him to know that when you came here you were not very good . . . apart from your hair, and that was without lustre. Now it shines. She has made you fit for the Pasha, and now that you are as you are, you should be sent to him. He will be thankful to the man who brought you, who was the Chief Eunuch, but it is Rani who has nursed you back to health. But . . . as I say . . . we have a week."

"What could we do? Please tell me."

"Your friend will have to take care."

"What would they do to him if they knew he had written to me?"

"Most certainly make a eunuch of him. They may do that in any case. That is the fate of a number of the young men who are sold to the Pasha. They are put into the gardens and there for a while they are normal young men, but if they are needed to work in the harem . . . well, how could he trust a normal young man among so many women? Hence the eunuchs. It would very likely be the fate of your friend. He will not be in the gardens forever. Eunuchs make good servants. They can go among the harem women

177

without temptation."

"I cannot see what can be done."

"You will do what you are told to do. You must remember that if you start this you may be discovered, and if you are . . . anything would be better."

"I wonder if Simon will be ready to take such risks. When I think what might happen to him . . . "

"If you are going to escape," she said, "you must not dwell on failure. Soon Rani will send you to the Pasha. Remember that."

I was silent, wondering how I could endure such a fate. Moreover, Nicole was talking in riddles. What plans could there be?

She was vague. Sometimes I thought she was talking so to comfort me.

As the days passed, my apprehension naturally grew greater. I told myself that I must in due course face the inevitable.

The Pasha was back. I noticed Rani's eyes on me, speculatively. She rubbed her hands together with a certain satisfaction and I knew the time had come, and when the Chief Eunuch visited Rani that evening I knew my fate had been decided.

As was the custom, five others were selected with me, for it would not do for Rani to choose for the Pasha; he must make his own decision as to which one he would honour.

Among the five was a very pretty young girl whose name I discovered was Aida. She must have been about twelve years old, slender but just budding into womanhood; she had long dark hair and big eyes which managed to combine an impression of virginal innocence and dawning knowledge which I imagined would be very attractive to a man whose senses might well be jaded by excess.

I was interested in Aida because I was pinning my hopes on her. I felt certain that she had a good chance of being selected. The girl was so excited; she danced round the gardens, making no secret of her glee. Fatima grumbled that she was already giving herself airs.

I said to Nicole, "She is very pretty. Surely he will prefer her?"

Nicole shook her head. "Pretty, yes, but so are hundreds of others . . . and very like her. All the same hair . . . eyes . . . delight . . . eagerness. You will stand out among them. And as I've already told you, Chief Eunuch says the Pasha is very interested in England. He admires the English Queen."

I felt sick with fear. What was the Pasha like? He must be fairly young. He had only recently become his father's heir. He spoke a little English, so Nicole had learned from the

Chief Eunuch. Perhaps I could talk to him, tell him about England, become a sort of Scheherazade, holding him off with my interesting tales of English life.

That day seemed endless. There were moments when I almost convinced myself that I was dreaming. How could this be happening to me? How many girls living quietly conventional lives in England had suddenly found themselves transported to a Turkish harem?

Then I told myself I must prepare for my fate. The Pasha would notice the difference in me. First I must pray that he did not choose me. If he did not, it might be decided that I was unfit for the harem. What then? Perhaps I could persuade them to let me go. Aida was so pretty. She was so suited to this way of life, and moreover she enjoyed it.

Rani came to me. It was time for the preparations to begin.

She smoothed my hair with her hands, almost crowing over it. She seized it and pulled it slightly; she stroked it. Then she clapped her hands and two of her girls appeared.

She stood up and beckoned.

I was taken to the bath and submerged under jets of perfumed water. When I was dry I must lie down while unguents, smelling of musk and patchouli, were rubbed into my skin. My hair was scented. The smell of it made me feel sick, and I knew that I should never smell it again without recalling that numbing fear I felt at that time.

I was dressed in lavender silk garments with the wide trousers caught in at the ankles with jewelled bands. Over the trousers I wore a tunic which fell to the waist. It was silk with a layer of fine gauze over it. Sequins had been sewn in profusion over the silk and shone mysteriously through the gauzy material, giving a subtle sheen. I had to admit that the costume had great charm.

On my feet were sandals with curled points at the toes. They were of satin and bejewelled.

Then my hair was combed so that it fell about my shoulders and a garland of mauve flowers was put on my head and others about my ankles. My lips were reddened, my eyes carefully lined with kohl so that they looked enormous and a deeper blue.

I was ready for submission.

Wild thoughts came into my mind. What would happen if I refused to go or if I tried to escape from the harem? How? The gates were locked and guarded by the Pasha's eunuchs . . . big men, all chosen for their size. How could I escape?

I had to face the truth. There was no escape.

Rani took my hand and shook her head at me. She was admonishing me for some reason. It must be because I looked so miserable. She was telling me to smile, to show happiness and appreciation of the great honour which might well be mine this night.

That was something I could not do.

Nicole was standing by. She was one of those who had helped to dress me. She said something to Rani, who appeared to consider.

Then Rani nodded and gave Nicole a key. Nicole left us.

I sat on the divan. I felt quite helpless. I had been brought so far for this? I had a vision of myself: chosen by the Pasha . . . bearing a child who would be the rival of Samir and Feisal. I had a father who was an important man, a professor attached to the British Museum. I wanted to tell them that if the Pasha attempted to treat my father's daughter as though she were a slave girl, there would be trouble. I was English. The great Queen did not allow her subjects to be treated in this way.

I was trying to give myself courage. I knew I was talking a great deal of nonsense to myself. What did these people care who I was? They were the rulers here. I was nothing.

Perhaps I could tell him how eager the other girls were to share his bed. Why not take one of those who were so willing, and let this one go? Would it be possible to explain to him? Would he listen? And if he did, would he understand?

Nicole came back. She was carrying a goblet in her hand.

"Drink this," she said. "You will feel better."

"No. I won't."

"I tell you it will do you good."

"What is it?"

One of the other girls added her persuasion. She wrapped her arms about herself and swayed to and fro.

"She is telling you that it will make you want love. It will make things easier for you. In any case, it was Rani who ordered it. She thinks you are not eager and the Pasha likes woman to be eager."

A sort of aphrodisiac, I thought.

"I will not," I said.

Nicole came close to me. "Don't be a fool," she hissed. She was looking into my eyes, trying to tell me something. "Take," she went on. "You will find it good, just what you need now. Drink . . . drink . . . I am your friend."

There was some hidden meaning in her words. I took the goblet and drank the contents. It was revolting.

"Soon . . . " said Nicole. "Soon. . . . "

After a few moments I began to feel very ill. Nicole had disappeared with the goblet. I tried to stand but I could not. I felt giddy.

One of the girls called for Rani, who came in great consternation. I could feel the sweat running down my face, and I caught a glimpse of myself in one of the mirrors. I was very pale.

Rani was shouting to everyone. I was put onto a divan. I felt very ill indeed.

Nicole had reappeared. I fancied she was smiling secretively.

I was *not* presented to the Pasha. I lay on my divan feeling sick unto death. I really believed my last moment had come.

I thought of Nicole smiling her secret smile. She had done this. She had feared that I would please the Pasha and bear a child who would oust Samir. Could this be so . . . or was she truly my friend? Whatever the answer, she had saved me from the Pasha that night.

In a day or so I began to recover, and with my recovery came the belief that Nicole had done this to save me from what I had dreaded. True, at the same time she was helping herself. Why not? Nicole was French and took a realistic view of life. The fact that she could serve herself and me at the same time would make the idea doubly attractive to her.

As I began to feel better I realised I had not been so ill as I had believed. If I had I could not have regained my health so quickly.

Nicole told me that when Rani had sent her to the cupboard to bring the aphrodisiac which was given to some girls before they went to the Pasha for the first time, she had substituted a draught which she knew would make me too sick to be sent.

"Was it not what you wanted?" she demanded. "Did you not say that anything . . . anything . . . ?"

"I did. I did. And I thank you, Nicole."

"I told you I was your friend. Aida was the chosen one. She has not yet returned. She must be in high favour. She would never have been if you had been there."

"I am so glad. She longed to be chosen."

"The little horror will be unbearable when she comes back. It is a great honour to be kept in the Pasha's apartments. She will be too important to speak to us . . . insufferable. You will see."

I was slowly recovering from my sickness and Rani from her disappointment. But she was a little reconciled because Aida had found such favour.

After three days, Aida returned. She swept

into the harem, her manner completely changed; she was languid and regarded us all with contempt. She had a pair of beautiful ruby earrings and a magnificent ruby necklace about her throat. Rani's attitude towards her had changed. Little Aida had become one of the important ladies of the harem.

She was certain she was pregnant.

"Silly creature," said Nicole. "How could she know yet?"

All the same, Nicole was worried.

"It may be you are safe for a little while," she comforted me. "For if he liked her so much as to keep her for three days and nights he might send for her again. That was what happened to me in my day. The most grateful woman in the harem must be Aida, and that gratitude should be for you."

"Perhaps he wouldn't have chosen me. He might have liked her better."

Nicole looked at me disbelievingly.

It was with great relief that I heard, through Nicole, who had it from the Chief Eunuch, that the Pasha had gone away for three weeks.

Three weeks! A great deal could happen in that time. Perhaps I should hear something from Simon. If it were possible to devise some means of getting out of this place, if anyone could do it, surely he could.

★

A few days passed. Aida was making herself very unpopular. She wore her rubies all the time and would sit by the pool taking them in her hands and admiring them, reminding everyone of the favour she had found and how she pitied them all for not having the beauty and charm necessary to enslave the Pasha.

She appeared languid and assumed the ailments of pregnancy.

Nicole laughed at her. So did the others. One of them quarrelled with her so violently that they fought and Aida's face was maliciously scratched.

That sent Aida into floods of tears. When the Pasha returned she could not go to him with a wound on her face.

Rani was angry and the two girls were shut away for three days. Rani would have liked to beat them, Nicole told me, but she was afraid of bruising their bodies, particularly Aida's. One thing about a harem was that its inmates were not submitted to physical violence while they were part of it.

However, it was a relief, said Nicole, to be free of the arrogant little creature, if only for three days.

Aida emerged not in the least repentant. She was as languid as ever, even more sure that she was pregnant and carried a male child. She slept in the ruby necklace and kept the earrings in a jewelled case beside her bed. As soon as morning came she put them on.

In spite of myself, I was caught up in the intrigues of the harem, because of my friendship with Nicole. She told me that violent quarrels blew up now and then, and that there was great jealousy between the girls. Aida, like Fatima, was one who created trouble. They had been chosen and they could not forget it. If Aida were pregnant and bore a male child, that would add greatly to the rivalries.

"But Samir is the eldest," said Nicole. "He must remain first favourite son."

I said I was sure he would.

I sensed that Nicole was less confident. She was going to work all the time on Samir's behalf, but she knew the matter was one she must constantly bear in mind.

At this time Nicole's thoughts seemed to be fixed entirely on Aida. She was not the only one. Fatima's were too. They had been the main rivals, both possessing sons with a claim on the Pasha's wealth. Now they both watched Aida.

It was unusual for one girl to satisfy the Pasha for three nights in succession, also for her to be kept in his apartments. So there could be no doubt that Aida had made a certain impression on him.

Moreover, she had been long enough with him to become pregnant and there was a good possibility that she might have achieved this happy state. Therefore she was an object of concern to all, but especially to Nicole and Fatima.

It was in the early hours of the morning and I was half asleep. I was just aware of a sliver of a waning moon shining into the dormitory. Through half-closed eyes I thought I saw a movement in the room, an outline of a figure bending over one of the divans in the corner. Then sleep claimed me and I thought no more of the incident.

The next day there was consternation. Aida's ruby earrings had disappeared. She wore the necklace all the time, she reminded us, but the earrings had been kept in the jewelled box beside her divan.

Rani came into the dormitory, demanding to know what all the fuss was about. Aida was shrieking in her fury, accusing everyone. Someone had stolen her earrings. She would tell the Pasha. He would not have thieves in his harem. We should all be whipped and sent away. Her beautiful earrings must be restored to her. If they were not returned this day she would ask the Pasha to punish us all.

Rani was angry.

"Little fool," said Nicole. "Doesn't she

189

know yet that she must not anger important people? I suppose she thinks she is so important she can do without their support."

The dormitory was searched, but the earrings were not found.

Fatima said it was a terrible thing and even the children should be searched. There were some children who were born thieves, and if her Feisal were proved to be such, she would see that he was severely punished.

Rani said the earrings would no doubt soon be found. They could not be far off. There would be no point in anyone stealing someone else's jewellery. When would the thief be able to wear it?

I was with Nicole in the gardens.

She said, "Serves her right. The arrogant little idiot. She will not get very far."

"Someone must have taken the earrings."

"As a joke perhaps?"

I said slowly, "I remember something now. I was only half awake. It was someone standing in the room . . . yes . . . and it was by Aida's divan."

"When?"

"Last night. I thought I was dreaming. I was in that state when I was not sure whether I was awake or asleep. I have had strange dreams since I've been here, and particularly after taking that stuff you gave me to drink.

Half sleeping . . . half waking . . . hallucinations almost. I am not really sure whether I dreamed this."

"Well, if you saw someone at Aida's bedside and in the morning her earrings had gone, the chances are that you were not dreaming."

Just at that moment Samir came up. He was holding something bright in his hands. "Look," he said. "Maman, pretty things."

She took the jewelled box from his hands and opened it. There lay the ruby earrings.

Nicole exchanged a glance with me, fearful and full of meaning.

"Where did you find this, Samir?" she asked in a voice which trembled.

"In my boat."

His toy boat, the pride of his life. He was hardly ever without it. He used to sail it in the pools.

Nicole looked at me and said, "I must take them to Rani immediately."

I put out a hand to stop her. I looked at Samir hesitantly. She knew what I meant.

She said to him, "Go away and play. Don't tell anyone what you found. It's not important. But don't say a word. Promise, Samir."

He nodded his head and darted off.

I said, "It's coming back. It could have been Fatima whom I saw last night. What if she stole the earrings? The more I think of it, the more I believe that this is what it is all about. Didn't she say we should all be searched . . . and mention the children? Fatima is foolish sometimes. She has no subtlety. It is easy to read her mind. She wants to damage you and Samir. So she stole the earrings, put them in the boat, and wants it to be believed that Samir stole them."

"Why?"

"To make a thief of him."

"But he is a child."

"Then perhaps I am wrong. What would have happened if the earrings had been found in his boat? He would have said he did not know how they got there, but would he have been believed? It might be reported to the Pasha. Aida would have reported it, if she went back to him . . . as she well might. Perhaps the boy would be punished. The Pasha would be displeased with him. Do you see what I mean? But perhaps I am wrong."

"No . . . no. I do not believe that you are wrong."

"I think she may say that Samir stole them and that when the theft was discovered he was afraid and gave them up."

"Then what?"

"Let's get rid of them . . . at once. Drop them . . . anywhere. It would not do for them to be found with you. What explanation could you give? How did they come to be in Samir's boat? they would ask. Samir must have put them there, they would say. It would be an unpleasant business. Leave them . . . near the pool. The case will be conspicuous and soon found; then Samir will not come into it. I feel sure it is better that he does not."

"You are right," she said.

"Then the sooner it is out of your possession the better."

She nodded. Cautiously she put the case down by the pool and we walked away.

I said, "I feel sure it was Fatima. I am trying to remember what I saw in the night. It would have been so easy for her to slip off her divan when everyone was asleep and take the case."

"It was Fatima. I know it. She was the one. Oh, how I hate that woman! One day I will kill her."

The case was found. Aida said she could not understand it. She had left it beside her divan. Someone must have taken it and then become frightened and thrown it away.

Rani said the earrings were found and that was an end of the matter.

But it was not really so. The enmity between Fatima and Nicole grew alarmingly.

It was almost certain that Aida was not pregnant, and that deepened the rivalry between the mothers of Samir and Feisal. Aida was sullen. Someone said she had pretended her earrings were stolen to call attention to the fact that the Pasha had once liked her enough to present them to her. There was a great deal of wrangling and petty spite in the harem, perhaps because there was so little for the women to do.

Nicole was undoubtedly grateful to me. She could clearly see the danger through which she and Samir had passed, for if the boy had been branded as a thief, his favour might have been tarnished with the Pasha, if not lost forever. It was a mean act and worthy of Fatima, Nicole was sure.

She became more open with me. I had always known that there was a special friendship between her and the Chief Eunuch, but now she told me that they had been on the ship together and there had been a friendship between them then. She did not say that they had been in love, but the seeds of it may have been sown. When she had been taken into the harem he had been sold to the Pasha at the same time. They had then been in urgent need of eunuchs and that had been his fate. He was tall, handsome, and clever, so he had risen quickly to his present rank. Nicole passed on information to him from the harem, and he gave her news of what was happening outside. They had both made the most of the life into which they had been thrust.

Now I knew how close they had been before they had been taken into captivity, I understood their relationship much better. It had taken some time for them to become resigned to this life, but he had become Chief Eunuch and she planned to be Chief Lady of the harem in due course.

The relationship between myself and Nicole had deepened. I had saved her son from a situation which could have been damning to their chances. It was clear to me that I was accepted as her friend, and she wanted to repay me for what I had done for her.

I tried to make her understand that there should be no thought of payment between friends. She replied that she realised that, but, if she could do anything for me, she would; and she knew that what I wanted most of all was to escape from my present position. Some time, long ago, she had felt exactly the same, and that gave her a special understanding of my case.

The first thing she did was to bring me a note. I think she had told her friend the Chief Eunuch the story of the earrings and enlisted his help, and for her sake he helped to bring this about.

The note was smuggled to me as before, and when I was quite alone I read it.

Don't give up hope. Through a friend of mine I have heard what is happening on the other side of the wall. If an opportunity comes, I'll be ready. So must you be. Don't despair. We have friends. I do not forget you. We shall succeed.

What a comfort it was to read that!

Sometimes, in a pessimistic mood, I asked myself what he could do. Then I assured myself that he would do something. I must go on hoping.

Nicole was watchful of Samir. I found myself watching him too. He and I had become friends. He knew that I was with his mother a good deal and that there was a special understanding between us; it seemed to me that he wanted a share in it.

He was an enchanting child, good-looking and healthy; loving all people, he believed they loved him too.

When I was sitting by the pool alone he came up to me and showed me his boat. We floated it on the pool and he watched its progress with dreamy eyes.

"It's come from a long, long way," he said.

196

"From where?" I asked.

"From Mar . . . Mar . . . "

I said, on sudden inspiration, "Martinique?"

He nodded happily.

"It's going to a place in France," he said. "It's Lyons. There's a school there."

I guessed his mother had told him her story, for he went on, "Pirates." He began to shout. "They are trying to take us but we won't let them, will we? Bang, bang. Go away, you horrid pirates. We don't like you." He waved his hand at imaginary vessels. He turned to smile at me. "All right now. Don't be frightened. They've all gone." He pointed to a tree and said, "Figs."

"Do you like figs?" I asked.

He nodded vigorously.

His mother came up. She had heard the last remark.

"He is greedy where figs are concerned, aren't you, Samir?" she said.

He hunched his shoulders and nodded.

I remembered that later.

I was sitting by the pool, thinking that the days were passing quickly and wondering when the Pasha would be coming back. Could I hope to escape again? There could not be another draught like the last. Rani would surely suspect if there were. And if I did take it, what effect would it have on me? How much did Nicole know about such potions? Moreover, I imagined that Rani would prepare the aphrodisiac this time herself. She was no fool. It might well be that she had a suspicion of what happened. Was there any hope? I wondered. Could Simon offer me anything but words of comfort?

Samir came up to me. He was holding a fig.

"Oh," I said. "What a nice fig, Samir."

"Yes," he answered. "Fatima gave it to me."

"Fatima!" A shiver of alarm ran through me. "Give it to me, Samir," I said.

He held it behind his back. "It's not yours. It's mine."

"Just show it to me."

He stepped back a pace and, bringing out his hand, held up the fig.

I went to take it from him, but he ran and I went after him.

He ran full tilt into his mother, who caught him laughingly and looked at me.

"Fatima gave him a fig," I said.

She turned pale.

"He's holding it now. He wouldn't give it to me."

She snatched it from him. His face puckered. "It's all right," she said. "I'll find you another."

"But that's mine. Fatima gave it to me."

"Never mind." Her voice shook a little. "You shall have a bigger and better one. This one's not very nice. It has worms in it."

"Show me!" cried Samir excitedly.

"First of all, I'll get you a nice one."

She put the fig into my hands. "I'll be back," she said.

She took Samir off and a few minutes later returned without him.

"What do you think?" I asked.

"She's capable of anything."

"So think I."

"Rosetta, I am going to test this."

She sat on the stones holding the fig in her hand and staring moodily before her. One of Fatima's little dogs came into sight.

She laughed suddenly and called to him. He came up and looked. She held out the fig to the dog, who swallowed it at one gulp and looked at us hopefully for more.

"Why should she give him a fig?" she asked.

"She might have been sorry about the earrings and wanted to please him."

She looked at me scornfully. Then her eyes went to the dog. He had crept into a corner and was being sick.

She was triumphant.

"She is wicked . . . wicked . . . she would

have killed Samir."

"We can't be sure."

"It's proof enough. Look at the dog."

"It might have been something else."

"He was well enough before he took the fig."

"Do you think she would go so far? What would happen to her if she were discovered?"

"Death for murder."

"She would think of that."

"Fatima never thinks ahead. She would only think of getting rid of Samir so that Feisal could be the Pasha's favourite."

"Nicole, do you seriously believe she would go to such lengths?"

The dog was now writhing on the ground. We stared at it in horror. Suddenly its legs stiffened and it lay on its side.

"It could have been Samir," whispered Nicole, "if you hadn't seen him with the fig. . . . I will kill her for this."

Aida came up. "What's the matter with the dog?" she said.

"He's dead," said Nicole. "He ate a fig."

"A what?"

"A fig."

"How could he die of that? It's Fatima's dog."

"Yes," said Nicole. "Go and tell her that

her dog has died through eating a fig."

I was really alarmed. I had been apt to feel somewhat contemptuous of these rivalries, but when they led to attempted murder, that was another matter.

It was not to be expected that that would be the end of the affair. Nicole was not the sort to let such a thing pass.

Her remarks about the fig and the death of the dog would be enough to show Fatima that she suspected her. And she had been the one who had given the fig to Samir — the fig which afterwards had poisoned the dog.

There was open warfare between Nicole and Fatima. Everyone was talking about Fatima's little dog, who had died after eating a fig.

Rani was worried. She hated trouble in the harem and liked to believe she could keep everything in order.

Smouldering looks passed between Nicole and Fatima, and we were all waiting for the trouble to start.

I begged Nicole to be careful. It would be best for her to tell Rani or the Chief Eunuch what she suspected and they could deal with the matter.

She said, "*I* want to deal with Fatima. They might not believe she did what she did. They will say it was some other thing which caused the dog's death. They wouldn't want the Pasha to know that there had been attempted murder in the harem."

I said fearfully, "He will be back soon. Surely he will hear something about it then?"

"No. He would not hear such a thing. Besides, they will try to make it all die down before he gets back. But I am not going to let it. She tried to prove my son a thief and when that failed she tried to poison him."

"At neither time did she succeed."

"No. Thank God. And it was due to you. You have been my good friend, and when I can I will repay you. Yes, I will repay you for the good you have done me and her for the evil. But repayment there shall be."

It could not go on.

Fatima approached Nicole in the gardens.

She said, "You are spreading evil tales about me."

I had picked up enough of the language to understand a little now and then, so I could make out roughly what was being said.

"Nothing could be more evil than the truth," cried Nicole. "You tried to kill my son."

"I did not."

"You liar! You poisoned a fig and tried to kill him. Instead, your dog died. It was proved."

"I did not give the fig to him. The child is a liar as well as a thief."

With that Nicole brought up her hand and dealt Fatima a stinging blow on the side of her face.

With a cry Fatima leaped upon her. I was terrified, for in her hand I saw a knife. Fatima had come prepared for battle.

Several women screamed.

"Fetch Rani," someone said. "Fetch the Chief Eunuch. Call them."

Fatima had plunged the knife into Nicole's thigh and her trousers were drenched with blood. It seemed to be spurting all around.

Rani had come and was shrieking to them to stop. With her was the Chief Eunuch. He was a big strong man and was soon dragging a kicking, screaming Fatima away from Nicole, who lay on the ground, bleeding profusely.

Two other eunuchs who were tending the gardens appeared. Rani ordered them to take Fatima away. The Chief Eunuch knelt beside Nicole. He said something to Rani. Then he lifted Nicole tenderly in his arms and carried her into the building.

I was horrified. I had known there would be trouble sooner or later between them, but I had not thought of fighting with knives. There had of course only been one knife, and that had given Fatima the advantage. Now I was worried about Nicole. I had grown fond of her. She was the only one with whom I could communicate. She it was who had made life tolerable for me.

Then I thought of Samir. Poor child, what would become of him?

He was bewildered and came to me to be comforted.

"Where is my maman?" he asked plaintively.

"She is ill."

"When will she be better?"

"We must wait and see," I told him — one of the most unsatisfactory answers possible, as I remembered from my own childhood.

Fatima was under restraint. I wondered what would happen to her. The incident would not be lightly passed over, of that I was sure. To do so would be to undermine law and order in the harem, and that was something neither Rani nor the Chief Eunuch would allow.

From what little I could understand, the women were discussing the poisoned fig and Fatima's attack on Nicole; Aida and her pretensions were no longer the main topic of conversation.

Rani was seething with anger because Fatima obviously had access to her closet where the drugs were kept. I wondered how often these had been used with discretion to remove some unwanted person from the harem. I imagined orders coming from the Pasha — through the Chief Eunuch, of course — that someone was to be quietly removed. It must have happened now and then. The secrets of the closet should be closely guarded and the fact that Fatima had succeeded in gaining access must give cause for alarm.

The Chief Eunuch was in constant communication with Rani. I saw him frequently in the harem.

Nicole was kept in a room by herself. I was allowed to visit her, presumably because she asked that I should. They were very anxious that she should recover and were ready to do anything to help her to that end.

I was shocked at the sight of her. Her thigh was encased in bandages and she was very pale; there were dark bruises on her forehead.

"That snake would have finished me, if she could — and she nearly did," she said. "How is Samir?"

"He asks for you."

A smile illuminated her face. "I did not want him to see me . . . like this."

"I think he would like to see you anyway."

"Perhaps, then. . . . "

"I'll tell him. He will be overjoyed."

"You are looking after him for me?"

"As well as I can, but it is you he wants."

"That wicked witch is shut away, I know. That is a great relief to me."

"Yes. She is not with us any more."

"Thank God for that. I could not lie here knowing she was there . . . and I powerless. How much does Samir know of the danger he was in?"

"He is too young," I said.

"Children are sharper than you think. They listen. There is little they miss. Sometimes they put the wrong construction on things, but Samir will know something is wrong. He will sense danger."

"I will look after him. You must not worry about him . . . and when you think he should come to see you, I am sure they will allow it."

"Oh, yes. They do not want me to die. The Pasha would ask questions. He would wonder how well Rani was looking after us. She might be replaced. That is always in her mind. He would remember me because I am the mother of his boy."

"And what of Fatima? She also is the mother of his boy."

"He never really liked Fatima. She is a fool. She always was. She is the mother of Feisal, true. But that is all. Feisal is a good-looking boy, but that does not mean Fatima will be kept in favour because of that if she is a menace in the harem. I did not have a knife. She was the one who produced it. She might have killed me. It was what she intended to do. As it is, I have lost a lot of blood. The wound is deep. It is going to take a long time to heal."

The next day I took Samir to her.

He leaped onto the divan and they hugged each other. I felt the tears in my eyes as I watched them. The child's joy was great. She was there. She was still ill, he knew, but she was there.

He sat beside her and she asked what he was doing. How was the boat going?

"The pirates nearly took her," he said.

"Really?"

"Yes, but I saved her in time."

"That is good news."

"When are you getting up?"

"Very soon."

"Today?"

"Well, not today."

"Tomorrow?"

"We'll have to see." There it was again. Samir sighed, recognising the vagueness of the reply.

"You've got Rosetta," she told him.

He turned and smiled at me and held out his hand. Nicole was biting her lip and lowering her eyes. She was as touched as I was, and in that moment I was sure she felt as great an affection for me as I did for her.

The next day when I was with her, Rani brought in the Chief Eunuch.

Nicole spoke to him in French. She told him what I had done and that it was my prompt action which had saved Samir. "I owe Samir's life to her," she said. "I must repay her for what she has done for me."

He nodded, and I believe the look which passed between them was one of love.

The tragedy of their lives was brought home to me more vividly than ever. But for that one incident which had befallen them, everything could have been so different. In my imagination I saw the ship. I could picture the meetings, the friendship which sprung up as it can on board ship where people see each other every day if they wish. Relationships blossom in such an atmosphere. And that was how it would have been with those two young people. What would have happened if they had been allowed to stay together? I pictured them at sea: warm evenings sitting on deck, the starlit sky, the gentle swishing of the calm sea as they drifted along. Romance in the air. And then shipwreck, sold into slavery, and the end of a love story which had only just begun.

Could I not understand better than anyone? Had it not happened to me?

And poor Nicole! Cruelly separated, yet to live not far apart. Actually to see each other often: she the member of a harem to bear a child to an imperious master; he to lose his manhood because he was tall and strong and could be of use to that ruthless man. How dared some people inflict such horror on others! How dared they take us from a civilised world and submit us to their barbarous way of life! But they did dare. They had the opportunity and for the moment the upper hand — and with it they tampered with our lives.

Nicole was getting better. She was exceptionally healthy and Rani was a skilled nurse. She knew exactly how to treat the wounds. I wondered how much practice she had had in a community where very idleness bred violence.

I took Samir to see Nicole every day. He was happier now. He was no longer afraid. His mother was ill for a while but she was there, he could see her, and I was a fair substitute.

One day she said to me, "The Chief Eunuch has just been to see me. He tells me much. They are eager to get this matter settled before the Pasha returns. Fatima will be sent away. Rani will let it be known that she had to be sent back to her family. For some time Rani has been complaining of her conduct. The Pasha will probably be told that there was trouble in the harem, and that Fatima attacked me with a knife. In the circumstances it seemed wise in the eyes of the Chief Eunuch and Rani to send her to her home."

"What of Feisal?"

"He will remain. He is the Pasha's son. He cannot leave."

"Oh . . . poor child."

"He will be better off here than with his foolish mother."

"Who will care for him?"

"The other women will. No one has any quarrel with Feisal. He cannot help having such a mother. Fatima will remain locked up for the time being. Quite right, too. She is a wild animal."

"But what a terrible punishment for the child."

"Fatima deserves to lose her life. She would have taken Samir's. Every time I think of that, I remember how much I owe you. I do not care to owe. I have spoken to Jean — the Chief Eunuch. He understands; it may be that he can help. Yes . . . I think he will help."

My heart started to beat so fast I could scarcely speak.

"How — " I stammered.

"The Pasha has been delayed. He will not be back for two more weeks. It must be done before then."

"Yes?"

"I told you, Fatima will be sent away. A carriage will come to take her. The Chief Eunuch will unlock the gates. The carriage will be waiting outside. It is to take her back to her family. Her presence is no longer required in the harem."

"Does that happen often?"

Nicole shook her head. "It is the ultimate disgrace. If she had killed me it would have been death. It may be that she will decide to kill herself," she added with relish.

"Oh, no!" I cried.

She laughed at me. "She must not, for if she did it would spoil our plans. Listen."

She paused for a few seconds. I could not hide my eagerness to hear more. Hope was suddenly surging up within me.

"All women are heavily veiled when they go out. It is only the lower classes who are not. One woman, therefore, looks very like another. Oh, I shall miss you . . . for we are good friends, are we not? But it is what you want. You would never have been a true harem woman. You have too much *esprit*. You cannot forget your pride, your dignity . . . no, not for all the rubies in the world."

"Nicole, tell me exactly what is planned. Don't keep me in suspense. You have been such a good friend to me. I don't forget that you saved me once with that potion you gave me."

"And made you most uncomfortable for a while."

"It didn't matter. It saved me. It gave me a respite."

"A bagatelle. Did you not save Samir for me?"

"We have helped each other. Now, please . . . please, tell me what is to be done."

"The Chief Eunuch will help . . . if it can be done."

"How? What?"

"He will come to take Fatima away. She would be heavily cloaked and wearing a yasmak . . . and if behind those concealing garments it was not Fatima but Rosetta . . . why, what of that?"

"Is it possible?" I breathed.

"It might be. He would take you through the gates. Nobody would have any idea that it was not Fatima but you. Everyone would have heard she is going back to her family."

"And where is Fatima to be at this time?"

"In her room. She is to be ready at a certain time, but the carriage will come half an hour early. It makes no difference, the Chief Eunuch will say, and he is the one who makes the arrangements. He will come to see me. You will be here in this room . . . ready and waiting. He will walk out with you and if anyone sees you — a few might dare to but they will be warned to stay in and not spy on Fatima's shame — they will think you are Fatima. The Chief Eunuch will unlock the gates and you will walk through with him. He will then lock the gates and you will get into the carriage which is waiting outside. It will all go according to plan, except that you will be the one who leaves instead of Fatima."

"Where would he take me?"

"To the British Embassy. You will tell your story. They will send you home. You cannot give the name of the Pasha because you do not know it. Besides, a foreign country cannot interfere in the affairs of another. The duty of the Embassy would be solely to get you home."

"I can't believe it. It sounds too easy."

"It is not easy. It is clever and well planned. The Chief Eunuch is a very clever man."

"And when it is found out what he has done, what will happen then?"

"It was a natural mistake. Everyone knew of your reluctance. You managed to pose as Fatima. He came to get a woman from the harem. The only one who could make trouble would be Rani, and she will not be so foolish as to quarrel with the Chief Eunuch. She may suspect what she will, but she can do nothing. It is not as though the Pasha knows of your existence. You were to be a surprise for him. So there is no difficulty on that score. And depend upon it, very soon after you have gone, Fatima will be sent off."

"Oh, Nicole, I can't believe this! For so long I have hoped and tried to think of possibilities. And now you and the Chief Eunuch are planning to do this for me. I'm not dreaming, am I?"

"As far as I know you are wide awake."

"The Chief Eunuch is risking such a lot for me."

"No," she said softly. "For me."

"Nicole, what can I say to you? That you should do this for me. . . ."

"I like to pay my debts. This has to work or I shall not have done so."

"You owe me nothing. . . . Anything I did — "

"I know what you mean. But you have done so much for me and it is my joy to give you what you most want."

"Oh, Nicole, I wish you could come with me. Your escape could have been arranged."

She shook her head. "I would not . . . if I

could. My life is now here. Years ago, before Samir came, it would have been different. I have felt all you feel now, but fate was too much for me. There was nothing I could do — and now this is my life. Samir is to be the Pasha. That is what I want now, more than anything. That is what I pray for."

"And I pray you will succeed."

She nodded fiercely. "I intend to," she said. "You may think I have impossible ambitions. But it did happen once . . . some time ago. There was a girl like myself. Her name was Aimée Dubucq de Rivery. She came from Martinique, as I did, and was on her way home from her school in France. She was shipwrecked and sold into a sultan's harem. I read of her long ago, and it has often seemed to me that I am reliving her story. I knew how she felt . . . how desperate at first until she became reconciled, how she sublimated everything to her son's future. She succeeded, and he became sultan. You see, her fate is so like mine. She succeeded, and so will I."

"You will, Nicole," I said. "I know you will."

I could not sleep. I could not eat. I went over and over the plan in my mind. To be free once more! Not to have this terrible fear hanging over me. . . . It was a relief too great to be

215

realised at first. To be mistress of my own destiny once more, an individual who made her own decisions, no longer a minion depending on the whim of a master who could command my presence and submission at any time he thought fit.

I thought of Simon. How was he faring? When I was free I must let it be known what had happened to him. He must be rescued. People should not be sold into slavery. That had been abolished. There should be no slaves in the civilised world. Oh . . . but I had forgotten. Simon did not want to be found. He was in hiding. He might be working as a slave in the Pasha's garden, but at least he was not on trial for a crime he had not committed.

And what of Lucas? What had happened to him?

But I must not think beyond escape. I must remember that this was what I had longed and prayed for and that it was now about to happen. Miraculously, I had acquired powerful friends and they were in a position to help me and would do so.

It would be hazardous, I knew, but I must not allow my mind to be sidetracked. I must hold myself in complete readiness for when the moment came.

The day had come.

Ever since her injury, Nicole had had a small room to herself, apart from the dormitory. The clothes I was to wear had been smuggled into this room on those occasions when the Chief Eunuch had come to see how she was progressing.

I dressed in them and then I looked like any other woman who might be encountered in the streets. I was a little tall, it was true, but I suppose some could be found who were my height.

The Chief Eunuch arrived. He saw that I was ready.

He said, "We must be careful. Follow me."

I went with him out of the room, taking one last farewell of Nicole. No one was about. He had given orders that everyone must stay in the dormitory and there must be no spying. No one was to see the departure of the disgraced member of the community.

It was simpler than I had dared hope. We went towards the gates together. I lowered my head, as though in humiliated sorrow.

A guard unlocked the gates and we passed through, the Chief Eunuch ahead, I a pace or two behind. The carriage was waiting. The Chief Eunuch pushed me in and hurriedly got in beside me. The driver immediately whipped up the horse and we drove away.

We came to the road and drove on for some

minutes. Then the carriage pulled up.

I wondered what was happening. Surely I was not going to be put out here, so close to the Pasha's domain? I was too bewildered at this stage to think clearly, but I was filled with apprehension at the notion.

The Chief Eunuch got out of the carriage and at the same time the driver leaped down from his seat. The Chief Eunuch immediately took his place and the driver got into the carriage beside me.

I thought I was dreaming.

"Simon!" I whispered.

He just put his arms round me and we clung together.

In those moments I felt I had awakened from a long nightmare. Not only was I free of all the fears which had beset me since my capture, but Simon was here.

I heard myself say, "You . . . too!"

"Oh, Rosetta," he whispered. "There is so much to be thankful for."

"When . . . ? How . . . ?" I began.

"We'll talk later," he replied. "For now . . . this is enough."

"Where is he taking us?"

"We'll see. He is giving us a chance."

We did not speak further. We just clasped hands tightly as though we feared we might be separated.

It was not yet dark and through the carriage window I recognised some of the landmarks I had noticed on my journey to the Pasha's domain. I glimpsed the Castle of the Seven Towers, the mosques, the tumbledown wooden houses.

I felt a great relief when we crossed the bridge which I knew separated the Turkish from the Christian part of the city. We were then on the north side of the Golden Horn.

We went on for some little while before the carriage stopped abruptly and the Chief Eunuch descended from the driver's seat. He signed for us to get out. He lifted his hand in a gesture which somehow signified that this was the end of his obligation.

"We don't know how to thank you," said Simon in French.

He nodded. "Embassy over there. Tall building. You see."

"Yes, but —"

"Go . . . go now. They may look for you."

Almost abruptly he climbed up into the driver's seat.

"Good luck!" he cried, and the carriage started back.

Simon and I were alone in Constantinople.

I felt a great elation. We were free . . . both of us. We only had to walk into the Embassy and tell our story and we should be kept in safety, our families informed of our whereabouts and then we should be sent home.

I turned to Simon. "Can you believe it!" I cried.

"It's hard. I'll take you to the Embassy. You'll have to explain that you have escaped from a harem."

"It seems so incredible."

"They will believe you. They know what goes on . . . particularly in the Turkish section."

"Let's go, Simon. Let's tell them. Soon we'll be on our way home."

He stood still and looked at me steadily. "I can't go with you."

"What?"

"Have you forgotten that I am escaping from English justice? They would send me back to . . . you can guess what."

"Do you mean you are going to stay here?"

"Why not? For a while, perhaps, till I make plans. It's as good a place as any for a fugitive from justice. But I think I shall try to make my way to Australia. I've had experience on a ship. I think that is the most likely place."

"Simon. I can't go without you."

"Of course you can. You'll be sensible . . . when you have thought about it."

"Oh, no. . . ."

"Rosetta, I am going to take you to the Embassy right away. You'll go in. You'll explain. They'll do everything possible to help you. They'll get you home . . . soon. We were brought here to the Embassy for that purpose."

"For both of us," I said.

"Well, how were they to know I could not take advantage of it? But you can. And you would be foolish beyond all reason not to . . . and without delay. In fact, I shall insist that you do."

"I could stay here with you. We'd find a way — "

"Listen, Rosetta. We've had great good luck . . . the greatest in the world. You can't turn your back on this chance now. It would be utter folly. We found valuable friends: Nicole for you, the Chief Eunuch for me. You were of service to her and I was lucky enough to strike up a friendship with him. Our cases were similar. It gave us something in common. He had been taken . . . the same as I was. We could talk in his language. When he knew that you and I were together, it seemed significant: he with the French girl . . . you with me. It gave us a fellow feeling. Don't you see? It's stupendous good fortune. We might have spent our lives in that place: you a slave girl at the Pasha's command . . . me guarding the harem with the eunuchs, perhaps becoming one of them. It could have been like that, Rosetta. And we have escaped. Let us thank our guardian angels for taking such good care of us. Now we have to make sure it was not done for us in vain."

"I know. I know. But I can't go without you, Simon."

He looked about us. We were next to a church which, on closer inspection, proved to be an English one.

There was a tablet on the wall. Simon drew me to it and we read that the church had been built as a dedication to those men who had fallen in the Crimean War.

"Let's go in," said Simon. "There we can think and perhaps talk."

It was quiet in the church. Fortunately there was no one there. I should have looked incongruous in my Turkish garb. We sat in a pew near the door, ready to escape if necessary.

"Now," said Simon, "we have to be sensible."

"You keep saying that, but — "

"It is so necessary to be."

"You can't ask me to leave you, Simon."

"I shan't forget you said that."

"It has been so long. I have wondered and wondered what was happening to you, and now that we are at last together . . . "

"I know," he said. There were a few moments of silence; then he went on. "The Chief Eunuch kept me informed. I knew the French girl had saved you from the Pasha by giving you a dose of a certain medicine. He supplied the medicine for her to give to you."

"He told you that!"

"Yes. I had spoken of you. I had told him of our shipwreck . . . how we had been together that time on the island. He said then it reminded him of his own experience. And . . . the French girl had been taken into the harem. I think because our stories were so similar and there was a chance for us, he wanted us to have it. He used to say, 'It will be the same story for you unless you get out of here.' There seemed no hope then. Then this chance came. What fantastic good fortune we have had, Rosetta!"

"I can't believe that we're here together now. It seems from the start we have been looked after. First the ship, then the island, and now this."

"We have had our opportunities and taken them. And now we must not turn away from this one when it is offered to us."

"I cannot leave you here."

"Remember, it was my original plan to get away from England. What would happen if

I returned now?"

"You cannot stay here. They may look for you. What if they found you? The penalty for escaping is . . ."

"They won't find me."

"We could prove you were innocent. Together we could do it."

"No. It is not the time."

"Will it ever be?"

"Perhaps not. But if I went back with you I should be arrested at once. I should be in the same position that I was in before I got out."

"Perhaps you should never have gone."

"Just think: If I hadn't we should never have met. We should never have been on that island together. Looking back, it seems like a sort of paradise to me."

"An uncomfortable paradise. Do you forget how hungry we were . . . how we longed for the sight of a ship?"

"And then we found we were in the hands of corsairs. No, I am not likely to forget."

"The island was no paradise."

"But we were together."

"Yes," I said. "Together, and that is how we should stay."

He shook his head. "This is your chance, Rosetta. You have to take it. I am going to make you take it."

"But I want so much to stay with you,

Simon. More than anything I want that."

"And I want you to be safe. It will be so easy for you."

"No, it will be the hardest thing I ever did."

"You are letting your emotions of the moment get the better of your good sense. Tomorrow you would regret it. There will be a bed for you at the Embassy. There will be sympathetic listening to your story and all the help necessary to get you comfortably home."

"And leave you behind!"

"Yes," he said shortly. "Now I will take you to the Embassy. Oh, Rosetta, don't look like that. It's best for you. That is what I want. It's a great opportunity . . . such as comes once in a lifetime. You must not fail to take it. You are emotionally overwrought. You do not understand your true feelings. Later you will be able to assess them. Now you must go. I ask it. I have to fend for myself. That will be difficult enough. But I shall manage . . . alone."

"You mean I would be a burden."

He hesitated and then looked at me steadily. "Yes," he said.

I knew then that I had to go.

"It is best for you too, Rosetta," he went on gently. "I shall never forget you. One day perhaps . . . "

I did not speak. I thought: I shall never be happy again. We have been through too much . . . together.

He took both my hands in his and held me against him for a few moments.

Then, together, we left the memorial church and made our way to the gates of the Embassy.

Trecorn Manor

In a few days I had passed out of the fantastic unreal world into normality. I was amazed by the manner in which I had been received at the Embassy. It almost made me feel that for a girl to be shipwrecked and sold into a harem was not such an unusual occurrence as I had imagined it to be.

Piracy must have been abolished almost a century ago, but there were still some who continued to ply their evil trade on the high seas, and potentates still maintained their seraglios behind high walls guarded by eunuchs, as they had in days gone by. Certain acts might not be performed openly, but they still existed.

The Embassy was a small enclave, a little bit of England in a foreign land, and from the moment I entered its portals I felt that I had come home.

I was soon divested of my foreign garments and conventional clothes were found for me. I was questioned and I gave my account of what

227

had happened. It was well known that the *Atlantic Star* had foundered and there had been few survivors. Immediate contact would be made with London. I told my story of our escape with the help of one of the deckhands, and how we had reached the island, where we had been picked up by corsairs who had sold us into slavery. I knew that I must say nothing about Simon's having escaped with me. My story was immediately accepted.

I was to stay in the Embassy for a while. I must try to relax, I was told, and to remember that I was now safe. I saw a doctor, an elderly Englishman, who was very kind and gentle. He asked me a few questions. I told him how I had been befriended and had been unmolested all the time I had been there. That seemed to give him great relief. He said I appeared to be in good health but I must take care. Such an ordeal as I had suffered could have had an effect on me which might not at first be discernible. If I wished to talk of it I was to do so; but if not, my wishes would be respected.

I was thinking a great deal about Simon, for naturally I could not get him out of my mind. This made me preoccupied and those about me probably thought I was brooding on the horror from which I had escaped.

Moreover, I could not help wondering what

was happening at the seraglio and what Rani's reaction had been when she had discovered that I had gone instead of Fatima. And what would have happened when Simon's departure had been discovered? Fortunately the Chief Eunuch had been involved, and he would doubtless see that there was as little fuss as possible. Rani would be very angry, I was sure. But even she had to bow to the Chief Eunuch.

I wondered about Nicole. Her debt was handsomely paid, and I fervently hoped that she would be rewarded for all she had done for me and keep herself and Samir in high favour with the Pasha.

But I should never know. They had passed out of my life as suddenly as they had come into it.

Then I would be overcome by the wonder of freedom. I should soon be home. I should live the life of a normal English girl. I must never cease to be thankful that I had come safely through that ordeal — except that, on achieving freedom, I had lost Simon.

Those days I spent in the Embassy seem vague to me now. I would wake in the morning for a few seconds believing I was on my divan. The terrible apprehension would come flooding back. Will it be today that the summons will come? I had not realised until this time what a strain I had lived under.

Then I would remember where I was and a feeling of relief would sweep over me . . . until I thought of Simon. How was he faring in this strange city? Had he been able to find a ship on which he could work his way to Australia? I supposed it was one of the best places he could go to in the circumstances. How could he survive? He was young and strong as well as resourceful. He would find a way. And one day when he was able to prove his innocence he would come home. Perhaps I should see him again and we could resume our friendship from where it had been cut off. He had hinted that he loved me. Did he mean in a special way or was it just that affection which naturally grows up between two people who have endured what we had together?

Free to go home, back to the house in Bloomsbury. Or was the house still ours? What had happened to my parents? Were Mr. Dolland, Mrs. Harlow, Meg, and Emily still in the kitchen? How could they be if my parents were not there? I had often pictured the scene, Mr. Dolland at the end of the table, his spectacles pushed up onto his forehead, telling them about the shipwreck. But if my parents had not returned, what would have happened to my friends in the kitchen?

Sometimes life here seemed as uncertain as it had within the walls of the seraglio.

The Ambassador asked me to go and see him one day, which I did. He was tall, dignified, with a ceremonial manner. He was very kind and gentle to me, as was everyone at the Embassy.

He said, "I have news. Some good . . . some bad. The good news is that your father survived the shipwreck. He is at his home now in Bloomsbury. The bad news is that your mother was lost at sea. Your father has been informed of your safety and looks forward to your homecoming. Mr. and Mrs. Deardon are going home in a few days when their leave falls due. It seems a good idea and would be most convenient if you travelled with them."

I was only half listening. My mother dead! I tried hard to remember her but could only think of her absent-minded smile when her eyes alighted on me. "Ah . . . the child" and "This is our daughter, Rosetta. She has had no tuition as yet." I could remember Felicity on that occasion far more distinctly. And now my mother was dead. That cruel ocean had claimed her. I had always thought of her and my father together and I wondered what he would be like without her.

Mrs. Deardon came to me. She was a

plump, comfortably cosy woman who talked continually, which I often found a relief as I had no wish to say much myself.

"My dear," she cried. "What an ordeal you have suffered. All you have been through! Never mind. Jack and I will look after you. We shall take ship from Constantinople to Marseilles and then travel through France to Calais. What a journey! I always dread it. But there it is. Needs must. But you do know that every minute you are getting nearer home."

She was the sort of woman who gives you a summary of her life in five minutes or so. I learned that Jack had always been in the Service, that he and she had gone to school together, married when they were both twenty, and had had two children, Jack Junior, who was now in the Foreign Office and Martin, who was still at university. He would assuredly go into one of the Services. It was a family tradition.

I could see that she was going to relieve me of making conversation and perhaps saying something I might regret. My great fear at this time was that I might be led into some indiscretion which would involve Simon. I must at all costs respect his desire for secrecy. I must remember that if his whereabouts were betrayed he would be brought back to face a death sentence.

In Mrs. Deardon's company I went out to buy some clothes. We sat side by side in the carriage while she chattered all the time. She and Jack had been in Constantinople for three years.

"What a place! I was thrilled when Jack first heard of the posting; now I'd do anything to get out. I'd like a nice *cosy* place: Paris . . . Rome, somewhere like that. Not too far from home. This place is *miles* away and so *foreign*. My dear, the customs! And what goes on on the Turkish side. Heaven alone knows, you have experience of that! I'm sorry, I shouldn't have mentioned it. My dear, I know how you feel. *Do* forgive me. Look! You can see across the water to Scutari. That was very much in evidence during the Crimean War when wonderful, *wonderful* Florence Nightingale took out her nurses. I do believe *they* played a bigger part in the eventual victory than people know. We're on the north side of the Golden Horn, dear. The other side is quite sinister. Oh, there I go again. . . . We're not far from Galata, that's the merchants' quarters, founded by the Genoese centuries ago. Jack will tell you all about that. He's interested in that sort of thing. Mind you, the streets are incredibly noisy and dirty. Our people wouldn't risk going there. We're in the best neighbourhood: Pera, you know. Most of the embassies are there, the legations and the consulates. There are some fine houses too."

While she was talking, I would go into a kind of dream. Pictures of the island would flash in and out of my mind: of going off with Simon, leaving Lucas to watch for a sail, and then the arrival of the galley. On and on . . . and I would come back to the questions: Where is he now? What will become of him? Shall I ever know?

"Now here is a very good tailor. Let's see what he can do. We have to get you presentable for home."

Her discourse went on. The great charm about it was that she did not expect replies.

It seemed a long time before we sailed from Constantinople. To board the ship — much smaller than the *Atlantic Star* — to gaze across the Bosphorus at historic Scutari, where our men had suffered so much in that hospital which from a distance looked like a Moorish palace, and to look back at the towers and minarets of Constantinople was an emotional experience.

Mr. Deardon was a tall man with greying hair and a dignified manner. He was the archetypal English diplomat — rather aloof, giving the impression that nothing could ruffle his composure or break through his reserve.

The journey to Marseilles was, as Mrs. Deardon had predicted, uncomfortable. The *Apollo*, being many times smaller than the *Atlantic Star*, took a battering from rough seas as severe as those I had previously suffered, and there were times when it seemed like a dream and that it was going to start again. If the *Atlantic Star* had succumbed to such a storm, I wondered how the frail *Apollo* could survive.

Mrs. Deardon took to her bunk and did not emerge. I missed her discourse. Mr. Deardon accepted the fury of the storm with the equilibrium I expected of him. I was sure he would remain serene and dignified, no matter what the disaster.

I could now go on deck and I recalled vividly that occasion when Simon had found me there during the great storm and had chided me and sent me down. I thought, All my life there will be memories of him.

At length the ordeal was over. Mrs. Deardon quickly recovered and was her old garrulous self. Mr. Deardon listened to her perpetual chatter with composed resignation, but I was glad of it. I could listen to it vaguely while inwardly following my own thoughts, secure in the knowledge that if I betrayed inattention I should be immediately forgiven on account of the ordeal through which I had passed.

There followed the long journey through France and finally the arrival at Calais and the Channel crossing.

The sight of the white cliffs of Dover affected us all. Tears came to Mrs. Deardon's eyes and even her husband, for the first time, showed a certain emotion by the twitching of his lips.

"It's home, dear," said Mrs. Deardon. "It's always the same. You just think of Easter and the daffodils . . . and the green grass. There's no green like our green. It's what you think of when you're away. And the rain, dear, the *blessed* rain. Do you know in Egypt they go for a year or even two without seeing a drop? Just those horrible sandstorms. We were in Ismalia — how many years, Jack, was it? . . . Surely it wasn't that many — and hardly ever saw rain. That's what it is, dear. It's the white cliffs. Home. It's good to see them."

And after that, London.

The Deardons insisted on delivering me.

"You must come in and meet my father," I said. "He will want to thank you."

Mrs. Deardon was eager to do so, but Mr. Deardon was firm, and in this he showed his talent for diplomacy.

"Miss Cranleigh will want to meet her family alone," he said.

I looked at him gratefully and said, "My father will most certainly wish to thank you personally. Perhaps you could come and dine with us soon."

"That," said Mr. Deardon, "would be a great pleasure."

So I said goodbye to them in the cab, which waited until I had rung the doorbell and the door was opened. Then, immediately and discreetly, Mr. Deardon ordered the cabby to drive on.

The door was opened by Mr. Dolland.

I gave a cry of joy and threw myself into his arms. He coughed a little. I did not realise at that moment that our household had changed. And there was Mrs. Harlow. I rushed at her. There were tears in her eyes.

"Oh, Miss Rosetta, Miss Rosetta," she cried, embracing me. "You're really here. Oh, it's been terrible!"

And there were Meg and Emily.

"It is wonderful to see you all," I cried.

And then . . . Felicity. We flew to each other and clung.

"I had to come," she said. "I'm here for two days. I said to James, 'I've got to go.' "

"Felicity. Felicity. How wonderful to see you."

There was a little cough. Over Felicity's

head I saw my father. He looked awkward and embarrassed.

I went to him. "Oh, Father," I said.

He took me into his arms and held me rather stiffly. It must have been the first time he had ever done so.

"Welcome . . . welcome home, Rosetta," he began. "I cannot express — "

I thought then, He does care for me. He does. It is just that . . . he cannot express.

A tall thin woman was standing a pace or two behind him. For half a second I thought my mother had been saved after all. But it was someone else.

"Your Aunt Maud is here," said my father. "She came to look after me and the household when . . ."

Aunt Maud! My father's sister. I had seen her only once or twice during my childhood. She was tall and rather gaunt. She had a look of my father, but she entirely lacked his obvious helplessness.

"We are all tremendously relieved that you are now safely home, Rosetta," she was saying. "It has been an anxious time for your father . . . for us all."

"Yes," I said, "for all of us."

"Well, now you are back. Your room is ready. Oh, it is such a relief that you are home!"

I felt numb with surprise.

Aunt Maud here . . . in my mother's place. Nothing would be the same again.

How right I was. The house had changed. Aunt Maud proved to be a strict disciplinarian. The kitchen was now orderly. There was no question of my having meals there. I should have them with my father and Aunt Maud in the proper manner. Fortunately, for those first few days Felicity was with us.

I could not wait to hear the verdict of the kitchen. Mr. Dolland discreetly said that Miss Cranleigh was a good manager and no one could help but respect her. Mrs. Harlow agreed. "Things were not really run right in the old days," she said. "Mind you, Mr. Dolland worked wonders, but there ought to be either a master or a mistress in a house — and a mistress is better because she knows what's what."

So Aunt Maud apparently knew what was what; but the old unconventional house had disappeared and I desperately longed to catch the old flavour.

Mr. Dolland still did the occasional turn, but *The Bells* had lost their horror for me. Having passed through some horrific adventures myself I could no longer get a thrill out of the murder of the Polish Jew. Meg and

Emily regretted the old days, but one thing I could rejoice in was the fact that some of those who had shared them were still here.

Meals were naturally different. Everything had to be served in the correct manner. The conversation was no longer dominated by ancient finds and the translation from some piece of papyrus. Aunt Maud discussed politics and the weather, and she told me that when my father had got over mourning for my mother, she proposed to give a few dinner parties for his colleagues from the Museum . . . professors and such like.

I was glad Felicity was with us for these first days, apart from my joy in seeing her. I knew that if she had not been there I should have wanted to shut myself away in my bedroom and avoid those interminable meals. But Felicity did lighten the conversation with amusing stories about life in Oxford and the exploits of her son Jamie, now aged three, and little Flora, who was not yet one.

"You must come and see them, Rosetta," she said. "I am sure your father will spare you after a while. Now, of course, you have just come home — "

"Of course, of course," said my father.

I could talk more freely to Felicity and I needed to talk. But I must do so guardedly, even to her. It was very difficult to speak of my adventures because Simon had played such an important part in them, and the fact that I must not betray him made me very reticent, lest by some odd remark I might do so.

But Felicity and I had been so close she guessed something was on my mind.

On the day after my arrival she came to my room. It was clear to me that, sensing some problem, she wanted to help me with it. If only someone could do that!

"Tell me frankly, Rosetta," she burst out suddenly. "Do you want to talk? I know how difficult it must be to discuss what has happened. Do say if it is. But I think it might help."

I hesitated. "I'm not sure. . . . "

"I understand. It must have been very frightening. Your father told us how you were lost when you went back for his notes."

"Oh, yes. It's strange how little things like that can change one's life."

"He blames himself, Rosetta. I know he doesn't betray his emotions, but that does not mean they are not there."

"Everything is so different now," I said. "The house . . . everything. I know it can never again be as it used to."

"It really is a very good thing that your Aunt Maud is here, Rosetta."

"We never saw much of her when I was

young. I scarcely recognised her. It seems so strange that she should be here now."

"I gathered she and your mother did not get on. That's easy to understand. They were so different. Your parents were so immersed in their work, and your aunt is so efficient in running a house."

I gave her a wry smile. "I liked ours as it was: inefficient."

"Your father misses your mother, terribly. They were so close in everything they did . . . always together. It is a sad blow for him. He cannot . . . "

"Cannot express," I said.

She nodded. "And you, Rosetta, when you feel more settled you must come and stay with us. James would be delighted and you would love the children. Jamie is a very independent young gentleman and Flora is just beginning to toddle. They are adorable."

"It would be lovely to come."

"You only have to say. I shall have to go back the day after tomorrow. But I had to be here for your return."

"How glad I am that you were!"

"By the way, did you hear about Lucas Lorimer?"

"Lucas . . . no!"

"Oh, didn't you? I suppose you wouldn't. He came back, you know."

"He came back . . . " I repeated.

"Obviously you haven't heard. He told us the story. We thought you had all been drowned, and it was a great relief to hear that you had escaped the wreck. But we were terribly worried to hear you had fallen into the hands of those wicked people. I've had nightmares wondering what had happened."

"Tell me about Lucas."

"It's a very sad story. That it should happen to him! I've only seen him once since he came back. James and I went down to Cornwall. James was lecturing at a college in Truro, and we called at Trecorn Manor. I don't think he is very pleased to see anyone. Trecorn Manor is a lovely old place. It's been in the family for years. Lucas's brother Carleton inherited. That was another sore point. It's always a bit of a strain for a man like that to be a second son. He used to be such a vital person."

"What happened to him?"

"As you know he was captured with you, but he somehow made a bargain with those people. He persuaded them to free him in exchange for some family jewels. How it was done I don't quite know. He obviously didn't want to talk about it, and one can't ask questions . . . not too many, in any case. However, they let him go. It was a sort of ransom. Poor

Lucas, he'll never be the same again. He so loved to travel; James always said he was something of a dilettante. It's his leg, you see. It was terribly hurt in the wreck. Of course, if it had had attention at the time. . . . He's been to various bone people getting advice — all over the country and abroad, Switzerland and Germany — but it is always the same story. It was neglected at the vital time. He limps badly and has to walk with a stick and he's in considerable pain. He is a little better, I believe, but the leg will never be right. It's changed him. He used to be so witty and amusing; now he is quite morose. He is the last person this should have happened to."

I was back in the past. I saw him clinging to the lifeboat . . . our clumsy efforts to set his leg . . . lying on the island, keeping watch for a sail while Simon and I went off to forage and talk secrets.

"So you don't see him often."

"No. It's not really all that far away. I've asked him to come and stay, but he declines my invitations. I think he doesn't want to go anywhere . . . or to see anyone. You see, it is a complete change. He used to live such a busy social life, and he seemed to enjoy it."

"I should like to see him again."

"Why, yes. He might be interested in that. Or perhaps he wouldn't want to be reminded.

It may be that he is trying to forget. I tell you what I will do. Come and stay and I'll invite him too. He might make the effort to see you. After all, you were together on that island."

"Oh, please arrange it, Felicity."

"I certainly shall . . . and soon."

I felt excited at the prospect, but even to Lucas I could not talk of Simon. That was our secret . . . shared only by us two. Simon had told me because he trusted me. I must respect that trust. If he were hunted down and brought back through me, I should never forgive myself. To Lucas, Simon must remain the deckhand who saved our lives.

Felicity had to go home and the house seemed dull. There was an air of such normality about it that I was forced to look facts in the face and make a logical conclusion.

I had deluded myself into thinking that when I was home I should be able to prove Simon's innocence. How? I asked myself now. How did I set about it? Go to his home? Get to know people who had played a part in the drama which had led up to the shooting? I could not go to Perrivale Court and say, "I know Simon is innocent and I have come to uncover the truth and solve the mystery." How could I behave as though I were an investigator from Scotland Yard!

I needed time to think. I was obsessed by the need to prove his innocence so that he could come back and lead a normal life. But suppose I did achieve this seemingly impossible task, where should I find *him?* The whole scheme was wildly fantastic. It had no place in this logical world.

Aunt Maud's influence on the house was very marked. The furniture was highly polished. Floors shone, brass gleamed, and everything, however small, was in the place designed for it. Daily she went to the kitchen to consult Mrs. Harlow on meals and both Mrs. Harlow and Mr. Dolland had assumed a new dignity; even Meg and Emily did their work in a more orderly fashion — not cutting it short to sit over meals and listen to Mr. Dolland's discourse on the old days of the drama — and I was sure that if they did indulge in these diversions, they would be interrupted by an imperious ringing, and Mr. Dolland would have to leave his performance to don his black coat and make his ceremonial appearance abovestairs.

I think I minded it more than they did. We had all been so happy-go-lucky in the past but I came to realise that good servants prefer a well-run house to a happy one.

I often found Aunt Maud watching me speculatively. I knew that in due course I should be dragooned into her scheme of things, and in Aunt Maud's eyes there would be only one course to pursue since I was a young and nubile woman: marriage. These dinner parties she had hinted at would have a definite purpose: the search for a suitable husband for me. I pictured him: earnest, slightly balding, learned, erudite, perhaps a professor who had already made his mark in the academic world. Someone rather like James Grafton only not so attractive. Perhaps he would be attached to the British Museum or Oxford or Cambridge. It would keep me in the circle in which my family moved. Aunt Maud might think my father was absent-minded — and I gathered that she had had little respect for my mother as a housewife, which was the reason we had seen so little of her during my mother's lifetime — but he was well respected in his profession and therefore it would be wise for me to marry into it. I was sure she felt that, schooled by her, unlike my mother, I might make a professor's wife *and* a good housewife at the same time.

She would preside over the affair and therefore it would be conducted in the most orthodox manner. Aunt Maud hated to waste anything — including time. I believed that, but for my strange adventure, operations would have been commenced long ago. As it was, I was allowed a little respite.

The doctor had evidently warned Aunt Maud that I must be treated with a certain care. The ordeal through which I had passed must not be forgotten and I needed time to rehabilitate myself to a civilised way of life in my own way. Aunt Maud followed his instructions with brisk efficiency, and my father did the same, remaining aloof. Mrs. Harlow did so by making sure that I was comfortably seated and speaking to me rather as she used to when I was five years old. Even Mr. Dolland lowered his voice, and I would find Meg and Emily regarding me with awe-struck wonder.

Only once did my father refer to the shipwreck. He told me how they had been caught up in a crowd going for the boats. They had wanted to wait for me, to go back and find me ... but one of the officers had taken their arms and more or less forced them to go with the crowd.

"We thought you would join us at any minute," he said piteously.

"It was such chaos," I said. "It couldn't have been otherwise."

"I lost your mother while they were pushing us into the boats. . . ."

"We mustn't brood on it," I said.

"If you hadn't gone back for those notes we

should all have been together. . . . "

"No, no. You and my mother were parted
. . . so should we have been."

He was so distressed I knew we must not
speak of it. He must try to forget, I told him.

All this affected me deeply, and I felt a
great desire to escape, to go down to Cornwall, to find Perrivale Court and begin the
impossible task of finding out what really happened. I needed time. I needed a plan. I
wanted desperately to take some action, but I
was not sure how to begin.

I went down to the kitchen to try to recap-
ture the spirit of the old days. I asked Mr.
Dolland for "To be or not to be" and the
speech before Harfleur. He obliged but I fancied he lacked his previous flair and they were
all watching me rather than Mr. Dolland.

I said to him, "Do you remember . . . just
before I went away . . . there was a murder
case?"

"What was that, Miss Rosetta? Let me see.
There was that man who married women for
their money."

"And then done 'em in," added Mrs. Harlow.

"I wasn't thinking of that. I mean the case
of those brothers . . . one of them was shot in
an empty farmhouse. Didn't someone run
away?"

"Oh, I know the one you mean. It was the Bindon Boys case."

"Yes, that's the one. Did you ever hear what happened?"

"Oh . . . the murderer got away. I don't think they ever caught him."

"He was smarter than the police," added Mrs. Harlow.

"I remember now," said Mr. Dolland. "It all comes back to me. It was Simon Perrivale, adopted when he was a child. He shot the brother. There was a woman, I believe. Jealousy and all that."

"I know you keep newspaper cuttings, Mr. Dolland. Do you have any of that case?"

"Oh, it's only theatre things he cuts out," said Mrs. Harlow. "This play and that, and what actor and actress. That's right, ain't it, Mr. Dolland?"

"Yes," replied Mr. Dolland. "That's what I keep. What did you want to know about the case, Miss Rosetta?"

"Oh, I just wondered if you kept cuttings, that's all. I knew you had albums . . . you see, it was just before I went away. . . . " I trailed off.

Glances passed between them.

"Oh, I reckon that's all done with now," said Mrs. Harlow, as though soothing a child.

"The police never close a case," added Mr.

250

Dolland. "Not till they've found the murderer and it's settled and done with. They keep it on their files, as they say. One of these days they'll catch up with him. He'll make a false step. Perhaps only one is needed, and then, hey presto! — they've got him."

"They do say," said Mrs. Harlow, "that murderers can never resist coming back to the scene of the crime. That's what this Simon whatever-his-name-is will do one of these days. You can bet your life on it."

Would he ever come back? I wondered.

What could I do? I had only this wild dream that I should prove his innocence and then he could come back without fear. He would know freedom again and we should be together.

Several weeks had passed. After living in perpetual fear and apprehension, the predictably peaceful days seemed to go on interminably.

Aunt Maud tried to interest me in household matters, all the things which it was good for a girl to know. She believed firmly that it was her duty to do what my parents failed to do: prepare me for my marriage. I must learn how to deal with servants. My manner towards them left much to be desired. It was necessary, of course, to maintain a certain friendliness but it should be aloof. I was too familiar, and it encouraged them to be so with me. One could not blame *them*. What I needed was a mixture of indiscernible condescension and amiability without familiarity, so that, however friendly one felt towards them, the line between upstairs and downstairs was never allowed to slip. She did not blame me. *Others* were responsible. But there was no reason why I should continue in this unsatisfactory strain. I must first of all learn how to deal with servants. I should listen to her, Aunt Maud, ordering the meals; I might be present on one or two occasions when she paid her daily visit to the kitchen. I must try to improve my needlework and practise more on the pianoforte. She hinted at music lessons. Soon, she told me, she would launch her scheme for bringing people to the house.

I wrote to Felicity.

Please, Felicity, I want to get away. If you could invite me . . . soon.

There was an immediate reply. *Come when you can. Oxford and the Graftons await you.*

"I am going to stay awhile with Felicity," I told Aunt Maud.

She smiled smugly. With Felicity I should meet young men . . . the right sort of young men. It did not matter from which spot the scheme was launched. Operation Marriage could begin just as well in Oxford as in Bloomsbury.

To arrive in Oxford was an exciting experience. I had always loved what little I had seen of it, that most romantic of cities standing where the Cherwell and the Thames — Isis, here — meet, its towers and spires reaching to the sky, its air of indifference to the workaday world. I loved the city, but what was most pleasant was to be with Felicity.

The Graftons had a house near Broad Street close to Baliol, Trinity, and Exeter colleges, not far from the spot where the martyrs Ridley and Latimer were burned to death for their religious opinions. The past was all around one and I found peace from Aunt Maud's efficiency and the far from subtle care which everyone in the house seemed determined to bestow upon me.

With Felicity it was different. She understood me better than the others. She knew that there were secrets which I could not bring myself to discuss. Perhaps she thought I should one day. In any case she was perceptive enough to know that she must wait for me to do so and make no attempt to prise them from me.

James was tactful and charming and the children provided a great diversion. Jamie chattered quite a lot; he showed me his picturebooks and proudly pointed out a pussycat and a train. Flora regarded me suspiciously for a while but eventually decided that I was harmless and condescended to sit on my lap.

The day after I arrived Felicity said, "When I knew you were coming I wrote to Lucas Lorimer. I said how delighted we should be if he came for a visit and I guessed you and he might have many things to talk about."

"Has he accepted?" I asked.

"Not yet. When I saw him before, he clearly did not want to talk of his adventures. It may be that he is afraid it will bring it all back too painfully."

"I should like to see him."

"I know. That's why I asked him."

All that day I thought of his being taken aboard the corsairs' galley after that moment on the island when they had seemed to hesitate whether to take him or not. I hadn't seen him again after that first night.

There was so much I wanted to ask him.

The next day we were at breakfast when the mail was brought in. Felicity seized on a letter, opened it, read it, smiled, and looked up waving it.

"It's from Lucas," she said. "He's coming tomorrow. I'm so glad. I thought he would want to see you. Aren't you pleased, Rosetta?"

"Yes. I am delighted."

She looked at me anxiously. "I daresay it will be a little upsetting, perhaps . . . ?"

"I don't know. We're both safe now."

"Yes, but what an experience! Yet I am sure it is better for you both to meet and talk openly. It doesn't do to bottle these things up."

"I shall look forward so much to seeing him."

Felicity sent the carriage to the station to meet him. James went with it. We had debated whether we should go too, but we finally decided it would be better for us to wait at the house.

My first sight of him shocked me deeply. I had, of course, seen him in worse condition — on the island, for instance, and when we had dragged him into the lifeboat — but I was contrasting him with the man whom I had first met. There were shadows under his eyes, and that certain cynical sparkle was replaced by a look of hopelessness. The flesh had fallen away from his features, which gave him a gaunt look. The tolerant amusement with which he had seemed to look out on the world had disappeared. He looked weary and disillusioned.

Our meeting was an emotional one. His

expression changed when he saw me. He smiled and came towards me, leaning on his stick. He held out his free hand and took mine. He held it for some time, looking intently at me.

"Rosetta," he said, and his lips twitched a little. The obvious emotion he felt made him look different again . . . defenceless, in a way. I had never seen him look like that before. I knew he was remembering, as I was, those days we had spent in the open boat, the island where Simon and I had left him to watch while we had gone off together, the arrival of the corsairs.

"Oh, Lucas," I said. "It is good to see you here . . . safe."

There was a short silence while we continued to gaze at each other, almost as though we could not believe that we were real.

Felicity said softly, "I know you two will have lots to say to each other. First . . . let's show Lucas his room, shall we?"

She was right. There was a great deal to talk about. The first evening was something of a strain. James and Felicity were the perfect host and hostess, full of understanding, skating over awkward pauses with skill and ease.

Felicity was the soul of tact. She knew that there would be things of which we would want to talk to no one but each other — and only then when we were ready — so the following day when James went off to his college, she told us she had an engagement which she must fulfil.

"Do forgive me," she said. "I'll have to leave you two to entertain each other this afternoon."

There was a pleasant part of the garden, walled in with mellow red bricks with a pond in the centre — the Tudor type of intimate small garden-within-a-garden. The roses were in bloom and I suggested that I show them to Lucas.

It was a mild afternoon, pleasantly warm without being too hot, and we made our necessarily rather slow progress there. There was a stillness in the air, and within the walls of that garden we might have stepped back two or three centuries in time.

"Let's sit here," I said. "The pond is so pretty and it is so peaceful." There was silence and I went on. "We'd better talk about it, Lucas. We both want to, don't we?"

"Yes," he agreed. "It's uppermost in our minds."

"Does it seem to you like a dream?" I asked.

"No," he said sharply. "Stark reality. I have a perpetual reminder. Here I am now . . . like this."

"I'm sorry. We didn't know how to set it . . . and we had nothing that would help us."

"My dear girl," he said almost angrily. "I'm not blaming you, only life — fate — whatever you like to call it. Don't you see? I have to spend the rest of my life . . . like this."

"But at least you are here, at least you are alive."

He shrugged his shoulders. "Do you think that is a matter for great rejoicing?"

"For some at any rate: your friends, your family. You are lame, and I know there is pain now and then, but so much worse might have happened to you."

"You are right to chide me. I am selfish, disgruntled, and ungrateful."

"Oh, no, no. Do you think . . . it is possible . . . that something may be done?"

"What?"

"Well, they are very clever nowadays. There have been all sorts of medical discoveries — "

"The bone was broken. It was not set. It is too late to do anything about it now."

"Oh, Lucas, I'm so sorry. If only we could have done better, how different it would have been."

"You did a great deal and I'm a selfish creature thinking of my own misfortunes. I just cannot bear to contemplate what happened to you."

"But I escaped. My fears were only in the mind."

He wanted to know in detail what had happened, so I told him of my friendship with Nicole and how she had given me the drug and saved me from the Pasha's attentions, and how the drug had been supplied by the Chief Eunuch who was a great friend of hers. He listened intently.

"Thank God," he said. "That could have scarred you as deeply as I have been, perhaps more so. And what happened to that man . . . John Player?"

It seemed as though the silence went on for a long time. I heard the buzz of a bee and the high-pitched note of a grasshopper. Be careful, I was telling myself. You could so easily betray him. Remember, it is not only your secret, it is yours and Simon's.

I heard myself say, "He . . . he was sold to the same Pasha."

"Poor devil. I can guess what his fate would be. He was a strange man. I always had an odd feeling about him."

"What sort of feeling?" I asked apprehensively.

"I felt that things were not all they seemed. Now and then I had a fancy that I had seen him before somewhere. Then sometimes he seemed as though he were hiding something."

"What do you mean? What could he have been hiding?"

"Anything. I've no idea. That was just the impression he gave. He wasn't the sort of man you'd expect to find swabbing the decks, was he? He was very resourceful, I must say."

"I think we could both say that we owe our lives to him."

"And you are right. I wish I knew what had happened to him."

"A great many men were employed in the gardens. He was big and strong."

"He would have fetched a fair price, I daresay."

There was silence again. I was afraid to speak lest I should betray something. He went on musingly, "How strange that we were all on that island together, never knowing whether we should be found before we died of starvation."

"How did you manage to get home, Lucas?"

"Well, I'm a wily old bird, you know." He smiled, and when he did so he was the man I had first met. "I seized my opportunities. I had a smattering of their language, I found. It helped a lot. I had picked up a few words when I was travelling round the world some years ago. It is amazing how being able to communicate helps. I offered them riches . . . for the three of us. I said that in my own country I was a very wealthy man. They believed me because they knew I had travelled a good deal. They wouldn't consider releasing you or Player. You were too valuable. I was not. Being crippled I was useless."

"You see, there is some advantage in everything."

"There have been times when I wished they had thrown me overboard."

"You must not say that. It is accepting defeat . . . no, welcoming it. That is not the way to live."

"You are right, of course. Oh, it is good to be with you, Rosetta. I remember how resourceful you were when we were on the island. I owe a lot to you."

"But most to — "

"To that man Player. Well, he was a sort of leader, wasn't he? He was cut out for the part, and it fell to him. He played it well, I'll admit. And I was the impediment. I was the one who slowed down the progress."

"You did nothing of the sort. How could you have done on the island? Tell me the rest."

"When I saw that I could not save you and nothing would make those men part with you and Player, I concentrated on my own case. They were more amenable in that direction. What price could they get for me, a man in my state? Nothing. I told them that if they would let me go, I would send them a valuable jewel. If they tried to sell me they would get nothing, for who would want a man who can't even walk without a stick? If they threw me overboard that would be equally unproductive. But if they took my offer of the jewel, then they would at least have something for their pains."

"So they agreed to let you go for the promise of a jewel?"

"It was simple logic really. They had two alternatives. Throw me overboard or despatch me in some other way and lose everything, or take a chance that I would keep my word and send the jewel. It would occur to them — as it would to any — that I might not keep my side of the bargain. And if I did not, well, they might just as well throw me overboard. The wise thing, of course, would be to take a chance, for at least if they did there could be a hope of getting something. So I was dropped in Athens, a street or so away from the British Embassy. The rest was simple. My family were informed and I was on the way home."

"And the jewel?"

"I kept my word. It was a ring which belonged to my mother . . . really one of the family jewels, you might say. They were divided between my brother and myself. It had been my mother's engagement ring and my father's mother's before her. If I had become engaged it would have been my fiancée's."

"Of course, you need not have sent it."

"No. But those people have long memories. I did not want to spend the rest of my life wondering if fate would throw me in their way again. Moreover, suppose some other poor devil was caught by them and tried my tactics? Once deceived, they might not have given the chance again. Then again, the ring would probably have lain idle for a very long time. It is not likely that anyone would want to marry me . . . in my condition."

"Did you take it yourself and where to?"

"They had arranged where it should be taken. There was an old inn on the Italian coast. I was warned not to swerve from the instructions. It was to be taken to this inn — I think it was one frequented by smugglers — and there it would be collected. I did not go myself. I was scarcely in a fit state and they recognised that. I told them who would bring it: Dick Duvane, my batman during my spell in the Army. He's a valet . . . confidant . . .

and frequently fellow traveller. He's not just a servant, he's one of the best friends I ever had. I don't know what I'd do without him. I trust him absolutely."

"I'm glad you got away, Lucas."

"I suppose I am myself, only . . ."

"I know. I do understand."

We fell into silence. We were still in the garden when Felicity came out to find us.

The visit to Oxford was of considerable help to me. Lucas's logical outlook on life — bitter though it was — brought me down to earth. What could I do? How could I prove Simon's innocence? I was not even on the spot. I knew nothing of the family at Perrivale Court except what I had gathered from Simon and had read in the newspapers at the time of the murder. If only I could find some means of meeting them, of going to Perrivale Court! What hope was there? I thought of Lucas. What if I asked his help? He was resourceful. The manner in which he had extricated himself from a dangerous situation showed that. He was not very far from Perrivale Court; he was not on terms of friendship or even casual acquaintance with the family, even though he had once, long ago, visited the place. I wished I could have discussed Simon with him, perhaps enlisted his help. Dare I? I wondered.

But I could not be sure what his reaction would be.

I felt as helpless as ever, but that visit did cheer me a little.

He left Oxford the day before I did. When he said goodbye he looked forlorn and rather vulnerable and I felt a great desire to comfort him. I thought at one stage that he was going to make a suggestion for a further meeting, but he did not.

Felicity and I went with him to the station. He seemed reluctant to leave us and stood at the carriage window watching us on the platform as the train steamed away, taking him back to the West Country.

"It is so sad," said Felicity. "There is a changed man."

The next day I went home.

Aunt Maud wanted to know whom I had met in Oxford.

I told her there had not been a great deal of entertaining because Felicity had thought I needed a restful time. When I was at dinner with her and my father it slipped out that Lucas Lorimer had been staying in Oxford while I was there.

My father was immediately interested. "Oh, yes, the young man who was with us on the *Atlantic Star*." He turned to Aunt Maud.

"It was most extraordinary. He discovered a stone in his garden in Cornwall. Ancient Egyptian. How it got there is a mystery. But it was quite an exciting discovery. Yes, he was with us on the *Atlantic Star*."

"He was one of the survivors," I told Aunt Maud.

I followed her line of thought. I *had* met a man in Oxford then? Who was he? Was he of good family? Was he in a position to support a wife?

I said shortly, "He is crippled. He was hurt in the wreck."

Aunt Maud looked disappointed, then resigned; I could imagine her mustering her ideas to bring eligible young men to the dinner table. How I missed Felicity and the peace of Oxford!

Aunt Maud relentlessly pursued her policy. There followed several dinner parties to which men whom she considered suitable were asked. She harried my father into bringing some of his associates home to dine; to my amusement and her chagrin, most of them were middle-aged, so fanatically devoted to their work that they had no plans for putting any impediment in the form of a wife to that, or cosily married with erudite and energetic wives and a family of prodigies.

The weeks passed into months. I was

restive and I did not see any escape.

Felicity paid us a flying visit. It was difficult to leave the children for long. The nanny was good and she enjoyed the responsibility of being in sole charge of the nursery, but Felicity hated to leave them. I was sure she came only because she was worried about me.

I was able to tell her how I missed the old days in our pleasantly disorganised household. I knew I should be grateful to the indefatigable Aunt Maud, but there was more to life than polished furniture and meals on time. Aunt Maud was such an overpowering person that she subdued us all, and her influence was particularly felt in the kitchen where I had spent so many happy hours.

Felicity said, "Rosetta, have you something on your mind?" I hesitated and she went on. "Wouldn't you like to talk about it? You know I'd understand. But I won't press you. I know that, terrifying as an ordeal can be while you live it, at times what can happen afterwards can be equally important. It's happened, Rosetta. It's over. Don't think I don't understand what it was like in that harem. It must have been quite terrible. But you escaped. It was a wonderful piece of luck. It's left its mark, though. I worry about you . . . and about Lucas, too. I always liked him. He used to be so amusing. He's travelled so much and talked so easily about it. He was always so lighthearted in a blasé sort of way. And now I think he's shutting himself in with his bitterness. It is all wrong. It's agonising for him, of course. He was always so active. I'm going to be rather bold. James is going to Truro again to lecture at that college. I shall go with him and I shall suggest that, as we are in Cornwall, we call on him. It would be nice if you came with us. What do you think?"

I could not hide my enthusiasm for the plan. To go there, to be not far from Perrivale Court . . . well, however far it was, I should be comparatively near! What I should do when I got there I was not sure. There was one thought uppermost in my mind: I must not betray Simon.

"I can see the idea appeals to you," said Felicity.

When the matter was broached Aunt Maud seemed mildly pleased. Her own attempts to bring me into contact with marriageable young men had not been very successful. She was probably hoping that this visit would be more productive.

The Graftons moved in the right circles. James Grafton was "something at Oxford." Aunt Maud was not well informed about such details. People were either suitable or unsuitable, and the Graftons — in spite of the fact that Felicity had been a governess — were eminently suitable. Aunt Maud was in favour of the idea. So was my father, when he was told by her that it would be good for my future.

So it was arranged that I should accompany James and Felicity to Truro.

On the instigation of Felicity, James had written to Lucas to tell him that we should be in Cornwall and he thought it might be an opportunity for us to call and see them while we were in the Duchy.

There was a prompt reply that we must certainly do so. We must stay a few days at least. Trecorn Manor was too far from Truro for us to come for a day.

The change in me was obvious.

Mrs. Harlow said, "You always did get on with that Felicity. I remember the day she came and we was expecting some stuck-up madam. From the moment she stepped out of that cab I took to her . . . and so did you, I'd say."

"Yes," I said. "She is a wonderful friend. How lucky we were that she came to us."

"I'd say you'd got the right bull by the horns there."

Oh, yes, indeed, I owed a great deal to Felicity.

Trecorn Manor was a pleasant Queen Anne mansion built in an age noted for its elegance. It was set in well-kept grounds. I was thinking how interesting it would be to see Lucas against the background of his own home.

We were warmly welcomed by him.

"It is so good of you to come," he said, and I felt he meant it.

We were introduced to his brother, Carleton, and Carleton's wife, Theresa. Carleton looked a little like Lucas, but they were of very different temperaments, I soon discovered. Carleton was bluff, easygoing, completely immersed in the running of the estate — in fact, the typical squire — and Theresa was entirely suited to be his wife. She was absorbed in her family, carrying out her duties on the estate with charm, tolerance, and total efficiency, clearly the excellent wife and mother.

There were two children, twins, a girl and a boy, Henry and Jennifer, aged five years. I knew that Carleton and his wife would be admired and respected throughout the estate, that she would work indefatigably in the affairs of the church and the general community. She was the sort of woman who would do her duty unstintingly and make a pleasure of it.

I could not quite see Lucas fitting into this environment.

When we were alone, Felicity said, "Lucas couldn't have a better home to come back to."

I wondered. This display of well-being might be galling to a man in his position. It was something I felt he would never have wanted before the shipwreck. Indeed he had, by his frequent absences, shown that he could not tolerate it. It was sad that such virtues as those of Carleton and his wife and Aunt Maud, so admirable in themselves, create a less than perfect atmosphere for those around them.

We planned to stay in Cornwall for about a week, which was all the time James could spare, and I knew that Felicity did not want to leave the children for longer than that.

We were given rooms on the first floor overlooking moorland. James and Felicity's room was next to mine.

Theresa took us up.

"I hope you'll be comfortable," she said. "It's a pity you can only stay a week. We love having visitors. Unfortunately we don't often. I'm so glad you came. Lucas is pleased you are here. . . . " She trailed off.

"We hesitated about suggesting a visit," said Felicity. "It was rather forward of us."

"We should have been most put out if you had come all this way without seeing us.

Carleton worries about Lucas . . . so do I. He is so changed."

"Well, it was a terrible ordeal," said Felicity.

Theresa laid her hand on my arm. "And for you, too. I heard about it. Lucas doesn't talk much. Carleton says it is like getting blood out of a stone to get information out of him. He was so active. And this has hit him hard. But he did cheer up quite a lot when he heard you were coming."

"He likes to talk to Rosetta," said Felicity. "After all, they were together. I always think it helps people to talk."

"It is wonderful that you both came through. We had been so worried about Lucas. And when we knew he was coming home we were so happy. And then . . . he was so different. And Lucas being the man he is . . . it was never easy for him to be the younger brother." She shrugged her shoulders and looked faintly embarrassed, as though she thought she was saying too much.

I knew that she was right. Before the accident Lucas had been constantly preoccupied by the fact that his elder brother was head of the household when their father died. He was a man who liked to lead and it could never have been easy for him to take second place. So he had travelled widely after he left the

Army, and of course while he was in it. He had tried archaeology. He had written a book, inspired by his discovery, and had been on the point of lecturing about it when disaster had struck. It must have seemed then that he was making a life away from Trecorn Manor which was what he had wanted; and then he was brought back . . . as he was now. I could understand that he was disillusioned with life. I looked forward to more talks with him. Perhaps I could try to make him see the future differently. Perhaps I could inspire him with a little hope. I did not think there was a very good chance of this, but I could try.

He could still ride, which was a blessing. True, he needed a little assistance in mounting and dismounting, but when he was on his horse, he was all that he had been before. He had always been an excellent horseman, and I noticed at once that there was a strong relationship between him and his mount, Charger, who seemed to understand that his master had changed and needed to be looked after.

Theresa said, "We never worry about Lucas when he goes off for long spells. If he's on Charger we know he will be brought home when he wants to come."

The first night at dinner he wanted to know if I rode.

273

"There was little opportunity at home," I told him. "But when I was at school we had riding lessons. So I cannot call myself quite a novice but . . . somewhat inexperienced."

"You ought to get in a bit of practice while you're here," suggested Carleton.

"Yes," agreed Lucas. "I'll undertake to be your tutor."

"It will be a little boring perhaps for such a practised rider," I said.

"I know it will be a pleasure," he replied.

Theresa beamed on us. She was such a kindly woman. I realised how happy she was that I was here because she thought it would be pleasant for Lucas and that we were good for each other.

It had been arranged that after two days at Trecorn Manor, James should go back to Truro to do his work while Felicity and I remain behind to wait for him. He would return to the Manor when his work was done, and after a day or so we should all leave together.

I soon settled into a routine. Lucas and I rode together and talked a good deal, often about our adventure. We often went over the same ground, but I am sure it did us both good. As far as I was concerned, it made me all the more eager to find out something about Perrivale Court.

I found myself drawn into life in the nursery. Jennifer seemed to have taken a liking to me. I had had little to do with children and was unsure how to deal with them, but Jennifer solved that. She informed me that her name was Jennifer Lorimer and that she lived at Trecorn Manor. She was five years old. All this was told as if in great confidence and it was almost as though we shared a special understanding. Although the girl in the twinship, she was the leader. She was vivacious and chattered a good deal. Henry was much quieter, a serious little boy; he always followed Jennifer and, as she had decided that she liked me, he must do so too.

Moreover, there was Nanny Crockett, another ally. I think it must have been because I got on well with the twins that she accepted me. She was by no means young, but a power in the nursery. Ellen, the fourteen-year-old nursery maid, behaved towards her as though she were the Queen. I gathered she was in her late fifties. She had iron-grey hair which was plaited and worn round her head in a rather severe manner. Her grey eyes were alert and she had a way of pursing her lips if she disapproved of anything; then she could be indomitable. She was a woman of definite opinions and once they became hers she determined to stick to them.

"We were lucky to get her," said Theresa. "She's a very experienced nanny. She's not young, of course, but that's all to the good. She's as active as a young woman and there's the experience as well."

Nanny Crockett liked to have a little chat now and then and when the children had their afternoon nap. If I were not with Lucas, I would be with her.

Felicity and Theresa had interests in common — the running of a home and the care of a husband and children. They were ideal companions. I imagine when they were together they discussed Lucas and me. They thought we were "good for each other," and we were certainly thrown together on every possible occasion. Not that their efforts were necessary, for Lucas showed clearly that he preferred my society to that of anyone else. It was a fact, I believed, that since we had arrived he had become a little more like the man he used to be. He laughed occasionally now and then and sometimes would deliver a witty quip, but alas, very often with a hint of that bitterness which seemed to have become a feature of his conversation.

I knew this routine must soon be interrupted by the return of James. I was enjoying my stay, but ever present was the need to find out the truth about Simon, and there were times when I felt a deep frustration and despair.

It was maddening to be so near to his old home, but how could I get to it without arousing suspicion? I was afraid to make outright enquiries. The very fact that Lucas had met him at some time implied that it would be very easy to make a false step and reveal to him who John Player really was. And if he discovered, how did I know what action he would take? True, John Player had saved our lives, but if Lucas believed him to be a murderer, a fugitive from justice, what would he feel he ought to do about it?

It would have been such a relief to talk to him about Simon, but I feared I could not do it. Sometimes I thought of telling Felicity. I was indeed often on the verge of doing so, but I always drew back in time.

But I was getting desperate, and that day at luncheon I had to speak. I said tentatively, "Wasn't there a murder somewhere about here?"

Theresa wrinkled her brow. Then she said, "You must mean that affair at Perrivale Court."

"Yes," I said, hoping I did not show the emotion I always felt when the subject was raised. "I . . . I think that was where it was."

"It was the adopted son," said Lucas.

"He'd been cared for all his life," Carleton added, "and he showed his gratitude by murdering one of the sons of the house."

"I think we mentioned it before," I said to Lucas. "Didn't you say you'd met him?"

"Oh, yes . . . years ago . . . and briefly."

"How far is the place from here?"

Theresa looked at Carleton, who pondered for a few moments. "As the crow flies, I'd say seven or eight miles, but if you are not a crow it could be a little longer."

"Is it near some place, some town . . . or village?"

Carleton said, "It could be near . . . where would you say, Lucas? Perhaps Upbridge is the nearest town."

"It's a mile or two from there," said Lucas. "The nearest village would be Tretarrant."

"Well, that is little more than a hamlet."

"Yes. Upbridge is the nearest big town."

"If you can call it big," added Lucas. "It's hardly a teeming metropolis."

"Oh, it's a pleasant little place," said Theresa. "Not that I've been there much."

"I daresay it seemed more important . . . after the death of that man."

"Well, of course the *Upbridge Times* was in great demand," said Lucas. "They had inside information. They knew the family well. I see you have a morbid interest in the place,

Rosetta. I tell you what we'll do. Tomorrow, we'll ride out there, and you can see the notorious town of Upbridge for yourself."

"I should like that," I said, my heart beating with triumph.

It was progress.

The next day Lucas and I set out. When he was in the saddle, I could almost believe that he had not changed since our first meeting.

"It's all of eight miles from here, you know," he said. "Do you feel up to it? Eight miles there and eight back? I'll tell you what we'll do. We'll have a meal there. Perhaps in good old Upbridge. Now I come to think of it, I believe there's quite a good place this side of Tretarrant. Do you feel you can do that?"

"Of course. It's a challenge."

It was, in more ways than one.

Then I was admonishing myself. What good would it do just to look at the place? Still, who knew what might come out of it?

Lucas went on. "The inn I'm thinking of is called The King's Head, I believe. Original, you'll think? The King in question is William IV — not the most popular of monarchs except in the matter of inn signs. I am always hoping to find one with Charles I. The Severed Head instead of merely The King's Head. But, brewers being the most tactful of men, he has never appeared."

I found myself laughing with him. He could forget bitterness for a while, but there was often something on hand to remind him.

We passed some blackberry bushes.

"There'll be a good crop this year," he said. "Do you remember how thrilled we were when we found some on the island?"

"We were thrilled to find anything edible."

"Sometimes I marvel . . ."

"Yes, so do I."

"I wonder what would have happened to us if the pirates had not come along?"

"Heaven knows."

"But it proved to be out of the frying pan into the fire."

"At least we escaped the fire."

"You and I did. I wonder about Player."

"Yes, I do too."

I was silent. I felt that before long I would be telling him, in spite of my determination not to. The temptation was great.

"I expect he'd be all right. He looked like one of nature's survivors to me."

"He would need to be," I said. "By the way, how far are we?"

"Getting tired?"

"Oh, no."

"I'll tell you something. You'll be a champion rider one day."

"I only want to be a reasonably good one now."

"Then you are almost there."

"Coming from you, that's a great compliment."

"Tell me the truth. Am I what is called an old curmudgeon?"

"Coming towards it. You could become entitled to it before I become a champion rider."

He laughed. "That's right," he said. "Be frank. Don't cushion me. I'm tired of being protected. Carleton and Theresa . . . I can *hear* them thinking, Now what shall we say, not to upset the poor devil?"

"Well, I shall say what I think."

"It's good to be with you, Rosetta. I hope you won't leave Trecorn for a long time."

"Well, I shall go back with James and Felicity. Felicity hates to leave her children."

He sighed. "We must make the most of the days you are here. What an excellent idea it was coming out like this. I only hope it won't be too long for you."

"Didn't you say I'd be a champion rider one day? Well, that day may not be far off."

"Good. We'll go across this field. I think it might be a shortcut."

When we had crossed the field, he pulled up.

"There's a view for you. Pleasant bit of coast, isn't it?"

"Pleasant! It's spectacular and very rugged. I'd hardly say pleasant. That doesn't fit somehow."

"You're right. Along that coast the wreckers used to ply their evil trade, enticing ships in rough seas onto the rocks out there so that they could steal their cargoes. I'll bet you anything the locals hear the cries of shipwrecked sailors on rough nights. Winds can make strange noises, and if they fall on susceptible ears, there are your ghosts!"

"Were you born a cynic?"

"I expect so. We couldn't have had two saints in the family."

"You're referring to Carleton as a saint. Why are people always slightly patronising about saints?"

"There's an easy answer to that. Because we find it so difficult to follow in their footsteps. We sinners have to feel we are slightly superior because we're having a better time."

"Do sinners have a better time than saints?"

"Oh, yes. At the same time they feel it is unfair that they should do so. That is why they have to take up that patronising attitude towards sainthood. Carleton is a good sort. He always did the right thing: learned the management of the estate, married the right girl, produced Henry the heir and the charming Jennifer; he is adored by the tenants, and the estate is more prosperous under him than it has ever been. Oh, yes, he has all the virtues. Well, you can't have too many good people around. They'd overcrowd the market and would lose much of their glory. So you see, sinners have their uses."

"It is a great advantage that Carleton is such a good squire."

"Everything about Carleton is good."

"You have your points . . . just as he has."

"Oh, but he has two sound legs to go with his."

The bitterness was there, always ready to come to the surface. I was sorry that I had allowed the conversation to get to this point.

"Everything goes right for Carleton," he said. "It always has done. Oh, don't mistake me. I know it comes right because of his nature."

"Lucas," I said soberly, "you've had bad luck. But it's done with. Nothing can change it now. There is still a lot left."

"You're right. I often think of Player and wonder what happened to him. It shows my evil nature that I can get a modicum of comfort out of it. At least I'm free."

"Yes," I said. "You're free."

"Oh, look. You can see the house over there."

"The house?"

"Perrivale Court. Look straight ahead and turn a little to the right. That's it."

At last I had seen it. It looked grand and imposing, built on a slight incline facing the sea.

"It's quite impressive," I said.

"Very ancient. Trecorn is modern in comparison."

"Could we take a closer look?"

"We could."

"Let's go, then."

"You'll sacrifice Upbridge if you do, by the way."

"I'd prefer it."

"Getting a little tired, I believe."

"Perhaps," I admitted. And all the time I was thinking, This was Simon's home since he was brought here at the age of five.

We rode on. I could see the house clearly now. It was almost like a castle — grey stone with a tower and castellations.

"It looks medieval," I said.

"Part of it undoubtedly is, but these old places are restored down the ages and sometimes you get something of a mixture."

"You went there once, didn't you?"

"Yes, but I don't remember much of it. It had completely slipped my memory until the murder. That brought it back, of course."

I was hoping that someone would emerge. Perhaps the brother who had survived or the beautiful woman who might have been the cause of it all. I should like to have had a glimpse of her.

Lucas said suddenly, "I am sure The King's Head is not far off." And as the winding road took a turn away from the coast he cried, "Ah, there it is. Only it's not The King's Head. The right place but the wrong name. It's The Sailor King. Same monarch but with a different soubriquet. Come on. We're going to leave the horses in the stables. They can do with a rest, I daresay. And while they're refreshing themselves we'll do the same. If there is time after — though I doubt it — we'll look in on Upbridge. But you mustn't be disappointed if we don't."

I assured him that I was having a thoroughly enjoyable day and should not be in the least disappointed.

I helped him dismount as unobtrusively as I could, and after seeing that the horses were in good hands we went into the parlour. There was no one else there and it was pleasant to have the room to ourselves.

The host came bustling in. "Now what shall it be, sir . . . my lady. It's only cold, I'm afraid. But I can promise you some prime beef and ham. And there's hot lentil soup."

We said that sounded just what we needed, and cider in pewter mugs was brought to us. Then we settled down to the meal.

A maid brought the food, which was excellent, and while we were eating, the host's wife came over to see that we had all we needed.

She was clearly a garrulous woman who enjoyed chatting to her customers.

She wanted to know how far we had come.

We told her we came from Trecorn Manor.

"Oh, I know it well. A fine old place . . . not so old as Perrivale, of course."

"Oh, Perrivale Court," I said eagerly. "We passed that. Is it occupied now?"

"Why, bless you, yes. The Perrivales have been there since time was. Come over with the Conqueror, so they boast, and they liked it so much they've stayed ever since."

"There are a lot like that," said Lucas. "They are pleased they got in at the start."

"Oh, there's been Perrivales round here forever. There's only Sir Tristan now, Mr. Cosmo having been — "

"Didn't I read something in the papers about that?" I said. "Oh, it was some time ago."

"That's right, you did. And at the time people could talk of nothing else. They forget quick like. People be fickle. You ask 'em about the Perrivale murder now and some of these young 'uns . . . they don't seem to know anything. I say it's history, that's what it is, and people should know it."

"Some might think you have a morbid mind to absorb and retain such knowledge," said Lucas.

She looked at him as though she thought he was a little mad and I could see the mischief rising in him so that he wanted to convince her that he was entirely so.

"Well," she said defensively, "when it did happen the place was swarming with people: reporters, detectives, and such like. Two of them stayed right under this roof. Making their investigations, they did say. So you do see, we be right on the spot."

"Very conveniently placed," put in Lucas.

"Well, I must go and see to things. Mustn't stop and chatter."

She went away and I said, "It was getting interesting. I wanted to hear more."

"Lookers-on often get a distorted vision."

"At least they are close to the scene."

Trifle was brought by the maid. It was delicious and well laced with sherry. I was glad that the hostess found it difficult to resist further gossip and while we were finishing the trifle she came up for a little more.

"People don't come here much," she confided. "Well, we get the locals like, but visitors like yourselves, they don't come this way much. It was different at the time . . . you know . . . what happened at Perrivale."

"Murder is good for business," said Lucas.

She looked at him warily and I prompted, "You must have known a good deal about the family."

"Well, being here all my life, I could hardly help it, could I then? I was born in this inn. My father had it, and then when I married William he took over. My son . . . another William . . . he'll do the same one day, I shouldn't wonder."

"A dynasty of innkeepers," murmured Lucas.

I said quickly, "It's very good to keep it in the family. It gives you a certain pride, doesn't it?"

She beamed on me. I could see that she was thinking I was nice and normal enough to enjoy a bit of gossip in spite of my companion.

"Do you see much of the Perrivales?" I asked.

"Oh, yes, they be always in and out. I can go back years. I remember when that Simon was brought here. That's the one . . . you know."

"Yes," I said. "I know."

"It must have been all of twenty years ago

288

when he came. Me and William was just married. There was a bit of a scene, I can tell 'ee, when Sir Edward brought him into the house and said he'd be staying there. Well, it stands to reason there'd be fireworks. What woman's going to stand for that, I ask you?"

"I quite agree," I said.

"Now why does a man like that bring a strange child into his home? Everyone said her ladyship was a saint to put up with it. And she wasn't the quiet sort either. A bit of a tartar by all accounts. But Sir Edward was the sort of man who didn't say much, but he'd have his own way. He said the boy would stay and stay he did."

"That was Simon," I said.

"Well, what can you expect? Can't make a silk purse out of a sow's ear, they tell you. Nor can you."

"You mean . . ."

"Well, where did he come from, I ask you? Some back street somewhere, I shouldn't wonder."

"Why should Sir Edward let him live in a back street and then decide to bring him to Perrivale Court?"

"Well, people get things on their consciences, don't they? Anyways, he came. Treated like one of them, he was. Time came they had a tutor . . . that was before they went away to school. A nice fellow, he was. He used to tell some tales about the life up there. Then he faded out and it was school for them. Simon, he went too, just like Cosmo and Tristan. And how did he repay them? He murders Mr. Cosmo. There's gratitude for you."

"But can you be sure that he was the one who committed the murder?"

"Plain as the nose on your face. Why else did he run away?"

"It certainly seems conclusive," said Lucas.

"There could be other reasons," I protested.

"Oh, a definite sign of guilt," commented Lucas.

"Yes, he was guilty all right. Jealous he was. Of course there was that widow woman, Mirabel. She was Mrs. Blanchard then. Now, of course, it's Lady Perrivale. She came down here with her father, the major, and a nicer gentleman you could not wish to meet. Her father and that young Kate; there's a piece of mischief for you. Then Mrs. Blanchard. Oh, she was a beauty . . . one of them red-haired ones. You couldn't help looking twice at her. She set her cap at Mr. Cosmo and we all knew it wouldn't be long before she was mistress of Perrivale. Cosmo was mad about her. Tristan liked her too, to say nothing of Simon. There they were, the three of them, all in love, they said, with the same widow woman. And what does Simon do? He lures Cosmo to that old farmhouse — Bindon Boys, they call it — and he just shot him. Through the head, they said. Might have got away with it too, if Mr. Tristan — Sir Tristan now — hadn't come in and caught him red-handed."

"Where is the farmhouse?"

"Oh, just along the coast. It's still there. A bit of an old ruin. They were going to put it right when this happened. After that they just let it slide. Nobody would want to live in a house where there'd been a murder. Well, I'm talking too much. William says I always do."

"It's been very interesting."

"Well," she said proudly, "it's not every place that's had a murder committed on its doorstep, you might say. Mind you, it's not everybody as wants to hear about it. When it happened people didn't want to talk about anything else."

My feelings were mixed as we came out of the inn. I was a little depressed by the opinion she had expressed of Simon. Apart from that, I had been excited to talk to someone who had actually lived near him at the time all that happened. I suspected that she had no doubt of his guilt. I was afraid that would be the general verdict. He had damned his case by running away.

As we rode off, Lucas said, "You seemed to enjoy our garrulous hostess. Did you find it so absorbing to gather a little local colour?"

"I did find it interesting."

"Murder fascinates most people. It is the mystery of this one. Though is it so mysterious?"

"Why? What do you think is the truth?"

"It's clear enough, isn't it? He ran away."

There was nothing I dared say. I wanted to shout out, He's innocent! I know he's innocent! It was hard to stop myself.

I was tired when we reached Trecorn Manor. I had so looked forward to seeing Perrivale Court, but I had discovered nothing and it had been brought home to me what strong feeling there was against Simon. Of course I had heard only one person's opinion. But always against him would be the fact that he had run away.

I was having one of my cosy sessions with Nanny Crockett. The twins were having their afternoon nap which, said Nanny Crockett, was good for them. It was Ellen's free afternoon and she had gone to visit her parents in a nearby village.

I was learning a little about Nanny Crockett's background. She had come from London to take up her first post in Cornwall.

"It was a bit of a wrench at first," she said. "Couldn't get used to it. Missed all the life. Then you get your little ones and they starts to mean something to you. I got quite caught up with the place, too, the moors and the sea and all that. You want to have a look at the place while you're here. It's worth looking at."

I was telling her I enjoyed my ride. "We went a long way. Near to a place called Upbridge. Do you know it?"

"Know it!" cried Nanny Crockett. "I'd say I know Upbridge. I lived in the place at one time. I was close to it before that."

"Did you know Perrivale Court?"

She was silent for a moment. There was a strange expression on her face which I did not understand. Then she said, "I should think I do. I lived there for nigh on eight years."

"You mean . . . in the house?"

"I do mean in Perrivale Court, Miss."

"You really lived there!"

"Well, I was nanny to the boys, wasn't I?"

"You mean Cosmo . . . Tristan . . . Simon . . . ?"

"I do. I was there in the nursery when little Simon was brought in. I remember that day. Never to be forgotten. There he was, handed over to me. Sir Edward said, 'This is Simon. He's to be treated like the others.' And there he was, a little scrap of a thing. I could see he was frightened . . . bewildered like . . . so I took him by the hand and said, 'Don't you fret, lovey. You're with Nanny Crockett and everything's all right.' Sir Edward was pleased with me and that was something rare, I can tell you. He said, 'Thank you, Nanny. Look after the boy. He'll feel a little strange at first.' We took to each other . . . Simon and me . . . from that moment."

I could scarcely suppress my excitement. "What a strange thing to do, to bring a child into the house like that. Was there any explanation?

"Oh, Sir Edward wouldn't give explanations. He was the one who said what was what and that was the end of it. If he said Simon was to be in the nursery, that was where he would be."

"Tell me about the boy. What was he like?"

"A nice little fellow, sharp as they come. Pining, he was, for someone he called Angel. I could only think it was his mother. I got little scraps from him, but you know how it is with children. They don't always see things the way we do. He talked about Angel, and there was an Aunt Ada who struck terror into his little heart. It seemed they'd buried Angel and he had been brought to Perrivale then. He couldn't abide to hear the church bells toll as they did for a funeral. I found him once hiding under the bed, hands over his ears, to shut out the noise. He'd thought this Ada was going to take him away . . . and then Sir Edward had brought him to Perrivale."

I listened. I was back there on the island, and it was Simon's voice I heard telling me how he had hidden under the table when Aunt Ada came.

"Well, there he was and there was a regular lot of gossip about that, I can tell you. Who was the boy? Why should he be brought in? Sir Edward's, they all said, and I reckon they were right. But it was strange because he wasn't the sort of man to go chasing women. All very proper he was . . . stern and upright."

"Sometimes such people have a secret life."

"You can say that again. But somehow you just couldn't picture Sir Edward up to that sort of lark. It's difficult to make you see him. Wanted everything run like clockwork. Meals on the dot . . . quite a to-do if anyone was late. You know the sort. There was a footman who'd been in the Army. He said it reminded him of a military camp. So you see, Sir Edward was not the sort who'd go chasing girls. Not like some I've heard of, where no young woman in the house was safe. They were safe enough in Perrivale Court, even the prettiest."

"Was he kind to the boy?"

"Not kind . . . not unkind. He just brought him in and said he was to be treated like the other two. Then he seemed to forget him. The servants didn't like it. You know what servants are . . . afraid someone's going to get above themselves. They didn't think young Simon had a right to be there in the nursery with the other boys, and I reckon they showed it."

"Did he mind?"

"Who's to know what goes on in their little heads? But he was a sharp one. I reckon he knew all about it."

"But you loved him."

She smiled reminiscently and tenderly. "Of all the children I ever had, he was my special boy. As for him . . . I reckon I took the place of this Angel. I was the one he'd run to if there was any trouble — and there was bound to be that. Mind you, he was older than the other two . . . just a year or two, that was all. When they were little, it was an advantage. But they soon got to know the difference. They were the sons of the house and he was the outsider. You know what children are. Cosmo — he was the eldest — gave himself airs, he did. He thought he was *Sir* already. And Tristan could be a little tartar. I've often found that with younger sons. You know what I mean? Ah, but Simon . . . he was my special one. Of all my children, he was the one. I don't know what it was. . . . perhaps being brought in like that . . . missing his mother . . . and then to think that he got himself into that mess — "

"You knew them so well," I said earnestly. "What do you think happened?"

"What I think is . . . no, what I *know* is . . . he didn't do it. He wasn't the sort. He couldn't have."

"He ran away," I said.

"Oh, that's what they all say. Well, so he did, but he'd have his reasons. He could look after himself. He was always like that. He'd find a way out of anything. That's what I remind myself . . . because I worry a bit. I wake up in the night and think, Where is he? Then I tell myself that, wherever he is, he'll know how to look after himself. I feel better then. He'll manage. When the two boys played tricks on him, he'd always get the better of them. He was clever, you see, and being in the position he was in . . . well, it made him able to look out for himself. He'd do what was best for himself at the time . . . and I reckon he'd be the one to know what was best."

"I was in the inn, The Sailor King. Mr. Lucas and I had something to eat there. The woman there seemed to think he was guilty."

"That would be Sarah Marks. What does she know? The old gossip. Thinks just because she's the wife of the landlord she knows everything. It's all for a bit of gossip with her. She'd tear anyone's reputation to bits if it gave her something to talk about. I know her . . . and I know Simon. I'm ready to stake my life on his innocence."

"Oh, Nanny, where do you think he is?"

"Well, there's no knowing, is there? He got away, all right. He'll be biding his time."

"You mean he'll come back when he's found some light to throw on the affair?"

"I think that could be."

"Would he write to you, do you think?"

"He might. He'd know it would be safe enough with me. On the other hand, he wouldn't want me to be involved. Isn't there something in the law about that?"

"I believe it's called being an accessory."

"That would be it. Though *I* wouldn't mind. I'd give a hundred pounds — if I had it — just to have a word from him."

I warmed towards her. She was an ally. I had lured her to talk. And after that I was often in the nursery when the children were asleep, so that I could chat with Nanny Crockett.

My friendship with the twins was growing. Jennifer had marked me as hers and had

298

assumed a proprietorial attitude towards me, which gave me a great deal of pleasure. I was treated to confidential details about her dolls. I learned of their foibles, of the good ones and the bad ones. There was Reggie the bear who would not take his medicine, and one-eyed Mabel — she had lost an eye in some mysterious accident — who was afraid of the dark and had to be taken into Jennifer's bed at night. I invented adventures for them to which both children listened entranced.

The time was passing too quickly and I was not looking forward to going away, but of course we should have to leave before long. Felicity was getting restive, but she did feel that our being there was good for me . . . and for Lucas, and being the unselfish creature she was, she curbed her own wishes and rejoiced for us.

Even she could not guess how much good it did me to be near Simon's home and especially to discover Nanny Crockett's involvement. Felicity was just happy to see me with Lucas and my enjoyment of the nursery.

Then one day events took a dramatic turn.

The day began ordinarily enough.

At breakfast the talk was about the heavy rainfall during the night and it turned to old Mrs. Gregory, the mother of one of the farmers.

"I owe her a visit," said Theresa. "It's nearly a month since I was there. She will be thinking I have deserted her."

I gathered that Mrs. Gregory was bedridden and her great treat was to have a visitor who would chat with her. Theresa, with her knowledge of neighbourhood affairs, was especially welcome. She told me that she visited the old lady as regularly as she could, taking some little gift of cakes or sweets or a bottle of wine . . . anything she felt might please her. But the great thing was to stay for an hour or so and chat.

"Then," put in Carleton, "there's that little matter of Mason's roof. If you get an opportunity, you might drop in and tell them that Tom Allen will be along this week."

"I'll go over in the trap this morning," said Theresa.

After breakfast Lucas and I rode out together. It was a pleasant morning, blandly mild . . . not too hot, ideal for riding. Lucas seemed more lighthearted than usual, and we took the road towards Upbridge.

He looked at me and smiled. "Your favourite ride," he said. "I believe old Snowdrop goes there automatically without waiting for instructions. I think you have a morbid mind and are fascinated by that murder."

"It's a pleasant road," I said.

That day I really did feel that I was making progress. We were a few miles from Upbridge and had decided we would turn back or we should be late for lunch. We could go on and have something at The Sailor King, but as we had not mentioned that we should not be back, we thought we had better return.

We were passing along a narrow winding road when we turned a bend and saw right ahead of us a shepherd with a flock of sheep blocking the road. We pulled up and watched and as we did so another rider came up behind us. It was a young woman of remarkable good looks. Her black riding hat was set jauntily on her red hair and her long green eyes, heavily black-lashed, regarded us with the amused look people usually wear when confronted by such an obstruction.

"The hazards of country life," she said.

"Which we must accept," replied Lucas.

"Have you come far?"

"From Trecorn Manor."

"Oh, you must be Mr. Lorimer, who was shipwrecked."

"The very same. And this is Miss Cranleigh, who was shipwrecked at the same time."

"How interesting! I'm Mirabel Perrivale."

"How nice to meet you, Lady Perrivale."

I was so overcome that I could only marvel. She was decidedly beautiful. I could imagine how impressed they must all have been when she came among them.

"Thank the sheep," she said. "Oh, hello . . . they're nearly off the road."

We moved forward. At the end of the lane the road branched in two directions. She took the one to the left; we turned right.

"Good day," we said and she had gone.

"What a beautiful woman," I said. "So she is Mirabel . . . the *femme fatale*."

"And looks the part, you must admit."

"I do. Indeed, I could do nothing else. How strange to meet her like that."

"Not really. She lives close by."

"And when you mentioned Trecorn she knew who you were."

"Well, I'm notorious in my way as she is in hers. The survivor of a shipwreck is worthy of a little notice. It's not like being concerned in a murder case, it's true, but still it is something."

When we reached Trecorn Manor one of the grooms came running out.

"There's been an accident," he said.

"Accident?" cried Lucas. "Who?"

"It's Mrs. Lorimer. The trap . . . they've just brought her back."

It was a house of mourning.

Early that day Theresa had been full of life;

now she was dead. We were all too stunned to take in this tragic truth.

Apparently she had paid her visit to Mrs. Gregory and delivered her gifts; she had chatted with her for an hour and then left. On her way to Mason's farm she had taken the hilly path. It was a road she had taken many times and had not been considered dangerous. But there had been a heavy fall of rain and there was a sudden fall of earth from the hillside. It must have dropped right in front of the horse, which took fright and bolted, taking the trap down the slope into the valley below. And thus . . . Theresa had been killed and Trecorn Manor had become a tragic household.

Felicity said to me, "I'm glad we're here. Not that we can do anything to comfort Carleton. They were so happy together . . . so suited . . . and what on earth will he do now?"

"Poor, poor Carleton. He is too shocked to realise fully what has happened. Do you think we should stay awhile?"

"Well, I suppose we must wait a bit. We couldn't discuss anything with them at the moment. Perhaps after the funeral . . . let's wait and see how things go."

When the opportunity came I asked Lucas if he thought we should go.

"Oh, not yet, please," he said. "My poor brother is in a state of numbed misery. I don't think he can accept what's happened just yet. We have to think of him first of all. He relied on Theresa more than even he realised. They were quite devoted to each other. I'm afraid we all took Theresa too much for granted: her good nature . . . her unselfishness . . . her way of playing down all the good she did to us all. We now see what a wonderful person she was. Carleton has been lucky . . . but that means it is going to be so much worse for him to face up to what he has lost. He'll miss her every minute of the day. We shall all miss her terribly. Please don't go yet, Rosetta."

"James will have to go back to his work."

"Yes . . . and he'll be coming here soon to collect Felicity."

I nodded.

"But that doesn't mean *you* have to go."

"But of course I shall have to go with them. I shall have to leave when they do."

"I can't see why. *You* haven't work to get back to."

"I . . . I don't think I should be wanted here . . . at a time like this."

"That's nonsense. I know your presence will help."

I told Felicity what he had said.

"He's right," was her verdict. "You've made a difference to him. I think you've been able to talk to him about that terrible time."

"But I couldn't stay here without you."

She wrinkled her brow. "I daresay your Aunt Maud would think you ought to go home. But, after all, I don't see why you shouldn't stay on a little. James will have to go back, of course, and I shall go with him."

It was left at that, and James arrived very soon after. His shock was great. By this time we were all learning something of the enormity of the tragedy which had overtaken this house.

Nanny Crockett said, "The place will never be the same again. Mrs. Lorimer was the one who saw it all went like clockwork. This is going to make a very big difference. But it's the children I'm most worried about. They're going to miss their mother. Oh, they've got me and they've got you now, but by golly, they are going to miss her. She was always in and out of the nursery. They used to wait for her visits. I don't know what this is going to do to them."

It was such a sad time. I was so desperately sorry for Carleton. He walked about bewildered like a man in a dream. Lucas said it was impossible to discuss anything. He could only talk about Theresa.

Lucas himself was deeply affected. "This is the worst thing that could have happened to Carleton," he said. "I've been a selfish brute moaning about my own troubles, telling my-self he was the lucky one, everything fell to him and so on ... and now there he is. There's no comforting him."

I was dreading the funeral. People came to the church from all over the neighbourhood. This was genuine mourning. Theresa had been loved and respected by so many.

Nanny Crockett kept the children in the nursery. I wondered what they were thinking as I listened to the dismal tolling of the bell. I thought of Simon who, years before, had heard a similar bell. To him it had meant the sound of doom, the loss of Angel and the plummetting into the unknown.

When everybody had left and the house was quiet, I went up to the nursery. Nanny Crockett was dressed in deep black. She shook her head sadly.

"They keep asking questions," she said. "What do you tell such little ones? They don't understand. 'She's gone to Heaven,' I say. 'When will she be back?' they ask. 'Well,' I say, 'when people go to Heaven they stay a little while.' Jennifer said, 'It would be bad manners to go away too soon, wouldn't it?' I nearly broke down. Then she said, 'She's having tea with God, I think, and the angels will be there.' It breaks your heart."

The children had heard us and came running out.

They stood still, looking at me, their faces solemn. They sensed that something terrible was happening and everyone was very sad about it.

Jennifer looked at me and her face suddenly crumpled.

"I want my mummy," she said.

I held out my arms and she ran to me. Henry followed her. I held them tightly.

That decided me. I could not leave immediately. I must stay for a while.

I was glad I stayed. I felt I was doing something useful and that I brought a modicum of comfort to that stricken household.

I spent a great deal of time in the nursery with the children at that hour when it had been their mother's custom to be with them, and between us Nanny Crockett and I managed to get them over the first tragic days of heartbreak. They were too young to understand fully what had happened and we smoothed away some of that uneasiness which they would inevitably feel; there were times when they would be absorbed in something and forget, but sometimes one of them would wake in the night and cry for Mummy. The other would wake and share the terrible loss. But usually either Nanny Crockett or I was there to offer comfort.

Carleton continued to be dazed. The blow was all the sharper for being unexpected. Fortunately there was a good deal of work to be done on the estate; that kept him busy and he was met with sympathy and understanding wherever he went. I knew he would never be the same again. He was particularly shattered because his life had followed an even stream of contentment and he had expected it to go on doing so. I knew at times he found it hard to believe that this had really happened to him, and he seemed unable to grasp that Theresa was no longer there and never would be again.

Lucas had grown philosophical. *He* did not expect life to flow peacefully. Tragedy had already struck him and he was not surprised that it had come again. Perhaps that was why he was able to face it more realistically.

He said to me, "You have done a great deal for us. It was fortunate for us that you were here when it happened."

"I wish I could do more," I told him.

"You and Nanny Crockett have been wonderful with the children. As for Carleton . . .

only time will help him."

We took short rides together, and the days began to pass.

The Governess

I could not stay at Trecorn Manor indefinitely and I was not by any means looking forward to returning to London. I had come to Trecorn Manor with the hope of discovering something which would help me unravel the mystery; now I was seeing how ridiculously optimistic I had been.

Theresa's death had temporarily forced that other tragedy into the background of my mind, but my obsession was returning. I sometimes felt that if I could get into Perrivale Court, really become acquainted with some of the main actors in the drama, I might make some progress. I had been foolish to hope that just because I was staying near the house I might accomplish this. I felt inadequate and alone. There were times when I was on the verge of taking Lucas into my confidence. He was clever, subtle; he might have ideas. On the other hand, he could dismiss my belief in Simon as romantic folly. In his realist way he would say, "The man was found with the gun in his hand and he ran away and would not face investigation. That speaks for itself. Simply because he happened to show a certain resourcefulness and helped save our lives does not make him innocent."

No, I could not entirely trust Lucas, but how I longed to confide in someone . . . someone who would work with me, join in the search . . . someone who believed in Simon's innocence.

There was no help for it. I should have to go home. I had already stayed on two weeks after Felicity had left with James, and in the first place I had only intended to stay one.

When I thought of returning to Bloomsbury and the domination of Aunt Maud I was distinctly depressed. I could not face that. Moreover, I had to consider my future. My fantastic adventure had put a bridge between my childhood and my adult life.

I felt lost and lonely. If only, I kept saying to myself — if only I could prove Simon's innocence. If only he could return and we could be together.

We had forged a bond between us which it seemed could never be broken. Lucas had shared that adventure with us but he was not involved as we were. Close as he had been to us during those days, he had never shared the secret and that set him apart. He was very perceptive. I often wondered whether he had guessed anything.

How many times a day I was on the point of pouring out my feelings to him . . . telling him everything!

He might have helped a great deal in solving the mystery. But did I dare tell him?

And so I pondered, and as each day drew to a close I knew that I could not go on in this way. I should have to make some decision sooner or later. Should I give up this quest which seemed hopeless? Should I return to Bloomsbury and let myself fall into Aunt Maud's capable hands?

One of my greatest comforts was talking to Nanny Crockett. She was my strongest link with Simon. She loved him as, I admitted now, I did; and that was a great bond between us.

She was a compulsive talker, and the murder at Bindon Boys was as absorbing a topic to her as it was to me. As a matter of fact she would return to the subject without my prompting her, and gradually certain facts began to emerge which were of vital importance to me.

She even knew something about the present Perrivale household.

She said, "I used to go over now and then. That was just before it all blew up. You see, when the boys went to school I took a post in Upbridge . . . quite close really. A dear little thing she was, named Grace. I got very fond of her. She helped to make up a bit for the loss of my boy. Not that that was a dead loss. Simon wasn't the sort to let that happen. He used to come over to see me, and sometimes I'd go over to Perrivale and have a cup of tea with the housekeeper there. Mrs. Ford . . . she was a friend of mine. We'd always got on. She ran things over there . . . still does. Even got the butler under her thumb. She's that sort of woman — good-hearted enough but knows how to keep things in order. Well, that's what a housekeeper should do, I reckon. Not that I'd have had her interfering in the nursery. She never tried that on me, and we were the best of friends always — or almost always — and I'd be over there for a cup of tea and it was nice to catch up with the news."

"So it was only when you came here that you didn't see them."

"Oh, I still go over now and then. If Jack Carter's taking a load of something over Up-bridge way he'll come and pick me up. He'll drop me at the house and when he's done his business come for me and bring me home. It makes a nice little outing, and it keeps me in touch with them over at Perrivale."

"So you still go over to Perrivale Court!"

"Well, it's a month or two since I was last there. And when all that was on I didn't go at all. It wouldn't have seemed right somehow . . . there was the police and everyone prying . . . if you know what I mean."

"When was the last time you went?"

"It would be three months ago, I reckon. It don't seem the same now. Never has . . . since Simon went."

"That's some time ago."

"Yes . . . some time. When there's been a murder in a place it seems to change everything."

"Tell me about the household. I'd like to hear."

"You're like everyone else, Miss. You can't resist a murder."

"Well, this is a mysterious one, isn't it? And you don't believe Simon did it."

"That I don't. And I'd give a lot to prove it."

"Perhaps the answer is somewhere in the house."

"Now what do you mean by that?"

"Someone must have killed Cosmo, and perhaps someone in the house knows who did."

"Someone somewhere knows the truth, that's for sure."

"Tell me about the house."

"Well, there was Sir Edward, wasn't there?"

"He's dead now."

"Yes. Died about the time of the murder, didn't he? He was very ill before it happened . . . not expected to live."

"And old Lady Perrivale?"

"She was a bit of a tartar. One of them Northerners, different from us. She'd been used to having her own way and Sir Edward he let her . . . except when it was something like bringing the boy into the house. She didn't want that . . . natural like, but he said it was to be and be it was. Well, there she was, never forgetting that it was *her* money that saved Perrivale. Mrs. Ford said the wood-worm and deathwatch beetle would have done for the place, and pretty quick, if she hadn't come into the family in time. And she had her boys, Cosmo and Tristan. She was proud of them. And then Simon comes. It might have been better for the poor little mite if there'd been open ructions, I used to think some-times, rather than all that snide picking on him. It wasn't only her ladyship. There were the servants and others. I wouldn't have had that in my nursery . . . but I've told you all this before."

"I like to hear it, and a bit more comes out every time."

"Well, as I was saying, up at Perrivale it wasn't a very happy house. Things wasn't quite right between Sir Edward and her ladyship. You can always tell. Mind you, he was always very proper . . . always treated her like the lady of the house . . . but you could tell. Her ladyship was one of those women who'd have had her own way with any other man. But Sir Edward, he was a funny one. He was the master but it was her money that had saved the place. She didn't want anyone to forget that. And Sir Edward, he was that strict. If a girl got up to a bit of foolishness with one of the men, it would be wedding bells for them before there was the first sign of a bundle of trouble. It was prayers in the hall every morning and everybody in the house had to attend."

We were silent for a while. She sat there, smiling into the distance, seeing the past, I knew.

"Then came the day when the boys went away to school and they didn't want Nanny Crockett any more. But I got this job in Upbridge . . . a stone's throw away, you might say, so I didn't feel quite cut off. A nice little thing, Grace was. Her parents were the Burrowses, highly respected in Upbridge. Doctor Burrows was her father. She was the only one. I was with her right till the time they sent her

316

to school. She used to say to me, 'You'll be nanny to my babies, won't you, Nanny Crockett . . . when I get some?' And I used to tell her that nannies get old like everyone else and there comes a time when they have to give a little thought to their own comfort as they once did to that of their little ones. It's sad, saying goodbye to them. You get attached. They're your children while you've got them. That's how it is."

"Yes, I know. The wrench is very sad."

"I've been lucky with mine. Simon used to come over to see me, and now and then I'd walk over and have a cup of tea with Mrs. Ford."

"And after Grace Burrows, you came here?"

She nodded. "It was in my last year at the Burrowses that it happened."

"So," I said, hearing the note of excitement in my own voice as I spoke, "you were close when it happened?"

"I saw her once or twice."

"Saw whom?"

"The young widow."

"What did you think of her?"

She was silent. Then she said, "With a woman like that around, things happen. There's something dangerous about them. Some said she was a witch. They go in for that sort of thing round here. They like to think of people riding out on broomsticks and cooking up mischief. Well, there was mischief at Perrivale after she appeared on the scene."

"So you think she was involved in it?"

"Most seem to think so. We hadn't seen many of her sort down here. She looked different, even. All that red hair and them green eyes that didn't go with the hair somehow. All of a sudden there was this widow among us with a child . . . and the child was almost as strange as the mother. Now her father, he was different. Oh, everybody liked the major. He was jolly with everybody. Always passed the time of day. A very nice gentleman. Quite different from her."

"Tell me about the child. You know a great deal about children. What did you think of her?"

"It's my own I know, all their little ways and habits; I can read them like a book. But that one . . . well, I never had much to do with her . . . nor should I want to. I reckon she'll be another like her mother. Kate, her name is, I think. A nice ordinary sort of name. Different from her mother's: Mirabel."

"Mine is Rosetta. You probably think that's odd too."

"Oh, no. That's pretty. It's Rose really and what's nicer than a nice rose?"

"Tell me what you found out about Mirabel and Kate?"

"Only that they were a peculiar pair. They came with her father and took Seashell Cottage, and it was clear that the widow woman was looking for a nice rich husband. So she settled on the Perrivales. They said she could have had any of them, and she picked Cosmo. He was the eldest. He'd get the estates and the title . . . so it had to be Cosmo."

"Did the family approve of this woman coming from nowhere? I should have thought Sir Edward, with his conventional tastes, might have objected."

"Oh, Sir Edward was too far gone. As for Lady Perrivale, she was as taken with Mirabel as any of them. Story was that the major was an old friend of hers. He'd married her old school friend and Mirabel was the result of that marriage. She had wanted them to come and settle in Cornwall in the first place. I don't know how true that is, but that's how the story goes. The major was always up at Perrivale. Oh, she was very taken with him. He's the sort who'd get on with anyone. Oh, yes, Lady Perrivale was all for the marriage."

"And then . . . it happened."

"They all thought Simon, like the others, was smitten by her. That was where the motive came in."

319

"He didn't do it, Nanny," I said earnestly. "Why should he have done? I don't believe he was in love with that woman."

"No," she said. "He'd have too much sense. Besides, it didn't mean that because Cosmo was dead she would turn to him. No . . . that was not the answer. How I wish I knew what was."

"You believe in Simon's innocence, don't you, Nanny? I mean you believe absolutely?"

"I do. And I know that boy better than any."

"Do any of us really know other people?"

"I know my *children*," she said staunchly.

"If you could help him, would you, Nanny?"

"With all my heart."

And then I told her. I went through the whole story, beginning with our encounter on deck, to the time when we parted company outside the Embassy in Constantinople.

She was astounded.

"And you've been here all this time and not told me before?"

"I couldn't be entirely sure of you. I had to protect Simon. You understand?"

She nodded slowly. Then she turned to me and gripped my hand.

"Nanny," I said solemnly. "More than anything, I want to solve this. I want to find the truth."

"That's what I want," she said.

"You know a great deal about them. You have access to the house."

She nodded.

I said with a sudden upward surging of hope, "Nanny, you and I will work together. We're going to prove Simon's innocence."

Her eyes were shining. I felt happier than I had for a long time.

"We'll do it," I said, "together."

What a difference it made to share my secret with Nanny Crockett. We talked continuously, going over the same ground again and again, but it was surprising how ideas occurred to us as we did so. We had convinced ourselves that someone in that house knew who had killed Cosmo Perrivale, and we shared the burning desire to find out the truth and prove Simon's innocence.

A few days after I had taken Nanny Crockett into my confidence, Jack Carter left a message at the house to say he was taking a load over Upbridge way and if Nanny Crockett would like a lift he'd be more than happy with the company and do her a good turn at the same time, for he knew how she liked the little trip.

It seemed like an answer to our prayers. Nanny Crockett said that if I would look after

321

the children, she would go; and she set off in a state of great excitement.

It seemed a long day. I did not see Lucas, as I spent the whole time with the children. I played with them, read to them, and told them stories. They were quite content, but I was counting the minutes till Nanny's return.

I do not know what I expected she would find out in that short time.

She came back in a mood of suppressed excitement, but she would tell me nothing until the children had had their supper of milk and bread and butter and were safely tucked up in bed.

Then we settled down to our chat.

"Well," she said. "It was a blessing that I went. It seems that Madam up there is in a bit of a state."

"You mean Lady Perrivale?"

"I mean *young* Lady Perrivale."

She folded her hands on her lap and surveyed me with great satisfaction, and, like some people who have exciting news to impart, she seemed to derive a certain pleasure in holding it back for a while, savouring the pleasure she was going to give me.

"Yes, yes, Nanny," I prompted impatiently.

"Well, it's nothing unusual to them up there. It happens regular, but they are getting desperate. It's Madam Kate."

"Do tell me what she's done, Nanny, and what has it to do with us?"

She pulled herself back in her chair and smiled at me knowingly, which was irritating to me, being so very much in the dark.

"Well," she went on, "it's like this. The governess up there has walked out again. It's a regular way with governesses up there. None of them can stand young Kate for more than a week or so. But it throws the household in a turmoil. Really, this Kate must be a bit of a demon if you ask me. Well, there's Mrs. Ford telling me that they're all praying for a governess who gives Kate the education she ought to have — and keeps her out of the way of the grown-ups, I wouldn't mind reckoning. And how they can't, how they're all in despair, and young Kate is laughing her head off because the last thing she wants in the house is a governess. There's been goodness knows how many . . . and not one stayed. Mrs. Ford reckons that soon it will get round and they wouldn't even give it a trial. She's a little imp, that Kate. Wants her own way. Mrs. Ford said if they don't get someone to control her sometime, governesses won't be the only ones who are leaving. Well, that's how it was up at Perrivale."

She paused and looked at me steadily.

"I said to Mrs. Ford, 'I wonder . . .' and she looked at me sharply and said, 'What do you wonder, Nanny?' I said, 'Now I don't know whether I'm speaking out of turn . . . but an idea has just come to me.'"

"Yes, Nanny," I said, a little breathlessly.

"I said to her, 'Well, I don't know. I may be speaking out of turn so don't bank on it,' I said, 'but there's a young lady staying at the house . . . a well-educated young lady. Best schools and all that. Well, she was saying the other day she thought she'd like to do something. Not that she needs to, mind. But she was just feeling a bit restless like. Well, she's very good with my two . . . likes teaching them things. Well . . . I don't know, I'm sure. It's just a thought that came into my head.' You should have seen Mrs. Ford's face. I reckon it would be a feather in her cap if she could find them a governess."

"Nanny, what *are* you suggesting?"

"Well, we always said if you could get into the house. . . . We reckoned the secret was tucked away in there somewhere. And there's no way of finding out when you're outside it."

As the possibility swept over me I felt enormously excited.

"Do you think they would take me?"

"They'd jump at you. You should have seen Mrs. Ford's face. She kept saying, 'Will you

324

ask her? Do you think she would?' I played it very cautious. I wanted to make them think you might need a bit of persuading. 'I can only just mention it,' I told her. 'I can't vouch for anything. . . . I don't know, I'm sure.' But she wouldn't leave it alone. She was on it like a ton of bricks."

"I've had no experience. How do I know if I could do it?"

"Look how you are with the twins."

"They're only five years old."

"That's true enough. But when Mrs. Ford told me, I thought it sounded like manna from Heaven, as they say."

"It does look rather like that. I've longed and longed for an opportunity."

"Well, now here it is."

"What else did Mrs. Ford say?"

"She did wonder how long you'd stay . . . if you came. She didn't understand how any-body — particularly someone who didn't have to work — would want to be governess to Miss Kate. I couldn't tell her that there was rather a special reason. Then she stopped talking like that, being afraid I might put you off. She said, 'Well, perhaps Miss Cranleigh might be able to manage her . . . perhaps it's because the others haven't been much good,' going on like that. Ever so anxious, she was, to get me to ask you. She'd be in high favour with her ladyship if she was the one to find a governess who stayed. I told her not to hope for too much but I'd have a word with you."

I had been so astounded by the suggestion that it was difficult for me to take in its implications at first. I was trying to be calm. I should go into a strange household as a sort of higher servant. What would my father think? Or Aunt Maud? They would never allow it. Moreover, what would my position be with a child who had a reputation for making life intolerable for past holders of the post?

And yet . . . only a few hours before I had been praying for a chance. I had seen clearly that unless I could get a footing in that house, unless I could learn something about its inhabitants, I should never discover the truth behind the murder of Cosmo Perrivale.

Even while I hesitated I knew I had to seize this God-given opportunity with both hands.

Nanny Crockett was watching me intently; a slow smile spread across her face.

She knew that I would go to Perrivale Court.

It was soon quite clear that I should be very welcome at Perrivale Court. Lady Perrivale must have despaired of ever getting a governess for her daughter, and the suggestion that I might take the post was received with enthusiasm.

Lady Perrivale sent the carriage over to Trecorn Manor to take me to Perrivale Court so that we could discuss the matter without delay.

I was relieved that Lucas was not there when I left, my trepidation overcome by the elation I felt at the prospect of making headway in my self-appointed task.

I had sworn Nanny Crockett to secrecy about the project, for I was anxious that Lucas should not know anything about it until it was definitely settled. I knew he would be astonished and would ask awkward questions and of course attempt to dissuade me, for, not knowing my reasons, he would naturally find it difficult to understand why I should take such a post.

I had ceased to marvel at the amazing turn of fate which had brought me this opportunity. So many strange things had happened to me in the recent past that I was prepared for anything. I supposed that when one stepped out of the conventional life one must be prepared for the unexpected and unusual. And there I was, speeding along the road in a splendid carriage drawn by two noble horses, one black, one white, and driven by a coachman in the smart Perrivale livery.

We arrived at Perrivale Court. In the distance I could see the sea. It was a light blue today, in a gentle mood, smooth and benign. Whenever I came face to face with the sea — whatever its mood — I would visualise that raging angry torrent which had played such havoc with my life and that of many others. I would never trust the sea again. And if I lived at Perrivale I should see it every day. I should be reminded.

If I lived at Perrivale? I must. I was becoming more and more certain how imperative it was that I should secure this post.

There was an air of timelessness about the place. The grey stone walls, battered by the winds of centuries, gave it the impression of a fortress, and the machicolations the look of a castle. Lucas had said it had been restored so often it had lost its original identity. That might be so, and I found it difficult to analyse my feelings as I passed under the gatehouse into a courtyard where the carriage drew up.

A door was immediately opened and a woman appeared. She was middle-aged, verging on the elderly, and instinct told me that this was Mrs. Ford.

She had come to welcome her protégée personally and she showed clearly that she was very pleased that I had come.

"Come along in, Miss Cranleigh," she said. "I am Mrs. Ford. Lady Perrivale would like to see you at once. I am so glad you could come."

It was an effusive greeting, hardly the sort that a governess would expect, but when I reminded myself of the reason for it I was less euphoric.

"Nanny Crockett has told me *all* about you," said Mrs. Ford.

Not all, I thought. I could imagine Nanny Crockett's glowing terms, and I was sure she credited me with qualities I did not possess.

"I'll take you to her ladyship right away," she said. "Will you follow me?"

We were in a hall, long and lofty, the walls of which were adorned with weapons, and there was a huge fireplace with inglenooks and seats on either side; the floor was tiled and our footsteps rang out as we walked across to the stairs. It was typical of many such halls except for the stained glass windows at one end with their beautiful shades of ruby red and sapphire blue which were reflected on the tiled floor. Placed strategically at the side of the staircase like a sentinel was a suit of armour. It seemed lifelike and I could not help glancing uneasily at it as I followed Mrs. Ford up the stairs.

We went along the corridor until we came to a door at which Mrs. Ford knocked.

"Come in," said a voice.

Mrs. Ford threw open the door and stood

aside for me to go in.

She called, "Miss Cranleigh, my lady."

And there she was, seated in a thronelike chair which was covered in dark velvet. She wore a gown of emerald green which was very becoming to her red-haired beauty. I noticed a gold necklace in the form of a snake about her neck. Her glorious hair was piled on top of her head and her green eyes glittered with pleasure.

"Miss Cranleigh," she cried. "Do come in. Thank you, Mrs. Ford. Sit here, Miss Cranleigh, and we can have our little talk."

She was immensely affable. Clearly she was very eager that I should accept the post. She must be desperate, I thought, and I shuddered to think what the child might be like.

"Mrs. Ford tells me that you want to come here to teach my daughter."

"It was suggested to me that you were in need of a governess," I replied.

"Kate's last governess had to leave in rather a hurry, and naturally I do not want her studies to be interrupted too long."

"No, of course not. I must tell you that I have never taught before."

"Well, we all have to start somewhere."

"Your daughter is eight years old, I believe . . . or is it nine?"

"She is just nine."

"She will be in need of advanced education soon. Do you propose to send her to school in the near future?"

I saw a look of dismay in the green eyes. Was she imagining this daughter of hers being expelled from school after school?

"We had no plans for a school yet."

We? That would be Tristan, the girl's step-father. Images flashed into my mind. I saw him coming into the farmhouse . . . finding his brother dead and Simon standing there with the gun in his hand. I must stop my mind from wandering on. This house would be full of such reminders. But this was what I had wanted. Those people who had been nothing but names to me were now going to take on flesh and blood, and I had to assess their part in the drama if I were to find out the truth.

She was saying, "Mrs. Ford tells me you are very good with children."

"She would be referring to the two at Trecorn Manor. They are only five years old."

"Oh, yes . . . Trecorn Manor. You are visiting there. We met, didn't we? Those sheep. What a terrible time Mr. Lorimer had. That ghastly shipwreck."

"Yes," I said. "I was shipwrecked too."

"What a dreadful experience! I heard about it from Mrs. Ford. But you have emerged, fortunately, in better shape than poor Mr. Lorimer."

"Yes, indeed I was more fortunate."

She was silent for a few seconds, denoting sympathy. Then she said brightly, "We should be so happy if you came. It would be good for Kate to have a . . . lady . . . to teach her. Mrs. Ford tells me that you have had an excellent education."

"There was nothing outstanding about it."

This was becoming a most unusual interview. I seemed all the time to be stressing why she should not employ me and she seemed determined at all cost that she should.

"We have rather pleasant nursery quarters here. You know, the family's children have been brought up there over the years. That makes a difference . . . somehow."

I was trying to shut out of my mind images of that frightened little boy being brought into the nursery by a determined Sir Edward and by good fortune falling into the hands of loving Nanny Crockett.

It was obvious that my next words unnerved her.

"Perhaps I could meet your daughter."

It was the last thing she wanted. There was apprehension in the green eyes. She was clearly thinking that one look at the little monster would be enough to make me decline. I felt almost sorry for her. She was so anxious to find a governess — any governess, I imagined — for her daughter.

Never could a prospective governess have been in such a position. I was amused at the feeling of power which came over me. It would be entirely my decision. I knew I was not going to enjoy my work, but at least I should not have to cringe before my employer. I knew I was coming to this house for Simon's sake and I was certain that I should discover some of its secrets which, with luck, might lead me to the truth.

"She may not, of course, be in her room," she said.

"I think we should meet before we make the decision," I said firmly, and somehow managed to convey that this was an ultimatum.

Reluctantly she went to the bell rope and in a few moments a maid appeared.

"Would you bring Miss Kate to me?" she said.

"Yes, my lady."

Lady Perrivale looked so nervous that I wondered what I was going to discover. If she is quite impossible, I thought, I shall at least have a chance to look around, and it it is really bad I can always follow the example of the other governesses and leave.

When she came, I was surprised rather

agreeably, but that was perhaps because I was expecting something worse.

She was very like her mother. Her hair was a little less bright, her eyes a little less green. There was a hint of blue in them but that might have been because she was wearing a blue dress; her lashes and brows were inclined to be sandy and her mother owed a great deal to her dark brows and luxuriant lashes for her arresting good looks. But it was obvious at once that she was her mother's daughter.

"Kate, my dear," said Lady Perrivale. "This is Miss Cranleigh. If you are lucky she may be your new governess."

The girl looked at me appraisingly. "I don't like governesses," she said. "I want to go away to school."

"That's not very polite, is it?" asked Lady Perrivale mildly.

"No," said her daughter.

"And shouldn't we be?"

"Perhaps you should, Mama. I don't want to be."

I laughed and said boldly, "I can see you have a great deal to learn."

"I never learn unless I want to."

"That's not very clever, is it?"

"Why not?"

"Because you will remain ignorant."

"If I want to be ignorant, I'll be ignorant."

"It is your choice, of course," I replied mildly, "but I never heard of any wise person wanting to be ignorant."

I looked at Lady Perrivale and I could see that her fear I would reject her daughter was growing.

"Really, Kate," she said. "Miss Cranleigh has come all the way from Trecorn Manor to see you."

"I know. And it's not 'all the way.' It's not really very far."

"You must assure her that you will try to be a good pupil or she may decide not to come."

Kate shrugged her shoulders.

I was surprised to find myself feeling almost sorry for Lady Perrivale. I wondered why she, who looked as though she might be the sort of woman to have her own way, could allow a child to behave so.

I fancied Kate felt a certain antagonism to her mother and at the root of her behaviour might be a wish to discountenance her. I wondered why.

I said, "If I am coming to teach Kate, I think we should get to know each other. Perhaps she could show me the schoolroom."

Kate turned to face me. I could see she was finding me very different from the governesses to whom she was accustomed, poor needy women desperately eager for the post and fearing to do anything that might mean losing it.

I felt more alive than I had for a long time. I was actually in Simon's old home and these were the people who had figured in the drama. Moreover, I was a little stimulated at the prospect of battles to come with this child.

"If you think . . . " began Lady Perrivale uneasily.

"Yes," said Kate. "I'll show you the schoolroom."

"That's good," I said.

Lady Perrivale rose as if to accompany us.

I turned to her. "Shall Kate and I get to know each other . . . alone?" I suggested. "We shall know better then whether we can get along."

I was not sure which was greater, her relief or her apprehension. She was glad to end this interview but she was afraid of what would ensue when I was alone with Kate.

The girl led me up the stairs, taking two at a time.

"It's a long way up," she said over her shoulder.

"Schoolrooms usually are."

"Miss Evans used to puff and pant coming up the stairs."

"Miss Evans being the unfortunate lady who tried to teach you before?" I asked.

She gave a little giggle. Poor Miss Evans! I thought. At the mercy of such a creature.

"It's not very nice up there," she went on. "It's haunted, you know. Are you afraid of ghosts?"

"Never having made the acquaintance of any, it is difficult to say."

Again she giggled. "You wait," she said. "They're very frightening. There are always ghosts in old houses like this. They come out in the night when you are asleep — particularly if they don't like you, and they never like strangers."

"Oh, don't they? I should have thought it was members of the family whom they would come back to see."

"You don't know anything about ghosts."

"Do you?"

"Of course. I know they do horrid things . . . like clanging chains and frightening people in the night."

"Perhaps you have been listening to gossip."

"You wait," she said ominously and with plans in her eyes. "If you come here, you'll be frightened out of your wits. I promise you."

"Thanks for the promise. So this is it?"

"It's at the top of the house. You can look right down into the well . . . because the stairs go round and round. Someone hanged herself once from these banisters. She was a governess."

"Perhaps she had a pupil rather like you."

That made her laugh and she looked at me with some appreciation.

"Moreover," I went on, "it would have been rather a difficult operation and she must have been very skilful. So this is the schoolroom. What books have you?"

"A lot of boring old things."

"You mean they bore you. That's probably because you don't understand them."

"How do you know what I understand?"

"Well, I gathered from you that you never learn anything unless you want to, and I surmise that very often you don't want to, which would account for your ignorance."

"You're a funny sort of governess."

"How do you know? I haven't been a governess yet."

"I'll give you a piece of advice," she said conspiratorially.

"That's good of you. What is it?"

"Don't come here. I'm not very nice, you know."

"Oh, yes. I had already discovered that."

"Why . . . ? How . . . ?"

"You've told me yourself, and in any case it's rather obvious, isn't it?"

"I'm not so bad really. Only I don't like to be told what to do."

"That's not very unusual, you know. You're

just going along with the common herd. But there are people who want to learn and they do. They are the people who have rewarding lives."

She stared at me with a puzzled look.

I said, "I have seen the schoolroom. Now I will go back to your mother."

"You're going to tell her how awful I am and that you don't like me and you won't come here."

"Is that what you want me to tell her?" She did not answer, which mildly surprised and pleased me. I went on. "Do you often tell people what they are going to do?"

"Well, of course you're not coming. You're not poor like Miss Evans. You don't *have* to. Nobody would come here unless they had to."

"If you would like to take me to your mother, I should be pleased. If not, I daresay I can find my own way."

We surveyed each other like two generals on a battlefield. I could see that in spite of herself she was mildly interested in me. I had not behaved like an ordinary governess, and she had certainly not acted like a prospective pupil. But I sensed that she had — as I admitted to myself that I had — enjoyed our little bout of sparring. I thought her a spoilt child, but there was another reason — as there usually is — why she behaved as she did. I could not grasp what her attitude towards her mother was, but I felt a growing curiosity and I wanted to find out.

Oddly enough, this difficult girl, who had driven governesses away in despair, attracted me in an odd way. I wanted to know more of her. I knew I was coming to the house in any case, but, having met Lady Perrivale and her daughter, I was finding myself intrigued by their personalities.

Kate pushed past me and started to go downstairs. "This is the way," she said.

I followed her back to the room where we had left Lady Perrivale. She looked up anxiously as though she were ready to accept defeat.

I said, "Kate has shown me the schoolroom. It is very light and airy and in such a pleasant spot . . . at the top of the house."

I paused, savouring my power with a certain complacency, then I went on.

"I have decided that, providing we can agree on the usual details, I should like to come on trial . . . on both sides . . . for, say, a month and if at the end of that time we feel the arrangement is satisfactory we can plan from there."

Her smile was dazzling. She had made up her mind that a short time with Kate would have decided me. She was ready to promise anything, and the salary she offered I was sure was beyond what was normally paid to a governess.

"When — ?" she asked eagerly.

"What about Monday, the start of the week? You see, I have not far to come."

"That would be admirable."

Kate was looking at me in astonishment. I said coolly, "If the carriage could take me back to Trecorn Manor . . . ?"

"But of course," said Lady Perrivale. "We shall look forward to seeing you on Monday."

I felt triumphant as I was driven back. I was going to succeed, I knew. I was going to find Cosmo's murderer. And then I should have to find Simon. How, I did not know. But I'd think of that when the time came.

I kept thinking how lucky it was that I had confided in Nanny Crockett, for that had certainly taken me along a few steps further. I was certain that I was on the only possible road to discovery.

Nanny Crockett was waiting for me, and she could hardly restrain her impatience. I did not keep her long in suspense.

"I'm starting on Monday," I said.

She flew at me and hugged me. "I knew you would. I knew it!"

"Lady Perrivale was determined. No applicant for a post can ever have had such an extraordinary interview. You would have thought she was the one who wanted the job."

"Well, Mrs. Ford told me how it would be." She looked at me anxiously. "Did you see . . . the girl?"

I nodded. "She's a challenge," I said. "And if it is possible to find the truth, I have to."

"For Simon's sake. Poor lamb . . . out there in the wilds somewhere. If only he could come home to us."

"We're going to succeed, Nanny. We are on the way."

Now that I had come so far, I had to face the difficulties. I should have to tell my father that I was taking a post as governess. That would bewilder him. And I did not forget Aunt Maud. I was sure she would be most disapproving because becoming a governess would not enhance my chances of what she would call a good marriage. But by the time they heard, I should be installed in Perrivale Court.

I should have to write to Felicity. I wondered what her reaction would be. If she knew the truth behind it, of course, she would understand, for she did realise how restless I was. She herself had been a governess, but I had been a very different child from Kate, and

Felicity and I had had good times together from the beginning.

I was unprepared for Lucas's reaction.

I did not see him until dinner that evening. It had become a dismal meal since Theresa's death. We were all conscious of the place where she used to sit at one end of the table opposite Carleton. Now that place was empty and every now and then one of us would gaze furtively towards it. Conversation was laborious and there would be certain gaps when Lucas and I sought for something to say. In the past we had lingered over meals; now they were occasions which everyone wished to be over as soon as possible.

Lucas said, "I haven't seen you all day. I looked for you this afternoon."

"No," I said. "I went to Perrivale Court."

"Perrivale Court!" he echoed disbelievingly.

"Yes . . . as a matter of fact I'm going to work there."

"What?"

"As a governess. Lady Perrivale has a daughter, Kate. I am going to act as her governess."

"Whatever for?"

"Well, it's something to do, and — "

"It's a ridiculous idea!" He looked at Carleton, who was staring gloomily at his plate. "Did you hear that?" he said. "Rosetta plans to go to Perrivale Court as governess to the girl there."

"Yes, I heard," said Carleton.

"Well, don't you think it's crazy?"

Carleton coughed slightly.

I said, "I shall be starting on Monday. I have to do something, and I thought this would be a start."

Lucas was speechless.

Carleton said, "It was good of you to stay with us so long. The children are so fond of you. We knew of course that you would only be here temporarily until they had recovered a little. . . ."

Then we all fell into silence.

As soon as dinner was over, Lucas hustled me into the drawing room.

"I'd like to talk," he said.

"Yes?"

"It's about this nonsense — "

"It's not nonsense. It's perfectly reasonable. I want to do something."

"There are lots of things you could do. If you're so eager to look after children, what's wrong with the two here?"

"It's not the same, Lucas."

"What do you mean, not the same? Do you realise what you are letting yourself in for?"

"If I find it intolerable I shall just leave."

"That place! There's something about it. You there! I just can't imagine it."

"Lots of young women take posts as governesses."

"You're not qualified."

"How many of them are? I have had a fair education. I could teach some things."

"It's absurd. Tell me, Rosetta, why are you doing this? There must be a reason."

I was silent for a few seconds. I longed to tell him. On impulse I had told Nanny Crockett, but then I had seen that she was emotionally involved and it was obvious that I had then taken a step in the right direction. I wavered. But I was uncertain of Lucas. He should feel grateful to the man who had saved his life, but Lucas was a calm realist, and I was unsure of what action he would take.

He answered for me. "After going through all that . . . well, it's natural that you should feel unsettled. Life at home seems dull . . . predictable. You are reaching out for change. I can only think it was that which made you take this ridiculous action."

"I don't see it as ridiculous, Lucas."

"You get on so well with the twins, and you and Nanny Crockett seem to be in some conspiracy or other. You're always together."

I caught my breath. Conspiracy? It was almost as though he guessed.

He said sharply, "How did you know that they wanted a governess at Perrivale? Through

345

Nanny Crockett, I suppose. I've heard she is still friendly with someone up there."

"Well, yes. . . ."

"I thought so. And you concocted this between you. I tell you, it's madness. That place! There's something unsavoury about it since the murder. It's not the sort of place you should go to. All that trouble . . . and that woman being engaged to the victim and then promptly marrying the other — "

"That has nothing to do with the governess."

"Governess!" he said contemptuously. "*You* a governess?"

"Why not?"

"You're not the type."

"What types are governesses? There are all sorts, I do assure you."

"Well, you don't fit into any of the categories. You'd better marry me."

I stared at him. "*What* did you say?"

"You're restless. Since you've been back, everything seems dull after such hair-raising adventures as you have experienced. You want something to happen. Very well. Marry me."

I burst out laughing. "Really, Lucas, who is being absurd now?"

"Still you. I'm as calm and sensible as ever. The more I think of the idea the more I like it."

"You don't care for me."

"But I do. Next to myself I love you best in the world."

That made me laugh again, and I was glad of the light relief.

"I am not taking you seriously, of course," I said, "but this must be the most unusual proposal anyone has ever received."

"It's honest, anyway."

"Yes, I grant that."

"And it is not so unusual either. It's just that people don't tell all the truth. Most people love themselves passionately and when they declare their love for someone it is always for their own comfort and pleasure. So you see, I am just the same as most other people — except that I am more honest."

"Oh, Lucas, it is good of you, but — "

"It's not good at all, and *but* . . . I knew there would be a but."

"I really can't take you seriously."

"Why not? The more I think of it the better solution it seems. You are in the doldrums, whichever way you turn. Everything has changed for you. Your forthright aunt has entered your old home and changed it. You have recently come through an almost incredible adventure. Nothing like it will ever happen to you again, so therefore life seems a little flat. You are not sure which way to turn. But

347

turn you will — to anything, anywhere — to take you out of the slough into which you have fallen. If governessing in a house of somewhat shady reputation is considered, why not marriage with a curmudgeon who is a poor thing but at least cares for you and understands?"

"You don't put it very romantically."

"We are not discussing romance but reality."

I couldn't help laughing again, and he joined in with me.

"Oh, come, Rosetta," he said. "Give up this mad idea . . . and at least consider the other proposition. It has certain advantages. We are good friends, aren't we? We've faced death together. I understand you as few people ever will. And do you want to go back to Aunt Maud and her plans for you?"

"I certainly don't want to do that," I replied. "You are right in a way. You do understand me . . . to some degree."

"Then abandon this idea. I'll send Dick Duvane over to Perrivale to tell them to look for a new governess. Think about what I suggested. Stay here for a while. Let's enlarge our acquaintance. You don't need to leap into this. Let's make plans."

"You are so good to me, Lucas."

I placed my hand in his and he put it to his lips.

"It's true, you know, Rosetta," he said earnestly. "I am fond of you."

"I really am second with you?"

He laughed and held me against him for a moment.

"But . . ." I went on.

"Yes, I know about that 'but.' You're going to Perrivale, aren't you?"

"I must, Lucas. There's a reason."

Warnings of danger flashed into my mind. Once again I was on the point of telling him why I must go to Perrivale. He would understand then.

He saw that I was really determined.

He said, "Well, I shall be close. We'll meet at The Sailor King. And when you find it quite unbearable, you only have to walk out and come to Trecorn."

"That is a great comfort to me," I told him. "And, Lucas . . . thank you for asking me. It means a great deal to me."

"It's not the last time I shall ask. There'll be others. I don't give in as easily as that."

"It was a great surprise to me. I think it was to you."

"Oh, it has been smouldering in my mind for a long time, even on the island perhaps. . . ."

"Do you think often of that time now?"

"It's always there, in the background. I am constantly ready to be reminded. I often think of John Player, too. It would be interesting to know what happened to him."

I was silent, apprehensive as I always was when he referred to Simon.

"I wonder if he is still in the seraglio. Poor devil. He came out the worst of the three of us . . . though none emerged unscathed."

His face hardened. The grudge against fate for making a cripple of a healthy man was never far away.

"I'd give a good deal to know what became of him," he went on.

"We must remember we should not be here if it were not for him," I said. "Perhaps one day we shall hear something."

"I doubt it. When that sort of thing happens people disappear from your life."

"We didn't disappear, Lucas."

"It is rather miraculous that we are here like this."

"Perhaps he will come back too."

"If he escaped . . . which seems impossible."

"I did, Lucas."

"That's quite a story, but who is going to let him out? No, we shall never see him again. Yes, while we were there . . . on that island, the three of us . . . we became very close to each other. But that is over now. We've got to grow away from it. And let me tell you,

you'll do that far better as Mrs. Lucas Lorimer than as governess to some hateful little brat in a household which was once the centre of a murder case."

"We shall have to see, Lucas," I said.

My first days at Perrivale Court were so crowded with impressions and suppressed emotions that they left me quite bewildered. The house itself was fascinating. It was full of unexpected features. It seemed vast, like a medieval castle in some places, a Tudor manor in others, and in some rooms a note of modernity had crept in.

Lady Perrivale had greeted me warmly but briefly and had handed me over to Mrs. Ford, who from the first showed herself to be my ally. I was her protégée; she had won the gratitude of Lady Perrivale for producing me, and she was going to take me under her wing and do her utmost to keep me in the house.

She took me to my room. "If there's anything you want, Miss Cranleigh, let me know. I'll see you're as comfortable as I can make you. Nanny Crockett said I was to take care of you, and I promise you, I will."

My room was next to the nursery, and Kate's was next to mine. It was a pleasant room with a window that looked down onto a courtyard. Across the courtyard other windows faced me. I immediately had the impression that I was being watched and I was glad of the heavy drapes.

From the first I felt as though I had slipped into a dream. I was overwhelmed by the knowledge that I was actually living in the house where Simon had spent the greater part of his boyhood, and my determination to prove his innocence intensified.

It soon became clear that Kate felt an interest in me. She was certainly determined to find out all she could about me.

No sooner had Mrs. Ford left me to unpack than she came into my room. She did not knock, feeling, I was sure, that there was no need to stand on ceremony with a mere governess.

"You came then," she said. "I didn't think you would, and then I did . . . because you wouldn't have said you'd come if you didn't mean to, would you?"

"Of course not."

"A lot of people say they'll do things and don't."

"I'm not one of those."

She sat on the bed. "Horrible old room, isn't it?"

"I think it's pleasant."

"I suppose as a governess you haven't

been used to much."

"In my home in London I have a very pleasant room."

"Why didn't you stay in it then?"

"You are not very well mannered, are you?"

"Oh, no. Actually, I'm very ill mannered."

"Well, at least you are aware of it ... which is a point in your favour. But as you appear to take a pride in it, that's one against you."

She laughed. "You are funny," she said. "I do and say what I like."

"I had gathered that."

"And nobody's going to change me."

"Then you'll have to do the job yourself, won't you?"

She looked at me curiously and I went on. "And would you mind getting off my bed? I want to sort out my things."

To my surprise she moved and stood watching me.

"Is that all you've got?"

"Yes."

"It's not much, is it? I suppose you think you're going to marry the master of the house, like Jane Eyre. Well, you can't, because he's married already ... to my mother."

I raised my eyebrows.

"Don't look so surprised," she said. "It's what a lot of governesses think."

"I was expressing surprise at your erudition."

"What's that?"

"In your case, a certain knowledge of literature."

"Did you think I didn't know anything?"

"I gathered you had difficulties with your governesses."

"I like reading books about people. I like it when awful things happen to them."

"I'm not surprised at that."

She laughed. "What do you think you're going to teach me?"

"We shall do some history, English literature . . . grammar, too . . . and of course mathematics."

She grimaced. "I shan't do what I don't like."

"We'll have to see about that."

"You *are* like a governess sometimes."

"I'm glad that you recognise that."

"I like the way you talk. It makes me laugh."

"I think you must be rather easily amused."

"You're not like Miss Evans. She was ever so silly. Right from the first she was just frightened all the time."

"By you?"

"Of course."

"And you took advantage of your position."

"What do you mean?"

"She was trying to do her work and you did all you could to prevent her. You made her so miserable that she had to leave."

"I didn't want her here. She was a bore. I don't think you're going to be a bore. I wonder how long you'll stay."

"As long as it suits me, I imagine."

She smiled secretly. Clearly she was planning her campaign.

Oddly enough, I found her stimulating and I was quite enjoying our verbal battles. She went with me to the schoolroom and I inspected the books that were in the cupboard. It was well stocked. There was a blackboard, several exercise books, slates, and pencils.

"I shall have to ask you to show me some of your previous work," I said.

She grimaced.

"When?" she asked.

"There is no time like the present."

She hesitated and seemed poised for flight. I wondered what I should do if she refused to stay with me. I knew she was quite capable of that and deeply I pitied my predecessors, whose ability to earn a living rested on the whims of this creature.

I wanted to stay for as long as it was necessary, but at least my living did not depend on it.

At the moment, however, she was mildly intrigued by me and she decided to cooperate; we had an interesting half hour when I discovered that she was not as ignorant as I had feared she might be; in fact she was exceptionally bright. She had read a great deal, which was a help. In that, at least, we had something in common.

During the first day I learned a little about the household. There were three estate managers, Mrs. Ford told me. "Because ever since . . . you know what, Miss Cranleigh; we don't talk about it. You see, Mr. Cosmo had gone and so had Mr. Simon. There'd been three of them, and now there was only Sir Tristan left. Well, it was too much for him. There'd always been one agent, even . . . before . . . and afterwards there were two more. Perrivale's a big estate, the biggest round here. Of course, it's all different since . . . *that* happened . . . and Sir Edward being gone."

During that first day I had a glimpse of Tristan, and from the moment I saw him I began to suspect that he knew something of what had really happened in the old farmhouse.

He looked the part of the stage villain. He was very dark: his hair was smooth and shiny, so sleek that it looked like a black cap, particularly as it came to a point in the middle of his forehead, which gave him a rather mysterious and sinister appearance.

Our meeting was brief. Kate had taken me out to show me the gardens and I met him coming with Lady Perrivale from the stables. She looked beautiful in a dark blue riding habit, with top hat in the same colour. Her hair looked brilliant under the dark hat.

She said, "Oh, Tristan, this is Miss Cranleigh, the new governess."

He took off his hat and bowed in a courtly manner.

"She and Kate are getting along so well together," said Lady Perrivale with more optimism than proof.

"I've shown her the schoolroom," said Kate. "And now I'm showing her the gardens."

"That's very good," said Lady Perrivale.

"Welcome to Perrivale," put in Sir Tristan. "I hope your stay with us will be a long and happy one."

I saw Kate smirk and wondered what she was planning for my discomfort.

And there and then I illogically assigned to Tristan the role of murderer, telling myself that I might not have any evidence against him, but my conclusions were due to my sixth sense.

I was very thoughtful as I examined the gardens. Kate had noticed this. I was beginning to realise that there was little she missed.

"You didn't like Stepper," she said.

"Who?"

"My stepfather. I call him Stepper. He doesn't like it much. Nor does my mother."

"I suppose that is why you do it."

Again that hunching of the shoulders, the grimace, as she laughed. "I always give people names," she said. "You're Cranny."

"I'm not sure that I approve of that."

"You don't have to approve. People have no choice when it comes to names. They have to have what's given them. Look at me: Kate Blanchard. Who wants to be Kate? I should have liked to be Angelica."

"That would make people think of angels," I reminded her. "Hardly apt in your case."

She was laughing again. There was quite a lot of laughter that morning.

I said to her, "We'll start lessons tomorrow morning at nine thirty and we shall finish at twelve noon."

"Miss Evans started at ten."

"We shall start at nine thirty."

Again that grimace, but it was still good-tempered.

I really thought we were getting on much better than I had thought we should. She seemed interested in me. I wondered whether I should be able to get her to work at her lessons.

I was soon to have a rude awakening.

It was understandable that on my first night at Perrivale Court I should find that sleep evaded me. The events of the day kept crowding into my head. Here I was at last, in Simon's home, almost at the scene of the crime, one might say; and I was dedicated to the monumental task of proving his innocence. I felt greatly comforted by the thought of Lucas, to whom I could turn at any time. I was touched that he had offered to marry me. I had been truly amazed. I had never thought of him in such connection, or only vaguely, when Aunt Maud had had that speculative look in her eyes when she knew I had seen him at Felicity's home.

I was turning over in my mind how I should begin my research. This was what would be called a wild goose chase, and it was only because of the fantastic adventures through which I had passed that I could contemplate embarking on it.

In the meantime I had to cope with Kate, quite a task in itself. The beginning had been easier than I had thought it would be, but that was merely because I had managed to make her mildly interested in me. I could visualise her quickly becoming bored and then the campaign against me would begin. I hoped she would not make my life intolerable before I had made some progress in my search.

I must learn something about Cosmo, who had been engaged to marry the fascinating Mirabel who had become a definite personality to me. I was getting my cast together. Simon, I knew well; I had glimpsed Tristan. How enamoured had Simon been of Mirabel? Having seen her, I could imagine how attractive she would be to most men.

I must have dozed, for I was awakened suddenly by a sound outside my door. I opened my eyes and saw the door handle slowly turning. The door was silently pushed open and a figure glided into the room. It was covered with a sheet and I knew at once who was underneath.

She stood by the door and said in a sibilant whisper, "Go away. Go away . . . while there is still time. No good can come to you here."

I pretended to sleep on. She came closer to the bed. My eyes were half closed, and when she came near enough I caught the sheet and pulled it off.

"Hello, ghost," I said.

She looked deflated.

"It was a poor impersonation," I added.

"And a sheet . . . obviously a sheet. Couldn't you have done better than that?"

"You were pretending to be asleep. It wasn't fair."

"You were pretending to be a ghost and all's fair in love and war, and war is what this is, isn't it . . . since it certainly isn't love."

"You were scared."

"I wasn't."

"Just for a minute?" she said almost pleadingly.

"Not for a second. You could have done better than that. In the first place, if you planned to stage a haunting, it wasn't very clever to talk so much about ghosts when we first met. You see, you put me on my guard. I said, 'This girl fancies herself as a governess baiter.'"

"A *what?*" she cried.

"You see, you have such a limited vocabulary. I'm not surprised, as you won't learn. You like taunting governesses because in comparison with them you feel ignorant. You think that for a moment they are in a weak position and you are in a strong one. That's rather cowardly, of course, but people who are unsure of themselves do things like that."

"I frightened Miss Evans."

"I've no doubt you did. You don't care about other people at all, do you?"

She looked surprised.

"Didn't it occur to you that Miss Evans was trying to earn her living, and the only reason she would want to teach an unpleasant child like you was because she had to?"

"Am I unpleasant?"

"Very. But if you gave a little thought to others beside yourself, you might be less so."

"I don't like you."

"I don't greatly care for you."

"So you will go away, will you?"

"Probably. You don't think anyone would want to stay to teach you, do you?"

"Why not?"

"Because you have stated so clearly that you do not want to learn."

"What of that?"

"It shows you have no respect for learning, and only stupid people feel like that."

"So I am stupid?"

"It would seem so. Of course, you could change. I tell you what. Why don't we make a truce?"

"What's a truce?"

"It's a sort of agreement. You make terms."

"What terms?"

"We could see if you like the way I teach and if you are prepared to learn. If you don't, I'll go and you can have another governess. It will save you racking your brains for methods to make me uncomfortable. Let's go about it in a civilised way without all these childish tricks to make me go."

"All right," she said. "Let's have a truce."

"Then go back to bed now. Good night."

She paused at the door. "There *are* ghosts in the house, though," she said. "There was a murder here . . . not long ago."

"Not in this house," I said.

"No, but it was Stepper's brother. One was killed and the other ran away. They were all in love with my mother before she married Stepper."

She was very observant. She had noticed the change in me. She came back and sat on the bed.

"What do you know about it?" I asked. "You weren't in the house at the time."

"No, I came here when my mother married Stepper. Before that we were at Gramps's house."

"Whose?"

"My grandfather's. He's in the Dower House now. He went there when my mother got married. He had to have a better house then because he was the father of the lady of the manor. Gramps didn't like living in a little cottage anyway. He's really a very grand gentleman. He's Major Durrell, and majors are very important. They win battles. We used to live in London but that was years and years ago. Then we came here and everything changed."

"You must have known them all, the one who was killed and the one who went away."

"I knew them . . . in a way. They were all in love with my mother. Gramps used to laugh about it. He was ever so pleased because when she married Stepper we moved out of the cottage. But first there was all that fuss. And then Cosmo was killed and Simon ran away because he didn't want to be hanged."

I was silent and she went on.

"They do hang them, you know. They put a rope round their necks and they . . . swing. It hurts a lot . . . but then they're dead. That was what he was afraid of. Well, who wouldn't be?"

I could not speak. I kept seeing Simon stealthily leaving the house . . . making his way to Tilbury . . . meeting the sailor, John Player.

She was watching me closely. "Ghosts come back when people are murdered. They haunt people. Sometimes they want to know what really happened."

"Do you think something happened . . . which people don't know about?"

She looked at me slyly. I was unsure of her. She could be teasing me. I had betrayed my

364

interest and she had noticed. She would already have guessed that I was extraordinarily interested in the murder.

"I was there, wasn't I?" she said. "I remember. I was with Gramps . . . my mother was upstairs. Someone . . . one of the grooms from Perrivale . . . came to the door and said, 'Mr. Cosmo's been found shot. He's dead.' Gramps said, 'Oh, my God.' You're not supposed to say oh, my God. It's taking the Lord's name in vain. It says something in the Bible about it. And Gramps went upstairs to my mother and he wouldn't let me go up with him."

I tried to think of something appropriate to say but nothing came.

"Do you ride, Cranny?" she asked, seemingly irrelevantly.

I nodded.

"I tell you what. I'll take you to Bindon Boys . . . the scene of the crime. You'd like that, wouldn't you?"

I said, "You're obsessed by that murder. It's all over now. Perhaps one day we'll ride out to that place."

"All right," she said. "It's a pact."

"And now," I said, "good night."

She gave me a grin and, picking up the sheet, left me.

I lay for a long time, wide awake. I had come to teach Kate, but there might be a good deal she could teach me.

Kate had long decided that the lives of governesses should be made so uncomfortable that they found it impossible to stay, so they left, which gave her a period of freedom before the next one came and she had to start her eliminating tactics once more.

I was different from the others, mainly because she sensed that it was not imperative for me to keep the job as a means of livelihood. That took a little spice out of the baiting and gave me the advantage. I tried to tell myself that all children have a streak of cruelty in them because they lack experience of life and therefore an ability to imagine the extent of the suffering they cause.

Apart from the fact that I was becoming sure that she could be of use to me in my quest, I wanted to take up the case of other governesses who had suffered before me and in particular those who would suffer after me. I wanted to teach Kate a little humanity. Oddly enough, I did not despair of her. I believed something must have happened to make her the callous little creature she had become, and I had a feeling that it must be possible to change her.

The next morning, rather to my surprise, she was in the schoolroom at the appointed time.

I told her I had worked out a timetable. We would start with English, perhaps for an hour or so; we would see how that worked. I should want to test her reading ability, her spelling, her grammar. We should read books together.

I had found a collection in the cupboard. I picked up *The Count of Monte Cristo* and when I opened it I saw *Simon Perrivale* written on the flyleaf in a childish hand. I felt my own hands tremble a little.

I managed to hide my emotion from her alert eyes. I said, "Have you ever read this book?"

She shook her head.

"We'll read it one day and — oh, here's another. *Treasure Island*. That's about pirates."

Her interest was aroused. There was a picture on the frontispiece of Long John Silver with his parrot on his shoulder.

She said, "In that other book, that was his name . . . you know, the murderer."

"We don't know that he was," I said, and stopped myself abruptly, for she was looking at me in surprise. I should have to go carefully. "We shall then do history, geography, and arithmetic."

She was scowling.

"We'll see how they fit in," I said firmly.

The morning passed tolerably well. I discovered that she could read fairly fluently and I was pleased to discover that she had a definite taste for literature. The personalities of history interested her but she shut her mind to dates. There was a revolving globe in the cupboard and we had an interesting time discovering places on it. I showed her where I had been shipwrecked. The story intrigued her, and we finished off the morning by reading a chapter of *Treasure Island;* she was absorbed by the book from the first page.

I was amazed at my success.

I had decided that we should work until midday. Then she could follow her own pursuits if she wished until three o'clock, when we might visit the gardens and learn something about plant life or take a walk in the surrounding country. We could resume lessons at four and work until five. That was our scholastic day.

In the afternoon she showed no wish to be on her own and offered to show me the surrounding country. I was rather pleased that she sought my company and seemed to retain her interest in me.

She talked about *Treasure Island* and told me what she thought would happen. She wanted to hear about my shipwreck. I began to think that it was this which had made her ready to accept me . . . perhaps briefly . . . as had not been the case with the other governesses.

She took me to the top of the cliffs and we sat there for a while, watching the sea.

"We have rough seas here," she said. "There used to be wreckers along these coasts. They had lights and they lured the ships onto the rocks, pretending that it was the harbour. Then they stole the cargo. I'd like to have been a wrecker."

"Why do you want to be evil?"

"Being good is dull."

"It's better in the long run."

"I like short runs."

I laughed at her and she laughed with me.

She said suddenly, "Look at those rocks down there. A man was drowned down there not very long ago."

"Did you know him?"

She was silent for a moment. Then she said, "He was a stranger here. He came from London. He's buried in St. Morwenna's churchyard. I'll show you his grave. Would you like to see it?"

"Well, I suppose it is hardly one of the local beauty spots."

She laughed again.

"He was drunk," she said. "He fell over the cliffs and right down onto the rocks."

"He must have been very drunk."

"Oh, he was. There was a fuss about it. They didn't know who he was for a long time."

"How you love the morbid!"

"What's that?"

"Unpleasant . . . gruesome."

"I like gruesome things."

"It's not the wisest of preoccupations."

She looked at me and laughed again. "You are funny," she said.

Looking back over that day when I retired to my room that night, I could say it had been unexpectedly satisfactory. I had some hope — however flimsy — of coming to an understanding with Kate.

A few days passed. To my secret delight, I was discovering that my somewhat unorthodox methods of teaching were more successful with a pupil like Kate than more conventional ones might have been. We were reading together a great deal. In fact, I held those reading sessions as a sort of bribe for good conduct during the less attractive projects. She could have read by herself but she preferred that we do it together.

She liked to share her enjoyment, which was a sign in her favour, I thought; moreover, she liked to talk about what we had read afterwards; then sometimes she might be held up because she did not know the meaning of a word. She was avid for knowledge, in spite of the fact that she had expressed her contempt for it; and she was completely intrigued by *Treasure Island*.

It was too much to expect a complete change in the child merely because our relationship had progressed more favourably than I had dared hope. I think it was on my fourth morning when she did not put in an appearance in the schoolroom.

I went to her room. She was looking out of the window, obviously expecting me, and I could see she was preparing to enjoy a battle.

I said, "Why are you not in the schoolroom?"

"I don't feel like lessons today," she replied jauntily.

"It doesn't matter how you feel. This is lesson time."

"You can't make me."

"I certainly would not attempt to take you there by force. I shall go to your mother and tell her that you have made up your mind not to learn and there is no point in my being here."

It was a bold step. I could not bear the thought of leaving now. Yet I knew I could get nowhere unless I had some authority over her.

She looked at me defiantly. My heart sank

but I hoped I hid my feelings. I had gone too far to turn back.

"You really mean you'd go?" I saw the fear in her eyes mingling with disbelief. I sensed that she was as uneasy as I was.

I said firmly, "If you will not come to the schoolroom I have no alternative."

She hesitated for a moment. "All right," she said. "Go, if you want to."

I walked to the door. I must not show my despair. If this was to be the end, what good had I done? But there was no turning back now. I went out. She did not move. I started down the stairs. Then I heard her. "Come back, Cranny."

I paused and turned to look back at her.

"All right," she said. "I'll come."

I felt flushed with victory as we made our way to the schoolroom.

She was in a difficult mood all day. I wondered why. Perhaps she felt she had been good too long and it was not in her nature to be so.

I found a dead shrew mouse in my bed that night. I carefully wrapped it up in tissue paper and went along to her room.

"I think this poor little thing belongs to you," I said.

She looked aghast. "Where did you find it?"

"Where you put it. In my bed."

"I bet you screamed when you found it."

"I did not think it frightening or funny. It's just a silly cliché."

I could see her pondering the word cliché. She loved discovering new words, but she was not in the mood to ask me what it meant.

I went on. "I wonder how many times some mischievous child has put a shrew mouse in someone's bed. It's really rather silly. You do the expected thing, Kate."

She was a little downcast. Then she said, "Well, you brought it back, didn't you? You were going to put it in my bed."

"I should have done no such thing. I merely wanted you to know that your silly trick has not had the effect you thought it would. Now, if we are going to have a truce, we should put an end to these childish tricks. It would be more interesting to get on well together. There are many exciting things we could do. We don't want to waste time having tantrums and playing silly tricks. We can talk — "

"What about?"

"About life . . . people — "

"Murder?" she put in.

I thought, yes, about one. I said, "What we can do is finish *Treasure Island*."

" 'Fifteen men on the Dead Man's Chest,' " she sang, " 'Yo-ho-ho, and a bottle of rum!' "

I smiled. "There are lots of books we can

read. You haven't read *The Count of Monte Cristo* yet. I saw it in the cupboard. It's about a man who was wrongfully imprisoned and escapes to have his revenge."

Her eyes were round with interest.

"Well," I went on, "if we don't waste our time in silly ways, we might tackle that. And there are many more."

She did not answer, but I felt I had won another battle.

I said, "What shall we do with this poor little mouse?"

"I'll bury it," she said.

"That's right. And bury all your silly prejudices against governesses with it. Then perhaps we can start to enjoy our lessons."

On that note, I left her. I was victorious and triumphant.

My handling of Kate was the wonder of the household. At last someone had been found who could turn the *enfant terrible* into a normal child — or at least who had found a way to control her.

Mrs. Ford fêted me. She was delighted. She mentioned my name in an awed whisper, as though I were a battle hero covered in military glory. I was quite an important figure in the household.

About a week after my arrival, Lady Perrivale asked me to come to her in the drawing room.

She was most gracious.

"You and Kate seem to be getting along very well," she began. "That is very good. I knew all would be well if only we could get the right person."

"I am quite inexperienced of governessing," I reminded her.

"Well, that is just the point. These old women have too many rules. They are too set in their ways to understand the modern child."

"Kate is rather unusual."

"Well, of course. But clearly you understand her. Are you completely satisfied with everything? Is there anything . . . ?"

"I am satisfied, thank you very much," I replied.

Sir Tristan came into the room as though on a cue. It amused me to think he had been called in to add his praise to that of his wife. Kate must have plagued them a good deal.

The thought crossed my mind that it was odd that a man who could murder his brother should be nonplussed by a wayward child. I pulled myself up sharply. It was nonsensical to have settled on Sir Tristan as the murderer, just because of his saturnine looks. Though, of course, he had inherited the title, the estates . . . and Mirabel.

His shrewd dark eyes were assessing me. I felt guilty. I wondered what he would say if he could read my thoughts.

"I hear you are managing Kate," he said, and added, with a little laugh, "Quite a feat. It's very clever of you, Miss Cranleigh, to do what your predecessors so lamentably failed to."

"She's not an easy child," I said.

"We are well aware of that, aren't we?" he replied, looking at his wife.

She nodded ruefully.

"I think she needs a great deal of understanding," I told them. I was wondering what Kate's relationship was with these two. She had not given me an inkling. What of her father? What had happened to him? How did she feel about her mother's engagement to Cosmo, and then, very soon after his death, the marriage to Tristan? These were matters I should like to know about. I believed they might help me solve the mystery.

"And you seem to be able to supply that."

"As I have explained, I have never been a governess before."

"You are too young, of course," he said, smiling at me warmly. "And too modest . . . is she not, my dear?"

"Far too modest," added Lady Perrivale.

"Miss Cranleigh, I hope you will not be bored here." She looked at her husband. "We were going to say that, perhaps . . . now and then . . . when we have a dinner party, you might care to join us. As a matter of fact your friends are quite close neighbours of ours."

"You mean the Lorimers?"

"Yes. So sad about the accident. I daresay they would not be in the mood for visiting just yet. But perhaps later we might ask them . . . and then, of course, you must be among the guests."

"That would be very pleasant."

"We don't want you to feel . . . isolated."

I was thinking: this is what happens to some governesses when the family are short of a guest and want to make up numbers; if the governess is fairly presentable, she is called in to fill the gap. On the other hand, they were clearly very anxious to keep me. How strange it was that I was the only one who had found a way to make this recalcitrant child less objectionable.

I said, "You are very kind. There is one thing . . . "

They were eager to know what.

"If I could occasionally have a free afternoon, I should like to visit the Lorimers. You see, there are children there. I was with them at the time of the accident. I stayed on awhile after the friends with whom I was travelling left."

I was amused to see the light of alarm in Lady Perrivale's eyes. Children? Might they be needing a governess? Really, I thought, I shall get a very high opinion of myself . . . and all because I had for a time found a way of making Kate behave mildly reasonably.

"Of course," said Sir Tristan quickly. "Certainly you must take the time to visit your friends. How will you travel? It is quite a few miles to Trecorn Manor, is it not? You are a rider, are you?"

"Oh, yes."

"Well, that's settled. Ask Mason down at the stables to find a suitable mount for you."

"You are most kind. Kate has mentioned riding and I think she would like us to do it together."

"Excellent. I believe she is quite good on a horse."

"I am sure she is. I look forward to outings with her."

It was a most satisfactory interview.

The next day Kate and I went for a ride. She had a small white horse of whom she was very fond. It pleased me to see the care she lavished on him — an indication that there was some capacity for affection in her nature.

The head groom, Mason, had found a chestnut mare for me. Her name was Goldie, he told me. "She's a good little thing. Treat her right and she'll treat you right. Good-tempered . . . easygoing . . . make a bit of fuss of her . . . and she likes a lump of sugar after the ride. Give her that and she'll be your slave."

Kate was a good little horsewoman, inclined to show off at first, but when I told her I knew she was aware of how to manage a horse, and in any case she would not have been allowed to go without a groom if she did not, she stopped doing so.

I was wondering how I could pose tactful questions about her home life, for I knew I had to be very careful. She was extremely observant, and she was watching me as closely as I was watching her.

She announced that she was going to take me to Bindon Boys.

"You know," she said, "the old farmhouse where the murder took place."

"I remember."

"You'll like that, Cranny. You know how you love anything about that old murder."

I felt uneasy. I had betrayed my interest and she had noticed.

"It's an awful old place. People won't go there after dark . . . I mean they won't even go near it. I reckon quite a lot would want to go in daylight . . . but never alone."

"Bricks and mortar can't hurt anyone."

"No. It's what's inside. Once it was a real farmhouse. I can remember it before . . . before that happened."

"Can you?"

"Well, of course I can. I wasn't all that much of a baby."

"And you lived near . . . when you came from London?"

"That's right. The cottage we lived in was close to Bindon Boys. It was the nearest cottage to it. And the sea was just down the slope. I'll show you when we get there."

"Is it far?"

"No, about a mile."

"That's easy."

"Come on. I'll race you."

We galloped across a meadow and when we emerged we were very close to the sea. I took deep breaths of the invigorating air. Kate came up close to me.

"There," she said. "You can see it just down there. That's the old farmhouse and there, not very far off, Seashell Cottage. Seashell . . . what a silly name! Someone had done the name on the soil outside the door in seashells. SEASHELL COTTAGE, all in shells. I used to pull them up. I took off the Seas and made it HELL COTTAGE."

I laughed. "Just what I would expect of you."

"Gramps thought it was funny. I tell you what. After you've seen the farmhouse I might take you to see Gramps. He'd like to meet you. He likes meeting people."

"I shall find it all most interesting, I am sure."

"Come on. The farmhouse first."

We rode down the slight incline, and there it was. It was in a state of dilapidation. The roof looked as though it was falling in. The heavy door was slightly ajar. The bolt had evidently gone.

"It looks as if it is on the point of collapse," I said.

"Coming in? Or are you scared?"

"Of course I want to go in."

"We'll leave our horses here."

We dismounted near an old mounting block and tethered the horses. We pushed open the door and stepped straight into what I presumed was a living room. It was large, with two windows, the panes of which were cracked. Several floorboards were missing. Threadbare curtains hung at the windows and dusty cobwebs hung from the ceiling.

"They didn't touch it . . . after the murder," said Kate. "This is where it was, in this room. It's haunted, isn't it? Can you feel it?"

I said, "It's eerie."

"Well, that's because it's haunted. You'd better keep close to me."

I smiled. She was eager not to be too far away from me in this place.

I was seeing it all clearly: Simon, tying up his horse at probably the same spot where we had tied ours, unsuspecting, coming in and finding Cosmo lying on the floor, the gun beside him. I saw Simon picking up the gun and just at that moment Tristan bursting in. It was too neat.

"You look funny," said Kate.

"I was thinking about it."

She nodded.

"I reckon Simon was waiting for him. And as soon as he came in — bang, bang! It was a good thing Stepper came in, though, and caught him red-handed. He ran away." She came close to me. "What do you think Simon is doing now?"

"I wish I knew."

"Perhaps the ghost is haunting him. Can ghosts travel? I reckon they can go a little way. I wonder where he is. I'd love to know. What's the matter with you, Cranny?"

"Nothing."

"Ever since you came in here, you've had a funny look in your eyes."

"Nonsense."

Then suddenly I thought I heard a movement overhead.

"The fact is you're scared, Cranny." She stopped suddenly. Her eyes widened as they turned towards the stairs. She had heard too. She came closer to me, and as I gripped her hand I heard the creak of a floorboard.

Kate was dragging on my arm, but I did not move.

"It's the ghost," whispered Kate, and there was real fear in her face.

I said, "I'm going to look."

She shook her head and drew back in alarm.

For a second or two she stood very still. Then she came to me and I started up the stairs with her following close behind.

We were on a landing. I could hear deep breathing. So could she. She gripped my hand tightly.

There were three doors on the landing and all of them were closed. I stood listening. Then again I heard the sound of breathing. I stood very still, listening. Behind the door nearest to me I knew someone was waiting.

I went to the door and turned the handle. I pushed open the door and stepped into the room.

A man was standing there, unwashed, unkempt, and there was a pile of rags on the floor with a paper bag beside it. I noticed crumbs on the floor and relief swept over me. This man was human anyway. I did not know what I had expected. Perhaps like Kate I feared the ghost of Cosmo. And this was just an old tramp.

"I be doing no 'arm," he said.

Kate was beside me. "It's Harry Tench," she said.

Harry Tench. The name was familiar. I had heard it mentioned in connection with the murder.

"Who be you?" he demanded. "I know who that one be." He pointed at Kate. "And what do 'ee want 'ere? I b'ain't doing no 'arm."

"No," I said. "No. We just came to look at the farmhouse. We heard a noise and came up."

"Nobody comes prying round 'ere. What 'arm be I doing?"

"None, none. I'm sorry we disturbed you."

"It was just a place to sleep. Drove out, I was. There's no 'arm done. Don't 'ee get no ideas about having me put out."

"We haven't any ideas about doing that," said Kate, who was fast recovering from her fright and was almost herself. "We thought you were a ghost."

His lips were drawn back in a grin, showing yellow teeth.

"Don't worry," I said. "Come on, Kate."

I took her hand and we went out of the room. I shut the door on Harry Tench and we went downstairs.

"Come on," I said. "Let's get out of here."

As we rode away, Kate said, "You were really scared, Cranny."

"Not half as much as you were. You were going to run, remember."

She was silent for a while and then went on. "He's rather brave . . . sleeping there, in a place where a murder happened. You wouldn't want to, would you, Cranny?"

"I would like to be more comfortable than that poor man obviously was."

We rode on and after a few moments she said, "Look, there's Seashell Cottage. That's where we all used to live."

It was a neat little place with a well-kept garden and clean lace curtains at the windows. We rode close enough for me to see that the SEAS had been replaced in the shells so that it was now respectable SEASHELL COTTAGE again. It was difficult to imagine Lady Perrivale living in such a place; and her daughter and father had been with her too.

I wondered about Kate's own father. Could I ask her? Perhaps at the appropriate moment I could put a few carefully chosen questions. I must remember how shrewd Kate was and be very careful.

"Come on," she said. "Let's go and see if Gramps is at home."

The Dower House was very different from Seashell Cottage. I had seen it in the distance, for it was not very far from Perrivale Court. There was a copse between the two and we rode through this.

It was a charming residence. I imagined it had been built during Elizabeth's reign for it was definitely of Tudor architecture — red brick with latticed windows. Virginia creeper grew on some of the walls and there was a neat lawn before it bordered by flower beds.

We slipped off our horses, tethered them, and walked through the gate. The house seemed quiet.

"I bet you he's in the garden," said Kate.

She led the way round the side of the house, past a small orchard, to a walled garden reminiscent of the period, with plants climbing over the red brick wall and beds of what I guessed to be aromatic herbs surrounding a pond, in the centre of which was a small fountain. What struck me most was the aura of absolute peace. A man was sitting on a carved wooden seat close to the pond.

"Gramps," cried Kate.

I was amazed that he looked so young. I realised later that he must have been in his

386

fifties; but he looked ten years younger than that. He was straight-backed, very upright, and undoubtedly handsome. I noticed the resemblance to Lady Perrivale and Kate. His hair was similar in colour to theirs but had a little white at the temples, and there was a hint of green in his eyes. But, like Kate, he lacked those dark brows and lashes which made Lady Perrivale such a startling beauty. *His* brows were so light as to be almost invisible, which gave him a look of youthful surprise.

When he saw us he came striding towards us. Kate flew at him. He picked her up in his arms and swung her round. She laughed gleefully, and I thought with pleasure, Here is someone she really cares about. I was glad to see she was capable of affection.

"Hey, young Kate," he said. "You're forgetting your manners. What about an introduction? Don't tell me. I know, of course — "

"It's Cranny," cried Kate.

"Rosetta Cranleigh," I said.

"Miss Cranleigh. What a delight to meet you. Your fame has spread to the Dower House. My daughter, Lady Perrivale, has already told me of what wonderful work you are doing with our miscreant here."

"What's a miscreant?" demanded Kate.

"It's better for you not to know, don't you

agree, Miss Cranleigh? I am so pleased that you have come to visit me."

"This," said Kate, "is *Major* Durrell. Majors are very important, aren't they, Gramps?"

"If you say so, my dear," he said, raising one of those pale eyebrows in a conspiratorial manner in my direction. "Now, come and sit down. Refreshments?"

"Oh, yes, please," said Kate.

"A little wine, eh?"

"And some of those wine biscuits," she said.

"But, of course. Look, my dear. You go and tell Mrs. Carne that you're here and tell her what's required."

"All right," said Kate.

As she ran off he turned to me.

"Mrs. Carne comes in every weekday morning to look after me. She also comes two afternoons a week as a special favour. Fortunately this is one of the afternoons. Apart from that I look after myself. You learn in the Army. I'm quite a handy man . . . which saves a lot of trouble. Come and sit down, Miss Cranleigh. Don't you think this is a delightful spot?"

"Oh, I do indeed. It is so peaceful."

"That's what I feel, and peace is a very desirable acquisition when one reaches my age. You can believe that, I'm sure."

"I think it is desirable at any age."

"Ah, the young prefer adventure. They want any excitement, no matter what they have to pay for it. I have had my share and now . . . thank Heaven . . . I can appreciate peace. I am so pleased you have come to teach my granddaughter and are making such a success of it."

"It is too early to say. I have only been with her a short time."

"But they are all delighted. There have been so many trials. Poor child, it has not been easy for her. She's a good little thing underneath it all, you know. The trouble is you have to find a way to that goodness. She needs understanding."

I felt drawn to him. He was clearly fond of Kate and he was confirming what I had thought of her.

"Yes," I said. "I do agree. One has to find the way to understand her."

"You know what I mean: uprooted . . . a stepfather. A child has to adjust herself, and with one of Kate's nature that's not easy."

There was something so frank about him. He was so much easier to talk to than either Kate's mother or her stepfather could possibly be.

He went on. "If there are any difficulties at any time . . . you know, with Kate . . . I hope you will not hesitate to come to me."

"That is good of you," I said. "It is a great comfort to me."

He made me feel that we were allies, and it was remarkable that he could have done this in so short a time.

Kate came out. Mrs. Carne would be bringing out the wine and biscuits soon, she said.

"Now come and sit comfortably by the pond. There are some new goldfish, Kate. Can you see them?"

"Oh, yes. They're lovely."

"Your gardens are well kept," I commented.

"I'm a keen gardener myself. There's peace in a garden, I always think."

How he harped on peace! Well, why not? It was a good state to be in.

Mrs. Carne came out with the refreshment. She was just as I had imagined her — plumpish, rosy-cheeked, middle-aged — and clearly had an affection for her employer, which did not surprise me. She was protective, admiring, and authoritative towards him.

"There we are, Major, and the biscuits were baked this morning."

"Mrs. Carne, you are an angel."

She bridled. "Well, it's a pleasure, I'm sure."

He went on. "This is Miss Cranleigh."

There seemed to be no need to explain my

reason for being with Kate. I expected Mrs. Carne was well aware of all that went on at Perrivale Court.

She nodded in my direction and was gone.

"She's a good sort," said the major. "Treats me like a babe in arms sometimes, but I confess I like to be spoiled. So you like my garden? I do a lot of it myself . . . the designing and planting and all. There's a man who comes in every morning and does the mundane jobs."

"Have you been here long?"

"Since my daughter married. The house was a sort of wedding present. Unusual, you are thinking, for the father of the bride to be so pampered, but Mirabel couldn't have her old father living in a little cottage. She made it as though coming to live here was a favour to her."

"We saw Seashell Cottage only this afternoon."

"It's quite charming in a way. Not much garden, of course. Not to be compared with the Dower House."

"I told Cranny how I took the Seas out of Seashell and made it HELL COTTAGE."

"There you see, Miss Cranleigh, what I have to contend with."

"You thought it was funny, you know you did, Gramps."

"Well, perhaps I did. What was I saying? Oh, a great improvement on the cottage, and I am very happy to be here."

"How comforting it must be to be so contented."

"Yes, particularly after a rather chequered career. Army life is no bed of roses, believe me. And then I come to this: my daughter happily settled . . . and my granddaughter now firmly placed on the straight and narrow path with her most excellent governess."

He raised an eyebrow at me again. I could see the gesture was a habit with him.

"Gramps has been all over the world," Kate informed me. "He's been just everywhere."

"A mild exaggeration, you will understand, Miss Cranleigh."

I smiled.

"Majors are the most important people in the Army," went on Kate.

"My dear granddaughter brushes aside all those generals, field marshals, colonels, and the rest who are under the impression that they are the ones."

"Well, *you* were," she said.

"Who can be so churlish as to contradict such a loyal supporter? It is true that I have done a bit of travelling. India, Egypt, wherever my duty lay."

"Tell us, Gramps," pleaded Kate.

Over the wine he talked a great deal. He spoke of his life in India as a young officer. "Those were the days . . . but the climate . . . uncertainty too. I was too young for the Mutiny, but the feeling was always there."

As he talked, Kate kept glancing at me to make sure that I was duly impressed. It was clear that he was a hero to her. He talked of Egypt, the Sudan, and India. At length he said, "But I'm talking too much. It's Kate's fault. She always lures me to talk, don't you, Granddaughter?"

"I like it," said Kate. "So do you, don't you, Cranny?"

"It is quite fascinating," I said.

"I'm glad you find it so. I hope it will tempt you to come and visit me again."

"I wish I'd been there," said Kate.

"Ah. Sometimes things are better to talk about than live through."

"You must miss all this adventure," I said.

"I was telling you how much I appreciate the peaceful life. I've had enough adventuring. What I want now is to settle down and enjoy the visits of my family . . . and to know that they are well and happy."

"It seems a very noble ambition," I said.

"And how the time has flown. We must be on our way back, Kate."

"Promise you'll come again."

I thanked him and Kate leaped up and flung her arms about his neck. I was astonished by her conduct. She was like a different child. And I was delighted to see this affection between her and her grandfather.

As we rode home, she said, "Isn't Gramps wonderful?"

"He has certainly had a very interesting life."

"It's the most interesting life anyone ever had. Of course, you were shipwrecked . . . that counts for something. You ought to have told him about it."

"Oh, his adventures were far more interesting, I am sure."

"Oh, yes. But yours are not bad. You can tell him next time."

And of course there would be a next time. I was glad of that.

When I was in bed that night I kept going over that afternoon's adventure. It had been quite eventful. First Harry Tench and then the major. Both of those men would have been here at the time of the murder.

I imagined the major living in Seashell Cottage with his daughter and granddaughter. I might learn quite a lot from him. A man like that would know what was going on and probably had his own theories.

I must cultivate the acquaintance of the major.

I believed it had been a profitable afternoon.

The Sailor's Grave

The visit to the major appeared to have been a great success in more ways than one. Kate became more friendly. I had liked the major and she had made up her mind that the major liked me; and as he was a hero in her eyes, I rose considerably in her estimation.

She talked of him freely, telling me of the wonderful adventures he had had, how he had fought battles single-handed and was solely responsible for the success of the British Empire. Kate could never do or think anything halfheartedly.

But I was delighted by the growing friendship between us.

Lessons had become quite painless. It had been a wise stroke to introduce her to books with a good strong narrative. We had almost finished *Treasure Island*, and *The Count of Monte Cristo* was lying in wait for us.

I used the books blatantly as a sort of

unconscious bribe.

"Well, I know these sums are a little difficult, but when we get them right, we'll see what's going to happen to Ben Gunn."

My success with her amazed me as much as everyone else. I was beginning to see that Kate was more than a rebellious girl bent on making trouble. I supposed there were reasons behind everything. And I was determined to discover more about her.

Through all this I did not forget for one moment the reason why I was here. I wished I could see the major alone. It would be difficult to ask leading questions in Kate's presence. She was already a little suspicious because of my intense interest in the murder. I could not call on the major, of course. Perhaps, I told myself, the opportunity would come, and when it did I must be ready to seize it.

I had always known that Kate had an interest in the morbid, so I was not particularly surprised when I discovered what a fascination the graveyard seemed to have for her.

The church was an ancient one, famed for its Norman architecture. It was not far from Perrivale Court and we often passed it.

"Just imagine," I said as we rode up to it. "It was built all those years ago . . . about eight hundred years."

We were, as Kate said, "doing" William the Conqueror, and she was getting quite an interest in him since learning of the particular manner in which he had wooed his wife, Matilda, by beating her in the streets. Such incidents delighted Kate, and I found myself stressing them whenever I found them, to stimulate her interest.

"He built a lot of places here," she said. "Castles and churches and things. And all those people in the graveyard . . . some of them must have been there for hundreds of years."

"Trust you to think of that instead of the beautiful Norman arches and towers. The church is really interesting."

"Let's go in," she said.

We tied up the horses and did so. The hushed atmosphere subdued her a little. We studied the list of vicars, which dated back a long way.

"There's a wonderful feeling of antiquity," I said. "I don't think you get that anywhere as much as you do in a church."

"Perrivale's very old."

"Yes, but there are people there. Modernity creeps in."

"Let's go into the graveyard."

We came out and were immediately among the tottering gravestones.

"I'll show you the Perrivale vault if you like."

"Yes. I'd like to see it."

We stood before it. It was ornate and imposing.

"I wonder how many are buried there," said Kate.

"Quite a number, I suppose."

"Cosmo will be there. I wonder if he comes out at night. I'll bet he does."

"How your mind dwells on the macabre."

"What's macabre?"

I explained.

"Well," she said. "That's what makes graveyards interesting. If they weren't full of dead people it would be just like anywhere else. It's the dead who are ghosts. You can't be one until you are dead. Come on. I want to show you something."

"Another grave?"

She ran ahead and I followed her. She had come to a standstill before one of the graves. There was nothing ornate about this one — no engraved stone, no ornamental angels or cherubs, no fond message. Just a plain stone with the name Thomas Parry and the date. A rough curb had been put round it to separate it from the others, and on it was a jam jar containing a few sprigs of meadowsweet which looked as though they had been picked from the hedges.

"Who was he?" I asked. "And why are you so interested in this grave?"

She said, "He was the one who fell over the cliff and was drowned."

"Oh . . . I remember. You did mention him."

"They said he was drunk."

"Well, I suppose he was. I wonder who put those flowers there? Someone must have thought of him. Someone must remember him."

She did not speak.

"Who was he?" I asked. "Did you ever know?"

"He didn't live here. He just came here and went over the cliff."

"How foolish of him to get so drunk that he did such a thing."

"Perhaps someone pushed him over."

"But you say he was drunk . . . ?"

"Well, someone could push him. I reckon he walks by night. He gets out of his grave and walks about the graveyard talking about murder."

I laughed at her. She turned to me and her face was serious.

Then she shrugged her shoulders and started to walk away. I followed her, turning once to look at the pathetic grave, untended but for a jam jar filled with meadowsweet.

Dick Duvane rode over from Trecorn Manor. He had brought letters for me, together with a note from Lucas. I studied him with interest, having heard so much of him. He fitted Lucas's description. He gave an immediate impression of capability and strength. I could imagine he would welcome adventure and be completely unruffled when confronted with any situation, however bizarre. He regarded me with obvious interest, and I am sure Lucas must have talked of me to him, too.

He said he would wait for a reply.

The letters were from London, one from my father and the other from Aunt Maud.

I opened Lucas's note.

Dear Rosetta,

How are you getting on in the governess role? Aren't you tired of it yet? Say so and I will come over and fetch you. In any case, I must see you. Could we meet tomorrow afternoon? We could see each other at The Sailor King. Should we meet there or would it be all right for me to come to the house? I could bring a horse for you. I want to talk.

Always devoted to your interests,

Lucas

I remembered my interview with Lady Perrivale, who had said I might be free to take time off when I wanted to. So I wrote a hasty note telling Lucas that I would meet him at The Sailor King the following afternoon at half past two.

Then I took the letters to my room to read them. They were both as I expected. My father's was rather stilted. He could not understand why I had thought it necessary to take a post. If I had wanted some work he could have found something congenial for me, perhaps at the Museum. He hoped that I would soon be home and we could talk about what I wanted to do.

I could not imagine myself explaining to my father. I was sorry for him. I guessed Aunt Maud had urged him to write in a disapproving manner.

There was no doubt of her feelings.

My dear Rosetta,

How could you? A governess! What are you thinking of? I know some poor females are forced into such a position but such is not the case with you. If you take my advice you will give up this nonsense without more ado. Do so quickly. People need never know . . . or if it came out it could be called a mad prank. Of course, the ideal thing would be a London sea-

son for you, but you know that is out of the question. But you are the daughter of a professor, a highly respected man in academic circles. You would have had your chances . . . but a governess!

It went on in this strain for several pages, through which I lightly skimmed. The reaction was so much what I had expected that it left me unmoved.

I was far more interested in my coming meeting with Lucas.

I told Kate the following afternoon that I was meeting a friend.

"Can I come?"

"Oh, no."

"Why not?"

"Because you are not invited."

"What shall I do while you are gone?"

"You'll amuse yourself."

"But I want to come."

"Not this time."

"Next time?"

"The future's not ours to see."

"You are the most maddening governess."

"Then I match my pupil."

She laughed. We had indeed come a long way in the short time I had been here. There was a rapport between us which I would not have dreamed was possible.

She was resigned though disgruntled. She referred once to my desertion.

"I've shown *you* things," she grumbled. "I showed you Gramps and the grave."

"Both suggested by you. I did not ask. Besides, people have a private side to their lives."

"And this one you're meeting is in your private life?"

"As you have never met him . . . yes."

"I will," she said threateningly.

"You may . . . perhaps . . . one day."

She would have liked to make a scene but she dared not. I knew that her life had changed since I had come and it was due to me. She looked upon me, in a way, as her protégée. She enjoyed being with me, which was why she was making such a fuss because I was leaving for a few hours; but there was a real fear, which I had managed to instil in her, that I might leave altogether; and that restrained her.

In my room that night I looked over the last days and thought how far I had come, not, alas, in my main project — that had remained more or less static — but in my new life as governess to Kate Blanchard I had progressed amazingly. True, I had met people who had been close to the scene of the murder, and that gave me hopes of coming on some discovery.

404

I needed time to talk to them, to get to know them, and I must do this in a natural manner . . . so that they did not guess my real motive.

I wished I could find out something about Mirabel's first husband, Mr. Blanchard. What could he have been like? When had he died? How long was it after that time when she came down to Cornwall with her father and her daughter? They could not have been very well off, for the cottage was quite a humble dwelling . . . at least in comparison with Perrivale Court and the Dower House.

Idle curiosity, perhaps. But not entirely. Mirabel was one of the chief actors in the drama, and it would be advantageous to know as much of her as possible.

Then I was thinking of Lucas, remembering his proposal with a certain tenderness. I felt a great longing to tell him why I was at Perrivale and I knew that when I was with him that longing would be intensified.

I sat at my window looking at those across the courtyard. I was trying to persuade myself that Lucas would be a help to me. What a relief it would be to share this with him. He cared for me . . . next to himself. I smiled, remembering his words.

If I made him swear not to betray Simon . . . was it possible?

I must not yet, I told myself. It was not my secret. Simon had told me because it had seemed possible that we might never get off the island and he had felt it necessary to confide in someone. Besides, there was a special relationship between us. I had been aware of that — as he had.

Suddenly my eyes were caught by a light in one of the windows opposite. It was faint . . . from a candle, I imagined. It flickered and then was gone.

I was startled. I was remembering a conversation I had had with Kate some days ago. We had been standing at my window and we had looked out across the courtyard.

"Whose rooms are those over there?" I had asked.

"The ones next to the top floor, do you mean? Do you see something special there?"

"No. Should I?"

"I wondered if you'd seen Stepper's father's ghost."

"Your preoccupation with ghosts is becoming quite a mania."

"It's like that in big houses, especially when there's been a murder. That's Stepper's father's bedroom over there. Nobody goes in there much now."

"Why not?"

"Well, because he died there. My mother says you have to show respect."

"Respect?"

"Well, he died there."

"Someone must go in to clean it."

"I expect so. Anyway, no one goes there. . . . Stepper's mother's up there with Maria. They stay there most of the time."

"Maria?"

"Her maid. I reckon it's haunted. Sir Edward died there."

I thought it was just another instance of Kate's preoccupation and forgot about it. Yet when I saw the light a faint shiver ran down my spine.

I laughed at myself. Kate was affecting me with her obsession.

As she would have said, it was because there had been a murder connected with the house.

She was right. It was because of that murder that I was here.

Lucas was in The Sailor King waiting for me, and I felt extraordinarily happy to see him.

He stood up and took both my hands in his. We looked searchingly at each other for a few seconds, then he kissed my cheek.

"Governessing suits you," he said. "Well,

sit down. How is it going? I've ordered cider. It's too early for tea, don't you think?"

I agreed.

"So they allow you a horse to ride, do they?"

I nodded. "They are most gracious."

"And the pupil?"

"I'm getting her tamed."

"You do look proud of yourself."

"Lucas, how are they at the Manor? The children . . . ?"

"Very hurt by your desertion."

"Oh, not really."

"Yes, really. They ask for you twenty times a day. When is she coming back? I'm going to ask the same question."

"Not just yet, Lucas."

"What satisfaction do you get out of it?"

"I can't explain, Lucas. I wish I could."

I could feel confession trembling on my lips. But it is not your secret, I kept reminding myself.

"A governess! It's the last thing — "

"I have had letters from home."

"Aunt Maud?"

I nodded. "And my father."

"Good old Aunt Maud!"

"Lucas, please understand."

"I'm trying to."

The cider was brought and for a few seconds we were silent. Then he said, "You and I went through an extraordinary experience, Rosetta. It was bound to have an effect. Look at us. It has made you into a governess and me into a cripple."

"Dear Lucas," I said and, stretching my hand across the table, touched his. He held mine and smiled at me.

"It does me good to see you," he said. "If ever governessing becomes intolerable and you don't want to go back to Aunt Maud . . . well, there is a haven waiting for you, as you know."

"I don't forget it. It's a comfort. I am so fond of you, Lucas. . . ."

"I am now waiting for the 'but.' "

"I wish — " I began.

"I wish too. But don't let's be maudlin about it. Tell me of this place. There seems to be something of a mystery hanging about it."

"Well, of course. It is because of what happened."

"There is something about an unsolved murder. It's so very unsatisfactory. There's always a question mark. For all you know you could be living in the same house as a killer."

"That could be so."

"You speak with some conviction. No. It was all so obvious. Didn't the man run away?"

"He might have had other reasons for doing so."

"Well, it's not our affair. It is just that you are in this house. I don't like your being there. It's not only because of the murder. Do you see much of them?"

"I'm mostly with Kate."

"The little horror."

"Well, I'm finding her interesting. We're just finishing *Treasure Island*."

"What bliss!"

I laughed. "And we're going to start on *The Count of Monte Cristo*."

"I cannot express my wonder."

"Don't mock. If you knew Kate you'd realise what tremendous strides I've made. The child actually likes me, I believe."

"What's so extraordinary about that? Others like you."

"But they are not Kate. It's fascinating, Lucas. The whole place is fascinating. There seems to be something behind it all."

"I believe you are harking back to the murder."

"Well, there was a murder. I suppose when something violent happens it does something to people . . . to places."

"Now I see what interests you. Tell me, what have you discovered?"

"Nothing . . . or very little."

"Do you see much of the fascinating Mira-bel?"

"Occasionally."

"And is she so fascinating?"

"She is very beautiful. We saw her, you remember, when the sheep held us up. You must admit that she is outstanding."

"Hm."

"I only see her in my capacity as governess. She has made it clear that she is very pleased with me. Apparently I am the only governess who has been able to make her daughter behave with some resemblance to a normal girl. It was quite easy, really. From the first she knew that I did not *have* to come and I threatened to go if things became too difficult. It is amazing what strength there is in indifference."

"I've always known that. That's why I pretend to be indifferent to circumstances."

I leaned my elbows on the table and studied him.

"Yes, you have done that, Lucas. And all the time you are not as indifferent as you seem."

"Hardly ever. For one thing I'm not indifferent about this governessing. I feel very strongly about it. That's something I can't pretend about. Tell me more of them. They've behaved well to you, have they?"

"Impeccably. I can have time off when I want and, you see, a horse to ride. A special one has been chosen for me — a chestnut mare. Her name is Goldie." I laughed. I felt so happy that he had asked me to meet him.

"Sounds cosy," he said.

"It is. She wants me to know that they don't regard me as an ordinary governess. Professor's daughter and all that. It reminds me of when Felicity came to our house. It's very like that."

"Only she had an easier ride."

"Dear Felicity. We were friends from the start."

"Have you told her of your foolish exploits?"

"Not yet. I've been there such a short time really. I'm going to write to her. I wanted to work myself in first. I was telling you about Mirabel, young Lady Perrivale — there is an older one, you know. I'm inclined to think of her as Mirabel because that was what they called her in the papers. She is gracious and so is Sir Tristan."

"So you have made his acquaintance?"

"Only briefly, but it was he who suggested the mount for me. And I may be invited to join the occasional dinner party."

"A perquisite for a good governess . . . when it is a not very important occasion and someone is wanted to make up the numbers?"

"I think there might be one important occasion. They are thinking of asking you and Carleton. They have put it off because of Theresa's death."

I saw the interest in his eyes. "So you and I would be fellow guests?"

"You will come when they ask, won't you, Lucas?"

"I most certainly shall."

"Is Carleton any better?"

He lifted his shoulders. "I don't think he'll ever get over it. We're a faithful lot, we Lorimers."

"Poor Carleton. I grieve for him."

"I feel guilty. As you know, I used to envy him, even saying to myself, Why should everything go right for him? Why should this happen to me while he sails happily through? And now he is in a worse condition than I. I've got a useless leg, but he has lost the one who was more important to him than anyone else. I wish I could do something for him, but I don't know what."

"Perhaps he'll marry again."

"It would be the best thing for him. He needs a wife. He's lost without Theresa. But of course that would be in the future . . . far in the future. Trecorn is not a very happy household at the moment. If you came back it would relieve the gloom."

I said, "The children . . . they are happy?"

"They are too young to grieve for long. I think they still ask for their mother and cry for her . . . and then they forget. Good old Nanny Crockett is wonderful with them, but I don't forgive her for bringing all this about. Whatever possessed her to set it in motion?"

He was looking at me closely and I felt myself flushing.

"There must be a reason," he went on.

I was telling myself, Explain, you owe it to him.

But I could not. It was not my secret to divulge.

After a while he said, "I think I understand. We shall never be as we were before, shall we? Sometimes I look back to the first time we met. How different we were then . . . both of us. Can you remember me as I was?"

"Yes, perfectly."

"And was I very different?"

"Yes," I said.

"You were different too. You were at school: very young . . . eager . . . innocent. And then on the ship together . . . how we used to sit on the deck and talk. Remember Madeira? We were so unaware of the monstrous thing that was about to happen to us."

As he was talking I was living it all again.

He said, "I'm sorry. I shouldn't have reminded you. If we had any sense we'd do our best to forget."

"We can't forget, Lucas. We can't ever forget."

"We could . . . if we made up our minds. We could start a new life together. Do you remember when we talked of our initials? I said it was significant that life had brought us together, little knowing then what we were to endure. How close we have become since then. I said my initials spelt HELL — Hadrian Edward Lucas Lorimer — and as R.C. you could bring me back to the path of righteousness. Do you remember?"

"Yes, I do, very well."

"Well, it's true. You could save me. You see, it has come to pass. I was speaking prophetically. You and I . . . we could face everything together. We could make life better than it was before."

"Oh, Lucas, I wish — "

"We could go right away from here. Anywhere we fancied. . . . "

"You couldn't leave Trecorn, Lucas. Carleton needs you there."

"Well, would it matter where we were? We could help him together."

"Oh, Lucas, I am so sorry. I truly wish . . . "

He smiled at me ruefully. "I understand,"

he said. "Well, let's make the best of what is. Whatever happens, what we went through together will always make us special friends. I often think of that man Player. I wonder what happened to him. I should like to know, wouldn't you?"

I nodded, afraid to speak.

He went on. "I understand why you did this, Rosetta. It's because you want to move away from all that went before. You're right, in a way. So you have gone to that place. It's entirely new . . . new surroundings, new work . . . a challenge. Particularly the girl. You have changed, Rosetta. I have to say I think she is helping you."

"Yes, I am sure she is."

"It's brave of you to have done this. I think I'm something of a coward."

"Oh, no, no. You suffered more than I did. And you brought about your own freedom."

"Only because I was a useless hulk."

"You're not useless. I love you very much. I admire you, and I am so grateful because you are my friend."

He took my hand and held it firmly. "Will you always remember that?"

"Always," I said. "I'm so glad to have seen you. I feel so safe . . . to know that you are nearby."

"I shall always be there," he said. "And

416

perhaps one day you will call me in. Now. Let's get out of this place. Come. Show me your Goldie. Let's ride out to the sea and gallop along the beach. Let's tell ourselves that our good angels are smiling on us and all our wishes will be granted. There is a nice sentimental speech for an old cynic, is it not?"

"Yes, and I like to hear it."

"After all, who knows what will be waiting for us?"

"One can never tell."

And we went out to the horses.

Mrs. Ford caught me as I was going to the schoolroom for the morning lessons.

"Nanny Crockett is coming over this afternoon," she said. "Jack Carter is taking a load to Turner's Farm, so he'll be bringing her over for a couple of hours. She'll want to see you, so do come up to my room for a cup of tea."

I said I should be delighted to do so.

As we were talking, there was a commotion in the hall. I heard the voice of the head gardener; he was saying something about roses.

Mrs. Ford raised her eyebrows. "That man," she said. "You'd think the whole world depended on his flowers. He's making such a noise down there, I'd better go and see what it's all about."

Out of curiosity, I followed her.

Several of the servants were in the hall. Littleton, the head gardener, was clearly very angry.

Mrs. Ford said in a commanding voice, "Now, what is all this about?"

"You may well ask, Mrs. Ford," said Littleton. "Four of my best roses, in their prime — someone has stolen them right from under my nose."

"Well, who's done it?"

"That's what I'd like to know. If I could get my hands on them — "

"Her ladyship may have fancied them."

"Her ladyship never touches the flowers. I've looked after those roses. I've been waiting all this time to see them in bloom. Beautiful, they was. A sort of pinky blue, a rare colour for a rose. Never seen anything like them before. They was special, they was, and I've been waiting all this time for the flowers. Took a bit of rearing they did . . . and then someone comes and picks them without a by-your-leave."

"Well, Mr. Littleton," said Mrs. Ford, "I'm sorry, but I've not touched your roses. If you can find who has that's up to you, but I can't have you disturbing my servants. They've got work to do."

Littleton turned his agonised face to Mrs.

418

Ford. "They were my special roses," he said piteously.

I left them and went up to the schoolroom.

It was difficult to settle to lessons that morning. Kate wanted to hear about my meeting with Lucas on the previous day.

"I was staying with his family, you know," I told her. "So he thought he'd come over to see me."

"Did he ask you to leave here?"

I hesitated.

"He did," she said. "And you told him you would."

"I did not. I told him we were reading *Treasure Island* and that you and I get along moderately well. That's right, isn't it?"

She nodded.

"Well, now let's see if we can master these sums, and if we can we'll have an extra fifteen minutes' reading. Then I believe we could finish the book today."

"All right," she said.

"Get out the slate and we'll start right away."

Simon was very much in my thoughts that morning. The meeting with Lucas had been unsettling, and the prospect of seeing Nanny Crockett had brought back memories more vividly than usual.

When I reached Mrs. Ford's room, Nanny

Crockett had not yet arrived but she had a visitor. It was the rector, the Reverend Arthur James. Mrs. Ford was evidently a great church worker and he had come to consult her about the flower decoration for the church.

She introduced me.

"Welcome to Perrivale, Miss Cranleigh," he said. "I have been hearing from Mrs. Ford how well you are managing with Kate."

"Mrs. Ford has been very kind to me," I said.

"Mrs. Ford is kind to everyone. We have good reason to know that. My wife and I often ask each other what we would do without her. It is the decorations, you know. We rely so much on Perrivale for so many things. The big house, you see . . . garden fêtes and so on. It has been the same for generations. Sir Edward took a great interest in the church."

"Oh, yes, he was a real churchman," said Mrs. Ford. "He'd be at church twice every Sunday . . . and so were the rest of the family too. Then we had prayers every day in the hall. Yes, he was a real one for the church, was Sir Edward."

"Sadly missed," added the rector. "We don't have many like him nowadays. The younger generation haven't the same commitment. I hope to see you there with your charge, Miss Cranleigh."

420

"Yes," I said. "Of course."

"Miss Kate is a bit of a handful," said Mrs. Ford, "but Miss Cranleigh is working wonders. Her ladyship is very pleased. It was my idea that she should come, Rector. Nanny Crockett and I worked it out between us. Her ladyship can't thank me enough."

"Very gratifying."

"This is the list," said Mrs. Ford. "Mrs. Terris always likes to do the altar, so I've put her there. And the windowsills I thought could go to Miss Cherry and her sister — on one side of the church, that is — and on the other, Miss Jenkins and Mrs. Purvis. I thought if I added the flowers they're to use there'd be no squabbling."

He had taken out his spectacles and was studying the list.

"Excellent . . . excellent . . . I knew I could trust you, Mrs. Ford, to make the arrangements amicably."

They exchanged mischievous glances which implied that trouble could ensue, but for Mrs. Ford's skilful handling of the affair.

In due course the rector rose to go. He shook hands, repeated his hope that he would see Kate and me in church on Sunday, and departed.

Not long after he had left, Nanny Crockett arrived. She was delighted to see me, and

Mrs. Ford looked on benignly while we greeted each other.

"My word," said Nanny Crockett, "you do look well. And what's this I hear about you and Miss Kate getting on like a house on fire?"

"The change in Miss Kate is really remarkable," said Mrs. Ford. "Sir Tristan and my lady are very pleased."

"Miss Cranleigh has a way with children," said Nanny Crockett. "Some of us have it, some of us don't. I saw it right from the start with my two."

"How are the twins?" I asked.

"Poor little mites. To lose a mother . . . well, that's not something it's easy to get over. Though they're young; I'm thankful for that. If they'd have been a year or two older they'd have understood more what was going on. Now they think she's gone to Heaven and that to them might be like going off to Plymouth. They think she's coming back. They keep asking when. It breaks your heart. They ask after you, too. You must come over and see them sometime. They'd like that. Of course, there'd be tears when you left most likely. Well, I do what I can."

"And how is Mr. Carleton, Nanny?"

She shook her head. "Sometimes I think he'll never get over it. Poor man. He goes about in a sort of dream. Mr. Lucas . . . well, you never know with him. He broods a lot, I think. It's a sad household. I try to make it as merry as I can in the nursery."

She was looking at me intently, hoping of course to get a word with me so that I could report progress. What progress? I wondered. When I considered it I had not come very far, and apart from the fact that I was being moderately successful with Kate, my little exercise had been up till now really quite fruitless.

We chattered about things in general: the weather, the state of the crops, little bits of gossip about the neighbourhood.

Mrs. Ford did leave us together for a while. She said she had to go to the kitchen, something she had to attend to regarding the evening meal. She wanted a word with cook and it really couldn't wait.

"You two can look after each other while I'm gone," she said.

As soon as we were alone Nanny Crockett burst out. "Have you found anything?"

I shook my head. "Sometimes I wonder whether I ever shall. I don't know where the key to the mystery lies."

"Something will turn up. I feel it in my bones. If it doesn't, my poor boy will spend the rest of his life abroad . . . wandering about. That can't be."

"But Nanny, even if we discovered the truth and he was cleared, we shouldn't be able to get in touch with him easily."

"It would be in the papers, wouldn't it?"

"But if he's abroad . . . he wouldn't see them."

"We'd find a way. First we've got to prove him innocent."

"I often wonder where to begin."

"I think *she* had something to do with it."

"Do you mean Lady Perrivale?"

She nodded.

"Why should she?"

"That's what you've got to find out. And him too . . . he came into everything, didn't he? That would be the motive. You have to have a motive."

"We've gone into all that before."

"You're not giving up, are you?"

"No, no. But I do wish I could make some progress."

"Well, you're in the best place to do it. If there's anything I can do . . . at any time . . ."

"You are a good ally, Nanny."

"Well, we're not far apart. I expect you'll be coming over to Trecorn sometimes, and I can get Jack Carter to bring me here now and then. So we're in touch. I can't tell you what I'd give to see my boy again."

"I know."

Mrs. Ford came back.

"I do believe this place would go to rack and ruin without me. If I've told cook once I've told her twenty times that her ladyship can't abide garlic. She wanted to put some in the stew. She was with a French family for a few months and it's given her ideas. You have to keep your eye on them. I stopped her just in time. You two had a nice cosy chat?"

"I was saying that if I can get Jack Carter to bring me I'll come over again soon."

"Any time. You're welcome, you know that. Oh, look, Rector's left his spectacles behind. That man would forget his head if it wasn't fixed on his shoulders. He'll be lost without them. I'll have to get them over to him."

"I'll take them," I said. "I'd like a little walk."

"Oh, will you? I wonder if he's missed them yet. If he hasn't, he soon will."

I took the spectacles and Nanny Crockett said she must be going. Jack Carter would be here at any minute and he didn't like to be kept waiting.

"Then you'd better go down," said Mrs. Ford. "Well, goodbye, Nanny, and don't forget, come any time and there'll be a cup of my best Darjeeling for you."

I went with Nanny Crockett to the gate and

we had not been there more than a few minutes when Jack Carter drove up. Nanny Crockett climbed up beside him and I waved as the cart trundled off.

Then I made my way to the church. The Reverend Arthur James was delighted to receive his spectacles, and I made the acquaintance of his wife, who said with mock severity that he was always losing them and this would be a lesson to him.

I was invited in but I said I had to get back as Kate would be waiting for me. I came out of the rectory and found myself walking through the churchyard. It is strange the fascination such places have. I could not resist pausing to read some of the inscriptions on the gravestones. They were of people who had lived a hundred years ago. I wondered about their lives. There was the Perrivale vault. Cosmo was buried there. If only he could speak and tell us what really happened.

My eye was caught by the sight of a jam jar, for in it were four exquisite roses — pink roses with a bluish tinge about them.

I could not believe my eyes. I went close to look. There was the cheap headstone, inconspicuous among the splendour of the other graves, and I knew these were the roses the loss of which Littleton the gardener had been mourning this very day.

For some moments I stood staring at them.

Who had put them there? I thought of the meadowsweet, obviously picked from the hedges. But these roses . . . ?

Who had taken roses from the Perrivale garden to put in a jam jar on the grave of an unknown man?

Why had Kate shown me the grave?

I walked thoughtfully back to Perrivale Court. The more I thought of it, the more likely it seemed that Kate was the one who had taken the roses and put them on the grave.

She was waiting for me when I returned and I had not been in my room for more than a few minutes when she came in.

She sat on the bed and looked at me accusingly. "You've been out again," she said. "Yesterday you went to see that man and today you were with Mrs. Ford and when I went up there you'd gone again."

"The rector left his glasses behind and I took them back to him."

"Silly old man. He's always losing something."

"Some people are a little absent-minded. They often have more important things to think about. Did you hear all the commotion this morning about the roses?"

"What roses?" She was immediately alert

and I knew instinctively that I was on the right track.

"They were some special ones. Littleton had taken great care with them and was very proud of them. Someone took them. He was furious. Well, I know where they are."

She looked at me cautiously.

I went on: "They are in the graveyard on the grave of the man who was drowned. Do you remember? You showed me his grave. There was some meadowsweet in the jam jar then. Now there are Littleton's prize roses."

"I could see you thought the meadowsweet was awful."

"What do you mean?"

"Well, wild flowers. People usually put roses and lilies and that sort of thing on people's graves."

"Kate," I said. "You took the roses. You put them on that grave."

She was silent. Why? I wondered.

"Didn't you?" I persisted.

"All the others have things on them . . . statues and things. What are a few flowers?"

"Why did you do it, Kate?"

She wriggled. "Let's read," she said.

"I couldn't settle down to reading with this hanging over us," I said.

"Hanging over us! What do you mean?" She was bellicose, a sign of being on the defensive with her.

"Tell me truthfully why you put the flowers on that grave, Kate."

"Because he didn't have any. What are a few old roses? Besides, they're not Littleton's. They're Stepper's or my mother's. *They* didn't say anything. They wouldn't know whether they were in the garden or on the grave."

"Why did you feel this about this man?"

"He hadn't got anything."

"It's the first time I've realised you have a soft heart. It's not like you, Kate."

"Well," she said, tossing her head, "I wanted to."

"So you cut the flowers and took them to the grave?"

"Yes. I threw the wild flowers away and got some fresh water from the pump —"

"I understand all that. But why did you do it for this man? Did you . . . know him?"

She nodded and suddenly looked rather frightened and forlorn — quite unlike herself. I sensed that she was bewildered and in need of comfort. I went to her and put my arm round her and, rather to my surprise, she did not resist.

"You know we are good friends, don't you, Kate?" I said. "You could tell me."

"I haven't told anybody. I don't think they'd want me to."

"Who? Your mother?"

"And Gramps."

"Who was this man, Kate?"

"I thought he might be . . . my father."

I was astounded and for the moment speechless. The drunken sailor her father?

"I see," I said at length. "That makes a difference."

"People put flowers on their fathers' graves," she said. "Nobody else did. So . . . I did."

"It was a nice thought. No one could blame you for that. Tell me about your father."

"I didn't like him," she said. "I didn't see much of him. We lived in a house in a horrid street near a horrid market. We were frightened of him. We were upstairs. There were people living downstairs. There were three rooms with a wooden staircase down the back into the garden. It wasn't like this. It wasn't even like Seashell Cottage. It was . . . horrible."

"And you were there with your mother and your father?"

I was trying to picture the glorious Mirabel in the sort of place Kate's brief description had conjured up. It was not easy.

"He didn't come home much. He went to sea. When he came back, it was awful. He was always drunk . . . and we used to hate it. He'd stay for a while, then he'd go back to sea."

"And did you leave that place then?"

She nodded. "Gramps came and we went away . . . with him. That's when we came to Seashell Cottage . . . and everything was different then."

"But the man in the grave is Tom Parry. You are Kate Blanchard."

"I don't know about names. All I know is that he was my father. He was a sailor, and he used to come home with a white bag on his shoulder, and my mother hated him. And when Gramps came it was all different. The sailor — my father — wasn't there any more. He was only there for a little while anyway. He was always going away. Then we got on a train with Gramps and he took us to Seashell Cottage."

"How old were you then, Kate?"

"I don't remember, about three or four perhaps. It's a long time ago. I only remember little bits. Sitting in the train . . . sitting on Gramps's knee while he showed me cows and sheep in the fields. I was very happy then. I knew that Gramps was taking us away and we wouldn't have to see my father any more."

"And yet you put flowers on his grave."

"It was because I thought he was my father."

"You're not sure."

"I am . . . and then I'm not. I don't know. But he might have been my father. I hated him and he was dead . . . but if he was my father I ought to put flowers on his grave."

"And so he came back here?"

She was silent for a moment. Then she said, "I saw him. I was frightened."

"Where did you see him?"

"I saw him in Upbridge. Sometimes I used to play with Lily Drake and she'd come over to Seashell Cottage and play with me. Gramps used to think of lovely things for us to do. Lily liked coming to us and I liked going to her. Mrs. Drake used to take us into the town when she went shopping . . . and that was when I saw him."

"How could you be sure?"

She looked at me scornfully. "I knew him, didn't I? He walked in a funny way. It was as though he were drunk . . . though he wasn't always. I suppose he was drunk so much that he forgot how to walk straight. I was there with Mrs. Drake and Lily by the stall. It was full of shiny red apples and pears. And I saw him. He didn't see me. I hid behind Mrs. Drake. She's very big with a lot of petticoats. I could hide myself right in them. I heard him speak, too. He went up to one of the stall holders and asked if she knew a red-haired woman with a little girl. Her name was Mrs.

Parry. I heard the man at the stall say he knew of no such person. And I thought it was all right because my mother was not Mrs. Parry; she was Mrs. Blanchard. But I thought he was my father. . . . "

"Did you tell your mother what you'd seen?"

She shook her head. "I told Gramps though."

"What did he say?"

"He said I couldn't have. My father was dead. He'd been drowned at sea. The man I had seen was someone who looked like him."

"Did you believe him?"

"Yes, of course."

"But you said you thought this man was your father."

"Not all the time I don't. Sometimes I do . . . sometimes I don't. Then I thought if he was my father he ought to have flowers."

I held her very close to me, and she seemed glad that I did.

"Oh, Kate," I said. "I'm glad you told me."

"So am I," she said. "We had a truce, didn't we?"

"Yes," I said. "But the truce is over. We don't need it now. We're friends. Tell me what happened."

"Well, then the man I'd seen was drowned. He fell over the cliff when he was drunk. That was the sort of thing he — my father — would have done, so this man was very like him. It was very easy to make a mistake."

"His name was Parry. What was your name when you were living in that place . . . before your grandfather came?"

"I don't remember. Oh, yes, I do, it was Blanchard . . . I think."

"Do you think it might have been something else?"

She shook her head vigorously. "No. Gramps said I was always Kate Blanchard and that was my father's name and it wasn't my father I had seen in Upbridge. It was another man who looked like him. He was a sailor too. Sailors look alike. All those sailors in *Treasure Island* looked different, didn't they? But they were special ones. Oh, Cranny, I shouldn't have told you really."

"It was good to tell me. Now we understand so much about each other. We've found out that we are real friends. We're going to help each other all we can. Tell me what happened when the man was found on the rocks."

"Well, he was just found. They said he was a sailor and he didn't live here. He came from London. He'd been asking for someone . . . some relation. That was what they said in the papers."

"And you told your grandfather that you

thought he was your father."

"Gramps said it wasn't my father and I had to stop thinking he was. My father was dead and I didn't belong to that place where we used to live any more. My home was with him and my mother in our nice Seashell Cottage by the sea."

"There was quite a fuss when the man's body was found, wasn't there? Where did they find it?"

"On the rocks at the bottom of the cliff. The tide might have carried him out to sea, they said, but it didn't."

"What will you do now, Kate? Shall you go on putting flowers on his grave?"

I saw a stubborn look on her face.

"Yes," she said. "I don't care about Littleton's old roses." She laughed and for a moment was her mischievous self. "I'll take some more if I want to. They're not his. They're old Stepper's, really — *and* my mother's because she married Stepper and what is his is hers."

I thought, In her heart she believes the man in that grave is her father; and I was becoming more and more sure that I had made an important discovery.

Some
Discoveries

My thoughts were preoccupied with what I had learned from Kate, and I had a conviction that it must have some bearing on the mystery I was trying to solve.

I had made up my mind that the drunken sailor was Mirabel's first husband and, since she had been contemplating becoming the mistress of Perrivale Court, it was imperative that he should not find her.

A husband would ruin all her chances. And then he had conveniently been found at the bottom of a cliff. She would be the one who wanted to be rid of him. What if she had wanted to be rid of Cosmo as well? Why? She was to have married him. But she married Tristan immediately afterwards.

Of course, the man who had died might have nothing to do with Mirabel. There was only Kate's evidence to suggest this. I knew how imaginative she could be. She had been very young when she had last seen her father and this man who looked like him. She mentioned the way he walked as one of the reasons why she recognised him. Many sailors had that rolling gait. It was acquired through constantly adjusting their balance on an unsteady ship.

It was all very vague and I did not know what to believe, but on the other hand I felt I had taken a step forward, if only a short one.

The very next day Lady Perrivale sent for me. She was very affable. She looked so feminine that it was impossible to imagine her luring her first husband to the cliff edge and pushing him over. That was too wild a conjecture. I felt sure that the man was a stranger. Thomas Parry. How could he be the husband of Mirabel Blanchard? But it was possible that she could have changed her name. . . . And so ran my muddled thoughts.

"I believe you met your friend Mr. Lorimer the other day," she said.

"Oh, yes."

"Kate told me. She missed you very much." She smiled at me benignly. "There is no need for you to have to meet in The Sailor King, you know. He would be very welcome to come here to see you. I don't want you to feel you can't have visitors."

"That is most kind of you."

"As a matter of fact, I was thinking of asking him and his brother over to dine soon."

"I think his brother is too shocked at the moment to want to pay visits. It has been such a terrible blow to him."

"Oh, yes, indeed. However, I shall invite them both and perhaps Mr. Lucas Lorimer will accept."

"I feel sure he will be happy to do so."

"You will join us, of course. There won't be many guests. It will be just an informal occasion."

"It sounds very pleasant."

"I am sending a note over to Trecorn Manor today. I do hope they will accept."

I had an idea that she was arranging the party to show me that, although I was the governess, she did not regard me as such. I remembered so well, when Felicity came to us, that my parents had been anxious that she should not be treated like a servant because she had come to us through the recommendation of a man who could have been one of my father's colleagues — but then ours was not a conventional household.

I was pleased that Lady Perrivale should have been so sensitive of my feelings, but all the time she was talking to me I was seeing her in three sordid little rooms, escaping from them when Thomas Parry went to sea. I imagined his coming back and finding her and his little daughter flown from the nest . . . and setting out to look for them.

I wanted so much to talk to Lucas. How I wished that I could tell him all I knew. Perhaps I should. If Thomas Parry had been murdered by someone who was living in the neighbourhood today, why should that person not have treated Cosmo in the same way? And what could Simon have to do with Thomas Parry? I needed advice. I needed help. And Lucas was near.

I longed to see him and I was so anxious that he should accept this invitation to dinner that when I saw the messenger leave with the note for Trecorn Manor I hung about waiting for his return and managed to be in the courtyard when he came back.

"Oh, hello, Morris," I said. "Have you been over to Trecorn Manor?"

"Yes, Miss. No luck, though. They were out — both Mr. Carleton and Mr. Lucas Lorimer."

"So you couldn't deliver your note to them?"

"No. I had to leave it. Someone will bring the answer over later. A pity. Makes two journeys instead of one."

It was the next day when the answer came. I went down because I thought Dick Duvane would bring it, but it was not Dick. It was one of the Trecorn stablemen.

"Oh," I said. "I thought Dick Duvane would come. He usually does these things for Mr. Lucas."

"Oh, Dick's not there now, Miss."

"Not there?"

"He's gone abroad."

"Without Mr. Lucas!"

"Seemingly. Mr. Lucas, he be at the Manor, and Dick Duvane, he be gone. I did hear to foreign parts."

"Mr. Lucas will miss him."

"Aye, that he will."

"Shall I take the note to Lady Perrivale?"

"If you'd be so good, Miss."

I took it to her.

She said, "Mr. Carleton declines. He doesn't feel up to it. Poor man. But Mr. Lucas accepts with pleasure."

That was what I wanted to know. I was puzzled about Dick Duvane, though, for I knew that he and Lucas had been together for so long. However, I suppose they parted company sometimes. For instance, Dick hadn't been on the ship with Lucas.

The dinner party was to take place at the end of that week. I was glad there was not long to wait before I saw Lucas again.

Kate had been a little withdrawn after her confession. I think she must have been wondering whether she told me too much. We got through our lessons with moderate ease, but even *The Count of Monte Cristo* did not entirely hold her attention.

She was not very interested in the dinner party because she was not to attend. If I was doing something she liked to share in it. She may have regretted her confession, but in a way it had made ours a more intimate relationship.

The evening of the dinner party arrived. I dressed carefully in a gown of lapis lazuli blue which had streaks of gold in it, so that it really did resemble the stone. It was one of the dresses I had brought with me when I had visited Felicity. Aunt Maud had said there would certainly be dinner parties and I should have something becoming to wear.

I dressed my yellow hair high on my head and I noticed with pleasure that the colour of my dress made my eyes look more blue. I think I could say I was looking my best.

Kate came in to see me before I went down.

"You look quite pretty," she said.

"Thank you for the compliment."

"It's true. Is that a compliment if it's true?"

"Yes, it is. It's flattery that can be false."

"You sound just like a governess."

"Well, I am a governess."

441

She sat on the bed and laughed at me.

"It will be a boring old party," she said. "I don't know why you think it's going to be such fun. Is it because that old Lucas is going to be there?"

"He's not exactly old."

"Oh, he is. He's ever so old. You're old and he's even older than you."

"You think that because you are young. It is a matter of comparisons."

"Well, he's old and he can't walk straight either."

"How do you know?"

"One of the maids told me. He was nearly drowned and it almost killed him."

"Yes, she's right. I was nearly drowned too."

"But you're all right. He's not." I was silent and she went on: "The old Rev is going to be there with his awful wife . . . and the doctor . . . all the most boring people you can think of."

"They may be boring to you but not to me. I'm looking forward to it."

"That's why your eyes sparkle and look bluer. Tell me about it after."

"I will."

"Promise. . . . Everything."

"I'll tell you all I think you should know."

"I want to know *everything.*"

"All that is good for you."

She put out her tongue at me. "Governess," she said.

"Not the most pleasant part of your anatomy," I said.

"What's that?"

"Work it out for yourself. Now I'm going down."

She grimaced. "All right. Don't let that Lucas persuade you to go back."

"I won't."

"Promise."

"I promise that."

She smiled. "I'll tell you something. Gramps will be there, so it won't be so boring after all."

The guests were already assembling. I went down and very soon we went in to dinner. I found myself sitting next to Lucas.

"What a pleasure!" he said.

"I am so glad you came."

"I told you I would."

"What happened to Dick Duvane? I hear he has gone away."

"It's not permanent. He's just gone away for a spell."

"I'm surprised. I thought he was your good and faithful servant."

"I've never looked upon him as an ordinary servant, nor has he regarded himself as such, I believe."

"That's why I'm so surprised he's gone."

"Dick and I used to travel a lot together. We had an adventurous time. Now I'm stuck at home . . . can't get about as I used to. Poor Dick, he gets restive. He's gone off on his own . . . just for a spell."

"I thought he was so devoted to you."

"He is . . . and I to him. But because I'm afflicted and restricted, there's no reason why he should be. How are you getting along here . . . really? I suppose we can't discuss it here, right in the middle of the family. You must be getting to know them well."

"Not all. It is the first time I've seen the Dowager Lady Perrivale."

He looked along the table to where the old lady sat. She looked rather formidable. It was indeed the first time I had seen her. She had had to be helped downstairs, and I gathered that she spent most of her time in her own rooms. The major was sitting beside her carrying on an animated conversation with her, which she seemed to enjoy. Tristan at the other end of the table was talking to the doctor's wife.

Lucas was right: We could not speak of the family at their dinner table.

Conversation was general, embracing the Queen and her advancing years, the merits of

Gladstone and Salisbury, and such like.

I was not paying a great deal of attention. I so much wanted to be alone with Lucas. There was a great deal to say. I was longing to ask him what he thought about the drunken sailor.

I really believe that, had it been possible to talk intimately with Lucas then, I would have told him everything.

With the ladies I left the men over the port and went into the drawing room. To my surprise I found myself seated next to the Dowager Lady Perrivale. I thought perhaps it might have been arranged and she wanted to inspect Kate's governess.

She was one of those women who must have been formidable in her prime. I could see from her face that she was accustomed to having her own way. I remembered what I had heard of her — how she had restored Perrivale Court when she brought her money into the family — and I imagined she had a certain fondness for the place.

"I'm glad to have the opportunity of a chat, Miss Cranleigh," she said. "My daughter-in-law tells me that you are doing very well with Kate. My goodness, that is an achievement. The governesses that child has had! And not one to stay more than a month or two."

"I haven't completed a month yet, Lady Perrivale."

"I do hope you will . . . and many months. My daughter-in-law is so happy with the outcome. She said Kate is a different child."

"Kate needs to be understood."

"I suppose we all do, Miss Cranleigh."

"Some of us are less predictable than others."

"I expect you are very predictable, Miss Cranleigh. I am most unpredictable. This is what they call one of my good days. I shouldn't be down here if it were not. You look to me as if you have a very orderly mind."

"I try to have."

"Then if you try, you will. I have given up trying. Though I used to be the same. I could never endure mess and muddle. One grows old, Miss Cranleigh. Things change. How do you like Perrivale Court?"

"I think it is one of the most interesting houses I have ever been in."

"Then we agree. I was fascinated by it from the moment I saw it. I am so pleased Tristan is married and settled. I hope there will be grandchildren . . . soon enough for me to see them before I go. I should like several."

"I hope your wishes will be granted."

"I want this place to pass to my grandchildren: children of the Arkwright blood mingling with the Perrivale . . . you know what I mean. Arkwright money made it what it is to-day, so it is only right. It would be just the right mixture, you see. . . ."

I thought this was an odd conversation. I noticed that the old lady's eyes were slightly glazed and I wondered whether she had forgotten to whom she was talking. I saw Mirabel cast an anxious look in her direction.

The Dowager Lady Perrivale noticed Mirabel's glance. She waved her hand and smiled.

"Don't you think she is delightful, Miss Cranleigh? My daughter-in-law, I mean. Did you ever see anyone so beautiful?"

"No," I said. "I don't think I have."

"I knew her mother and her father, the dear major. It is so nice to have him as a neighbour. Her mother was my best friend. We went to school together. That was why the major came down here after her death . . . when he left the Army, of course. I said, 'Come and settle in Cornwall.' I'm thankful that he did. It brought dear Mirabel into the family."

"She lost her first husband," I said tentatively.

"Poor Mirabel. It's sad to be left a widow with a child to care for. Of course she had her wonderful, wonderful father . . . and he came out of the Army just at the right time. He has been a tower of strength to us all. Such a delightful man. Have you met him . . . I mean, apart from tonight?"

"Yes. Kate took me to see him at the Dower House."

"She would. She adores him. He's so good with children. Well, he's good with anyone. He's devoted to Mirabel. He was delighted with the marriage . . . so was I. It was just what I wanted. And it means the major is here with us, a charming neighbour . . . and a member of the family really."

"He has a lovely home there at the Dower House."

"He seems to like it. I'd like to go along and see him there but I can't get out now."

"What a pity."

"Yes . . . indeed. But old age takes its toll. I have a good woman. She has been my maid for years. She's my constant companion. I'm in the rooms next to those used by my husband when he was alive. It's almost a separate part of the house. My husband was a man who liked to be alone. He was very religious, you know. I always said he should have gone into the Church. Well, it has been nice to chat. You must come along and see me. Maria . . . that's my maid . . . will be pleased to see you. In fact, she keeps me informed."

"I don't think I've met Maria."

"No, you wouldn't. She's mostly in my part of the house."

"I think my room must be opposite yours."

"You're up in the nursery. Yes, that would be about it . . . across the courtyard. Oh, look, the men are coming back. They'll split us up now. I have enjoyed getting to know you. And thank you for what you're doing with Kate. That child did know how to make a nuisance of herself. My daughter-in-law tells me she is greatly relieved."

"I really don't deserve all these compliments."

Mirabel was coming towards us. She smiled at me. "Miss Cranleigh must come and talk to her friend," she said to the old lady.

Then she drew me to one side. "I hope my mother-in-law didn't confuse you. She rambles on a bit. It's rarely that she comes to things like this. But she seemed a great deal better and wanted to meet you. She's not always lucid . . . and talks wildly quite often."

"No, no," I said. "She talked normally."

"I'm glad. Oh, here's Mr. Lorimer."

Lucas was coming towards us. There was someone with him and the evening was almost over before I found myself alone with him.

"Oh, it's such a shame. I did want to say so much to you."

"You're making me very curious."

"But not here, Lucas."

"Well, then, we'd better meet. What about tomorrow at The Sailor King?"

"I'll manage to get there."

"Two thirty as before?"

"That's a good time."

"I'll look forward to it," said Lucas.

The evening was over. Kate came to my room as I was getting undressed.

"What was it like?" she asked.

"Interesting. I had a long chat with the Dowager Lady Perrivale."

"You mean Stepper's mother. She's an old witch."

"Really, Kate!"

"Well, a bit mad anyway. She stays in those rooms where Sir Edward died. She and that old Maria are up there all the time. She's with the ghost up there. I don't like her much."

"She seemed concerned about you."

"Oh, she doesn't like me. She likes my mother and Gramps, though. Did you talk to Gramps?"

"Not really . . . just greetings. It is amazing how little one can talk to people."

"What about old Lucas?"

"Why is everyone old to you?"

"Because they are."

"Well, they are certainly not nine years old. Go away now, will you? I want to go to bed."

"I want to hear all about it in the morning."

"There's really nothing to tell."

"I suppose you think you are going to go to parties here and find a rich husband."

"Most of the men seem to have wives already," I said with a smile.

"All you have to do is . . ."

"What?" I asked.

"Murder them," she said. "Good night, Cranny. See you in the morning."

And she was gone.

I was disturbed. What was actually in the child's mind? I wondered. What did she know? And how much did she make up when she did not know? I kept thinking about the sailor. I had almost made up my mind to tell Lucas.

When I met Lucas the following day, I was still wavering. But the first thing he said when we were seated was, "Now, out with it. What's on your mind? Why don't you tell me? You've wanted to for a long time . . . and in any case that's why you've brought me here today."

"There *is* something," I said. "Lucas, if you promise . . . promise you won't *do* anything that I ask you not to . . . "

He looked at me in puzzlement. "Is it something that happened on the island?"

"Well, yes . . . in a way."

"John Player?"

"Yes. But he isn't John Player, Lucas."

"That doesn't surprise me. I knew there was some mystery."

"Promise me, Lucas. I must have your promise before I tell you."

"How can I promise when I don't know what I'm promising?"

"How can I tell you if I don't know you will?"

He smiled wryly. "All right, I promise."

I said, "He's Simon Perrivale."

"What?"

"Yes, he left England on the *Atlantic Star* . . . taking the place of one of the deckhands."

Lucas was staring at me.

"Lucas," I said earnestly. "I want to prove his innocence . . . so that he can come back."

"This explains . . . everything."

"I thought it would. And I was afraid that you might think it your duty to tell the authorities . . . or someone."

"Don't worry about that. I've promised, haven't I? Tell me more. I suppose he confessed this to you on the island when I was lying there, unable to move?"

"Yes, it was like that. There is something else you must know. He was in the seraglio . . . or rather just outside it, working in the gardens. I told you how I became friendly with Nicole and she was the friend of the Chief Eunuch. Well, he . . . Simon . . . managed to ingratiate himself with the Chief Eunuch and — I think because of it and because of Nicole — he helped us both. Simon escaped with me."

Lucas was speechless with incredulity.

"We were taken away together and left close to the British Embassy. I went in . . . and in time came home. Simon dared not be sent home. He left me there. He was going to try to get to Australia."

"And you have heard nothing of him since?"

I shook my head.

"I understand now," he said, "why you have this crazy idea of proving his innocence."

"It's not crazy. I know he's innocent."

"Because he told you?"

"It's more than that. I got to know Simon very well."

He paused for a few seconds before he said, "Wouldn't it be better for him to come home and face things? If he is innocent . . . "

"He *is* innocent. But how could he prove it? They have all decided that he is guilty."

"And you think you are going to make them change their minds?"

"Lucas, I know there is some way of doing this. There must be. I'm certain of it. If only I could find the answer."

"This is the most important thing in the world to you, is it?"

"I want it more than anything."

"I see. Well, what good is it playing governess to that child?"

"I'm here. I'm close to the people who were involved in it. It's a way — "

"Listen, Rosetta. You're not being logical. You're letting your emotions get in the way of your common sense. You've had some fantastic adventures; you were plunged into a world so different from the one you knew, that you are not thinking clearly. What happened to you was melodramatic . . . beyond what you could have imagined before. Miraculously, you came through. It was a chance in a thousand . . . but because it happened you expect life to go on like that. You were in that seraglio . . . a prisoner . . . everything was so different there. Wild things could happen. You're in another sort of seraglio now, one of your own making. You're a prisoner of your imagination. You think you are going to solve this murder, when it is clear what has happened. The innocent rarely run away. You should remember that. He couldn't have said 'I'm guilty' more clearly. You're not being logical, Rosetta. You're living in a world of dreams."

"Nanny Crockett believes in him."

"Nanny Crockett! What has she to do with it?"

"She was his nurse. She knew him better than anyone. She says he is incapable of such a thing. She knows."

"That explains this friendship. I suppose she put you up to this governessing."

"We worked it out together. We didn't think of my being a governess until the possibility arose. Then we saw that it was a way of getting me into the house."

I was looking at him appealingly.

"Do you want my opinion?" he said.

I nodded. "Please, Lucas."

"Drop it. Give up this farce. Come back to Trecorn. Marry me and make the best of a bad job."

"What do you mean, a bad job?"

"Say goodbye to Simon Perrivale. Put him out of your thoughts. Look at it like this: He ran away when he was about to be arrested. That is too significant to be ignored. If he returned he'd be tried for murder and hanged. Let him lead a new life in Australia . . . or wherever he lands up. As you're so certain of his innocence, give him a chance to start a new life."

"I want to prove that he was wrongly accused."

"You want him to come back." He looked at me sadly. "I understand absolutely," he said. He shrugged his shoulders and looked grave, as though communing with himself. Then he said, "What discoveries have you made so far?"

"There was a drunken sailor."

"Who?"

"His name was Thomas Parry. He fell over a cliff and was drowned."

"Wait a minute. I remember something about that. There was quite a stir about it at the time. It was some while ago. Didn't he come down here . . . from London, I think? Got drunk and fell over the cliff. It's coming back to me."

"Yes," I said. "That's the one. Well, he's buried in the graveyard here. I discovered Kate putting flowers on his grave. When I asked her why, she said he was her father."

"What? Married to the glorious Mirabel?"

"One can't be sure with Kate. She romances. She said that she saw him in the market in Upbridge and he was asking if anyone knew a red-haired woman named Parry with a little girl. She was frightened and hid herself behind the woman she was with, the mother of a little girl she had gone to play with. She was frightened of him. Apparently she had memories of a father who was a brute."

"And he was found at the bottom of the cliff."

"You see, it seems so fortuitous. If Mirabel was hoping to marry one of the Perrivales and a husband from the past who is supposed to be dead turns up, it could be awkward."

"And as far as the glorious Mirabel was concerned, he was more useful at the bottom of the cliff than making trouble for her. It makes sense."

"Not completely. You see, I only have Kate's word for it. I asked her if she had told her mother she had seen him. She said no, but she had told Gramps. Gramps is her name for her grandfather, Major Durrell. He said she had made a mistake and she shouldn't mention it because it would upset her mother, and her father anyway was dead. He'd been drowned at sea."

"Why should the child think it was her father?"

"She's a strange child, given to fantasy. It occurred to me that she might miss a father and was inventing one."

"She has Sir Tristan as a stepfather."

"He doesn't take much notice of her. She calls him Stepper in a rather contemptuous way . . . but then she is contemptuous of most of us. It occurred to me that she had seen people putting flowers on graves and thought she would like to do it and so invented a father. The sailor had no relations so she put flowers on his grave and adopted him."

"It seems plausible . . . but how is all this going to solve Simon Perrivale's troubles?"

"I don't know. But just suppose someone now in the house did the murder . . . well, people who commit one might not hesitate at another. It might be part of the whole picture."

He looked at me in some exasperation.

I said, "I was afraid you'd take it like this. I hoped you might help me."

"I'll help," he said, "but I don't think it is going to get anywhere. Simon, it seems, was jealous of the other two. He killed one in a rage, and was caught by the other. That's it. As for the sailor, I think you may be right. The child wanted a father so she took up with a dead man who had no relations around."

"She cut the head gardener's prize roses to put on his grave."

"There you are. That bears it out."

"All the same . . ."

"All the same," he repeated, smiling at me quizzically, "if we are going to investigate, we have to pick up the most likely point, and there is a faint possibility that something might be lurking behind the untimely death of the sailor. At least that is something we could start with."

"How?"

"Find out something about him. Who was he? Who was his wife? Then if she should happen to be the present Lady Perrivale it might begin to look as though we were on to something. And if someone actually got rid of the sailor because he was making a nuisance of himself . . . well, there is a possibility that that person, having successfully accomplished one crime, might try another."

"I knew you'd help me, Lucas."

"So we begin to unravel the skein," he said dramatically.

"How?"

"Go to London. Look up records. What a pity Dick Duvane isn't here. He would throw himself into this with enthusiasm."

"Oh, Lucas . . . I'm so grateful."

"I'm grateful too," he said. "It relieves the monotony of my days."

I went back to Perrivale Court in a state of euphoria.

I knew I was right to have taken Lucas into my confidence.

Lucas was away for three weeks. Each day I looked for a message from him. Kate and I had settled into a routine. She still had her difficult moments, but she made no attempts to play truant. We read together, discussed what we read, and I made no reference to the sailor's grave, which she continued to visit. She did not take any more flowers from the garden but contented herself with wild ones.

A few days after Lucas had left for London, Maria, the Dowager Lady Perrivale's maid, sought me out and said that her mistress would like to have a chat with me.

Maria was one of those servants who, having been in the service of a master or mistress for a long time, feel themselves to be especially privileged. Moreover, they are usually too useful to their employers to be denied what they expect. They look upon themselves as "one of the family," and I could see that, as far as Maria was concerned, this might be to my advantage.

It was the first time I had been in that part of the house which, when I looked from my own window, I could see across the courtyard.

Maria greeted me, putting her fingers to her lips.

"She's fast asleep," she said. "That's just like her. She'll ask someone to come and see her and when they come she's dead to the world."

She beckoned me and opened a door.

There, sitting in a big armchair, was Lady Perrivale. Her head had fallen to one side and she was indeed fast asleep.

"We won't disturb her for a bit. She had a bad night. Gets them sometimes. Having nightmares about that Sir Edward. He was a bit of a tartar. Eee . . . but you know naught about that. She's up and down. Quite her old self sometimes. Then her mind goes wandering."

"Shall I come back later?"

She shook her head. "Sit you down here for a bit. When she wakes she'll ring or bang her stick. Oh, dear me, she's not what she was."

"I suppose that happens to us all in time."

"Reckon. But she went down when Sir Edward passed away."

"Well, I suppose they'd been married for a long time."

She nodded. "I was with her when she came south. Sorry to leave Yorkshire, I was. Ever been, Miss Cranleigh?"

"No, I'm afraid not."

"The dales have to be seen to be believed . . . and the moors. 'Tis a gradely place, Yorkshire."

"I am sure it is."

"Here? Well . . . I don't know. I could never get used to these folks. Full of fancies. Now that's something you couldn't accuse us of."

She looked at me in a somewhat bellicose manner which I thought was undeserved as I had no intention of accusing her of being fanciful.

"A spade's a spade up there, Miss Cranleigh. None of this fancy stuff. Airy-fairy: people walking out of their graves . . . little men in the mines . . . goblins and things sinking the boats. I don't know. Seems a funny way of going on to me."

"It certainly does," I agreed.

"Mind you, in a house like this, some people might get the creeps."

"But not a Yorkshire woman."

She grinned at me. I could see she was regarding me as . . . well, not quite as a kindred spirit, but, coming from London, at least I was not one of the fanciful Cornish.

"So you came here with Lady Perrivale when she married," I said.

"Well, I was with her before that. And what a to-do it was. Marrying a title. He had the brass, old Arkwright did . . . rolling in it. But brass ain't everything. And when she became 'my lady,' she was on clouds of glory. This house: what she did to it! It was in a right old mess. This house . . . and her ladyship too, if you please. Of course, she had to take Sir Edward with it."

"Was that such an ordeal?"

"He was a strange sort, he was. You never got to know him. She was used to having her own way. Old Arkwright adored her. Good-looking, she was, and all that brass of course. Only child . . . heiress. You could see what Sir Edward was after."

"How was he such a strange one?"

"He didn't say much. He was always so very proper. My goodness, he was strict."

"I've heard that."

"At church every Sunday, morning and evening. Everyone had to go, even the tenants, or it was a black mark against them. He was making sure of his place in Heaven . . . and then that boy! . . ."

"Yes?" I said eagerly, for she had paused.

"Bringing him in like that. If it was anyone else's you would have said . . . you know what I mean, men being what they are. But you wouldn't believe it with Sir Edward. I often wondered who that boy was. Her ladyship hated the sight of him. Well, you could understand it. Old Nanny Crockett used to stick up for him. I wondered her ladyship didn't get rid of her, but Sir Edward wouldn't have had that. He'd have put his foot down hard about that. Though mostly he didn't interfere about the servants . . . as long as they all went to church and attended the prayer meeting every morning in the hall. I've heard her ladyship storm and rage, say she wouldn't have the little bastard in the house . . . yes, she went as far as that. Well, you could understand it. I heard everything, me being her personal maid and all that, having been with her when we was in Yorkshire. She wanted her own maid and she settled on me. There's not much I haven't seen. Here, why am I talking to you like this? Well, I look on her as my child really. It's like talking about myself. And you're here . . .one of the family, you know. You must have seen a bit of life with that Miss Kate — "

She pressed her lips together and I had the impression that she was reproaching herself for having talked of such intimate matters to me, almost a stranger.

"You must have seen a great many changes here," I said.

She nodded. "I was always one for a bit of gossip," she said, still excusing herself. "And I don't get much chance of that up here all day. It gets a bit lonely. You've got one of them sympathetic natures, Miss Cranleigh, I can see that. You're an understanding sort."

"I hope so. I find it very interesting here . . . the house and the people."

"That's so. As you was saying, I've seen some changes. People don't come to this part of the house much. You know what they're like round here, as we were saying. . . . Sir Edward died here. They think he'll come back and haunt the place. There's talk about it. They've seen lights. They say it's Sir Edward looking for something because he can't rest."

"I saw a light once," I said. "I thought it was a candle. It flickered . . . and then I didn't see it any more."

She nudged me. "I can tell you what that was. That was her." She jerked her head towards Lady Perrivale's room. "She does that sometimes. Gets up in the night. She'll light a candle. I've told her many times, I've said, 'You'll set the place alight one day . . . your own nightdress perhaps.' She says, 'I have to look. I have to find it.' 'Find what?' I say. Then she gets a funny look in her eyes and shuts her mouth and won't say a thing."

"Do you think she is really looking for something?"

"People get notions when they get old. No . . . there's nothing. She's just got this notion in her head. Time after time I've told her. 'If there's something you've mislaid, tell me what. I'll find it for you.' But no, it's just some fancy that comes to her in the night. I have to watch out, though. She could start a fire and there's a lot of wood in a place like

465

this. What I do is hide the matches. But that don't stop her. I've heard her groping about in the dark."

"In her room?"

"No, in his room . . . Sir Edward's. They had separate rooms, you know. I always think there's something amiss with separate rooms."

"You must be kept busy here, looking after Lady Perrivale."

"Oh, yes. I do everything. Keep the place clean . . . cook her food. It's not often she goes down to parties like she did the other night. But she'd been better for the last week or so. They lead their own lives and she's very content with the present Lady Perrivale. She wanted her to marry one of the boys."

"Yes, I heard that she knew her mother."

"Yes, school friend, she was. She wanted the major to come here; she found Seashell Cottage for them and before long Miss Mirabel was engaged to Mr. Cosmo."

"He died though, didn't he?"

"Murdered. I can tell you, that was a time. It was that boy Simon. They'd always been against each other."

"He went away, didn't he?"

"Oh, yes. Ran off. He was a sharp little fellow, even when he was small. It was the only thing he could do . . . or hang by the neck. I reckon he'll fall on his feet. He was that sort."

"What do you think happened?"

"It's plain as the nose on your face. Simon had had enough. He had his eye on Mirabel. Not that he had a chance." She lowered her voice. "Perhaps I'm speaking out of turn, but I always thought she had her eye on the title, so she took Cosmo. I think Simon shot him in a temper."

"But why should he have the gun handy like that?"

"Now you're asking me. Looks like he took it there for a purpose, don't it? Eee. You never know. There's nowt as queer as folk, as we say in Yorkshire. And by gum, we're right. Well, everyone seems to have made up their minds it was jealousy . . . and jealousy's a terrible thing. It can lead anywhere."

"So then Lady Perrivale married Tristan."

"Yes. Well, they always had a fancy for each other, those two. I've got a pair of eyes in my head. I've seen things. And I'll tell you this: I said to myself, more than once, 'Ho, ho, there'll be trouble when she marries Cosmo because Tristan's the one she wants.' I've seen a thing or two."

She stopped abruptly and put her fingers to her mouth.

"I'm talking out of turn again. It's so nice to have a chat with someone who's interested."

"I am certainly interested," I assured her.

"Well, you're one of the family now, I suppose. And, after all, it happened some time ago. It's all over and done with now."

I could see that she would need but little prompting to overcome her qualms of conscience, and I continued to prompt her.

"Yes, of course," I said. "But I daresay everyone was discussing it all at one time."

"My goodness, yes. That's a fact."

"You were saying you'd seen a thing or two."

"Oh . . . I don't know. It was just that I noticed one or two things, so it didn't surprise me at all when she turned to Tristan. People said it was on the rebound . . . and, poor things, they comforted each other. Well, you know what people say. . . ."

She was frowning slightly. She was, I think, trying to remember how much she had said.

"Her ladyship and me, we used to have some fun together. She'd tell me everything . . . two girls together, that's what we were like . . . and then of course she changed. It's a long time since I've had a chat like this. Well, I'd better take a look at her. Catnaps, that's what she takes. Then she'll wake up suddenly and want to know what's going on."

She rose and went to the door. I was hoping that Lady Perrivale would not have woken up, for the conversation with Maria had been very interesting and illuminating. I had always been aware that servants knew as much as anyone did of a family's secrets — perhaps even more.

I heard a peevish voice. "Maria . . . what's happened? Wasn't someone coming?"

"Yes, you wanted to have a chat with the governess. She's been waiting here for you to wake up."

"I am awake."

"Now you are. Well, here she is: Miss Cranleigh."

Lady Perrivale smiled at me. "Bring a chair, Maria, so that she can sit down."

The chair was brought.

"Closer to me," said Lady Perrivale, and Maria complied.

We talked for a while, but I could see that her mind wandered. She was not nearly as lucid as she had been on the night of the party and was not sure which of the governesses I was, and then suddenly she remembered I was the successful one.

She talked about the house and told me what a state it had been in when she came and how she had repaired it and given it a new lease of life.

After a short while I saw her head nodding and she fell into a doze.

Quietly I rose and looked for Maria.

She said, "It's not one of her good days. She had a bad night. I'll bet she was wandering about in the dark . . . looking for something which isn't there."

"Well, I must go now. I did enjoy talking to you."

"I hope I didn't say too much. Got carried away by having someone to talk to for a bit. You must come again. I've always enjoyed a bit of a gossip."

"I will," I promised.

I went back to my room. It had not been a wasted afternoon.

A message from Lucas was sent to the house.

He was back and wanted to see me as soon as possible. I could not wait for the meeting and soon after I received the message was in the parlour at The Sailor King with him.

"Well," he said. "I've made some discoveries. I think Miss Kate must be romancing."

"Oh, I'm glad of that. I should have hated to think Lady Perrivale had murdered her first husband."

"It seems that this Thomas Parry was a sailor."

470

"That's the one."

"He married a Mabel Tallon. She was a chorus girl."

"Lady Perrivale, a chorus girl!"

"Might have been . . . before she acquired her airs and graces. But listen, isn't her father down here?"

"Yes, Major Durrell. Mirabel Durrell doesn't sound much like Mabel Tallon."

"A Mabel might call herself Mirabel."

"Yes, but it is the surname which is important."

"She could have changed that."

"But there is her father."

"Listen. There is a child. I looked that up. She was Katharine."

"Kate! Well, that could be."

"It's a fairly common name."

"But it's the only thing that might fit."

"And you want to hitch on to that?"

"No, I don't. I think Kate imagined the whole thing. She's lonely, really. I know by the way she so quickly became friendly with me. There's something pathetic about her. She wants a father. That's why she has adopted this sailor."

"You would have thought she would have looked for someone more worthy."

"She had to take what there was. He was there in the grave . . . unknown . . . and don't forget she had seen him in the marketplace."

"Had she, do you think? Or did she imagine that?"

"I think she must have seen him, because he was there and he was seeking information about his wife and child."

"We have proved that he had one and she happened to be named Katharine."

"Well, there are other diminutives for the name: Kathy, for instance."

"Yes, that's so. I suppose Kate is the more usual. But that alone is too flimsy to hitch on to. And Mirabel's father gives a touch of respectability. Major Durrell. She could hardly have involved him. No. Let's close the books on that one and look for another strand to unravel."

"I must tell you that I have made a little discovery while you've been away. I've spoken to Lady Perrivale's maid, Maria . . . that is, the Dowager Lady Perrivale."

"Ah. And what has she revealed?"

"Not a great deal that I didn't know already. But she was very garrulous."

"Just what we need."

"She remembered Simon's being brought to the house and the fuss and consternation because no one could figure out how he came to exist. With some it would seem obvious that there had been a misdemeanour on the part of the master of the house . . . but not Sir Edward. He was not the type to indulge in that sort of thing. He was God-fearing, a pillar of the church, eager that high principles be upheld."

"By others, but perhaps he was a little more lenient where he himself was concerned. Some people are like that."

"Yes, of course. But not Sir Edward. And this misdemeanour must have occurred before his marriage."

"Well, they do now and then."

"To people like Sir Edward?"

"Maybe. He came to repentance after it happened because he brought the boy into his house . . . but do you think there could have been some other reason why Simon was brought to the house?"

"Perhaps that is one of the things we have to find out."

"He might have been sorry for the child left alone with that aunt."

"Do you think the mother might have been some poor relation?"

"What was to prevent his saying so? As far as I can see he just brought the child into the house and let people draw their own conclusions. No, it just doesn't make sense. It must have been a lapse. Even the most virtuous have been known to stumble."

"But he was so insistent on morality."

"Repentant sinners are often like that."

"I can't believe it of him. There is something behind it."

"Listen to me, Rosetta, you're chasing shadows. You're believing something because you want to. You're dabbling in dangerous waters. Just suppose you are right. Just suppose there is a murderer in that house and suppose he — or she — discovered you are meddling. I don't like the idea. If this person murdered once, why shouldn't he — or she — do it again?"

"So you believe there is a murderer in the house?"

"I did not say so. I think the police version is the most likely one, and Simon the most plausible suspect. Running away seems to make it fit."

"I don't accept it."

"I know you don't . . . because you don't want to. You knew the man we were with all that time. That was different. We were all fighting for our lives. He was heroic and resourceful. We both owe our lives to him, but that does not mean that in different circumstances he might not be a murderer."

"Oh, Lucas, you can't believe that!"

"I did not know him as well as you did," he said ruefully.

"You were with him all the time. He dragged you out of the sea. He was most concerned for you."

"I know. But people are complex. When his passions of jealousy were aroused, he could have been a different person."

"You won't help me because you don't believe in him."

"I will help you, Rosetta, because I believe in you."

"I don't know what that means, Lucas."

"It means that I'll help you all I can, but I think you have set yourself a hopeless task and one which could be dangerous."

"If you think it could be dangerous you must believe in Simon's innocence. Otherwise the people in that house would have nothing to hide."

"Yes, that may be so. But I do want you to be careful. In your enthusiasm you might betray your thirst for knowledge. And just suppose you were right? Then it could be dangerous. Please be careful, Rosetta."

"I will. By the way, something came out of my talk with Maria. Apparently while Mirabel was engaged to Cosmo she was having some sort of flirtation with Tristan."

"Oh?"

"Well, according to Maria it was Tristan whom Mirabel preferred all along."

"That's interesting."

"I thought it might be a motive."

"She could have transferred her hand to the brother without murder."

"And lose the title and everything that went with it?"

"I am sure that would have been important to her, but would she have murdered for it?"

"They might have, Tristan and she between them. There was something to gain."

"Well, it's the best you've come up with so far. But I wouldn't rely too much on servants' gossip. By the way, I may be going back to London in a few days' time."

"Oh? So soon after . . . shall you be away long?"

"I'm not sure. As a matter of fact, I'm going to have an operation. I've been thinking about it for some time."

"You didn't mention it."

"Oh, I didn't want to bother you with such a thing."

"How can you say that! You know I am enormously concerned. Tell me about it."

"It's this fellow in London. Something very new, of course. It may work, it may not. He's quite frank about that."

"Lucas! And you just mention it casually like this?"

"I don't feel exactly casual about it. I saw

this man when I went up on my sleuthing operation concerning the drunken sailor. I killed two birds with one stone, you might say."

"And you've only just told me!"

"I thought I'd better explain my absence. You might have been expecting some messages. 'Come at once: Murderer discovered' or something like that."

"Don't be flippant, please, Lucas."

"All right. The fact is my leg is in pretty bad shape. It's getting worse. Well, this extremely clever bone man has introduced certain methods. He can't give me a new leg, alas, but he may be able to do something. If it's successful, I'd always walk with a limp but it could be an improvement. And . . . the fact is . . . I'm ready to take a chance."

"Lucas, is it dangerous?"

He hesitated just a second too long. "Oh, no. I couldn't be made more of a cripple than I already am, but — "

"Tell me the truth."

"To tell the truth, I'm a bit in the dark myself. There *is* a hope . . . a faint one, perhaps . . . but I want to take it."

"Why didn't you tell me before?" I demanded.

"I wasn't sure that I was going to do it. And then I thought, Why not? It can't be much

477

worse if it goes wrong, and it could be a lot better."

"And I'm going on about all this when you've got this on your mind!"

"Your concern touches me deeply, Rosetta," he said seriously.

"Of course I'm concerned. I care very much about you."

"I know. Well, I shall be leaving in a few days' time."

"How long will it take?"

"I'm not sure. If it's successful, perhaps a month. I'm going into this man's clinic. It's just off Harley Street."

"I shall hate to think you are not here."

"Promise me you'll be careful."

"About probing. Of course I will."

"Don't make it too blatant and don't take too much notice of servants' chatter."

"I promise you, Lucas. Will you give me the address of this clinic?"

He took a piece of paper from his wallet and wrote it down.

"I shall come to see you," I said.

"That will be pleasant for me."

"I shall keep in touch with Carleton. What is he going to feel about your going away like this?"

"I don't think my being here makes much difference. It doesn't bring Theresa back.

He'll be all right. He throws himself into his work, and that's the best thing for him."

The news had cast a gloom over the day for me. It was typical of Lucas that he should make light of a serious matter. What was this operation? Was it dangerous in any way? If it were, I knew he would not tell me.

I felt very uneasy.

We left The Sailor King and went out to the stables.

"I'll escort you back to Perrivale," he said.

We rode on in silence and all too soon the house came into view.

"Oh, Lucas," I said. "I wish you weren't going. I shall miss you very much."

"I'll remember that," he replied. "It won't be long before you'll see me galloping up to The Sailor King, a changed man."

I looked at him sadly.

Then he said seriously, "But I *am* concerned about you, Rosetta. Take care. Give up the search until I return. That's the best plan."

"I promise to be very careful, Lucas."

He took my hand and kissed it.

"*Au revoir*, Rosetta," he said.

I felt depressed. These meetings with Lucas had meant a great deal to me, and to be deprived of them made me wretched. Moreover, I was worried about him. What was the operation? I wondered. Had he been a little too secretive about it?

When I went riding with Kate I suggested we call in at Trecorn Manor one day.

"It's rather a long way. We couldn't do it in an afternoon. But why shouldn't we have a day's holiday? I will ask your mother if it would be permitted."

Kate was excited by the prospect and, as I had been sure, there was no difficulty in getting the required permission.

My riding had improved since my arrival. I could manage a long ride easily now, and Kate was quite capable of it.

I was delighted to see her so pleased at the prospect of our little outing.

"It's quite grand," she commented, when she saw the house. "Not so grand as Perrivale, of course, but it's all right."

"I am sure the Lorimers would be pleased by your approval."

"Are we going to see that old Lucas?"

"No. He's not there."

"Where is he?"

"In a clinic."

"What's a clinic?"

"A sort of hospital."

"What's he doing there?"

"You know he hurt his leg."

"Yes, in the shipwreck. He can't walk very well."

"They are going to see if they can do something about it."

She was thoughtful. "Who shall we see then?"

"His brother, I hope, and the twins and Nanny Crockett."

We left our horses in the stables and went to the house. Mr. Lorimer was on the estate but Nanny Crockett should be informed that we were here.

She came hurrying down.

"Oh, Miss Cranleigh. How nice to see you! And Miss Kate! Well!"

"Where are the twins?" asked Kate.

"Oh, they'll want to see you. They remember you, Miss Cranleigh."

"I hope I shall be able to see Mr. Lorimer before I leave."

"Oh, he's gone to London."

"I mean Mr. Carleton."

"I was thinking you'd come to see Mr. Lucas. They're going to do something about his leg." She shook her head. "They're *supposed* to be very clever nowadays. I don't know."

"I knew he was going. I wanted to talk to Mr. Carleton about it."

"He'll be back before long, I reckon. Come up to the nursery and see the twins."

Jennifer recognised me at once and ran to me. Henry was unsure, I could see, but he followed his sister.

"Now tell me how you've been getting on," I said. "This is Kate, who is my pupil now."

Kate was looking at the children with slightly scornful interest.

I asked Jennifer how one-eyed Mabel was and also Reggie the bear. She laughed and said they were as naughty as ever.

I talked with the children for a while and Nanny Crockett said why didn't they show Kate the dolls' house.

The twins jumped with glee. I looked anxiously at Kate, who might well state her lack of interest in such childish toys.

I think my glance must have been appealing for she said, "All right."

The dolls' house was in a corner of the nursery. The children went over to it and Nanny Crockett signed to me to sit down.

"Is there any news?" she asked in a whisper.

I shook my head.

"It's difficult. I can't find out anything. Sometimes I think it's an impossible task."

"I know you'll find something. I know there's something to be found . . . and it's in that house. That's where the secret lies. I wish

I could get there."

"I get little bits of information but they don't lead anywhere."

"Well, you go on trying. Have you tried talking to Mrs. Ford? She knows most of what's going on."

"Perhaps you could talk to her. You're on such friendly terms."

"I've tried but I don't get very far."

"Perhaps she doesn't know anything — or, if she did, thinks she shouldn't talk about the family."

"She might talk to someone in the house while she wouldn't to someone outside it. And you're there, you're one of them. I'm out of it now."

I could see that Kate was listening to what we were saying and I flashed a sign to Nanny Crockett. She understood at once and we talked of the children and how they would soon be needing a governess.

Kate called, "You won't come back here, will you, Cranny?"

So I knew she was taking note of what we were saying.

"Not while you continue to be a good pupil," I replied.

Kate grimaced. But it was clear that there could be no intimate conversation with Nanny Crockett.

In due course one of the maids came to say that Mr. Lorimer had returned.

I left Kate in the nursery and went down to see him. He looked very sad but he was pleased to see me.

I said, "I'm worried about Lucas. What do you know about this operation?"

"Very little. He went up to London recently to see this man and to have a thorough examination. Well, this is the result."

"What do they think they'll be able to do?"

"It's a little vague. They say they have made a lot of advances in that field. It is an attempt to put right what went wrong when his leg was left to set itself."

"I constantly regret that we did not know what to do. We could have prevented all this."

"It's no use blaming yourself, Rosetta, or the man who was with you. You did the best you could. You saved his life between you. You couldn't have done more. Believe me, he is eternally grateful to you. I know he talks lightly of these things, but he does feel more deeply than you would think."

"Yes, I know."

"He knows best what he should do. You see, this is a chance. He's ready to take it. It may be that if it fails he'll be worse than he was before, but if it succeeds he'll be a great deal better."

"It's rather a risk, I gather."

"I gathered that too."

"They will let you know the result of the operation as soon as they see how it is going, I suppose?"

"Yes, I'm sure of that."

"Carleton, when you hear, would you send a message to me?"

"Of course I will."

We were silent for a moment. Then Carleton said, "It was a great tragedy to him. He always hated it when anything went wrong with his health. And that sort of deformity . . . it hit him hard."

"I know."

"I wish . . . he could marry. I think that would mean a lot to him."

"Providing of course that it was a happy marriage."

"A happy marriage is the perfect state."

"Yes . . . if it's perfect. Otherwise it has to be a compromise."

I could see that Carleton was thinking of his own marriage.

"And then," he said sadly, "it can all end . . . suddenly . . . and you wonder whether it wouldn't have been better never to have known it."

"Carleton, I understand perfectly, but I

485

think you should rejoice in what you have had."

"Yes, you're right. Here I am, revelling in my misery. What do you think of the twins?"

"They're fine. Nanny Crockett is wonderful. They've grown, haven't they?"

"We'll have to be thinking of a governess for them." He looked at me speculatively.

"I'm not really a governess, you know."

"I hear you've done well with that girl."

"How my fame travels!" I said lightly.

"You must have some luncheon before you go back."

"Well, thanks. I suppose we should need something. It's a good ride to Perrivale from here. I'll call Kate."

"Yes. They'll be ready to serve it in a few minutes."

Kate was delighted to have lunch in the Trecorn dining room. Carleton was quite attentive to her and treated her like an adult, which she enjoyed. She did justice to the food and talked quite animatedly about Perrivale Court, which amused Carleton and seemed to lighten his spirits a little. So it was a successful visit.

He came out to the stables with us.

"Thank you for coming," he said, to Kate as well as to me. "I hope you'll come again."

"Oh, we will," Kate told him, which I

found gratifying, and so did he.

On the way back Kate said, "The lunch was nice. Those silly twins with their old dolls' house were a bore, though."

"Didn't you think it was rather a lovely dolls' house?"

"Cranny, I am not a child. I don't play with toys. He wants you to go back, doesn't he?"

"Who?"

"That old Carleton."

"I feel your vocabulary must be very limited. You use the same adjective to describe almost everyone."

"Which adjective?"

"Old."

"Well, he is old. He does want you to go back and teach those silly twins, doesn't he?"

"At least they are not old. Why should you think that?"

"Because Nanny Crockett wants you to go back."

"Not *old* Nanny Crockett?"

"Well, she's so old you don't have to say it. She said she'd keep in touch and so did Carleton."

"He meant about his brother. He's going to let me know about his operation."

"Perhaps they'll cut off his leg."

"Of course they won't; trust you to think of such a thing! They're going to make it better.

He's a great friend of mine and naturally I want to know how he gets on. So ... his brother and Nanny Crockett will keep me informed if they hear of his progress."

"Oh," she said and laughed.

Suddenly she burst into song.

> Fifteen men on the Dead Man's
> Chest —
> Yo-ho-ho, and a bottle of rum!
> Drink and the devil had done for
> the rest ...

I thought, I believe she really cares for me.

During the next days I felt very depressed. I was realising how important it was to me to know that Lucas was close at hand. I grew more and more worried about the operation. Carleton knew no more than I did, and it was typical of Lucas to be reticent about such a thing.

It was brought home to me how futile were my investigations. Lucas thought they were absurd and he was right. If only he were at hand and I could send a message over to Trecorn and arrange a meeting.

I wondered what this operation would do to him, and I greatly feared the result.

Kate sensed my melancholy and tried to

cheer me up. When we were reading my attention would stray, and this puzzled her. It was during this time that I began to be sure that she had some affection for me. That would have been very comforting at any other time but now I could think only of Lucas.

She would try to cajole me to talk and I found myself talking to her about the past. I told her of the house in Bloomsbury, of my parents and their preoccupation with the British Museum. She was amused that I had been named after the Rosetta Stone.

She said, "It is like that with me. I haven't got a father and my mother has always had other things . . . not the British Museum but . . . other things. . . ."

At any other time I should have questioned her about her feelings, but I was so obsessed by Lucas that I let the opportunity pass.

She wanted to hear a great deal about Mr. Dolland. I told her about his turns, and she was particularly interested in *The Bells*.

"I wish we had them here," she said. "Wouldn't it be fun?"

I admitted that it would and it had been fun in the old days.

She put her arm through mine and squeezed with a rare show of affection.

"It didn't matter about them only caring for the old British Museum, did it? It doesn't matter, if you have other things. . . ."

I was touched. She was telling me that my presence made up for her mother's neglect.

When I told her of Felicity's arrival she squealed with delight. I saw why. It was the similarity with my coming to Perrivale.

"You thought some awful governess was coming," she said.

"Old, of course," I added, and we laughed.

"Well, they are all old," she said. "Did you think of how you were going to make her go?"

"No, I didn't. I wasn't such a monster as you are."

She rocked back and forth in merriment.

"You wouldn't go now, would you, Cranny?" she said.

"If I felt you wanted me to stay . . . "

"I do."

"I thought you hated all governesses."

"All of them except you."

"I'm flattered and honoured."

She smiled at me rather shyly and said, "I'm not going to call you Cranny any more. You're going to be Rosetta. I think it's ever so funny, being named after that thing."

"Well, it was a rather special stone."

"An old stone!"

"The adjective fits this time."

"All those squiggly things on it . . . like worms."

"Hieroglyphics are not in the least like worms."

"All right. You're Rosetta."

I think because I had told her about my childhood she wanted to tell me about hers. And that, of course, was just what I wanted to hear.

"We must have been a long way from the British Museum," she said. "I never heard of it till now. We were always waiting for him to come home."

"Your . . . father?" I prompted.

She nodded. "It was awful. My mother was afraid . . . not so much as I was when I used to be there all by myself. It was so dark. . . . "

"At night, was this?"

She looked puzzled. "I can't remember. It was a horrid room. I had a bed on the floor in the corner . . . my mother was in the other bed. I used to look at her hair in the morning. It was like gold all spread out over the pillow. I used to wake up in the morning . . . I didn't know what to do. She'd be there . . . and then she'd be gone again. There was someone from downstairs; she used to look in to see if I was all right."

"And you were all alone there for a lot of the time."

"I think so."

"What was your mother doing?"

491

"I don't know."

I thought, A chorus girl. Tom Parry married a chorus girl.

"You had Mr. Dolland and Mrs. Harlow. . . ."

"Tell me, Kate . . . tell me all you can remember."

"No, no," she cried. "I don't want to. I don't want to remember. I don't want to remember." She turned to me suddenly and flung herself against me. I stroked her hair.

I said, "All right. Let's forget it. It's all over now. You've got me now . . . we'll have some fun together. We'll ride . . . we'll read . . . we'll talk. . . ."

I was learning so much . . . not about what I came to learn but about Kate. She was a lonely child; she behaved as she did because she had been starved of love and attention. She was trying to attract it in the only way she knew. I felt resentful against Mirabel, who had failed to give her the love she needed. She had had to work, perhaps . . . but not now.

Kate disengaged herself abruptly, as though ashamed of her emotion.

She said, "It was all right when Gramps came."

"Yes," I said. "Your grandfather. He loves you very much, doesn't he?"

A smile illuminated her face.

"He came and took us away. He brought us here . . . and then it was all right. He tells lovely stories, all about battles."

"It must have been wonderful when he took you away."

She nodded.

"I remember it was in the room . . . he sat on the bed. He said something about a contact — "

"A contact?"

"A contact in Cornwall."

"Oh, he meant a friend, I suppose."

She nodded. Her mood had changed. She was smiling. "We went in a train. It was lovely. I sat on Gramps's knee, and then we came to Seashell Cottage. I loved it . . . because Gramps was there. He was there all the time. He was there when it was dark. I liked the sea too. I loved to hear it banging against the cliffs. I could hear it ever so loud in my bedroom at Seashell Cottage."

"And then," I said, "there was Perrivale. You soon became friendly with them, didn't you?"

"Oh, yes. Gramps knew them and they liked him a lot. Well, everybody likes Gramps. They liked my mother too because she's so beautiful. Then she was going to marry Cosmo and we were going to leave Seashell Cottage and live in the big house. She was

493

ever so pleased. So was Gramps . . . though he wasn't going to live there, but he was pleased all the same. Then Cosmo died while we were still at the cottage. He died in Bindon Boys and the murderer ran away so everyone knew who'd done it."

"And what happened after that?"

She wrinkled her brows. "My mother went away."

"Went away? I thought she married Tristan."

"She did . . . but at first she went away."

"Where did she go?"

"I don't know. She was ill."

"Ill? Then why did she go away?"

"She was very sick. I used to hear her. She looked very white. Once when she was ill and she didn't know I was there, she looked in the glass at herself and said, 'Oh, God, what now?' I was little then. I thought God might say and I'd know what was the matter. Now I know people only say 'Oh, God' when they're frightened or angry. She was frightened because she was ill. Then Gramps said, 'Your mother is going away for a while.' I said, 'Why?' Gramps said because it would be good for her. And she went. Gramps went with her to the station. He was going with her just at first. I was to stay with Mrs. Drake for two days. Then Gramps came back and I went back to Seashell Cottage with him. I said, 'Where's my mother?' He said, 'She's visiting friends.' I said I didn't know we had any. Then he said, 'You've got me, my darling. I'm your friend.' And he hugged me and I felt all right. It was great fun in Seashell Cottage with Gramps. He used to do the cooking and I helped him and we laughed a lot."

She began to laugh at the memory.

"What happened after?" I asked.

"My mother came back and she was better. Her friends had done her good. Then she was engaged to Stepper and they were married and we went to Perrivale Court. I wished Gramps could come with us. But he went to the Dower House. He said it wasn't far away and I'd know where he was."

"And you never met the friends your mother went to?"

"Nobody ever talked of them. I know they lived in London."

"Did your mother or Gramps tell you that?"

"No. But it was the London train they went on. It always is at that time. I know they got on that one because Mrs. Drake took me to see them off. Gramps had taken me to her house the night before. I said I wanted to see them off so Mrs. Drake took me to the station and I saw them get on the train."

"They might have got off somewhere along the way."

"No. I heard them talking about going to London."

"And Gramps came back and left your mother there."

"He was only away one night. But she was gone what seemed like ages. It might have been about three weeks. I don't remember much about time. But I know how ill she was when she went . . . she didn't smile at all."

"She must have been very ill."

She nodded and started to tell me about the shells she and Gramps had found on the beach.

I had been up to see the Dowager Lady Perrivale on two or three occasions. Our chats were not very rewarding. I had hoped to discover something as she rambled on about the past and the days of opulence in her native Yorkshire.

I was always hoping for an opportunity to talk to Maria, and as Maria hoped for it too, it was inevitable that one day it should come about.

One day when I went up, I was greeted by Maria, who put her fingers to her lips and said with a wink, "Her ladyship is fast in the land of Nod. But come in, Miss Cranleigh, and we'll wait for her to wake up. I never like to rouse her. Another bad night, you see. I always know by the look of her. Roaming about, I expect, looking for something that's not there. In any case she can't get at the matches. I see to that."

We sat opposite each other.

"My word," she went on. "You and Miss Kate are getting on better than ever. Thick as thieves, you two are."

"I think we understand each other. She's not a bad child."

"Eee. I wouldn't go as far as that, but she's been better since you've been here. That's for certain sure."

"And how has Lady Perrivale been?"

"Up and down. One day she's clear enough . . . all there, you might say . . . and the next she's a ha'p'orth missing. Well, she's getting on in years; can't last much longer, I shouldn't wonder. When I think of her in the old days! Mistress of the house, she was. And then, hey presto! — overnight she's like a different person."

"Perhaps she was very fond of Sir Edward and the shock of his death was too much for her."

"Quite the reverse, I should have said. They weren't exactly what you'd call a Darby and Joan. Oh, dear me, no. There was differences between them right up to the end, I can tell you. I heard them arguing something shocking. She was in tears. He was laying down the law, but I couldn't quite catch his words."

I thought that was a pity, and so clearly did Maria.

"He died about the time of that shocking affair, didn't he? I mean the killing in the farmhouse."

"Oh, yes . . . the murder. He was on his deathbed then. I don't think he knew much about that, though. He was too far gone. Well, you wouldn't go to a man on his deathbed and say, 'Your son's been murdered, and by the boy you brought into the house.' I mean to say, nobody would tell him that. He didn't know anything about it. Passed away soon after."

"It's a very strange case, don't you think, Maria?"

"Well, murder's murder whichever way you look at it."

"I mean it was a very mysterious affair."

"Jealousy, that's what it was. He was jealous of Cosmo. Some said he was sweet on the present ladyship. Well, you've got to admit she's a handsome body."

"Very handsome. You told me that Sir Tristan was fond of her before his brother died."

She winked and nodded. "A funny business. But then love is a funny thing. She seemed all right with Cosmo. Well, she would be, wouldn't she? But I reckoned it was all pretence. I could see there was something between her and Tristan. You feel it, you know. That's if you know anything about such things."

"I heard someone say she was very ill and went away for a few weeks and when she came back she was her old self."

"I think that was just before the murder . . . just before. I noticed she was beginning to look a bit . . . well, if she'd been married, I would have said she might have been expecting."

"And when she came back?"

"Well, then it happened. It must have been a week or so after, as far as my memory takes me."

"And then she married Tristan."

"Well, it was some months after. They couldn't rush into it quite as fast as that. It was fast enough, though."

"Do you think she was relieved because she could have Tristan and the title and everything?"

Maria frowned. I thought, I'm going too far. I must be careful. Lucas warned me of this.

"Oh, I couldn't say that. Mind you, I believe there was something between her and Tristan, so I suppose she'd rather have had him. Cosmo was one for throwing his weight about. He was the great Cosmo. He'd be Sir Cosmo one day . . . only he didn't live long enough for that. The tenant farmers didn't like him much. They liked Tristan better . . . so she wasn't the only one. It was a quiet wedding. It had to be, didn't it? Her ladyship was chuffed when they married, though. She thought such a lot of Mirabel. She'd wanted her for a daughter-in-law. You should have seen her and the major together. Well, she'd always had a soft spot for him, hadn't she?"

"Yes, I believe you said she had."

"I knew that. Her ladyship's mother was supposed to be her best friend, but there was a bit of jealousy there. It was over the major . . . only he wasn't a major then. I didn't hear what he was . . . but he was always a bit of a charmer. He was younger than both of them, of course. Her ladyship was Jessie Arkwright then. She used to talk to me while I brushed her hair. She was sweet on him, just like her friend was."

"You mean the school friend who married him?"

Maria nodded. "There was a time when I

thought it would be Jessie who married him. But old Arkwright put his foot down, thought the charming young man was after Jessie's fortune. I thought it was the school friend he really wanted, but of course, like a lot of them, he had his eyes on old Arkwright's money. Well, Jessie had had a lot of her own way, but where his money was concerned, old Arkwright had his own ideas. Jessie was not going to throw herself away on a young adventurer who was after his money, he said. If she did marry him, there'd be no money. Poor Jessie was heartbroken, but she married Sir Edward, became Lady Perrivale, and came down here. And the major married the school friend. That's how it was. And then all those years later, when his wife was dead and he had a daughter — herself married with a little girl — he wrote renewing his friendship with her ladyship. She was over the moon with joy and wanted him to come down here. Seashell Cottage was found for them . . . and ever since, she's looked on Mirabel as her daughter."

"She wasn't jealous because the major had married her friend?"

"She'd got over that. The friend was dead and the major was here. She's pleased to have Mirabel now as her daughter-in-law, and the major's always in and out."

"And young Lady Perrivale's fond of her?"

"Oh, yes . . . well, it's nice for the old lady. I remember how upset she was when Mirabel went away . . . that was before the marriage. She was really worried. I remember seeing a letter from young Lady Perrivale to her: 'Darling Aunt Jessie' — she had called her Aunt Jessie when she first came down and it never changed. I can see that letter now. She was staying at a place called . . . what was it? . . . Oh, I remember. Malton House in a place called Bayswater in London. I remembered Malton because I was born close by. It's near York. That's why it stuck in my mind. When she came back, her ladyship made such a fuss of her. And then soon after that there was the murder. . . ."

"It must have been a terrible shock for Lady Perrivale to lose her son like that."

"Oh, it was . . . and Sir Edward dying at the same time. It was enough to finish her off. We were all surprised that she came through as well as she did. But it did something to her; her mind started wandering then, and there was all that prowling about at night."

She went on to talk about the difficulties she had with Lady Perrivale and gave examples of her strange conduct, to stress the change in her after the tragedy.

While we were talking the major arrived.

"Oh, hello, Major," said Maria. "Her ladyship's fast asleep. Been prowling in the night again, I'm afraid."

"Oh, dear, dear. Nice to see you, Miss Cranleigh. You haven't been over to see me lately. I must speak to Kate about that. I've told her to bring you any time you're passing. You're almost certain to find me in the garden."

"Thank you, Major. I should like that."

"Maria takes such good care of Lady Perrivale. What we should do without Maria, I do not know."

"I don't know what I'd do without her ladyship," said Maria. "We've been together so many years."

I said that I would go as I guessed that when Lady Perrivale awoke she would be delighted to see the major and would not want another guest to spoil her tête-à-tête with him.

He said politely that he was sure she would be most disappointed to miss me.

"Oh, I can easily look in tomorrow."

He took my hand and said, "Now, don't forget. I shall expect to see you soon."

When I went downstairs it was to find a message awaiting me.

It was from Carleton. It told me briefly that Lucas's operation was to take place on the following Wednesday. It was then Friday.

A Visit to London

I had made up my mind that I was going to London. I wanted to be there when Lucas had his operation. I wanted to see him before it took place, so I could assure him that I should be thinking of him all the time and that I was praying that the operation would be successful.

I could stay with my father, where I should not be very far from the clinic. I must be close at hand and I wanted Lucas to know that I was there.

I broached young Lady Perrivale.

I said, "I am very sorry, but I have to go to London. A very dear friend of mine is having an operation and I want to be there. Moreover, it is time I saw my father. I haven't seen him since I left with my friends Professor and Mrs. Grafton for Cornwall, and I really owe it to my family to explain a few things."

"Oh, dear," she said. "I'm afraid Kate will

be most upset. You two have got along so well together."

"Yes, but I have to go. I'll talk to her. I'll see that she understands."

I did talk to her.

"Why can't I come?" she said.

"Because I have to go alone."

"I don't see why."

"I do."

"What about me while you're away?"

"You managed before I came."

"That was different."

"I'll tell you what I'll do. I'll find some books for you to read, and you can tell me all about them when I get back. I'll set you some lessons, too."

"What's the good of that?"

"It'll pass the time."

"I don't want the time to pass. I don't want you to go unless I go with you.

"Alas. That is another lesson you have to learn. Things don't always turn out the way we want them to. Listen, Kate. This is something I have to do."

"You might not come back."

"I will. I swear it."

She brought a Bible and made me take an oath on it. She seemed a little more satisfied after that.

I was deeply moved to see that I meant

505

so much to her.

My father was pleased to see me. Aunt Maud was cool and disapproving — as I had expected her to be.

My father said, "This was a strange decision for you to take, Rosetta."

"I wanted to do something."

"There were so many more suitable things you could have done," said Aunt Maud.

"I could have found you something at the Museum," added my father.

"That would have been far better," said Aunt Maud. "But a governess . . . and in the wilds of Cornwall!"

"It is a very important family. They are neighbours of the Lorimers."

"I am so glad you are near them," said my father. "What are you teaching?"

"Everything," I told him. "It's not difficult."

He looked amazed.

"In any case," said Aunt Maud, "no matter what you teach and to whom, I think it is a very foolish thing to have done. A governess indeed!"

"Felicity was one, remember."

"You are not Felicity."

"No, I'm myself. I was just saying that she managed very well and was not the least bit ashamed of having once been a governess."

"It was with friends . . . and to oblige."

"Well, I'm obliging. They're very glad to have me."

Aunt Maud made an impatient gesture.

I had a very good welcome in the kitchen. Mr. Dolland looked a little older. There was a little more white at his temples. Mrs. Harlow seemed larger than I remembered her and the girls were the same.

"So you're a governess now, are you?" said Mrs. Harlow with a faint sniff.

"Yes, Mrs. Harlow."

"And you the master's daughter!"

"I enjoy it. I have a very bright and unusual pupil. She was quite unmanageable until I came."

"I wouldn't have believed it . . . nor would Mr. Dolland. Would you, Mr. Dolland?"

Mr. Dolland agreed that he never would.

"It used to be such fun down here," I said. "Do you still do *The Bells*, Mr. Dolland?"

"Now and then, Miss Rosetta."

"It used to frighten me so. I used to dream about the Polish Jew. I've told Kate . . . she's my pupil . . . about you. I'd love to bring her up to meet you all."

"We miss not having a young 'un in the house," said Mrs. Harlow reminiscently.

I went to her and put my arms round her.

She hugged me tightly for a few moments.

"There," she said, wiping her eyes, "we often talk about the old days. You were an old-fashioned little thing."

"You must do *The Bells* before I go back, Mr. Dolland."

"I heard Mr. Lorimer is in London."

"Yes. I shall go to see him while I'm here."

I intercepted a knowing look which passed between Mrs. Harlow and Mr. Dolland. So they were pairing me off with Lucas.

The next day I went to the clinic. Lucas was delighted to see me.

"I'm so touched that you came," he said.

"Of course I came. I wanted to be here while it was done, and I want you to know that I'll be thinking of you all the time. I shall come round tomorrow afternoon with my father or Aunt Maud and find out how it went."

"That might be too early."

"Nevertheless, I shall come."

His room was small with a single bed and a small table beside it. He was in a dressing gown. He said that he had been advised to rest for the last two days and was spending the time mainly reading. They had to prepare him, apparently, and this was what they were doing.

"I'm so glad you came, Rosetta," he said.

"There's something I wanted you to know. Sit down there, by the window, so that I can see you."

"Does the sound of the traffic disturb you?" I asked.

"No. I like it. It makes me feel there's a lot going on outside."

"What do you want to tell me, Lucas?"

"I took some action. It was a little while ago, before you confessed to me that John Player was Simon Perrivale."

"Action, Lucas? What action?"

"I sent Dick Duvane off to look for him."

"You . . . what?"

"I didn't have much to go on. Dick went off to Constantinople. I thought Simon might still be working for the Pasha and there might be a possibility of bribing someone to get him back. I know how these people work. It was just the sort of thing Dick would do well. If anyone could bring it off, he would."

"Why did you do it, Lucas?"

"Because I knew that he was the one you wanted. I used to tell myself that there was a sort of bond between the three of us. We'd been through so much together. That does something to people. But I was in a way the outsider. On the island I felt that."

"It was because you weren't able to walk. We had to go off together to see what we could find to eat. You were never the outsider, Lucas."

"Oh, yes, I was. It was to you he confessed his secret, and here you are, intent above everything on proving his innocence."

I was silent.

"There have been times when I thought you and I . . . well, it was what I wanted. Life has been different for me since you came to Cornwall. I've felt a certain optimism . . . just a thought that miracles can happen."

"We saw one miracle . . . more than one. It really seemed as if Providence . . . fate . . . whatever you call it, was looking after us. Look how we survived in those seas, and then on the island, and how fortunate I was in the seraglio. I did at times feel my good angel was looking after me. You too, Lucas. The way in which you came home was certainly . . . miraculous."

"Like this," he said, looking down at his leg.

"I don't think any of us escaped unscathed. But, Lucas, you did this for me! You were trying to find him to bring him back to me."

"I admit that at times I thought I was a fool. Let him go, I said to myself. Let him stay away forever. Then you and I could make something of our lives . . . together. That's the way I used to think. Then I thought,

She'll always hanker. She'll always think of him. So I came to the conclusion that I'd try to find him and bring him back . . . if that were possible."

"I shall never forget that you did this for me. You once told me that you loved me next best to yourself, and that all people loved themselves best and when they said they loved someone else it was because of the comfort and pleasure that person brought *them*. Do you remember? I don't think you have shown it is true . . . of you."

He laughed. "Don't make a hero of me. You'll be horribly disappointed if you do."

"Oh, Lucas!"

"All right, all right. No more. Don't let's get sentimental. I thought you ought to know, that's all. When you told me who he was and that he had said he would try to get to Australia, I wrote to Dick and he'll be on his way there now. It's a sparsely populated place. It might be a fraction easier to find him there. But even if we did . . . he can't come back, can he?"

"Not until we prove him innocent."

He looked at me sadly.

"You think I am never going to prove it, don't you?" I said.

"I think you have set yourself a very difficult task."

"But you are going to help me, Lucas."

"Rather a broken reed, you know."

"But you are going to be much better after
. . . you know you are. You're sure of it."

"Well, that's the whole purpose, isn't it?"

"I can't wait for tomorrow to be over."

"Thank you, Rosetta."

"It's got to be a success. It's got to be!"

He nodded. I kissed him on the forehead
and left him. I was unable to hide my emotion
and I did not want him to see how fearful I
was.

After I had left him I asked if I might have a
word with the surgeon and I was finally conducted to him. I said that I should be grateful
if he would tell me if there was any danger of
Lucas's not coming through the operation.

When he hesitated for a few seconds I felt
numb with terror.

"I believe you are his fiancée," he said. I
did not deny it. I thought in that role he
would be more frank with me. He went on.
"It is a long and delicate operation. If it is
successful, he will be able to walk with much
more ease and painlessly . . . although there
will always be a slight limp. Because it is long
and complicated, it could be a strain on the
heart, and that is where the danger lies.
Mr. Lorimer is strong and healthy. He is in
moderately good condition. There is a good

chance that he will come successfully through the operation. It is just that we should not forget the strain on the heart."

"Thank you," I said.

He laid a hand on my shoulder.

"I am sure it will be all right," he said.

I came out of the clinic feeling very disturbed. I wanted to go back to Lucas and tell him how much I cared for him, and at this time the most important thing in the world to me was that the operation would be a success.

The next day seemed as though it would never pass. In the late afternoon my father, Aunt Maud, and I went to the clinic. We saw the doctor whom I had seen on the previous day.

"He has come safely through," he said. "It is too soon yet to see how successful the operation is. But Mr. Lorimer is doing well. You might look in and see him, but don't stay more than a few minutes. Just Miss Cranleigh, of course."

I saw Lucas. He was lying in his bed, his leg under a frame. He looked very different from how I had ever seen him before . . . defenceless, vulnerable.

"Hello, Lucas."

"Rosetta . . . !"

"They say you've done well."

He nodded and looked at the chair beside his bed. I sat down.

"Good to see you."

"Don't talk. They've told me I mustn't stay more than a few minutes."

He smiled faintly.

"I just want you to know that I'm thinking of you all the time. I'll come again as soon as they let me."

He smiled.

"And you'll be out of here soon."

A nurse looked in and I rose.

"Don't forget. I'm thinking of you," I said, and kissed him.

Then we went back to Bloomsbury.

Lucas was progressing "as well as could be expected." He was in bed and I gathered that the success of the operation was not yet known and would not be until he was able to put his feet to the ground. Visits had to be brief. It made the days seem long, and one day I decided to go and look at the place where Mirabel had stayed when she had come to London with her mysterious illness.

I could not forget that Maria had said, "If she had been married I should have thought she was expecting." She must have been wrong. There was no child. I wondered if there was some evidence hidden in the fact

514

that she had come to London in that way.

Malton House was in Bayswater. That was all I knew, but it might be possible to find the place.

Lucas had occupied my mind exclusively during the last week, and because I was unable to see him except very briefly, I needed something to occupy me and to take my mind from the fearful feeling of uncertainty that all might not have gone right with him after all.

I would take a cab one afternoon and go and see if I could find Malton House. I reminded myself that I must leave no stone unturned. Who knew, important evidence might be found in the least expected places.

It was true that the need to prove Simon innocent had taken second place to my anxiety about Lucas lately, but I had gone too far in my search to slacken now. The need to prove Simon's innocence was as strong as ever.

I knew the name of the house and the name of the district. I would hail a cab and ask to be taken to Bayswater. Cab drivers were very knowledgeable about London. They had to be. It was essential to their jobs.

It was early afternoon. My father was at work in his study. Aunt Maud was taking a nap. I came out of the house and hailed a cab.

The cabdriver looked a little dismayed when

I told him I wanted to go to Malton House in Bayswater.

"Malton House? Where's that?"

"In Bayswater."

"That all the address you've got?"

I told him it was.

"Well, we'll get to Bayswater. That's easy enough. Here . . . wait a minute, I know of a Malton Square."

"I think it would very likely be there."

"All right then, Miss. We'll go and see."

When we arrived at Malton Square he slowed down and studied the houses as we went along.

We saw a woman with a shopping bag. She was walking briskly along.

The cabdriver slowed up and touched his hat with his whip.

"Excuse me, lady. You know Malton House round here?"

"Why, yes," she said. "The one on the corner."

"Thank 'ee, Ma'am."

The cab stopped before a house.

I said, "Will you wait for me? I shall not be long."

"I'll just wait round the corner, into the next street," he said. "Can't very well stay here right on the corner."

"That will suit me beautifully."

And it did, for it occurred to me that he might think it odd that I had made the journey just to look at the place.

The house lay back from the road. Steps led to the door, and among the few rather dingy bushes in the front garden there was a board on which was printed MALTON HOUSE. MATERNITY NURSING HOME. And in the corner, MRS. B. A. CAMPDEN, with several letters after her name, the significance of which I was unsure.

I stood staring at the board for some moments, and as I did so a woman came up to me. I recognised her at once as the one whom the cabdriver had asked about the house.

"Can I help you?" she asked pleasantly.

"Oh . . . er . . . no, thank you," I said.

"I am Mrs. Campden," she said. "I saw you alight from the cab."

This was becoming awkward. She must know that I had meant to come here as the cabby had asked her the way. How could I tell her that I just wanted to look at the place?

She said, "Why don't you come in? It's easier to talk inside."

"I . . . er . . . I only wanted — "

She smiled at me. "I understand." Her eyes swept over me. I found myself following her up the steps. The door was open and we

517

stepped into a hall in which was a reception area.

"Come along in," she said.

I began to protest. "I only — " How could I tell her that I wanted to see what sort of place this was? She seemed to have drawn her own conclusions about me.

"Really I shouldn't waste your time — " I began.

She took my arm and drew me into a room.

"Now, let's be comfortable," she said. She pushed me into a chair. "You mustn't be embarrassed. So many girls are. I understand that. We're here to help."

I felt I was getting deeper and deeper into a ridiculous situation from which I must extricate myself as quickly as possible. What could I say? How to explain? She knew that I had purposely come to the place. It was most unfortunate that the cabdriver should have spoken to her. I tried to think of some reason why I should be here.

"I have to ask a few questions, of course," she was saying, while I was desperately racking my brains for some plausible excuse for being here. "Now don't be nervous. I'm used to this sort of thing. We'll put everything right. Have you any idea when conception took place?"

I was horrified now. I wanted to get out of

518

this place as quickly as I could. "You're making a mistake," I said. "I . . . I just came to enquire about a friend of mine."

"A friend? What friend?"

"I believe she came here. It was some time ago . . . I have lost touch with her and I wondered if you could help me. She was Mrs. Blanchard."

"Mrs. Blanchard?" She stared at me blankly.

I thought she would surely remember. Anyone would remember Mirabel. Her unusual beauty would make that inevitable.

A sudden thought came to me. On the spur of the moment I said, "Or perhaps she came as Mrs. Parry."

As soon as I had spoken, I wondered what I was thinking of. It was just that the thought had flashed into my mind that her visit here would be of a secret nature and she might not have used the name of Blanchard. There had always been a faint suspicion in my mind that she was in fact the wife of the sailor whose grave Kate visited . . . that she was in truth at that time Mrs. Parry.

I was losing my head. I just wanted to get away.

I said, "I thought if you could give me her address — "

"I must tell you right away that we never divulge the addresses of our patients."

"Well, I thought you might not. Thank you very much. I'm sorry to have taken up your time."

"What is your name?"

"Oh, that's not important. I was just passing and I thought . . ."

Just passing! In a cab which brought me here specially! I was making a mess of this.

"You are not the press, are you?" she asked rather threateningly.

"No . . . no, no, I assure you. I was just thinking about my friend and wondering whether you could help me find her. I am so sorry to have bothered you. I shouldn't have come in if — "

"If I hadn't come along just at that moment. Are you sure you are not in need of our services?"

"I'm quite sure. If you'll excuse me. I'm so sorry to have troubled you. Goodbye, and thank you."

I made for the door while she watched me through narrowed eyes.

I was trembling. There was something about the woman, about the place, which made me very apprehensive.

It was with great relief that I came out into the street. What a disaster! How was I to know I should encounter the proprietress! What bad luck that she should have come along at that precise moment. And I had been quite unprepared. I was hopeless in the role I had set for myself. Because I had managed rather well as a governess I fancied myself as a detective. I felt humiliated and shaken, and my desire was to get away as quickly as possible.

It was a lesson to me. My methods of investigation were both crude and amateur.

I ran round the corner to where the cab was waiting.

"That was quick," said the cabdriver.

"Oh, yes."

"Everything all right?"

"Oh, yes . . . yes."

I knew he was thinking: A girl in trouble going to one of those places. Maternity home, yes — but not averse to helping a girl in trouble.

I sat back, thinking of it all, going over every excruciating minute. Why had I mentioned Mrs. Parry? It had just come into my head that she might have gone there under that name. How foolish of me! One thing I did know, and that was that Mirabel must have been pregnant when she went there and not so when she came out. What could it mean? Whose child was it? Cosmo's? She was going to marry Cosmo at that time. Or Tristan's?

Was this an important piece of evidence?

It seemed to me that the chain of events was becoming more complicated and I was no nearer to the solution.

When I reached our house I was still shaken from the encounter.

The next day I went to see Lucas. When I knocked at his door it was opened by him. He stood standing there.

"Lucas!" I cried.

"Look at me." He took a few steps and I could see the difference.

"It's worked!" I cried.

He nodded, smiling triumphantly.

"Oh, Lucas . . . it's wonderful."

I threw myself at him and he held me close.

"You've helped a lot," he said.

"I?"

"Coming every day. Caring."

"Of course I came. Of course I cared. Tell me all about it."

"Well, I'm still something of a poor thing."

"You don't look it."

"This business has worked, they tell me. I've got to do exercises and such like. But I'm better. I feel better. I feel lighter. Less like an old hulk."

"Wonderful! It was all worthwhile."

"I have to be here for another week or two,

while they put me through my paces. I have to learn to walk again . . . like a baby."

I could only smile at him. I felt near to tears. I was so happy because the operation had been a success.

"You'll be here for a while?"

"Yes. I shall come and see you every day and watch for improvements."

"There are quite a few needed."

"But it's better, Lucas."

"I shall still be a bit of a cripple. There are things they can't put right. But they have done a great deal. This man is something of a genius. I think I was a bit of a guinea pig, but he's pleased with me — though not half as pleased as he is with himself."

"Don't let's grudge him his glory, Lucas. I'm so happy!"

"I haven't felt like this for a long time."

"I'm glad . . . so glad."

On the way out I was waylaid by the surgeon. His delight was obvious.

"Mr. Lorimer was such a good patient," he said. "He was determined, and that is a great help."

"We don't know how to thank you enough."

"My reward is the success of the operation."

When I went home and told them, my

father said how gratifying it was that modern medical science had advanced so far; Aunt Maud showed her pleasure in a manner which told me she was speculating on the possibility of a match between Lucas and me; but it was in the kitchen that I was able to celebrate with abandon.

Mr. Dolland, wise as ever, leaned his elbows on the table and talked about the wonders of medicine today with far more enthusiasm than my father had done; and Mrs. Harlow sighed romantically so I knew her thoughts were on the same lines as those of Aunt Maud, but it did not irritate me as Aunt Maud's speculation had done.

Then Mrs. Harlow told of her cousin's operation for appendicitis and how she had come near to death under the surgeon's knife. Mr. Dolland remembered a play in which a man was supposed to be a cripple unable to move from his chair when all the time he could walk with ease and was the murderer.

It was like old times, and I was happier than I had been for a long time.

It was not until a day or so later that I told Lucas about my unpleasant experience at the maternity home.

"But at least," I said, "I did find out that Mirabel was going to have a baby before Cosmo was killed and evidently she went to that place for an abortion."

"What an extraordinary turn of events! What bearing do you think this has on the murder?"

"I can't think."

"If it were Cosmo's child they could let it be thought that it was a premature birth . . . unless it was too late for that."

"Sir Edward wouldn't have approved, of course."

"But he was on his deathbed."

"It could have been Tristan's, and when she thought she was going to marry Cosmo she had to do something about it."

"That seems more likely. It's all very complicated. There is a possibility that you didn't go to the right place. After all, you only had the address . . . and verbally at that . . . from Maria."

"Well, I'm afraid it hasn't got us very far. There was something rather sinister about the place, and this Mrs. Campden was really very put out when she thought I was making enquiries."

"Well, I suppose she would be. She thought she had a client."

"She looked a little alarmed when she thought I might be from the press."

"Which suggests she might be in fear of them, as she is doing what is illegal. Listen to me, Rosetta. I suggest you drop this sleuthing."

"I must find out, Lucas."

"You don't know what you're getting into."

"But what of Simon?"

"Simon should come home and work out his own problems."

"How could he? He'd be arrested."

"I have a feeling that this is becoming more than a little unpleasant for you."

"I don't mind a bit if it's unpleasant."

"Moreover, you could be dealing with dangerous people. After all, it is a murder you are investigating, and if you believe Simon wasn't the murderer, then someone here probably is. How do you think the guilty person would feel about your probing?"

"That person would not know I am doing it."

"What about that woman? She didn't seem to be very pleased. And if she is dealing in abortions . . . at a good price, I imagine . . . she could be in trouble."

"She had a board outside. It was a maternity home. That is legal."

"It might be a cover. I have a feeling that you ought to stop it . . . keep out of it."

"I have to clear Simon."

He shrugged his shoulders. "All right," he

526

said. "But keep me informed."

"I will do that, Lucas."

The next day Felicity arrived in London. I was overjoyed to see her.

"I had to come up to see Lucas," she said. "And I guessed that you might be here too. How is he?"

"Coming along very well. The operation was a success. He'll be delighted to see you, as I am."

"I came straight from the station," she went on. "I thought I'd get the news of Lucas and see you at the same time."

Aunt Maud came in and greeted Felicity warmly.

"I'll see that a room is made ready for you," she said.

Felicity replied that she had been thinking of staying at a hotel.

"Nonsense," said Aunt Maud. "You must stay here. And if you'll excuse me, I'll go and see about it right away."

Felicity smiled at me. "Still the efficient Aunt Maud."

"Oh, yes. Mrs. Harlow says the household runs like clockwork."

"And what is all this about becoming a governess? Following in my footsteps?"

"You could say that."

She looked puzzled. "We have such a lot to talk about."

"Let's get you settled in first."

We went up. Meg was putting the final touches to the room. Felicity exchanged a few pleasantries with her and then we were alone. I sat on the bed while she put the few things she had brought with her into drawers and cupboards.

"Tell me honestly. Is Lucas really improved?"

"Oh, yes. There's no doubt of that."

"I'm glad you came up from Cornwall."

"I just had to."

She nodded. "Tell me all about this idea of being a governess."

"Well, there was this girl. No one could manage her. It was a sort of challenge."

She looked at me disbelievingly. And then suddenly it dawned on me that I might have confided in Felicity long ago. I could trust her completely; she was resourceful. Nanny Crockett and Lucas already knew, and I could not keep it from Felicity any longer.

So, having extracted a promise of absolute secrecy, I told her everything.

She listened incredulously. "I thought your stay in the seraglio was fantastic," she said. "And now this!"

"People have been sold into harems before," I said. "It happened to Nicole. It's just that it is more rare than it used to be."

"But this Simon . . . he really is Simon Perrivale?"

"Do you remember the case?"

"Vaguely. It raised quite a storm at the time, didn't it, and then it dropped out of the news. And you are convinced of his innocence."

"Yes, I am. You would be too, Felicity . . . if you could have known him."

"And you were alone on this island . . . "

"Lucas was with us, but he couldn't walk. He just lay in the boat and kept a lookout for a sail."

"It sounds like Robinson Crusoe."

"Well, all those who are shipwrecked and cast up on an island are like that."

"Are you . . . in love with this Simon?"

"There was a very strong . . . bond between us."

"Did you discuss your feelings for each other?"

I shook my head. "No, not really. It was just there. We were all so intent on survival. When we were on the island we thought we were doomed. There wasn't enough to eat or drink. . . . And then we were picked up and there was no opportunity."

"He left you at the Embassy and then you

came home and he stayed behind."

"He would have been arrested if he had come back."

"Yes, of course . . . and Lucas shared in all this, to a certain extent."

I nodded.

"I've always been fond of Lucas," she mused. "It was very distressing to see him when he came back. He had always been so full of vitality. James is fond of him too. James said he had a flare for living. I think Lucas loves you, Rosetta."

"Yes."

"Has he asked you to marry him?"

"Yes . . . but not very seriously; really . . . rather flippantly."

"I think he might be inclined to flippancy where his feelings are most concerned. You could do a lot for him and, I think, he for you. Oh, I know you think you don't need him . . . as he needs you . . . but you do, Rosetta. All that you went through . . . well, my dear, you couldn't really endure all that and remain as you were before."

"No, I couldn't."

"Lucas was there part of the time. There is so much he would understand."

I was silent and she went on. "You're thinking Simon was there too. And there was this special bond between you and him."

530

"It started before . . . when he was cleaning the decks."

"I know. You told me. And now you are dedicated to proving his innocence."

"I must, Felicity."

"If he came back . . . if you saw him with Lucas . . . you might decide. Lucas is really a wonderful person."

"I know, Felicity. I've learned that. This operation . . . when there was just a slight fear that he might not come through, I realised how important his friendship was to me. I have confessed to him what I am trying to do, Felicity, and he is helping me. He has sent Dick Duvane out to see if he can find him. He was going to bring him back if he could; he thought they might take a ransom for him as they did for Lucas himself. That was before he knew that Simon couldn't come back."

"And you will never be completely content if you don't see him again. He will haunt you forever. You could always remember . . . and perhaps build up something which was never there."

"He can't come back until his innocence is proved."

"How can he hope to prove it from afar?"

"But how could he do it if he were in prison awaiting death?"

"So . . . it is for you to find the solution."

"I want to do it. I shall never stop trying."

"I know. I remember your stubborn nature of old." She laughed. "Some would call it determination."

We went on talking about it. I daresay I went over the same ground again and again, but she said she wanted the complete picture. It was typical of Felicity to throw herself wholeheartedly into my affairs.

She said, "It would be interesting to know why Sir Edward brought him into the household."

"The obvious conclusion is that he was Sir Edward's son."

"It certainly seems likely."

"But the mystery is that Sir Edward was so morally conventional . . . a strict disciplinarian."

"That sort can have their lapses."

"That's what Lucas says. But from what I've heard Sir Edward was particularly censorious with those who erred in that respect."

"Well, as I say, that often happens, but it is just possible that the key to the mystery may be in the secret of Simon's birth. And when one is studying a case of this nature it is as well to know everything possible about the characters in the drama. See if you can remember more of what you have heard about Simon's beginnings."

"I've told you about Angel. You see, he doesn't even say she was his mother. She was just Angel."

"That's explainable. I expect she called him her angel as mothers do. It was probably the first thing he remembered. Then he transferred the name to her. I've known that sort of thing to happen with children. I know with mine. Was she his mother? Or was she someone who had adopted him as a baby? That's a possibility."

"What difference would it make?"

"Possibly none. But we don't know, do we? And every detail can be important. What else about his beginnings?"

"There was a wicked aunt. Aunt Ada was her name. He was scared of her and feared that when Angel died she was going to take him with her. Sir Edward seemed to sense his fear and stepped in. At least that is the impression he gave."

"Do you remember anything about the aunt? You haven't got a surname . . . just Ada."

"Just that. He thought she was a witch, and he and Angel went to visit her. It was a place called Witches' Home, and as it was her home they were going to that was significant."

"Did he say anything about the place?"

"He said there was water at the bottom of

the garden, I think. Yes, he did. It could have been a river."

"Is that all?"

"Yes. He must have been under five years old, because he was five when he came to Perrivale."

"Well," said Felicity. "We've got Witches' Home and presumably a river and Ada."

"What are you suggesting?"

"I was thinking that we could try and find Ada. A little talk with her might be rewarding."

"Felicity, you mean that you — "

"I have an idea. Why don't you come back with me and we'll spend a few days together before you go back to Cornwall. James and the children would love to see you."

"I do have my work. I've been away longer than I should."

"The *enfant terrible*. Oh, yes. By the way, how is she getting on without you?"

"Well, I hope. But I must get back. I can't take too much time, although they are very amenable."

"A few more days won't make much difference. In any case, they won't dismiss you. They'll be so pleased to have you back."

"Kate might revert to her old habits from which, I believe, I am weaning her."

"That will only make them appreciate you

all the more. I have a plan. We'll find out if there is a place called Witches' Home . . . or something like it. It could be on a river, or some sort of water. That could be useful."

"It might have been a pond at the end of the garden. All we really have is Ada and Witches' Home. It will be rather like Thomas à Becket's mother coming to England, her only knowledge of the English language being London and Gilbert and going through the streets of the capital calling Gilbert's name."

"I'm glad you remember the history I taught you."

"Well, London is rather different from Witches' Home and a great deal larger."

"I imagine Witches' Home is a small village where everyone will know everyone's business."

"And where are we going to find this Witches' Home?"

"We'll consult maps."

"Little villages are not marked on maps."

She was downcast but only for a few moments. Then her eyes sparkled. "I have it," she said. "Professor Hapgood. That's the answer."

"Who's Professor Hapgood?"

"My dear, I don't live in Oxford for nothing. Professor Hapgood is the greatest authority on the villages of England. It's his passion

. . . his life's work. He can go right back to the Domesday Book and beyond. If there is a place called Witches' Home in England, he will tell us in the winking of an eye. Ah, I can see your scepticism fast disappearing. Rosetta, trust me and Professor Hapgood."

How glad I was that Felicity knew. I was reproaching myself for not having told her before.

Felicity and I went to the clinic. Lucas was improving and was now walking with great ease. He said he was no longer in pain with every step; all at the clinic were very pleased with his progress. He still had to rest a good deal and would be going home in about a week.

I told him that I had taken Felicity into my confidence and we had plans for trying to locate Aunt Ada. He was amused at the prospect and said the information we had to go on was very flimsy; however, he was impressed at the mention of Professor Hapgood, of whose reputation he was aware.

I said that as Oxford was on the way I could go straight to Cornwall from there. I could not delay my return much longer and I should be at Perrivale Court perhaps a few days before Lucas returned to Trecorn Manor.

"I shouldn't hope for too much success in

this new venture," he warned me. "Even if you do find the place . . . and you might with Professor Hapgood's help . . . you've still got the search for Aunt Ada."

"We know," I told him. "But we're going to try."

"Good luck," he said.

The next day Felicity and I left for Oxford, where I was greeted in a most friendly fashion by James and the children. Felicity explained that she and I were taking a little trip and she would accompany me on part of the journey back to Cornwall, but only be away for a night or two.

James was always understanding about the close friendship between myself and Felicity, and he never raised objections to our taking a little time to be together. So that was easily settled and our first task was to get into touch with Professor Hapgood, who was delighted to help.

He took us to his study, which was lined with massive tomes, and it was clear that the prospect of a search delighted him.

He could find no Witches' Home, which we rather expected.

"You said a child under five mentioned the name. Well, it must be something that sounded similar. Witches' Home. Let me see. There's Witching Hill. Willinham. Willin-

under-Lime. Wodenham. What about Witchenholme? That might sound to a five-year-old
like Witches' Home. More than the others, I
think. And there's Willenhelme. Well, those
two would be the most likely."

"Holme sounds more like Home than
helme," I said.

"Yes," agreed the professor. "Let me see.
Witchenholme is on the River Witchen. . . .
It's hardly a river, a tributary of — let me
see — "

"A tributary sounds just right," said Felicity. "The boy said there was water at the
bottom of the garden."

"Let me look at Willenhelme. No, there is
no river there. It's in the north of England."

"That can't be the one. Where is Witchenholme?"

"Not far from Bath."

I looked at Felicity with delight. "In the
west," I said. "Much more likely."

"We'll try Witchenholme," said Felicity.
"And if it isn't the one, we shall probably be
troubling you again, Professor."

"It's a great pleasure," he said. "I pride
myself I can produce the smallest hamlet that
existed in England since the days of the Norman Conquest, and I like to have a chance to
prove it. Now, let me see. Your nearest town
would be Rippleston."

"Is there a railway?"

"Yes, there's a Rippleston station. Witchen-holme would be no more than a mile or so out."

"We're extremely grateful."

"Good luck in the search. And if it's not the one, don't hesitate to come back to me and we'll try again."

As we left him I felt amazingly optimistic.

"Now," said Felicity. "We shall have to go through Witchenholme as Mrs. Becket did through London, only we shall be calling not Gilbert but Ada."

We booked a room for the night at Rippleston, which proved to be a small market town.

"We may have difficulty in locating Ada and may need two days to do it," said Felicity.

It was good to have her with me. I remembered how she had always thrown herself wholeheartedly into any project. It was one of those characteristics which had made her such a stimulating companion.

All the way down in the train we chatted about how we would set about finding Ada and what we should say to her when we found her. We had both made up our minds that we were going to find her, which was perhaps a little naïve of us, but we were very happy to be together and somehow seemed to slip back into the old days when most things were so exciting.

When we arrived in Rippleston, we booked into our hotel and asked about transport. There was a trap and a man at the hotel who would drive guests where they wished to go. So that was settled quickly.

We decided to waste no time and were soon rattling along the road on our way to Witchenholme.

A hundred yards or so from the village was an inn called The Witchenholme Arms. Here we decided to stop and perhaps ask a few questions in the hope that someone might know of a Miss Ada Something who lived nearby. We arranged for the driver to wait with the trap at the inn.

There was a middle-aged woman at the counter serving ale and cider and we asked if she knew of anyone in the village named Ada. She looked at us as though she thought we were a little odd — as well she might — and said, "Ada . . . Ada who?"

"That's what we're not sure of," said Felicity. "We knew her long ago and we can't remember her surname . . . all we can think of is Ada."

The woman shook her head.

"Come in here much, does she?"

"We don't know," I answered.

"Ada. . . . " She shook her head. "It's mostly men who come in regular."

"I was afraid so," said Felicity. "Well, thanks."

We came out of the inn and started to walk into the village.

"Well, you'd hardly expect Aunt Ada to frequent The Witchenholme Arms, would you?" said Felicity.

The village was, as the professor had told us, very small. And there was a river, yes, and houses backing onto it.

I felt sure this was the place.

A man on a bicycle rode by. We were on the point of stopping him but I realised, as did Felicity, that he would think we were crazy if we stopped to ask if he knew someone called Ada. If only we had her surname, how much more plausible it would all have sounded.

Felicity said suddenly, "Oh, look, there's the village store. Now if anyone might know, they would know in there. Everyone would go in there at some time or other, surely."

We went into the shop. One had to step down and a bell overhead tinkled as the door was opened. There was a pungent smell of paraffin oil and the shop was crowded with goods of all descriptions — fruit, cakes, biscuits, bread, sweets in glass bottles, vegetables, hams and poultry, notepaper, envelopes, flypapers and much more.

"Yes?" said a voice.

Our hearts sank. It was a girl of about fourteen and her face was only just visible above the glass bottles of sweets on the counter.

"We've come," said Felicity, "to ask you if you know someone named Ada."

The girl stared at us in amazement.

"We're trying to find an old friend," went on Felicity, "and all we can remember is that her name is Ada. We just wondered whether she lived around here . . . she might come into the shop as most people would, I suppose?"

"What?" she stammered.

"Do you know any of the people round here?"

"No. I don't live here . . . always. I've just come for a bit. I'm helping my aunt."

"Perhaps we could see her?"

"Aunt," she called. "Aunt Ada."

Felicity and I exchanged glances of wonder.

"Aunt Ada," whispered Felicity.

"There's people here wants to see you," shouted the girl.

"Half a tick," said a voice. "I'm coming."

Was it possible? Could our search be ended? As soon as we saw the woman we knew this was not so. No one could mistake her for a witch. Never could this one have been Simon's Aunt Ada. She was very plump, shaped like a cottage loaf, with a rosy, good-humoured face, untidy greying hair, and alert blue eyes.

"Now what can I do for you ladies?" she said, beaming on us.

"It's a very strange request," said Felicity. "We are looking for someone who, we believe, lives here, and we can't recall her surname. All that we know is that her Christian name is Ada."

"Well, she's not me. I'm Ada. Ada Mac-Gee, that's me."

"Our Ada had a sister called Alice."

"Alice . . . Alice who?"

"Well, we don't know her name either. But she died. We just wondered if among the people here — and you must know most of them — there was an Ada."

I guessed she was the sort of woman who loved a gossip. She was naturally interested in two strangers who had come into her shop, not for apples or pears or a pint of paraffin oil, but because they were looking for an Ada.

"You must know almost everyone in Witchenholme," I said, almost pleadingly.

"Well, most of them come in at some time or other. It's a bit far to go into Rippleston to shop."

"Yes, I should imagine so."

"Ada," she said. "Well, there's Ada Parker down at Greengates . . . she's not Parker any more now; she married again. It's her third. We always call her Ada Parker . . . though not to her face. But Jim Parker was her first husband. Names stick here."

"Perhaps we'll call on her. Are there any others?"

"Well, there's Miss Ferrers. I've heard she was an Ada. I remember the Adas, seeing as I'm one of them. I've never heard her called Ada, mind . . . but I've got a notion that's her name."

"Yes, I can see why you remember the name. I think we were lucky we came to you."

"Well, I would help you find this friend of yours if I could, of course. Ada . . . yes, I'm sure Miss Ferrers is an Ada. I've heard it somewhere. Keeps herself to herself. A cut above the rest of us. I'm sure that's what she thinks anyway."

"Did she have a sister, do you remember?"

"Couldn't rightly say. She's been in that cottage for years. I don't recall a sister. It's a pretty little place and she keeps it like a picture. Rowan Cottage, it's called, on account of the tree outside."

"You've been so helpful to us," said Felicity. "Thank you very much."

"Well, I hope you find what you're looking for."

"Good day," we said, and came out. The bell rang as we opened the door and stepped into the street.

"Perhaps we ought to have bought something," I said. "She was most obliging."

"She didn't expect that. She enjoyed talking to us. I think we'll dispense with the much-married Mrs. Parker and go to her if the lady at Rowan Cottage fails us. I somehow feel that our Aunt Ada wouldn't have had three husbands."

"Look," I said. "The houses back onto the river."

We had walked through the street which seemed to be the whole of Witchenholme without finding Rowan Cottage. We stood blankly staring about us. Then we saw a house some short distance from the rest and, to our delight, the rowan tree.

"Well, she would be apart from the others," said Felicity. "Remember, she thinks herself 'a cut above.' I imagine she will be formidable."

"Simon thought so."

"Come on, let's beard the lioness in her den."

"What on earth are we going to say? 'Are you Aunt Ada? Simon's Aunt Ada?' How does one open a conversation like that?"

"We managed with the shop lady."

"I believe this one will be different."

Boldly I took the brass knocker and brought it down with an authoritative *rat-tat!* The sound reverberated through the house. There was a pause and then the door was opened.

She stood before us, tall and thin with greying hair severely drawn back from her face into a knot at the back of her neck. Her eyes behind thick glasses were shrewd and alert; her crisply white blouse came right up to her chin, held there by bone supports. A gold chain hung about her neck with what I presumed was a watch tucked in at her waistband.

"Please forgive the intrusion," I said. "Mrs. MacGee at the shop told us we should find you here."

"Yes?" she said, coolly enquiring.

Felicity took over. "We are trying to find a lady called Ada, but unfortunately we don't know her surname. Mrs. MacGee told us you were Miss Ada Ferrers, and we wondered if you were the lady we sought."

"I'm afraid I don't know you."

"No, you wouldn't. But did you by any chance have a sister named Alice who had a son called Simon?"

I saw her flinch behind her glasses; her

colour changed a little, and I knew then that we had found Aunt Ada.

She was suspicious immediately. "Are you from the press?" she asked. "They've found him, have they? Oh . . . is it all going to start again?"

"Miss Ferrers, we are not from the press. May we come in and explain? We are trying to prove Simon's innocence."

She hesitated. Then she stepped back uncertainly, holding the door open for us to pass into the house.

The hall was small and very neat, with a hatstand on which hung a tweed coat and a felt hat — hers, obviously — and on a small table there was a brass bowl and a vase of flowers.

She threw open a door and we went into a sitting room which smelt of furniture polish.

"Sit down," she said, and we did so. She sat facing us.

"Where is he?" she asked.

"We don't know," I said. "I must tell you that he was on a ship. I was also on that ship. We were shipwrecked and I survived with him. He saved my life and that of another man. We were taken to Turkey and there I lost sight of him. But during the time we were together, he told me everything. I am convinced of his innocence and I am trying to prove it. I want to see everybody who can tell me anything about him . . . anything that might be useful."

"How can you prove he didn't do this terrible thing?"

"I don't know, but I'm trying to do so."

"Well, what do you want of me? You're sure you're not from the newspapers?"

"I assure you we are not. My name is Rosetta Cranleigh. You may have read about my survival. There was something in the papers about it when I came home."

"Wasn't there a man who was crippled or something?"

"Yes, he was with us too."

She frowned, still disbelieving.

"I don't know," she said. "It sounds a bit odd to me. And I've had enough of it. I don't want to hear another word. I knew it would go wrong right from the beginning."

"You mean . . . when he was a boy?"

She nodded. "He ought to have come to me. I would have taken him in. Not that I wanted a child — I've never had anything to do with children — but someone would have had to have him and she was my sister. There were only the two of us. How could she have got caught up in that sort of thing?"

"It's that which we think might help us," I said tentatively. "If we could go back right to the beginning — "

"How's that going to prove he didn't do it?"

"We're hoping it might help. We feel we can't ignore anything . . . I got to know him very well. We were together in most extraordinary circumstances. We escaped in a boat and drifted onto an island, an uninhabited one. We had this tremendous adventure together. We got to know each other very well, and I'm convinced he couldn't have killed anyone."

"He was caught red-handed."

"I believe that could have been arranged."

"Who'd arrange a thing like that?"

"It's what we have to find out. I want your help. Please, Miss Ferrers, he's your nephew. You want to help him, don't you?"

"I don't see how *I* can. I haven't set eyes on him since he was taken away."

"By Sir Edward Perrivale?"

She nodded.

"Why did Sir Edward take him?"

She was silent. Then she said, "All right. I'll tell it right from the beginning. Alice was beautiful. Everyone said so. It was a curse in a way. If she hadn't been this wouldn't have happened to her. She was a fool, soft as they come. Gentle, loving, and all that . . . but she had no sense at all. Our father owned a nice little inn on the other side of Bath. It was a profitable place. Alice and I used to help with the guests. Then one night Edward Perrivale came. He saw Alice . . . and kept coming. I warned her. I said, 'He'll be no good to you.' She could have had John Hurrell, who had a sizable farm and wanted to marry her. But no, it had to be this Edward."

I looked at Felicity. The story was working out as we had expected. The good man had had his lapse and fallen into temptation, and, as was the general way, repentance came afterwards.

"I used to say to her time and time again, 'He's no good to you. He'll take what he wants, and then it will be goodbye. That's how his sort go on. He's not for you. His class don't marry innkeeper's daughters.' You could see what he was, a real gentleman, and we didn't get many of his sort at the inn. He'd just come in by chance one night . . . horse had gone lame or something. Otherwise he would never have come to a place like ours. But then he kept coming . . . because of Alice.

"She would say, 'He's different. He's going to marry me.' 'Not him,' I said. 'He's got you on a bit of string. That's where he's got you.' She wouldn't believe me . . . and it turned out she was right, in a way. They were married. I can testify to that. It was in the church . . . a simple affair, though. He wouldn't have it any other way. But married they were. I was there, so I know."

"Married," I said. "But — "

"Yes, they were married. We'd been brought up strictly. Alice wouldn't have gone with him in any other way. Nor would he with her. He was very religious. He made Alice turn to it. Oh, we had to go to church every Sunday. Father always insisted on that — but it was more than that with this Edward."

"So they were really married!"

"Really and truly married. He set her up in a nice little house and then he'd go away and come back. He paid regular visits. I said, 'Where does he go to, then?' And Alice said, 'Oh, he's explained all that. He's got a big house in Cornwall. It's been in the family for years. He said I wouldn't like it . . . and he wouldn't want me to be there. I'm better off here.' Alice was a girl who didn't ask questions. She liked everything to be peaceful. That's all she asked. Any trouble and she didn't want to know. So that's how it was. He would come to see her and they'd be like any other married couple. Then he'd go away for a spell. Then the boy came."

"I see," I said. "And when he was five years old, Alice died."

She nodded. "There was the question of where Simon would go. I guessed I'd have to have him, she being my sister. I didn't know what I'd do with the boy. Father had died a year or so before. He'd never liked that marriage, though he'd been to the church and seen that it was all properly done and this Edward never stinted her with anything. She was better off than any of us and there was no doubt he thought the world of her. When Father died, I was left comfortably off. Everything was for me. Father had said that Alice was well taken care of. I got this cottage. Alice came here once bringing the boy."

"Yes," I said. "He mentioned the place to me. That is how I found you."

"Well, it came out that the one who was murdered was Sir Edward's son. It was the first time I knew he was *Sir* Edward. At first I thought he had deceived our Alice and that when he'd gone to the church with her he was married already. But then it came out when there was a lot about the family in the papers that he'd married a Miss Jessica Arkwright and when — and that was *after* he'd married our Alice. The one who was murdered, his eldest son, was a year or more younger than Simon. It was all a bit fishy, I thought . . . but it was clear as daylight. Alice was his wife, and this other woman had no right to the title. Our Alice was the real Lady Perrivale. So the two boys he'd had after were the illegitimate ones, not Simon. I was well out of it then, and I did not want to hear another word about it. You don't believe me, do you?"

"Oh, yes, I do."

"Well, I can prove it. I've got the marriage lines. I said to Alice, 'That's something you want to keep by you always.' She was careless about that sort of thing. But I thought there was something odd even at the start. Husbands don't usually go off like that and leave their wives . . . not unless they're trying to get away from them. So I made her be sure to keep her marriage lines. Not that he wanted to get away from her. He was really sad when she died. Then I made sure that I kept the lines. I'll show them to you."

"Will you?" I said.

"Of course I will. She was married and no one's going to say she wasn't. I've got them upstairs. I'll go now and get them."

When we were left alone, Felicity said to me, "We didn't expect this."

"No."

"It seems incredible. That strong pillar of the church to commit bigamy."

"If this is a genuine certificate of marriage . . ."

"It must be. She was there at the ceremony. She's not the sort to say so if she wasn't."

"Might she have some idea about protecting her sister's honour?"

Miss Ferrers came back into the room, proudly waving the document.

We looked at it. There could be little doubt of its authenticity.

"I think," I said, "it may be that someone knew about this, and that Simon was the true heir to his father's estates and title. It makes a motive."

"But they didn't kill him."

"No . . . but he was implicated."

"You mean someone arranged to be rid of both the elder brother and Simon at the same time."

"It could be. It would be useful if we could have this proof of the marriage."

I could see at once that Miss Ferrers in no circumstances would allow the certificate to pass out of her hands. "You can see it in the church records," she said. "It's St. Botolph's in Headingly near Bath. You really do believe in his innocence, don't you?"

"Yes," I said firmly.

"It would have broken Alice's heart," she said. "I was glad she died before she could know that. But then if she'd been alive he would never have gone to that place. Alice would never have let him go. She loved him so much."

"You have helped us a great deal," I said.

"I can't tell you how grateful I am."

"If you can clear his name . . ."

"I'm going to try. I'm going to do everything in my power."

She insisted on making us a cup of tea. She talked to us while we drank it, going over everything she had already told us, but we did get an impression of the affection she had had for Alice, which was none the less genuine because it was faintly contemptuous. Alice had been soft . . . too trusting . . . loving unwisely . . . believing all that was told her. But Alice had been her dear sister, closer to her than anyone had been before or after.

I was glad we had convinced her of our sincerity.

And so we left Rowan Cottage with the knowledge that Sir Edward Perrivale had married Alice Ferrers, and the date on the certificate showed clearly that the marriage had taken place before the ceremony he had undergone with the present Dowager Lady Perrivale.

Encounter in a Copse

That night Felicity and I talked continuously of our discovery. It was beyond our wildest hopes.

"I still can't believe it!" I said. "How could Sir Edward, with his strong moral stance, enter into a bigamous marriage, have two sons whom he accepted as his own, while his legitimate son, though brought up in the house, was treated as an outsider?"

"We have to remember that he wanted the boy to be given every chance."

"Poor Simon!"

"Well, he had your Nanny Crockett."

"It would have been sad for him if he hadn't."

"Oh, there are always compensations. But why did Sir Edward not only break the law but go against his strong religious principles?"

"I think I can guess. You see, there is a great tradition in the Perrivale family. The old house is at the root of it. The place was falling down and Sir Edward was in financial difficulties. He had never brought Alice to Perrivale. Much as he loved her, he did not think she would be a suitable chatelaine. You see how strong the family tradition was. I daresay he had been brought up to believe that the great family of Perrivale was all important. It had been kept going all through the centuries by its members doing their duty. It was his duty, therefore, to save Perrivale. Along comes the ironmaster or coal owner, whatever he was, from Yorkshire. He will supply the money required to save the house. Sir Edward's financial problems can be solved . . . but at a cost, of course. The price is marriage to the rich man's daughter."

"But Sir Edward couldn't accept those terms. He had already married little Alice."

"But who knew? Only those people in the country. Alice was quiet and docile. She would accept everything he told her. She would not make trouble . . . even if she knew what was happening . . . but she didn't. He thought he could pull it off, and he did. I daresay it troubled him a great deal. But there was no other way of saving Perrivale. He had always been brought up to believe that his first duty was to tradition . . . to the family name. You can see how he was torn. He had to save his house;

the family must go on living in the style to which it was accustomed. Alice could not rise to what would be demanded of her. He had loved Alice . . . he had been led into the temptation of marrying her. But she was not suitable to be a Perrivale wife. I can see how it happened."

"You certainly make it sound plausible."

"I think Sir Edward could not die with this secret on his conscience. I think he may have confessed when he was near the end. And to whom would he confess but to the one whom it concerned most . . . the woman who thought she was his wife? Imagine it: 'I cannot go like this. I must tell the truth now. My heir is Simon, the boy I brought into this house. I married his mother, and that means I am not truly married to you.' That was how it must have happened. Maria said that she heard them quarrelling violently and that Lady Perrivale went very strange at the time of his death. It must have been because of this."

"Are you suggesting that she was involved in the murder? You can't think she killed her own son just to get Simon accused."

"Of course not. What she did was tell her sons. She would, wouldn't she? Or perhaps Sir Edward told them. Yes, of course, it would concern them most . . . next to Lady

Perrivale, of course."

"But it was Cosmo who was murdered."

"I always had a notion that Tristan was the murderer, that he killed Cosmo because he wanted the title and Mirabel. Just imagine what he would feel to be in second place and miss all the prizes. He had everything to gain. And there was Mirabel. She married him very soon after Cosmo was killed."

"And what of the child she seems to have got rid of?"

"I don't understand that, it's too complicated. But at least if Tristan was aware that Simon was really his father's heir, he would want to get him out of the way. So he kills Cosmo and arranges that Simon is blamed for it, and both encumbrances are removed. Sir Edward dies . . . there is nothing to say that Tristan is not the rightful heir."

"It's taking shape," said Felicity. "But how are you going to prove all this?"

"I don't know . . . yet. But we've taken a great step forward . . . thanks to you, Felicity. I think I shall know what to do when the time is right."

"And in the meantime?"

"I shall tell Lucas, when I see him, what we have discovered. He is very astute. He will suggest what action we take next. Something has occurred to me. Lady Perrivale . . . the

Dowager Lady Perrivale . . . is searching for something in Sir Edward's room. She lights candles at night — or she did before Maria hid them for fear she burned the house down . . . and goes prowling round. What is she looking for, do you think?"

"Simple logic would point to a will."

"Exactly. The last will of Sir Edward Perrivale, in which he states that Simon is his legitimate son and heir. He cannot go to his grave with that secret on his conscience."

"So to purge his own soul he plunges those who for years have believed themselves to be his only family into turmoil."

I nodded. "He knows that if someone gets his — or her — hands on the will while he is too ill to know what is happening, it will be destroyed. So he hides it, meaning to produce it to the solicitor or someone whom he can trust — when he gets the opportunity to do so. Now Lady Perrivale knows that this will exists. She must find it and destroy it for the sake of her sons if for nothing else. She is not very clear in her mind, but she hangs on to the fact that it exists. That is why she wanders about at night looking for it."

"Hm. Sounds likely."

"I often visit Lady Perrivale. There might be an opportunity . . ."

"You'd better be careful."

"That's what Lucas says."

"If this is true and Tristan killed once, he might not hesitate to do so again, and people who know too much might be in danger."

"I'll be watchful."

"I'm really serious, Rosetta. I'm worried about you."

"Don't be. I'll be careful. They don't suspect anything. I'm just the governess."

"But no ordinary governess."

"Oh, yes, I am, really. It just happens that I have found a way of getting on with Kate better than most could."

"Well, don't be rash."

"I promise."

"Now we'd better get some sleep, I suppose."

"Felicity, I can't tell you how grateful I am for your help."

"Oh, really . . . it was fun. I like a mystery as well as anyone."

"One of the nicest things that ever happened to me was when you came to teach me."

"Well, on that happy note we'll say good night."

When I arrived in Cornwall, Kate greeted me sullenly.

"You've been away a long time," she said.

"It wasn't really so long. I met my friend Felicity, who used to be my governess."

I had already told her about Felicity's coming to the house and how I had been imagining she would be an ogre, how they had all liked her in the kitchen and how she used to join us for meals.

Her mood changed. She was really very pleased to see me back.

"Did Mr. Dolland do *The Bells?*"

"Yes."

"I wish you'd take me up there."

"I might . . . one day."

"One day, one day," she mocked. "I don't want one day. I want now. You ought to have taken me with you."

I was glad when I was able to retire to my room. I wanted to brood on all that had happened. I was sure we were right in our theories. I could picture it all so clearly. Sir Edward, on the point of death, had made his startling revelations. If Tristan could kill Cosmo and have Simon hanged for murder, no one need ever know of the previous marriage. It would be between Tristan and his mother. He would certainly trust her to keep quiet. She would not want it to be known that, though she had lived with Sir Edward and borne him two sons, she had not been his wife.

How could the truth be brought out? How could Simon be exonerated? There was the marriage certificate in the hands of Miss Ada Ferrers. There would be the records in St. Botolph's Church. But even though Simon was proved to be the true heir to the Perrivale estate, that would not clear him of the murder charge. Even if the will — if there was one — were found, that would not be enough.

I felt we had come to an impasse. We had uncovered dark secrets, reasons for murder . . . but we had not found the identity of the murderer.

Still, if I could find that document . . .

Sir Edward could move only with difficulty, I imagined. It would be in his room. Where would he be likely to hide a document?

I was becoming more and more certain that it was a will for which Lady Perrivale was searching, and I was going to try to find it. That would be my next venture. There might be an opportunity of slipping into that room . . . perhaps if Lady Perrivale were asleep and Maria did not happen to be there. If I could produce the will I could at least prove a motive.

The next afternoon I went up to see Lady Perrivale. She was asleep but Maria was there.

"It's nice to see you back," she said. "Her

ladyship's been sleeping most of the day. That's how it is nowadays. The major came in to see her pretty often while you were away. She cheers up for his visits." She gave me a wink. "Well, she always had a soft spot for him."

"Even though he married her best friend."

"Ah, yes. She might have had him herself but old Joe Arkwright was a hard man when it came to the brass. She was heartbroken when her father put an end to it. Then of course she married Sir Edward. It was what Joe Arkwright wanted. Stands to reason: *Sir* Edward and the title and Jessie brought the brass. What people will do for brass!"

I went away with those words ringing in my ears.

It was indeed revealing . . . what people would do for money!

It was two days later when my opportunity came. I went up to see Lady Perrivale. Maria was not there and Lady Perrivale was in her chair snoring slightly.

My heart was beating fast as I slipped out of the room and into that which I knew to have been Sir Edward's.

I saw the big four-poster bed with a table beside it on which lay a very large Bible with leather covers and brass clasps.

I looked round the room. Where would he

564

be likely to put something he wanted to hide? Why should it be necessary to hide it? Because he did not trust the woman who for years had thought she was his wife.

There was a cupboard near the window. I went to and opened it. There were some clothes in it and a tin box. I picked up the box. It was locked.

I wondered what was in it, but it was impossible for me to open it; and in any case whoever was searching for a will would immediately look in such a place. I could be sure someone had opened that box and inspected the contents since Sir Edward's death.

For a moment I paused by the window and glanced across to my own room, and just at that moment the major came into the courtyard. He looked up and immediately I dodged back. I was not sure whether he had seen me. I did not think he had. But it was a warning. I must get out of this room. He would clearly be coming to pay one of his frequent visits to Lady Perrivale.

When I emerged, Maria was still not there and Lady Perrivale remained asleep. I hurried downstairs and was in the hall when Major Durrell came in.

"Good afternoon, Miss Cranleigh," he said. "And what a pleasant afternoon it is."

I agreed.

"I trust you had a good trip to London."

"Oh, yes, thank you. It seemed a long time since I had seen my family."

"And I hear Mr. Lorimer is progressing favourably."

"Yes, that's so."

"Then all's well with the world."

He smiled benignly on me as he started up the stairs.

It was the next day. Kate and I had been at lessons all morning, which had passed pleasantly enough. I was still brooding on my discoveries and felt frustrated because I did not know which way to go next. I had attached great importance to discovering the will, but if I did, what would that tell us which we did not know already?

I wanted to be alone to think. As soon as possible I must see Lucas. He would be home very soon. I expected he would be rather exhausted immediately after his return, but I was very eager to tell him what Felicity and I had found out.

However, the need to get away was imperative. I wanted to be by myself to think. I took an opportunity of slipping out of the house, unseen by Kate, who would have wanted to come with me, and I walked briskly away from the house. I was near the Dower House when I saw the major.

"Oh, hello, Miss Cranleigh," he called. "How nice to see you. You're looking well."

"Thank you."

"The trip to London was obviously a great success."

"Yes, I think it was."

"How's Kate getting on now?"

"Very well."

"I get rather worried about that girl. I've been wanting a little chat with you about her for a long time."

"What is worrying you?"

"Look. Why don't you come in? It's not easy to talk out here."

He led me up the path to the front door, which was ajar. I said the garden was looking beautiful.

"I take a great pride in it. I have to have something to occupy me now I'm free of the Army."

"It must be difficult to adjust to a civilian's life. But it is some time since you retired now, isn't it?"

"Yes, but one never really gets used to it."

"I can well imagine that."

The drawing room was quite large, with oak beams, latticed windows, and a big fireplace.

"It's a lovely house," I said.

"Yes, the Tudors may not have been so elegant as their successors, but they did seem to create a certain atmosphere. Do sit down."

I sat on the settle near the window.

"Are you comfortable there?" he asked solicitously.

I told him that I was very comfortable. "What worries you about Kate?" I asked.

"I'm going to give you a glass of wine first. It's always more cosy to talk over a drink."

"Thank you, but I'd rather not."

"Oh, come, I insist. I want you to try this. It's very good. I only serve it on special occasions."

"Oh . . . is this one?"

"Yes, because for so long I've wanted to talk to you and to thank you for what you are doing for Kate."

"You're very fond of her, I know, as she is of you."

He nodded. "Now, just a small glass, eh?"

"Well, thanks . . . just a small one."

He brought it to me and then went and poured one out for himself.

"To you, Miss Cranleigh. With my heartfelt thanks."

"Oh, really, you make too much of it. It's only a matter of getting to know her . . . understand her."

"There have been so many . . . and you

took the trouble. That's what I'm grateful for. Mirabel — my daughter, Lady Perrivale — said to me the other day, 'The change in Kate since Miss Cranleigh came is really remarkable.' "

"Then why are you worried?"

"That's what I want to talk to you about. What do you think of the wine?"

I took another sip. "It's very pleasant."

"Well, drink up. And have another. I told you it is very special."

Just at that moment there was a sound of footsteps coming round the house. The major looked startled.

"It's me, Gramps," said a well-known voice. "Rosetta's here, I know. I saw her come in."

I put my glass down on a small table near the settle as Kate entered.

"What are you doing here?" she cried. "I watched you leave. I followed you. You didn't see me, did you? I kept behind. I stalked you. Then I saw you speak to Gramps and come in here. You're drinking wine."

"Yes," said the major.

Although he smiled at his granddaughter, I fancied I saw a flicker of annoyance cross his face. It was understandable. He had wanted to talk to me confidentially about her. That would be impossible in her presence.

"Well, come and sit by Miss Cranleigh."

He took her by the arm and brought her towards the settle. I was not sure what happened because I was looking at Kate, who was so pleased with herself at having caught up with me. But as she sat down the glass toppled over and the wine went trickling all over the carpet.

"Damnation," muttered the major.

"Oh," cried Kate. "You swore!"

"Forgivable," he said. "That was my very special wine. I wanted Miss Cranleigh's opinion."

"It wouldn't have been of much significance," I told him. "I'm no connoisseur."

"And you shouldn't swear, Gramps. Your guardian angel will be writing it all down in a little book and you'll have to answer for it one day."

"If that is all I have to answer for, I am not particularly worried and in any case I am sure you would intercede for me."

Kate laughed and I looked down at the shattered glass. I stooped, but he said quickly, "Don't touch it. Broken glass can be dangerous. It's those horrible little splinters. Leave it. I'll get it cleared away. I'll give you a fresh glass."

We moved away from the mess on the floor to the window seat. Kate begged to have a glass of wine.

"Not suitable for little girls," said the major.

"Oh, Gramps, don't be mean."

"All right. Just a taste, eh? You see how she wheedles me, Miss Cranleigh."

"You can't resist me, can you, Gramps?"

"We are putty in the hands of our enchantress," he said.

I could see Kate was enjoying this.

About half an hour later we left and went back to Perrivale Court. I was yawning.

"What's the matter with you?" said Kate. "You look half asleep."

"It's due to the hard work I have to put in to keep you in order."

"No, it's not. It's the wine. You always say it makes you sleepy in the day."

"You're right. It does and it is."

"Then why do you drink it?"

"Your grandfather was rather insistent."

"I know," she said, laughing.

It was late morning. We had finished lessons and Kate and I were going into the gardens. As we came down into the hall the major was just arriving.

"Good morning, my dears," he said. "How nice to see you. Just on the point of going out, I see."

"Have you come to see old Lady Perrivale, Gramps?" asked Kate.

"That's so, and it is a great pleasure to see you as well. I did enjoy your visit. But it was too short. You must come again."

"We will," Kate assured him.

"And Miss Cranleigh will too?" he said, looking at me.

"Thanks. Of course," I said.

Just at that moment one of the grooms from Trecorn Manor came to the door.

"Oh, Miss Cranleigh," he said. "I've got a message for you. Mr. Lucas is back. He wants to know if you could meet him this afternoon. Two thirty at The Sailor King."

"Yes, yes. I'll be there. Is he all right?"

"Getting on a treat, Miss."

"Oh, I'm glad."

He left us and Kate said, "You're going off again this afternoon. You're always going to The Sailor King."

"Only in my own time, Kate."

"What a little slave driver she is," said the major. "You mustn't make a prisoner of Miss Cranleigh, Kate. You wouldn't like anyone to do that to you, would you? And if you do, she might fly away and leave us. Well, I shall see you soon, I hope. *Au revoir.*"

He went up the stairs.

"But you are always going to that inn," said Kate.

"I have to meet my friends now and then."

"Why can't I come?"

"Because you're not invited."

"That's no reason."

"It's the very best reason possible." She was a little sulky during our walk. But I could only think of meeting Lucas.

I left just before two o'clock. It did not take more than fifteen or twenty minutes to reach the inn. I could have walked, but I did like to exercise Goldie and I enjoyed the ride. Moreover, if I rode I could stay a little later and Lucas could ride back with me.

It was a lovely afternoon. There was only the slightest breeze to ruffle the trees. There was no one about. There rarely was at this hour. I took the coast road and turned inland. I had to go through a small copse. It could hardly be called a wood, but the trees grew closely together and I always enjoyed wending my way along the narrow path among them.

I was in good time. I should be there ten minutes before two thirty.

I don't know whether it was a premonition of danger, but as soon as I entered the copse I was aware of a certain uneasiness. I had the feeling that there was something strange about it on this day, that I was being watched. It was uncanny. Usually I went through without giving the solitude a thought.

I was aware of a sudden cracking of a branch, a movement in the undergrowth. Some small animal, I supposed, the sort of thing I must have heard a hundred times before and scarcely noticed. I was in a strange mood today.

I knew what it was. Felicity had said, What you are doing is dangerous. Lucas had said it too. What if Tristan knew what I was doing? What if he had been watching me . . . as I had been watching him?

Guilty people must be ever on the alert.

"Come on, Goldie," I said. "Let's get on."

Then I realised that someone was in the wood . . . very close to me. I heard the sound of horse's hoofs behind me and my impulse was to urge Goldie into a gallop, but that would have been impossible in the copse, where she had to pick her steps carefully.

"Hello," said a voice. "If it isn't Miss Cranleigh."

It was the major. He was right behind me.

"What a bit of luck. Just the one I wanted to see."

"Oh, hello, Major," I said with relief. "I was wondering who was in the copse today. One doesn't usually meet anyone at this time."

"All taking their afternoon nap . . . or siesta, perhaps they call it."

"I expect so."

"You're just the one I wanted to see. I did want to have a word with you."

"About Kate."

"Yes. She interrupted us when I thought I was going to have the opportunity I wanted."

"Something is worrying you, isn't it?"

"Yes."

"What? I think she's getting on very well."

"It's difficult to shout. Could we dismount and sit down on that tree trunk over there?"

"I haven't much time. . . ."

"I know. I heard you make your appointment this morning. But this won't take more than five minutes."

I dismounted and he did the same.

He came close to me and, taking my arm, led me to the fallen tree trunk.

"What is worrying you?" I said.

His face was close to mine. "You," he said.

"What do you mean?"

"Why did you go and see Mrs. Campden?"

"Mrs. Campden?"

"Of Malton House, Bayswater."

I felt suddenly cold with fear. I did not answer.

"You don't deny you went. You have very beautiful hair, Miss Cranleigh. Unusual colour. It's very noticeable. I knew who it was right away. And what are you doing at Perrivale? You're not a governess. You are an inquisitive young woman."

He turned my face to a tree. He held me there with one hand while with the other he produced a tie from his pocket. For a moment I wondered why, and then the awful truth dawned on me.

I had looked for my murderer and here he was. I had found him, but in doing so I was going to become another of his victims.

I thought of the sailor . . . of Cosmo . . . of Simon . . . and now I was the one.

"You've none but yourself to blame," he said. "I don't want to do this. I hate doing it to you. Kate will grieve. . . . Why couldn't you let sleeping dogs lie?"

A wild hope came to me. If he were going to kill me why didn't he do it? Why did he talk like this? It was almost as though he were putting it off. He was speaking the truth when he said he didn't want to do it. He was doing it because he thought he must, because he was already caught up in a maze of murder.

I said, "You are planning to do to me what you did to the sailor; you'll kill me and throw me over the cliff. Kate told me . . . about the sailor. I understand now."

"You understand. You understand too

much. I know what's happened. It was Harry Tench, wasn't it? He's talked. Oh, Miss Cranleigh, why did you have to meddle?"

I was suddenly aware that Goldie was walking away. I felt desperately frightened. He seemed to realise that he was wasting time. He might be thinking of Lucas, who could come to the inn and wait in vain.

With a deft movement he released his hand. He needed them both to strangle me with the tie. I attempted to dodge away . . . but he was watchful of me.

Any minute now. . . .

It must not be. I had found the murderer. I had succeeded. I would not die and let the secret die with me. I must make a superhuman effort to break away . . . to get to Lucas.

I was praying silently to Lucas . . . to Simon . . . to God.

I had to tell them. I had to save Simon. And Lucas was waiting for me.

He had the tie round my throat. Somehow I managed to get my two thumbs under it, which relieved the pressure. I lifted my leg and kicked backwards.

Luck was with me. He was not expecting that. He let out a cry of pain; the tie fell from his hands. I had a second or two in which to act, and I did. I broke away. I was agile and I was fighting for my life.

I had to get out of the copse before he caught me. Instinctively I knew he would not dare attack me in the open country. Someone could easily come into view.

Through the trees I dashed. He was after me, fully aware of the necessity to catch me before I emerged into the open.

I could hear him close on my heels. The branches caught at me, but somehow I managed to keep a step or two ahead of him, just out of his reach. If only Goldie were here . . . if only I could mount her.

The trees were thinning. There was not far to go. I was going to make it.

I could hear him close behind me, breathing heavily. He was not a young man, I thought exultantly. I had the advantage of youth.

I was thinking, Lucas! How right you were. I should have been more careful. I had had a warning with the wine. Of course, he was going to drug me and then throw me over the cliff . . . just as he must have done in the case of the sailor, Mirabel's husband. I had had a warning and I had been too blind to see. But . . . I had found my murderer. Success had been thrust upon me and it had nearly cost me my life.

I was out in the open. I dare not stop. I went on running as fast as I could. Cautiously

I glanced over my shoulder.

He was no longer there. I had escaped. And suddenly I saw Lucas galloping towards me.

"Lucas!" I panted. "Lucas!"

He leaped from his horse. He took me in his arms and held me tightly.

"Rosetta, my love, what happened?"

"I've found him, Lucas . . . I've found him. He was going to kill me."

"Rosetta, what . . . ?"

"He followed me into the copse. He was going to strangle me . . . and then he would have thrown me over the cliff . . . as he did the sailor."

"You'd better tell me all about it. I thought you'd had an accident when Goldie arrived at the inn without you."

"Goldie . . . yes, she wandered off."

"I was looking out for you when I saw her trotting along. She came straight to the stables."

"Oh, good old Goldie!"

"I'd better take you home with me."

"No . . . no, I must tell you. There isn't much time . . . or there may not be. . . ."

"You're distraught. I want to know everything that happened. Who — "

"Let's go into the inn. Tell them I took a toss. I can't let them know what really happened yet."

"Who was it, Rosetta?"

"It was Major Durrell."

"What?"

I put my hand to my throat. "He had a tie; he was going to strangle me. It was round my throat. I thought I couldn't stop him. But I managed . . . somehow . . . and I got away. He couldn't catch me. I ran faster than he did."

He stared at my throat.

"There are bruises," he said. "Rosetta, what in God's name is this all about?"

"I want to talk to you, Lucas. I've got the answer . . . I think. It hasn't been in vain."

I got up behind him and we rode back to the inn. My thoughts were in such a jumble that I did not know where to begin. I was deeply shocked, trembling violently, but I knew that something had to be done . . . quickly. And I had to get Lucas's help.

"Don't talk till we get to the inn," he said. "A good strong brandy would be the thing for you. You are shaking, Rosetta."

"I don't get nearly murdered every day," I said with an attempt at humour.

The innkeeper's wife came running out, followed by her husband.

"My patience me!" she cried. "When I saw that horse coming without you — well, I was in a shocking state, really!"

"Thank you," I said. "I wasn't badly hurt."

"Let's get Miss Cranleigh inside," said Lucas. "And I think some brandy please. That's the best for her."

"Right away, sir," said the host.

"I'm glad to see you in one piece, Miss," said his wife. "I shouldn't have thought that Goldie would have played tricks like that . . . and then to come walking back, meek as you like."

"I'm glad she came here," said Lucas.

"A real bit of luck."

I was in the inn parlour, the brandy was brought, and at last I was alone with Lucas.

"I'll begin at the beginning. I've been careless. I ought to have guessed something. . . . "

I told him about the wine.

"You see, he intended to drug me and throw me over the cliff as he did in the case of the sailor who was without doubt Mirabel's husband, who had come back to spoil her chances. But Kate came and foiled his plan, and at Perrivale this morning when your groom came over he heard me make arrangements to come here this afternoon. So he waylaid me."

"That was a daring thing to do."

"Yes, it would have been so much easier with the wine, but I think he thought he had to act quickly. He was annoyed, I realise now, when Kate spoiled that plan, which would have been so much easier to carry out."

I told him about our visit to Ada Ferrers and what we had discovered through her.

"But," I said, "it was the visit to the nursing home which betrayed me. You see, I mentioned Mrs. Parry."

Lucas caught his breath.

"I knew it was foolish, as soon as I said it. But I was caught up . . . and so embarrassed. I had only meant to look at the place. I made such a mess of it. But he must have known her fairly well and that was why he sent Mirabel there . . . and she described me and then he knew I was on the track and he planned to get rid of me . . . just as he had the sailor."

"So you think he killed Cosmo?"

"Yes."

"I thought you'd selected Tristan for that."

"I don't know whether he was concerned in it, too. Oh . . . by the way, he said something about Harry Tench. He said I'd been talking to him . . . or something like that. He was the one who came under suspicion in the beginning and was quickly dismissed by the police. He's the farmhand who lost his cottage because of Cosmo and hated him for it. He could of course have witnessed the murder."

"How?"

"Because it took place in Bindon Boys, and

that is where Harry Tench sleeps. He made the derelict farm his home, since he had no other. Lucas, that's what we have to do quickly; we have to talk to Harry Tench. We have to do it now."

"I'm going to take you back to Trecorn. You can't go back to Perrivale after this. That's the first thing."

"No, Lucas. I couldn't rest. I've got to see Harry Tench, and I want you to come with me."

"When?"

"Now, without a moment's delay. Who knows? We may have delayed too long already."

"My dear Rosetta. You have just been nearly murdered. You're deeply shocked."

"I can think about that afterwards. I *know* this is important. I've got to see him. I've got to talk to him without delay."

"Do you think you'll be all right?"

"I wouldn't be all right if I didn't go. I should be tortured by what might be happening. Already the major may have gone to him."

"Look, I'll go alone."

"No, Lucas. This is my affair. I started it, and I want to be in at the end. I hope this is the end."

He could see that I was determined, and at

length he agreed that we should go to Bindon Boys together.

I mounted Goldie. I was feeling shaken but somehow buoyed up by the thought of further revelations.

The farmhouse looked more desolate than ever. We dismounted. The front door was open. It was a long time since the lock had disappeared. The place sent a shiver down my spine. I kept thinking of Cosmo's coming here and facing death. I had very recently been made aware of how that could feel. I had faced it before, but it was not the same when one was being threatened by the elements. To be fighting for one's life against a murderer is a different experience.

A streak of sunshine shone through the dirty window. It accentuated the cobwebs and the accumulation of dirt and dust on the floor.

"Are you there?" called Lucas. His voice echoed through the house. There was no answer.

I pointed to the stairs and Lucas nodded.

We were on the landing and the three doors faced us. We opened one. The room was empty; but when we tried the next we found him there, lying on a pile of old clothes. He put his hand up to his face as though to shield himself.

"Hello, Harry," said Lucas. "Don't be afraid. We've just come to talk."

He lifted his head and leaned on his elbow. He was dirty, unkempt, and very thin. I felt a surge of pity for him.

"What you want?" he muttered.

"Just a word or two," said Lucas.

He looked bewildered.

Lucas went on. "It's about the day Mr. Cosmo Perrivale was killed."

Harry was really frightened now. "I don't know nothing. I weren't here. I didn't do it. I told 'em I didn't."

"We know you didn't do it, Harry," I said. "We know it was the major."

He stared at me.

"Yes," said Lucas. "So it doesn't matter about keeping quiet any more."

"What do you know about it, Harry?" I asked gently.

"He robbed me of my 'ome, didn't he? What 'arm was I doing? The place stood empty for three months after . . . my little 'ome."

"It was cruel," I said soothingly. "And then you came here."

"There was nowhere else. It was a roof. And then they was going to do it up. . . . I stayed here. I wasn't going till I 'ad to."

"Of course not. And you were here on that day."

He didn't answer.

I said, "It's all right now. You can talk. The major has told me now, so it doesn't matter."

"He were good to me, he were. I wouldn't have been able to get by but for 'im.'"

"Payment for your silence?" asked Lucas.

"He said not to tell. He said I'd be all right then. He said he'd kill me if I told . . . in a jokey sort of way . . . like he always had." He shook his head, smiling. I could see that the major had charmed him too.

"Tell us what happened on that day, Harry," I said.

"You sure?"

"Yes," I replied. "The major knows I know. So it's all right for you to talk."

"You sure?" he said again.

"Oh, yes, quite sure."

"I want to be left alone."

"You will be . . . when you've told us."

"I didn't do it."

"I know you didn't and nobody said you did."

"They asked questions."

"And they released you. They knew you didn't do it."

"I didn't tell them what I see."

"No. But you're going to tell us."

Harry scratched his head. "I mind that day

. . . never forget it. Dream about it sometimes. It was being 'ere when it happened.
Can't get it out of me 'ead."

"Yes, of course."

"I was 'ere. I didn't know when they was
coming in to measure an' all that. But there
was always time when I heard 'em come in to
slip down the back staircase to the back door
and out."

"And you heard Mr. Cosmo come in."

"No, it weren't Mr. Cosmo who come first.
It was the major. That's why I didn't get right
away. I thought it was one of them coming to
measure up. I didn't expect to see the major."

"What did he do?"

"Well, he came in and went over to the
door what leads down to the basement. He
opened it and went in. I wondered what 'e
were doing in the basement. But he didn't go
down . . . couldn't have. He was just waiting
behind the door. Then Mr. Cosmo came in.
There wasn't a word spoke. I saw the basement door open. The major stood there. He
lifted the gun and shot Mr. Cosmo."

"Then what happened?"

"Mr. Cosmo fell to the floor and the major
came out and he put the gun right down by
Mr. Cosmo. I was on the landing, wondering
what to do, when Mr. Simon come in. The
major had gone then . . . and Mr. Simon picks

up the gun just as Mr. Tristan comes in and finds 'im standing there with the gun in his hand. Mr. Tristan was very upset . . . so was Mr. Simon. Mr. Tristan starts shouting and says Mr. Simon's killed his brother . . . and Simon says Mr. Cosmo was dead when he come in . . . and I thought it was time I got out. So I went down the back staircase."

"So you were a witness to the murder," said Lucas.

"And the major . . . how did he know that you'd seen it all?" I asked.

" 'Cos he'd caught a look at me up there on the landing. He didn't give a sign he'd seen me, not then . . . only after. I wasn't at Bindon then. I was over at Chivers's. Old Chivers said he didn't mind me sleeping in one of his barns. The major gave me money and said he'd kill me if I told the police I'd seen him. Old Chivers were good to me. I knew I'd have to find someplace when they started on Bindon . . . but they never did after all that."

"Harry," said Lucas. "Will you tell this to the police?"

He shrank from us.

"I don't want none of that."

"But you will. You'll have to."

He shook his head.

"You should," I said. "It's your duty."

His face crumpled.

"It'll do you no harm," said Lucas. "Look, Harry, you come along and talk to the police, and I tell you what I'll do. I'll ask my brother if he can find a little place for you on Trecorn estate. Perhaps you could give a hand now and then on some of the farms. I'm sure there'd be work for you to do somewhere, and you'd have your own little cottage."

He stared at Lucas unbelievingly.

"I don't want you to think it has anything to do with this. I'm sorry that you had the bad luck to be turned out of your home. I'll speak to my brother in any case, but please . . . please come along and tell the police this."

"And if I don't you won't get this place for me?"

Lucas said, "I didn't say anything of the sort. I'm going to try and get this place for you whatever you do. I'll ask my brother, and I am sure when he hears how helpful you've been he'll want to do all he can. I'll do it in any case, I promise you. But you should talk to the police."

"We shall have to tell them what you've told us, Harry," I explained. "It's our duty. You see, an innocent man has been blamed for what he didn't do. So we have to. The police will question you. You have to tell them the truth this time. It's a criminal offence not to."

"I ain't no criminal. I didn't do nothing. It were the major. He were the one who fired the shot."

"Yes, I know. And you are going to tell the truth when they ask you."

"When?" asked Harry.

"I think," said Lucas, "now."

"I can't."

"Yes, you can," said Lucas. "You're going to ride on the back of my horse, and we are going to take you there . . . now."

How right he was. We must get there before the major had time to get to Harry. I wondered what he would do now that his attempt to murder me had failed.

"All right," said Harry.

The Return

The months which followed were some of the most wretched I have ever known. I witnessed much of the unhappiness at Perrivale Court, and I knew that, although I had acted as I had to bring justice to an innocent man, I was to a large extent responsible for this misery.

On the very day when the major had attempted to take my life he had gone back to the Dower House and taken his own.

He had realised that when I had escaped from him, I had taken from him his only chance of surviving in the manner which was important to him. When I had run out of the wood, I had destroyed all that he had spent his life trying to achieve. He had been ready to murder to keep it. When I looked back and had all the pieces of the puzzle in their place, I could see how much more sophisticated had been his plan to drug me and throw me over the cliff, as had been his first intention. It was ironic that the granddaughter who so dearly loved him, and whom he loved, should have been the one to defeat him. His plan had failed on a flimsy coincidence. She had happened to see me leave the house and followed me. If she had not, my death would have been just another mystery.

The second method was not so clever. But of course he had had to plan hastily. He dared not let me live. He was afraid of what information I might pass on to Lucas. I had betrayed myself so utterly when I had visited the nursing home run by his friend. He must have been in a panic. He had to dispose of me before I reached The Sailor King. He was convinced, I think, that Harry Tench had betrayed him.

I often wondered what he would have done if he had succeeded. Hidden my body in the copse . . . perhaps let my horse wander away? Perhaps throw her over the cliff with me, so that it would appear to be an accident? Fate worked against him when Goldie escaped and went to the inn, to which she had been so many times.

A great deal was revealed about him, and that was very distressing for the family at Perrivale Court, for there was no doubt that he had been greatly loved by his daughter as well as by Kate. He had been popular everywhere, which was an indication of how complex human nature can be when one considered that he was a cold-blooded murderer as well as a caring family man. His whole life was based on fantasy. He had never been a major, as he had led everyone to believe, but had served in one of the Army's catering corps as a sergeant-major. He had been cashiered from the Army because of certain nefarious deals regarding stores in which he had been involved. He had narrowly escaped prison. He was an extraordinary man, a man of great charisma who should have been successful. He had been a devoted husband, and the welfare of his daughter was very important to him, so much so that he was ready to murder for it.

A certain amount of this information came out through the press, but there was a good deal I learned later. He had left a note at the Dower House before he shot himself. He was anxious that his daughter and her family should not be involved in any way. Only he was to blame.

He had known that Cosmo would be at Bindon Boys that day and had waylaid him. Lady Perrivale, who had considered him to be her greatest friend, had confided to him that Sir Edward had confessed to a previous marriage. Thus, when Simon had been accused of Cosmo's murder, it had seemed like a heaven-sent opportunity to remove him from the scene, whereupon he would cease to be a threat to Mirabel's future. Cosmo had had to go because he had discovered that she had been unfaithful to him with his own brother, Tristan, and was threatening to make trouble and destroy everything that had been so carefully planned.

It was Mirabel herself who made me understand a great deal of this, for I became very close to her during the months that followed.

Kate was in such a state of depression, brought about by the death of her grandfather, that I was the only one who could rouse her from it. I found myself drawn into the family circle, and when the revelations about her father were made known by the press, Mirabel seemed to find some comfort in talking to me.

There was no longer any pretence. She was quite humble. It was all her fault, she said. She had made such a mess of her life. Her father had wanted so much for her. He had done everything for her.

She had been barely seventeen when she had married Steve Tallon. That was before her father had been turned out of the Army. Feeling it to be a respectable way of life, her father had apprenticed her to a milliner. She hated the life.

"Cooped up in rooms with three other girls

all learning the trade," she said. "Long hours at the workbench . . . no freedom. How I hated the sight of hats! I met Steve when I was out making a delivery. Not that we had much opportunity of meeting people. I used to creep out at night to be with him. The girls used to help me. It was a relief from the tedium. I was headstrong and so foolish. I thought I'd be free if I married him. He was only about a year older than I was. My father was bitterly disappointed — and how right he was. Poor Steve. He tried. He had a job in a foundry. We had very little money. I soon found out I'd made a terrible mistake. We had been married just over a year when Steve was killed. There was a terrible accident at the foundry. I must have been very callous, because the first thing I thought was that I was free.

"I got a job with a dance troupe. We toured the London music halls. Sometimes there was work . . . sometimes not. I dreamed of meeting someone, a rich man who would carry me away to luxury. It became an obsession. There was one . . . I believed him. He promised to marry me, but when I became pregnant with Kate, he went off and I never saw him again. I had made a mess of everything. When Tom Parry came along he was very keen to marry me, and because of the child I took that way out. I seemed to have a talent for landing in desperate situations. I had gone from bad to worse. I grew to hate him."

She closed her eyes as though she were trying to shut out memories. "Rosetta, it was terrible. Those awful rooms. I used to dread those times when he came home from sea. He drank a great deal. After Kate was born I went back to the troupe. I had the idea that if I could keep myself we'd get away. I used to have to leave Kate alone. I didn't get back until late. Then my father came out of the Army . . . disgraced. But it was better when he was there. He had some money he had saved. I felt a lot happier then. But there was Tom coming home. I was thankful that his leaves were not frequent. Kate was growing up, and there came a time when I could endure it no more. We would have to find a better way of life for her, if not for ourselves, my father said.

"He had the idea that we would go to Cornwall. He remembered Jessica Arkwright, who had become Lady Perrivale. She had been a friend of my mother, and according to what I had heard Jessica had at one time been very fond of my father.

"We'd get right away, he said. But we had to plan carefully. We had to make sure that

Tom Parry would not find us. I would change my name. I'd be Mrs. Blanchard. That did not bother me. I'd had three different names already. Instead of Mabel Parry I'd be Mirabel Blanchard. So that was how we came here.

"Everything was different. Lady Perrivale was very friendly. She made a great fuss of me and both the brothers liked me. My father was eager for me to marry Cosmo. It was like a fantastic dream to him. I would become the lady of the manor. I should have a title when Sir Edward died. It was all wonderful. There was of course Tom Parry. My father said we must forget all about him. It must be as though he had never existed."

"And you could agree to that?"

She nodded. "I was desperate. I would have done anything in order to get away from him. Then he came down here looking for me. I did believe that he fell to his death. He always drank too much, so it seemed reasonable. I would never have believed . . . my father . . . could have done that. He was always so kind and gentle; everybody said so."

"I know," I said.

"Even then, I spoiled things. You see, it was always Tristan I loved. He was the only one. There had been Steve Tallon, Tom Parry, and Cosmo. It had to be right next time. He felt the same about me. We couldn't help it. We loved each other. Then I became pregnant and I went to that dreadful nursing home. My father arranged it; he knew the woman who ran it. But Cosmo found out about Tristan and me. He had a violent temper. He was arrogant and vindictive. He could not bear to think that we had deceived him. He threatened to ruin us. He would get Tristan cut off without anything. We could marry if we wanted to and get out. I told my father. Then . . . it happened. . . . "

I was sorry for her. She had suffered enough. I hoped she would be happy with Tristan.

"I cannot believe my father did all those wicked things," she said. "He stole . . . he cheated . . . I understood that in a way. But that he should commit murder? All I know is that he was the kindest of fathers to me. He started with nothing. He spent all his life trying to get what he called a place in the sun. He said he didn't want to be out in the cold all his life. That was what he was doing: finding a place in the sun, for me . . . for Kate . . . for himself. And when he thought he had found it, it was about to be snatched away from him. You see, don't you? You see how it happened?"

I said, "Yes. I see."

Our friendship grew. We talked a good deal

about Kate. I said that Kate had been lonely. She had behaved badly in order to call attention to herself. She was asking to be noticed, to be loved.

"Yes," replied Mirabel. "I was so involved with my own affairs I neglected her."

"She admired you. But, you see, she was alone in that room when she was a child. Frightened at night, thinking nobody wanted her."

"It is difficult to explain to a child."

"She must have been terrified when Tom Parry came home. She needed comfort, assurance. . . ."

"My father gave her that."

I agreed that that was so.

"But now she has lost him," I said. "We must remember that. We must be very gentle with her."

"Thank you for what you have done," she said with real feeling.

What had I done? I had uncovered the truth, and my actions were responsible for the present situation.

Kate did not mention her grandfather to me. I wondered how much she understood of what was going on. We continued our lessons. We read a great deal. The mischief had gone out of her. She was subdued, a sad little girl.

The will was read. It was found by Maria

when she touched a secret spring in the cupboard close to Sir Edward's bed, revealing an aperture in the wall. Inside this, among other documents — none of which was of much significance — was the much-sought-after will. It was as we had thought. He had written a letter telling of his previous marriage and naming Simon as his heir. Tristan was left comfortably off, but the title and the house would go to Simon.

Lucas and I met often in the inn parlour of The Sailor King. I wondered how I could have lived through those melancholy months without him.

There was a certain tension between us. These were the waiting months. We knew something had to happen before too long and we were waiting for it.

Dick Duvane was in Australia and on the trail. But now the lawyers had taken over. They wanted to find Simon Perrivale and bring him back to England so that the estate might be settled. They advertised in papers all over Australia: no place, however remote, was left out; no possibility was forgotten.

I began to wonder whether he would ever come home. He might not have reached Australia. Something might have happened to him. Nanny Crockett was sure he would come back. She prayed every night that he would do so . . . soon.

And then — it was six months after I had almost lost my life in the copse — there was news. Dick Duvane had written home. He had found Simon living on a property just outside Melbourne. Simon was coming home.

There was a letter to me.

Dear Rosetta,

Dick has told me all you have done. I shall never forget it. Lucas too, Dick says. Both of you have done so much for me. I have often thought of you and now I am coming home. Soon I shall be with you.

Simon.

Tristan and Mirabel went to the station to meet Simon's train. Mirabel had suggested that I might accompany them, but I did not want our first encounter to take place in public. I guessed there would be several people at the station to give him a welcome, for it was well known that he was coming home.

I went to my room and waited. I knew that he would come to me soon, and, like me, he would want our meeting to take place in private.

He stood in the doorway. He had changed. He seemed to have grown taller; he was bronzed with the antipodean sun; his eyes

601

seemed a brighter blue.

He held out his hands.

"Rosetta," he murmured. He looked searchingly into my face. "Thank you for what you did."

"I had to do it, Simon."

"I thought of you all the time."

There was silence. It was as though there was a restraint between us. So much had happened to him . . . and to me. I supposed we had both changed.

"You . . . you are well?" I asked. It sounded banal. Here he was, standing before me, glowing with health. We had both passed through some horrific adventures and I asked him if he were well!

"Yes," he said. "You . . . too?"

There was another pause.

Then he said, "So much has happened. I must tell you about it."

"Now that you are home . . . everything will be so different for you."

"Just at first it doesn't seem quite real."

"But it is, Simon. You're free now."

And, I thought, I am free too. Once I was a prisoner within the walls of the seraglio, and when I escaped I built a wall about myself . . . a seraglio of my own making. My jailor this time was not the great Pasha but my own obsession. I did not see what was clear about me because I could only see one thing — a dream I had built up, forming it to fit my fantasy . . . blind to the truth.

He was saying, "And it was you who did it, Rosetta."

"I was helped by Nanny Crockett . . . by Lucas . . . by Felicity. They did a great deal, particularly Lucas."

"But it was you . . . you were the one. I'll never forget."

"It's wonderful to know it is over . . . it worked . . . and now you are here, free."

It *was* wonderful, I assured myself. It was my dream come true. I had waited a long time for this meeting . . . dreamed of it . . . lived for it. Now it was here, why must it be tinged by sadness? I was overexcited, overemotional, of course. It was only natural.

Simon said, "We'll talk . . . later. There's so much to say."

"Yes," I said. "We'll talk about it . . . later. Just now . . . it seems too much. And people will be waiting to see you. *They*'ll want to talk to you."

He understood.

It was true there were many people waiting to see him. His vindication had been much publicised. He was the hero of the day. Although it was some time since his innocence had been made known, his return to England revived interest in the case. So many people wanted to talk to him, to congratulate him, to commiserate with him on all his sufferings. I was glad he was so occupied. He was different, of course. Sir Simon Perrivale now, no longer humble deckhand, castaway, man on the run.

The first night I dined with the family.

"We thought you'd want to be quiet," said Tristan to Simon. "Just the family. Later, I daresay you'll be inundated with invitations and it might be difficult to refuse some. We shall have to invite people here — "

"It will pass," said Simon. "And quickly. I shall be a nine days' wonder."

The talk at dinner was mainly about Australia. Simon was enthusiastic. I could see that.

"I was lucky from the start," he said. "I soon found work. Labour is in demand over there. I worked hard. It helped me to forget so much. I saved. I became friendly with a fellow worker and soon we were able to acquire a small property of our own. Land goes cheap over there. We got excited about it. We made plans."

I saw him there, working, making plans for a new life . . . thinking he would never come home. But even then I supposed he would have been on the alert, never sure when his past was going to catch up with him. Now he was free. It was small wonder that he felt a little strange — just as I did. It must be a deeply emotional experience for him to come back to the house to which he had been brought as a frightened little boy ... the place where he had experienced the horror of being accused of murder.

Lucas came over the next day. He, too, had changed. He reminded me very much of the man I had first met at the house of Felicity and James. There was of course the limp, but even that was scarcely perceptible. He seemed to have regained that nonchalance ... that rather cynical attitude to life.

Simon said, "I have to thank you for what you did for me, Lucas."

"Small payment for a life, and I should have said goodbye to mine if you hadn't hauled me into the boat and looked after me when I was a burden to you. In any case, what I did was under Rosetta's orders."

"It wasn't like that, Lucas," I protested. "You were eager to do everything you could."

"Thank you, Lucas," said Simon.

"You're embarrassing me," replied Lucas. "So let's forget it. Too much gratitude embarrasses the one who gives it and the one who takes it."

"Nevertheless it's there, Lucas," I put in.

He did not stay long.

"Good old Lucas!" said Simon. "He doesn't really change much."

"No," I said, trying to smile brightly.

I kept thinking of Lucas. In fact, I could not stop myself thinking of him. He had truly loved me. He had helped bring back Simon . . . he had given Simon to me. That was true love, I supposed.

A few days passed. There was much coming and going at the house. Kate was subdued. She did not ask questions, but I could see she was watching Simon and me closely.

Since the death of her grandfather, she had changed a great deal. She had loved him so deeply, she had admired him so much, looked up to him, the major of the Guards who, she had once told me, had been the bravest man in the Army, the hero of every battle. It must have been a terrible shock to her. I knew that she would have learned a great deal about him, though she never spoke of him. She relied on me more than ever, I believed, and she was looking anxiously into the future.

Simon talked to me more freely now. We seemed to have recovered from that first restraint.

"Tristan is just made for this place," he

said. "He and Cosmo, they were brought up to believe it would be theirs. I never felt like that. I think poor old Tristan would be broken-hearted if he had to go away from here."

"Couldn't he stay? There's plenty to do."

"But he thought the place was his. He had complete control. It's a difficult situation. Do you know, I think I might go back to Australia. I could get a big property out there; I could have people working for me. I wonder . . . what you'd think of the place?"

I thought, It's coming. At last he is going to ask me. That thought was immediately followed by another, Australia? I should never see Lucas again.

He saw the look in my eyes. He said, "It was a dream of mine . . . all that time. I'd make a go of it and somehow I'd get a message to you. I'd ask you to come out and join me. We forget . . . people change. We're apt to think they go on just the same. I always thought of you . . . as you were on the island . . . and when I left you outside the Embassy. But you're different."

I said, "You're different too, Simon. Life changes people. So much happened to me . . . after . . . so much happened to you."

"You couldn't leave England," he said. "You couldn't *now*. Perhaps if we had gone together then, it might have been different.

What you want is here. You will have to do what is best for yourself. We mustn't either of us blind ourselves to our romantic and adventurous past. Perhaps we both dreamed of a future, forgetting that life was going on . . . changing us . . . changing everything around us. We are not the same people who said goodbye to each other outside the Embassy."

"You wanted to come back to England more than anything then."

He nodded. "You see," he said rather sadly, "we have to face the truth."

"You've explained it," I told him. "We're different."

"We've come through dangerous times, Rosetta. We must make sure we are on the right course now. You will always be a very special person to me. I shall never forget you."

"Nor I you, Simon."

I felt as though a great weight had been lifted from me.

I rode over to Trecorn Manor. Lucas heard me and came out of the house.

"I wanted to talk to you, Lucas," I said. "Simon and I have discussed things. We understand each other perfectly."

"Yes, of course," said Lucas.

"Simon wants to go back to Australia. It

608

seems reasonable. He likes the country, and he is now in a position to go ahead there."

"I understand. When will you be leaving?"

"Simon wants to go soon, but I . . ."

He was looking at me intently. He said slowly, "Naturally you want a little time."

"No, Lucas, I know exactly what I want. I want to stay here."

He took me by the shoulders and looked earnestly into my face.

"Don't you see what I'm telling you, Lucas?" I said. "How could I leave you?"

"Are you sure?" he asked.

"I am absolutely sure that this is the one thing I shall never want to do."

THORNDIKE-MAGNA hopes you have enjoyed this Large Print book. All our Large Print titles are designed for easy reading, and all our books are made to last. Other Thorndike Press or Magna Print books are available at your library, through selected bookstores, or directly from the publishers. For more information about current and upcoming titles, please call or mail your name and address to:

THORNDIKE PRESS
P.O. Box 159
Thorndike, Maine 04986
(800) 223-6121
(207) 948-2962 (in Maine and Canada call collect)

or in the United Kingdom:

MAGNA PRINT BOOKS
Long Preston, Near Skipton
North Yorkshire,
England BD23 4ND
(07294) 225

There is no obligation, of course.